THE
HUSBAND
TRAP

THE
HUSBAND
TRAP

A Novel

TRACY ANNE
WARREN

BALLANTINE BOOKS • NEW YORK

The Husband Trap is a work of fiction. Names, characters, places, and incidents are the products of the author's imagination or are used fictitiously. Any resemblance to actual events, locales, or persons, living or dead, is entirely coincidental.

An Ivy Books Mass Market Original
Excerpt from *The Wife Trap* by Tracy Anne Warren © 2006 by Tracy Anne Warren

Copyright © 2006 by Tracy Anne Warren

Published in the United States by Ivy Books, an imprint of The Random House Publishing Group, a division of Random House, Inc., New York.

IVY BOOKS and colophon are trademarks of Random House, Inc.

This book contains an excerpt from the forthcoming book *The Wife Trap* by Tracy Anne Warren. This excerpt has been set for this edition only and may not reflect the final content of the forthcoming edition.

ISBN 0-345-48308-1

Cover illustration: Jon Paul Ferrara

Printed in the United States of America

www.ballantinebooks.com

OPM   9   8   7   6   5   4   3   2   1

To my sister and best friend, Leslie

For all the wonderful things you do
both large and small.

But most especially for
never having a single doubt.
You believed even on the days I didn't.

This book, and all the rest to come, I owe to you.

Acknowledgments

My deepest thanks to Helen Breitwieser and Arielle Zibrak for their wisdom and support during this tremendous journey and for helping me turn dreams into reality.

Cyberhugs to my fellow writers Ruth Kaufman, Dorothy McFalls and Darlene Roberts, who've proven you don't have to "meet" somebody to become good friends.

And Marybeth Gezelle, who never minded schlepping around my heavy manuscripts. Thanks for wanting to read my stories.

Chapter One

London, July 1816

"I, Adrian Philip George Stuart Fitzhugh, take thee, Jeannette Rose, to be my wedded wife . . ."

Violet knew she was going to faint, or else be sick, right here at the altar in front of Adrian and the Archbishop. In front of everyone, nearly the entirety of the Haut Ton, assembled in St. Paul's Cathedral to witness what was being hailed as the wedding of the year.

One thousand people lined the aisles. Two thousand eyes locked in rapt fascination upon Jeannette Brantford, this Season's Incomparable—and last year's as well—as she exchanged vows with Adrian Winter, Sixth Duke of Raeburn, England's most eligible bachelor.

Trouble was, the bride wasn't Jeannette Rose Brantford.

The bride was Jeannette's identical twin sister, Jannette Violet Brantford, or Violet, as her family called her. And right now she thought perhaps she had gone a little insane.

She fixed her eyes upon her blue silk slippers, studied the intricate designs wrought upon the marble floors beneath the elegant shoes. Light swam around her in a brilliant mist. A few tiny motes of dust winking in the mix of candlelight and natural sunshine that cascaded through colorful stained-glass windows in intense shades of blues and greens.

The scents from the great bowers of blush roses and creamy white gardenias arranged for the ceremony curled inside her nostrils, their overly sweet fragrance only adding to her discomfort. She swallowed, her throat dry as sand. A trickle of nervous perspiration slid between her shoulder blades, making her long to wiggle her shoulders against the damp.

She should be a bridesmaid, she thought in dizzying panic. She should be waiting off to the side by now with the other attendants. Instead she was standing here next to Adrian in front of a pair of massive Baroque columns with their swirled bands of dark marble and mellow gold, the cathedral's great dome rising more than three hundred feet above her. Paintings of the life of St. Paul stared down at her from the ceiling, scornfully disapproving her every move, she imagined.

She willed herself to be calm.

Calm?

How could she possibly be calm when she was perpetrating the most appalling deception of her life? She kept expecting someone to notice who she really was, to stretch out an accusing finger and shout, "Fraud!"

But as her twin had accurately predicted, people saw exactly what they expected to see. Certainly her parents and the servants had earlier, accepting her as Jeannette when she'd presented herself in her sister's elegant wedding gown, a lustrous confection of ice blue silk with elbow-length half sleeves and an overskirt of snowy white organza, hundreds of seed pearls arranged in the shape of rose blossoms and trailing leaves sewn into the scoop-necked bodice. No one had questioned her identity, not even when she'd sent her sister's dresser into a tizzy by needing to have her hair arranged for a "second" time that morning, the servant forced to painstakingly rethread pearls and tiny sparkling sapphires into her upswept coiffure.

Oh, merciful God, Violet fretted for the hundredth time, *how had she gotten herself into such a fix?* Everything had been so blessedly normal when she'd awakened this morning. As normal as a wedding day could be, that is, the entire household thrown into a flurry of anxious activity. In hindsight, she would have been a lot more anxious herself had she realized it was to be *her* wedding day and not her sister's. She wished now she'd skipped the breakfast of eggs and kippers she'd eaten. The meal wasn't sitting too pleasantly in her stomach.

Oh, what an idiot she was. She'd never get away with it.

Her hand trembled inside the duke's, his clasp strong and masculine, so very warm against her own icy skin. Since walking up the aisle, she'd given him little more than a cursory upward glance, too nervous to dare look at him fully. She couldn't help but be aware of him as he towered beside her. Dark and beautiful, powerful, utterly resplendent in his formal wedding attire.

Did he know? she wondered. Did he suspect? Oh, Lord, what if he did? Would he denounce her right there in full view of the entire Ton? Or would he wait until they could be in private and demand the marriage be annulled forthwith? Either way, how would she ever be able to explain?

What could a woman say when her very identity was a lie?

Whatever had possessed her this morning? How could she have allowed Jeannette to talk her into such an appalling ruse? Isn't that why she had vowed years ago never to trade places again with her elder twin? Because it always led to trouble—for *Violet*!

Why, oh why, had she let herself be lured down such a treacherous path?

Was it because Jeannette had decided to renege on her promise to marry her rich, handsome, influential bride-groom barely two hours before the ceremony? An action sure to create a scandal so disastrous her family might never recover from the humiliation and shame of it.

Was it because Adrian had settled twenty thousand pounds upon Jeannette for the marriage—money their family had spent like water drained from a well to pay off their father's and wastrel younger brother, Darrin's, prodigious debts?

Or was it because she loved Adrian Winter? Had loved him since the moment she first laid eyes upon him at her come-out ball two Seasons before. Had continued to love him, aching and unrequited, even after he offered marriage to her sister. Even though he'd unknowingly captured her heart and left her to bleed.

"Ahem . . . my lady," the Archbishop whispered, "it is your turn."

"What? Oh, beg pardon. Y-yes, of course," she replied softly, cringing to realize she had been caught woolgathering.

She glanced upward, caught a glimmer of curious puzzlement in Adrian's gaze and immediately looked away.

The Archbishop recited the words for her to speak. "I, Jeannette Rose, take thee, Adrian Philip George Stuart Fitzhugh, to be my wedded husband."

"I, Jannette Vi . . . umm." She cleared her throat and coughed. What was wrong with her? If she didn't take herself in hand she would give the whole thing away without any need for thought from anyone else. *Try again,* she thought frantically, *concentrate.* She drew a deep breath. "I, Jeannette Rose, take thee, Adrian Philip George . . ." Her mind went suddenly blank. Oh, heavens, what was the rest of it?

"Stuart Fitzhugh," the Archbishop prompted gently.

". . . Stuart Fitzhugh, to be my wedded husband . . ."

The Archbishop recited the next line.

She listened intently, repeating the words when it was her turn. ". . . to have and to hold from this day forward . . . for better, for worse, for richer, for poorer . . ."

She raised her eyes again, met the steady regard in Adrian's rich, sable brown gaze.

". . . in sickness and in health . . ."

She felt some of her nerves melt away, knowing she meant each word.

". . . to love, cherish and obey, till death us do part . . ."

She did love him. Promised to cherish him all the days of her life. As for the obey part . . . well, she rather feared she might already have violated that one, but she'd try her best to make amends in the future.

". . . according to God's holy ordinance; and thereto I give thee my troth."

The Archbishop spoke again. This time to Adrian, who lifted her left hand and slid a slender gold band in place next to the immense emerald and diamond ring Jeannette had thrust onto her finger a little over an hour before. Her ring now.

"With this Ring I thee wed . . ." Adrian intoned, his honeyed voice deep, solemn. ". . . with my Body I thee worship and with all my worldly Goods I thee endow: in the Name of the Father, and of the Son, and of the Holy Ghost. Amen."

"Let us pray." The Archbishop lifted his prayer book in readiness.

Legs shaking, Violet knelt beside the man who was now nearly her husband. Bowing her head, she closed her eyes and said her own prayer, asking God to forgive her. She was weak and human but she loved this man at her side more than he could possibly imagine or would probably ever know. How could the falsehood she committed be so very great a sin when her heart adored with such steadfast devotion and truth?

It seemed to her God answered her silent entreaty when He allowed the Archbishop to conclude the ceremony unchecked. "Those whom God hath joined together let no man put asunder."

Adrian assisted her to her feet, keeping her right hand tucked within his own. A shiver raced through her as he curved an arm around her waist and drew her nearer.

"Your Grace," the Archbishop smiled, "you may kiss your bride."

Violet couldn't read the expression on Adrian's chiseled, saturnine features as he bent close, closer.

She had been kissed one time before, a stolen peck in the shade of an apple tree by one of her Brantford cousins when she was twelve. At the time she found the idea of the kiss far more exciting than the actual event, she had to confess.

Adrian's lips touched hers. Warm and smooth, hard yet tender. And proved to her she had never really been kissed before at all. A rushing hum filled her ears, blood thrumming like racing rivers in her veins as the world melted away; guests, the Archbishop, everyone. Instinctively she parted her lips to let him take more. And for a brief instant he did, intensifying the kiss in a way that stole the air from her lungs, blanked every thought from her brain.

Then suddenly it was over. He straightened and tucked her arm in the crook of his own to lead her back down the aisle.

"Smile, my dear," Adrian said for her ears only. "You look pale as death. Although that kiss seems to have put a touch of color back in your cheeks."

At his mention of the kiss, her blush deepened. Because he had asked, she planted a beatific smile upon her lips and beamed at the blurry mass of guests as they walked past. *Look happy,* she told herself. *Look like Jeannette.* She playacted and did her best to keep from shivering.

She kept pace as they retraced their steps down the long quire, past additional rows of smiling guests seated in the carved dark oak pews, before stepping into a crowd of well-wishers gathered in the cathedral's wide, domed transept.

Adrian kept her close at his side. She clung gratefully to his supporting arm and did her best to smile and chat instead of withdrawing into shy silence the way she longed to do.

Thankfully they were soon interrupted. One of the Archbishop's assistants appeared, drawing her and Adrian aside after a few murmured words to the duke. Words she wasn't able to overhear. Violet said nothing as the man led them into the quiet privacy of a nearby chamber, turning to inform them with grave politeness that the Archbishop would wait upon them directly.

Then he closed the door, leaving her and Adrian alone.

She shot a quick glance at her new husband from beneath her lashes, checking to see if his demeanor might hint at why they were here. He didn't look angry or upset. Although he was good at shielding his thoughts when he wished. She had come to understand him well enough over the past few months to know that much.

Had he guessed the truth? Had the Archbishop? Is that why the pair of them had been escorted here to await the clergyman? Because he knew? Because they all knew?

Legs weak, palms damp with perspiration, she sank down onto a nearby chair. One of two positioned in front of a massive walnut desk that had angels carved across the frontpiece and sides, cherubs along the legs. She could barely make out the fine detail, her close-up vision not much better than an indistinct blur without her spectacles.

Under other circumstances—and had she been allowed the use of her eyeglasses—she would have bent down to study the magnificent desk. But she'd had to forfeit her spectacles to her twin that morning. Jeannette, of course, had no need for the corrective lenses, her vision utterly perfect.

But without her glasses Violet could not fully appreciate the glorious furniture—a pity, considering her love of art. Painting, sculpture, architecture—she took pleasure in all things of beauty and creative distinction. The arts, music and literature were, she believed, some of the few things that truly lifted man above himself into the realm of the heavens.

At this moment, though, she had other more important concerns to attend to. Such as not being found out.

"La," she declared in her best imitation of her sister, " 'tis frightful warm, I must say."

"That likelihood was broached, as I recall, when the wedding plans were discussed," Adrian replied. "You are the one who decided to hold the ceremony in mid-July."

Insisted, more like. Violet remembered the incident and the hand-wringing it had caused the household, especially her mother. Any woman could be a June bride, Jeannette had declared, but only a woman of true distinction could persuade the members of the Ton to stay in London for two whole weeks after the end of the Season. Her wedding would be memorable, Jeannette promised. The most spectacular event held since the last royal wedding.

Adrian poured two small glasses of red wine from a crystal decanter on the side table, extending the first one to her. "Here, my dear, you appear as though you could use this." After she accepted, he took a drink of his own wine. "Are you all right?" he asked in a casual tone.

"In what way?"

"You looked near ready to pass out for a few moments during the ceremony. I could literally feel you shaking in your shoes."

Her mind raced, scrambling for a response. She decided to use one as close to the truth as possible. "Bridal nerves, if you must know. I've been feeling a bit peaked all morning. Couldn't eat, hardly closed my eyes last night. But I am nearly recovered now." She gave him a small, reassuring smile.

"Well, I'm relieved to hear it is nothing more serious than that. When you were so late arriving today I thought perhaps you had changed your mind."

She swallowed hastily, nearly sputtering on the small sip of wine she had just taken. Had he guessed about Jeannette's change of heart? Adrian was far more observant than her sister gave him credit for. The very reason she herself had had such doubts about the success of this insane plan.

"Whatever do you mean?" she asked, faintly breathless.

"I mean I wondered if you were about to desert me at the altar."

Now what was she supposed to say? Battling down a bubble of panic, she went with her instincts, tossed her head back and laughed. "Don't be absurd. Of course I wasn't about to desert you. Whyever would I want to do that?"

He drank another swallow of wine, obviously not yet convinced.

"It was my hair," she continued gamely.

"Your hair?"

"Yes. Jacobs—she is my dresser, you know—well, she could not get the style right. It took her simply hours, but I had to wait until my coiffure was perfect. I couldn't appear at my own wedding looking less than my best, now could I?"

He met her eyes for a long moment while she held her breath and awaited his response.

Abruptly he relaxed, smiled as humor shone in his gaze. "No, of course you could not, and your efforts were well worth the wait. You look beautiful. You are beautiful." He stepped close, lifted her hand into his own. "The most beautiful bride any man could have." He pressed his lips to the inside of her wrist against the delicate blue veins that traced just beneath her skin. She trembled, this time from something that had nothing to do with nerves.

The door opened and the Archbishop strode in, his vestments flapping around his ankles. "I apologize for keeping your Graces waiting. I know you must be anxious to proceed on with this very special of days. I have the marriage register just in the adjoining room. You have only to sign, then our business here will be happily concluded."

Marriage register? Violet realized both she and Adrian would have to sign the book to make their union official. *Oh, dear.* Well, she would have to forge Jeannette's name, that was all.

Yet when it was her turn to step up to the register, Adrian having inscribed his name first, she hesitated. To begin with, the heavy vellum page before her was a great muddled blur. She could barely make out what he had written on the line next to the one she was supposed to use. Now more than ever she bemoaned the loss of her spectacles.

As she prepared to sign her sister's name, an uncomfortable thought occurred to her. Legally, if she wrote down her twin's name, wouldn't it mean Adrian was really married to Jeannette? Even if she, Violet, was the one who'd actually gone through with the ceremony? Oh, Lord, she had no idea. She wasn't a solicitor.

Suddenly, forcefully, she was loath to give up the one last remaining trace of her own identity. Even if it might be a foolhardy risk.

Only a single letter separated her first name from her twin's. A simple *e* that gave the pronunciation of Jeannette's name an elegant French twist, and left her own sounding oh so plain and boringly English. Maybe if she made a messy scrawl of her first name and omitted her middle name entirely, the signature would pass muster. Assuming, of course, she could squint hard enough to see where she needed to place her pen.

She wished she could plead illiteracy and simply mark an X in the spot. But sadly, not even Jeannette— her less than scholarly sister—was that ignorant.

Knowing she dare not dally a moment longer, she bent to the task and scribbled her given name, *Jannette Brantford,* across the page. She wondered wistfully if it would be the last time she would ever be able to do so again.

"All finished, your Grace?"

She whirled. "Yes, yes, quite finished," she said, trying to act as if the Archbishop and his innocent question hadn't scared her near to death.

She waited, heart kicking like a hammer against an anvil, to see if he would read her signature, if he would notice the discrepancy. But after no more than a cursory glance, he dusted the vellum with a few fine grains of sand to dry the ink, brushed them away and closed the book.

"Allow me to be one of the first to offer my heartfelt wishes for your future happiness, your Grace," the clergyman told her with a smile, taking her hands in his own. "May your life and his Grace's be blessed."

There it was again.

Your Grace.

How odd that sounded. How frightening. What did she know about being a duchess? How was she ever to cope? Why had she gone along with Jeannette's impulsive scheme? Heaven knows, their hoax would lead to nothing but disaster.

Then she looked up at Adrian, where he waited a few feet away, and remembered why.

God help her, but she loved him. *May he never find out who she truly was.*

Chapter Two

The remainder of the morning and the long afternoon to follow passed by in an unreal haze. Some moments slow, other perilously fast as she waited, with every hand she pressed, every smile she exchanged, every murmured word of thanks, for someone to realize exactly who she was.

But they didn't.

And the longer they didn't the better able she was to portray her chosen role.

As children, she and Jeannette used to switch places occasionally. Despite their innate personality differences, the game of pretend had come easily to them both. Emboldened, adventurous, they'd tried out their tricks on their parents, their governess, the servants, even their friends, managing to fool them all. Afterward, they'd sit together in the nursery, arms clasped around their updrawn knees as they giggled and grinned at their prank.

Thinking back to those nearly forgotten times, she resurrected the old skills, the old bluffs, different now since she and Jeannette were no longer children, yet somehow comfortably, strangely the same.

Still, she quaked and quivered inside as she struggled to project an aura of elegant vivaciousness the way she knew her twin would have done. Smiling and chatting, she traded kisses and compliments with literally hundreds of people as the day wore on. Luckily, as the bride she was able to flit from group to group like a majestic butterfly, pausing only long enough to acknowledge them before winging away to the safety of a fresh location.

Her worst moment came when Jeannette's best friend, Christabel Morgan, caught up to her in between conversations, pulling her aside for a quick, private coze. Flirty and fashionable, Christabel was a Ton favorite, earning high marks for her famous wit and rapier tongue. As Violet knew, Christabel could be generous and kind, even sweet. But only if she liked you and deemed you worthy of her regard. Unfortunately, Christabel did not approve of young women like Violet who enjoyed scholarship and learning. Such matters Christabel maintained, were the rightful province of men. Parties and fashion, shopping and feminine fun—that was the proper milieu of a lady.

So what acute irony, Violet thought, to be included in a bit of intimate girl talk with the illustrious Miss Morgan.

If only Christabel knew the truth!

"Oooh," the girl squealed, linking their arms together as she maneuvered the two of them into semi-seclusion next to a leafy potted palm. "I am simply dripping with envy. How ecstatic you must be. Wife of the handsomest man in the entire country, and a duchess besides. And you look so beautiful today, have I told you that already? I suppose I shall have to address you as 'your Grace' from now on. How terribly droll."

Staring at her sister's friend, Violet fought the urge to pull her arm free. She lifted her chin in a perfect imitation of Jeannette, raised a single eyebrow. "Of course you shall refer to me as 'your Grace,' but only when we are out in Society." She smiled widely to soften the impact of her haughty statement.

Christabel smiled back, having obviously expected no other response.

"Would you look at that," Christabel remarked, inclining her head toward a tall, pale walking stick of a man across the room.

Violet recognized him instantly even without her spectacles.

Ferdy Micklestone, a notorious man milliner, known as much for his frequent calamitous accidents as he was for the temple-high shirt points he insisted upon wearing. Today was no different, his collar rising a full eight inches, giving him the look of a racehorse done up in blinders.

"Oh, he's spilled punch on Lord Chumley," Christabel gasped. "Quite ruined his suit, I should imagine."

Violet watched Ferdy brush frantically at the offending stain on the other man's shirtfront. Plainly disgusted, the older gentleman—a distinguished member of Parliament—brushed Ferdy's hands away, made some cutting remark, then stalked off. Ferdy turned bright as a ripe pomegranate, his head sunk so low that his chin vanished beneath his cravat.

"What a foolish little man," Christabel said. "He really ought to come with the word *hazard* stitched onto his lapel, do you not agree?"

Violet tittered because she knew it was expected. Inwardly, she felt rather sorry for him. She knew how it was to be mocked. How it felt to have interests and proclivities that set one apart from the crowd.

For the next several minutes, Christabel launched into an animated discussion of some delicious gossip she'd heard, when suddenly she paused, nudged her elbow softly into Violet's side.

"Look, across the room," Christabel whispered. "It's your sister and that dowdy bluestocking, Eliza Hammond. Whatever does Violet see in the girl? If I were you, I would forbid the association. A woman of your status shouldn't have to abide such a distasteful alliance. Only consider how it might reflect upon your plans to one day become a patroness."

Violet gritted her teeth, stifled the defense of her friend that sprang instantly to her lips. Sadly, she knew her twin would probably have agreed with Christabel. She couldn't count the number of occasions on which her sister and their mother had expressed similar sentiments, chastising her for her friendship with the unfashionable Eliza. Consorting with such a bookish nobody would do nothing but drive eligible suitors away, they'd warned. Stubbornly, she'd chosen to ignore them and continue her relationship with her friend. She liked Eliza, fashionable or not, and that was good enough for her.

"Ooh-hoo, my eyes may be deceiving me," Christabel observed, "but if I am not mistaken, Violet is giving the horrendous Miss Hammond the cut direct. Perhaps seeing you so splendidly married today has forced your sister to come to her senses at long last."

Not in this lifetime, Violet thought, watching helplessly as her twin turned a dismissive shoulder upon her best friend, then strode away. The confused hurt on Eliza's gentle face was apparent.

She wanted to rush across the room and console her friend. She wanted to explain to Eliza that it was Jeannette she had been speaking to and not her.

But she couldn't go to her, couldn't explain, all too aware how dangerous it would be to reveal her deception, even to a person as trustworthy as Eliza. One tiny slip and this house of cards she and Jeannette had built would come toppling down around them. She promised herself she would make it up to Eliza someday. Somehow she would find a way to make amends for Jeannette's slight.

Christabel sighed. "How eminently diverting. Did you not think so?"

Violet realized she was supposed to nod and chuckle in agreement, make some witty reply. But she couldn't, too sad inside to muster even a false humor. Instead she found herself staring into Christabel's limpid blue gaze.

Hateful girl, she thought. Slowly she retrieved the solitary use of her arm, unable to bear Christabel's touch any longer, pulling away as though escaping Medusa's reptilian clutch.

Christabel frowned and stared. "Is something amiss? You look peculiar all of a sudden. You aren't ill, are you?"

Her newfound bravado temporarily deserted her, her tongue welding itself suddenly to the bottom of her mouth. Silent, she shook her head, forced a smile, sure if she even attempted to speak she would give herself away.

Christabel continued to stare, obviously unconvinced, when Adrian appeared at Violet's elbow.

"Sorry to interrupt, ladies," he said, all congeniality. "I hope you do not mind, Miss Morgan, but I fear I must steal my bride away. It is time Jeannette and I begin the dancing." He showered them both with a debonair smile.

Reluctantly, Christabel curtseyed, and they exchanged parting nods.

Violet turned into his arms with a grateful inner sigh, allowed him to lead her away. He had no idea, she thought, the invaluable service he had just rendered her.

As they danced, his long arms enfolded her in a warm, stalwart embrace and she relaxed. Safe for the first time since she'd walked down the aisle on her father's arm that morning. Ridiculous, she scoffed, considering he was the one person with whom she need always to be on her guard. The one man who, should he discover her real identity, had the power to crush her, heart and soul. And yet she was his wife.

His wife.

What wonderful, improbable words. Until that morning, until those unbelievable moments of shock, denial, apprehension and hope after Jeannette had declared she would not marry Adrian, Violet had never dared to dream such a thing might be possible. Never let herself truly imagine he could ever be hers.

She thought back to those seconds just after Jeannette made her bold declaration not to marry Adrian, recalling the way she'd gaped and sputtered. And the way, after she'd had a moment to collect her wits, she'd argued. Much as she despised the idea of her sister marrying the man she herself loved, she'd realized instantly the ramifications of Jeannette's refusal.

Yet in spite of all her pleas that Jeannette reconsider, her twin had remained adamant.

"Her happiness," Jeannette declared, "was far too important to worry over mundane details like money and social strictures. For a time she'd fancied herself in love with Raeburn, but she'd been mistaken in her feelings. He was an uncaring bully and she would not be chained to him for a lifetime," she had stated with dramatic hyperbole. "She would not be used for the benefit of the family like some slave bartered at market."

Then Jeannette had uttered the words that had irrevocably altered their lives.

If you care so much about saving everyone, if you want to act the martyr and sacrifice yourself on the family pyre, why don't you marry him?

The statement had hung between them, dramatic as a cannon blast.

Marry Adrian? Dear God, Violet could think of nothing she would like better. But to deceive him? Beguile him by trading identities with her twin? To consign herself to living her life in a permanent game of pretend?

No, she'd reasoned, it would be wicked. A villainous crime no decent person would dare perpetrate, certainly not a shy, genteel young woman like her. Why, the very concept was laughable. No one would believe her capable of committing such a brazen hoax, she'd argued.

But wasn't that what made it all so perfect, so possible? Jeannette had urged. Who, after all, would even think to suspect?

Despite her reservations, her terror of potential discovery, her knowledge that what she contemplated was wrong, she had not been able to resist. Her one chance, her opportunity to be with the man she adored, how could she pass that up? If she refused now, Adrian Winter would walk out of her life as surely as the sun would set in the sky that evening.

What did it matter if he thought she was her sister, as long as she could be with him?

She considered her decision again now as they danced, as she smiled up into his beautiful, expressive eyes. *It's worth it,* she thought, *for however long it lasts.*

Somehow she made it through the rest of the day, due in great measure, she realized, to Adrian's rock-steady presence at her side. If not for his support, she feared she would have collapsed into a shivering heap, disgracing herself before one and all.

And if he noticed a difference in her, in *Jeannette,* he didn't remark upon it. Attributing her lapses, she prayed, to the unusual strain of the day. For despite doing her utmost to act like her sister, she worried her performance was a pale imitation. Dull as paste stones displayed next to diamonds.

Finally, after many long hours, after the dancing and the small talk and the elaborate meal—most of which she'd pushed around her plate, unable to eat—she was allowed to retreat upstairs to change into the clothing she would wear for the honeymoon trip.

"There you are, darling, nearly ready for your journey." Her mother, the Countess of Wightbridge, sailed into Jeannette's bedchamber. A pair of maidservants flitted around the room busily packing last-minute essentials. Her mother believed she was Jeannette. She couldn't falter now. She had to keep Mama believing. *Just a few minutes more,* Violet told herself, as nausea swelled like a queasy tide inside her belly.

"Oh, it will be so hard to see you go, my sweet child," her mother moaned. "How we shall all miss you."

"Yes, and I shall miss you," Violet said, striving for the breezy tone she was certain Jeannette would have affected. "But a woman must learn to accept these things once she marries and leaves to set up a household of her own."

"Oh, married and a duchess." Her mother clasped her hands together in delight. "Your father and I are so pleased. The wedding was everything to be hoped for."

"It was, was it not?"

"Although I still think it perfectly beastly of Raeburn to have canceled your wedding trip abroad. I know how crushed you are. How much you were looking forward to seeing the Continent—France and Holland and Belgium—now that that fiend Napoleon has finally been defeated and locked away. Problems on Raeburn's estate! *Pshaw.* I am sure they are far less serious than he claims. But then, men are stubborn about these things. Never understanding how important special occasions like a honeymoon are to a woman. And they claim to be the smarter sex."

Violet knew all about the canceled European tour. Every single member of the Brantford household did, down to the lowliest tweeny. Jeannette had cried and wailed and pouted over it for nearly the whole of last week, drying her eyes just in time for the wedding.

Only, Jeannette had not gone through with the wedding.

Violet pressed a palm against her stomach and struggled to focus on her mother's words, on the role she was supposed to be playing.

"Are you certain you want to give Jacobs to your sister?" her mother continued, referring to Jeannette's longtime lady's maid. "Violet can do quite well on her own, you know. She always has done. I couldn't bear to part with my own dear Miss Phillips."

Violet drew a deep breath before rushing into the speech she and Jeannette had agreed upon earlier. Jeannette, it seemed, could not be parted from her lady's maid any more than their mother could be parted from hers.

"Yes, she will be a great loss, you are right," she agreed. "But Jacobs is so very knowledgeable about all things Continental. With Violet off to Italy with Great-aunt Agatha in a few days' time, she will need her assistance far more than I. I wouldn't feel right leaving her to the ministrations of some *foreign* maid. Heaven knows the trouble that might ensue."

Violet fluttered a hand, imitating a regal gesture Jeannette had taken to using lately. "So I have decided to give Jacobs to Violet as a present. A wedding gift, if you will, one sister to another. I shall take Agnes for myself. She's new to the household but genteel. She should do quite well as a lady's maid, I am sure, once she is properly trained."

Actually, Jacobs had been handsomely compensated to soothe her ruffled feathers, the woman none too happy when she had learned she was not to be the Duchess of Raeburn's dresser, after all.

"Oh, you are so dear, Jeannette," her mother proclaimed. "So giving and loving. Violet is blessed to have you as her sister." The countess straightened and gazed toward the door. "Where is that girl anyway? I declare she is never around when you want her."

Violet cringed inside but said nothing.

"Here I am, Mama." The real Jeannette walked demurely through the doorway, attired in the ecru silk bridesmaid's gown she'd worn since their switch, spectacles and reserved glances firmly in place. Violet found herself staring for a long moment before she looked away.

What a curious sensation, she mused, to see herself as others must. Like gazing into a three-dimensional mirror except for the glint of mischief that peeked like a devil from inside her twin's eyes.

"Have you seen your sister's brush?" their mother questioned, turning to Jeannette. "You know, the one with the pearl handle. The maids say they can't find it anywhere, and your sister needs it for her trip. You didn't use it and leave it somewhere, did you?" The countess shot Jeannette a disapproving stare.

Jeannette linked her hands together in front of her. "No, Mama, I . . . I did not use the brush. It was on the dresser this morning, as I recall, when Jeannette was getting ready for the ceremony. I have not seen it since."

Her mother snorted derisively. "Well, you're of little help. See to your sister, then, since she must be leaving anytime now. Raeburn won't abide being kept waiting much longer. You know how men hate letting their cattle stand. I shall consult with Phillips," she went on, half speaking to herself. "Perhaps she will be able to shed some light on this mystery." Carried forward on a wave of rustling skirt, the countess departed, leaving the two sisters entirely alone.

Jeannette crossed the room, closed the door, turned the key in the lock.

Violet met her twin's gaze. "I suppose you have it."

"Of course I have it. It is *my* brush."

"Well, don't let any of them see you with it. You will be sorry if you do."

Jeannette came over, dropped down into a nearby armchair. "I don't care a fig what they think. I never have. You are the one who has always been the little timid doe, trembling at her own shadow."

Violet gritted her teeth at her sister's unflattering assessment of her character. Jeannette didn't understand the way it had been growing up, since she had always been the favorite, fussed over and cosseted by both of their parents. Violet, on the other hand, had simply been the *other* daughter.

Over the past twenty years of her life, she had often considered the subject, never able to understand what it was she did wrong. Why her parents made such a marked distinction between her and her sister.

Physically the two of them were indistinguishable. They shared the same ash blonde hair, the same peaches and cream complexion, the same radiant blue-green eyes. They both had pert noses and full rosy lips, cheekbones set high in perfect oval faces. Their figures were rounded in the hips and breasts, attractively slender everywhere else. Even their voices sounded exactly the same; only by their manner of dress and speech could they be told apart. Like a pair of fresh spring peas in a pod, their uncle Albert used to say of them.

Yet their personalities were markedly different, and had been from the time of their birth, so their mother was wont to say. Perhaps beneath the surface others saw what Violet could not see herself. Some essential ingredient, some basic character flaw that made her intrinsically unworthy. She had spent many long hours praying over it. Many hours searching her reflection in the mirror for signs of what it was she lacked.

"Still," she quietly warned Jeannette, "purloining the brush would be unlike me. And you having it might draw attention in directions that would not be wise. You are, after all, supposed to be me now."

Jeannette shrugged. "I know, I know. Don't fret over it. I won't get caught. No one has suspected a thing. And I must commend you. You have been putting on a fine performance. I told you none of them would know the difference if you simply applied yourself a bit. Now, there is something I must tell you before we part."

Violet frowned. Whenever Jeannette pulled her aside to tell her something, it usually led to trouble. "What?" she asked dolefully.

"I am not saying you will, but if you should receive any missives from a certain individual by the name of Kaye, you are to pass them along to me directly, unread, of course."

Violet frowned harder. "Who is this Kaye person and why should I need to pass along notes for you?"

"Because I asked you to. Because you are my sister and you love me. Now, will you do it or won't you?"

Was this Kaye person a man or a woman? Violet wasn't sure she wanted to know, was afraid to ask. Was Jeannette involved with someone? Someone other than Adrian? Is that why she had decided to call off today's wedding? Oh, it was too scandalous to contemplate.

She wanted to refuse Jeannette's request but knew it would only cause unpleasantness. And didn't she have enough to fret about right now without adding to the burden? If any of the notes came, she assured herself, she could always dispose of them.

She nodded. "Yes, all right."

Jeannette picked up an adorable chip-straw bonnet, one that had been made especially to complement her—now Violet's—traveling costume of pearl pink sarcenet. A sheer, long-sleeved pelisse of dotted white swiss buttoned over the dress, completing the outfit. Settling the fashionable hat upon Violet's head, Jeannette tied the candy-striped ribbon in a tight, saucy little bow, set off at a stylish angle to one side of her chin.

Violet waited as Jeannette stepped back to survey her work.

"Perfection," her twin declared. "Shame I couldn't wear that outfit myself at least once. Raeburn is bound to find you quite fetching in it."

"Do you think?"

"Oh, yes, definitely."

Violet turned around to take a look at herself in the dressing-table mirror, forced to squint at her image. "I wish I had my spectacles," she murmured low. "Everything is so frustratingly blurry."

"Well, you had best get used to that. Lord knows I would never wear them, not unless forced to, that is." Jeannette pointed to the eyeglasses perched on her face. "I have been doing a bit of thinking upon that issue. It seems to me that *Violet* may soon undergo a change of heart about wearing her spectacles. In fact, I believe she may soon undergo a change of heart about a great many things. This trip to Italy will do her a world of good."

Alarmed, Violet grabbed her sister's arm. "Oh, Jeannette, don't do anything rash."

Jeannette plucked Violet's fingers away. "Don't worry. *Violet* will change ever so gradually. No one will suspect."

Her stomach pitched in a long, slow roll, fresh tension slamming her like a hard wave in a raging tempest. Her hands began to perspire. "Perhaps we shouldn't do this, after all. There is still time to change back, change places again."

Her heart sank even as she spoke the words aloud. It would mean losing her chance with Adrian for good. But lying to him was so dreadfully wrong, wasn't it?

Jeannette's face hardened. "There is no changing back. You are the Duchess of Raeburn now. *You* married him, I did not. If you want to be a fool and reveal everything to everyone now, be my guest. But know this, it will all come raining down on your head. The scandal, the disgrace and the punishment. Mama and Papa will likely disown you. At the very least you'll be sent away somewhere dreadfully remote, Scotland or Ireland perhaps, and never be heard from again."

She was right, Violet thought, that is precisely how their parents would react, what they would do. Jeannette would be fine; nimble as a cat, she always landed on her feet. No, she was the one who would reap the brunt of the blame for the deception. She would be seen as the truly guilty party for having agreed to participate in the ruse at all.

When she'd slipped into Jeannette's wedding gown this morning and assumed her sister's identity, she had sealed her own fate. Made a choice from which there could be no retreat. Ever.

"So put away your guilty conscience and show some pluck," Jeannette encouraged. "Everything is going well, will go well, as long as you don't start confessing. Now, come along. Like Mama said, Raeburn's horses must be growing restive, and he anxious to be off."

Violet drew in a deep, rallying breath. She could do this, she repeated silently. Everything would be fine. Forcing her shaking hand to still, she reached for the doorknob.

A few doors down the corridor, Adrian stood conversing with his brother, Christopher. His words drifted her way. " . . . since I shan't be seeing you again before you leave for University. Have a good term and don't do anything foolish. You are there to study, remember, not drink and carouse to excess."

"Don't worry, brother," the younger, dark-haired man murmured. "I'll make you proud."

"See to it that you do," Adrian concluded, not sounding terribly reassured.

The men turned to watch her and Jeannette approach.

Just as she had done, Adrian had changed out of his wedding attire into clothes more suited to travel. Coat and trousers of the finest dark blue broadcloth. White shirt and tan waistcoat embellished with a modest gold stripe, his neck cloth tied in a mesmerizingly complex knot. A pair of gleaming Hessians on his feet.

Sophisticated, refined, breathtaking.

She swallowed and fought another minor skirmish for composure.

He was so beautiful, she thought, far too beautiful for her. What on earth did she think she was doing?

"Ready at last, my dear." Adrian approached to take her hand.

Tell him or not? she dithered. This was her very, very last chance to be honest.

Then she smiled as she thought Jeannette would, wide and full of confidence. She struck a small pose to show off her finery, holding her arms out to her sides. "And was it worth it, your Grace?" She shifted her hips to make her skirts sway.

He raked his eyes over her, smiled, long and slow. He bent to kiss her hand. "Most decidedly, my dear. Most decidedly."

Chapter Three

The well-sprung coach bowled along the southwest road away from London at an impressive speed, the elegant team of four that pulled it some of the finest horseflesh to be found in all of England. Inside, Adrian Winter, Duke of Raeburn, relaxed his long legs against the satin-covered seats and watched his new wife sleep.

She was exhausted. There had been no hiding that fact once they had been waved away from the reception hall by the cheers and congratulations of their family and friends. The rhythm of the coach and the stress of the day had soon combined, her hands growing limp in her lap, her eyelids heavy as leaden weights, until she had been helpless to deny the lure of Morpheus's command.

Adrian had been observing her for nearly half an hour now. Wondering if he had done the right thing. Knowing it was too late for regrets if he had not. As the vows said, he and Jeannette were married for life, for better or for worse, until death do them part. A sobering realization indeed.

She had surprised him today, especially at the reception, behaving in a far quieter, more reserved manner than he had ever seen her exhibit before. She had even listened with patient interest while his perpetually tongue-tied cousin Bertram took a full five minutes to stutter out best wishes on their nuptials. Most people began fidgeting the moment poor Bertie opened his mouth. Their eyes would wander, their full attention drifting away after no more than a minute or two at most.

Yet today Jeannette had been nothing but gracious politeness, pleasant consideration, to everyone she encountered. Perhaps the gravity of the step the two of them had taken today had acted as a sobering reminder for her as well.

He could but hope.

Lately, over the past few months of their engagement, he had been racked with doubts as to the wisdom of his choice of bride, finding her behavior annoyingly childish on occasion, such as the day she spent pouting when thunderstorms had ruined an intended picnic. And another time when she refused to join him for a ride in the park because the new matching bonnet for her favorite carriage dress had not arrived from the milliner's shop. Added to that was her all-consuming adoration of parties and entertainments. Once he had rendered her speechless by suggesting they cancel plans to attend a masquerade and spend a quiet evening together instead. He'd never bothered to make such a suggestion again.

Of a far more serious nature, Adrian had begun to suspect she was seeing another man. But although he had tried, he had never been able to catch her or even procure any tangible evidence. As he well knew, suspicions were not proof. A gentleman, no matter his reservations, did not call off an engagement with anything less than rock-solid proof demonstrating a grave indiscretion.

While they were courting, Jeannette had seemed so sweetly vivacious. Although, as he reconsidered the matter, her mother had left them little time alone. It was only after their engagement had been announced that he had begun to observe her other side.

Most particularly he recalled last week when he broke it to her that their much anticipated tour of Europe would have to be postponed for several months due to difficulties at Winterlea, his primary estate, in Derbyshire. He had thought for a moment, after he delivered the news, that she might burst into a messy fit of tears right there in her mother's silk-lined drawing room, her face had grown so flushed. And when he suggested a week by the seashore at one of his lesser estates, in Dorset, she'd gaped and stared at him as if he'd asked her to honeymoon inside a hermit's cave. Adrian had almost expected her to call off the wedding then and there. Perhaps a part of him had been hoping she would.

He could have chosen Brighton to placate her, to smooth things over, since word had it the Prince Regent would be relocating his Court to the popular seaside town in the next day or two. But Adrian didn't want to go to Brighton, where half the Ton would be descending to while away the last of their summer boredom. He wanted some privacy, away from Society's demands, and thought perhaps the quiet would give him and Jeannette some time to get to know each other better.

She shifted in her sleep on the opposite end of the seat from him, pushing her hat to one side, so the ribbon under her chin was yanked tight against one cheek. It looked far from comfortable. Taking pity, he leaned across and tugged the bow loose, letting the ribbons trail freely under her chin. Relieved of the pressure, she settled more deeply, breathed more evenly in her sleep.

He hadn't entirely believed her excuses concerning her late arrival at the church this morning. There was more to that story than a simple case of ill-arranged hair, but he had decided not to force the issue. She had done her duty, had not embarrassed him in front of his peers.

In the end, weren't those the things he really expected of her?

Duty and discretion.

The coach hit a rut, jostling them both despite the excellent springs in the vehicle. She roused briefly, giving a small cry of alarm. Her eyes fluttered open for a moment before drifting downward once more, her head coming to rest behind her at a very awkward angle.

He couldn't leave her like that, Adrian decided. A few minutes in such a position might result in a painfully stiff neck, one that could linger for days. His lips quirked upward at her decidedly humorous posture before he reached out and gently pulled her into an upright position. She sank forward against him, murmuring in her sleep. The brim of her elegant chip-straw bonnet dug sharply into his neck.

With the nimble fingers of a man well used to assisting women out of their garments, he tugged the little bonnet loose from its moorings. Then cast it across to the opposite seat with scant regard for its fashionable perfection. Settling back into his own corner, he tucked her against him so she could use his shoulder as a pillow.

He glanced downward, noting the way her pale golden lashes fanned out against the porcelain smoothness of her fair cheeks. Her lips, tinted a delicate, sunset pink, lay slightly parted, ripe for a kiss. Mere inches and his mouth would be on hers, stealing soft kisses at first then progressively harder ones until she awakened to find herself in his arms. But Adrian didn't know how far things might progress if he gave in to temptation now. And he did not want their first time together to be in the inside of a coach, even one as comfortable as this. There would be time for that sort of loveplay later, he consoled himself, plenty of time.

As if she sensed his intent regard, her eyes opened, her irises translucent as the finest aquamarine gemstones. Still more than half asleep, she locked her sights upon him. "Adrian? What are you doing here?"

He gave her a slow, indulgent smile. "Traveling with you, my dear, on our honeymoon journey."

She frowned slightly as if perplexed. Then she lifted a hand to his cheek, stroking up and down over his skin in a way that made his body ache with desire.

"Rough. You need to shave," she observed, her voice curious, as if she hadn't realized his whiskers actually grew.

His smile widened at her strangely innocent remark. "I will do so later, my dear. Now go back to sleep. You are dreaming."

It was her turn to smile. "Of course I am," she told him. "How else could I do this?" She rubbed her thumb over his lower lip. He had to restrain the impulse to kiss and suck her finger into his mouth.

"You are so beautiful," she murmured, then with a deep inhale of breath, her hand fell back into her lap. She burrowed her face once more against his shoulder, sound asleep.

Rigid with need, Adrian leaned his own head back and closed his eyes with a groan. He held her for the next two hours until the coach finally rolled to a stop.

Sunset was crowning over the horizon in an orange and magenta blaze. A redbrick country house with healthy green ivy growing on its walls rose tall across a modest courtyard. The house belonged to a friend of Adrian's, who was back in London, no doubt still at the wedding festivities drowning himself in champagne. Use of the house was a small wedding present and where they would spend the night.

"Jeannette," he said, "wake up." He shook her lightly. "Jeannette." No response. "Wake up, my dear." He nudged her again, straightening her into an upright position beside him. "We are here."

Her eyes blinked open. "Hmm? Here? Where is here?"

He smiled anew. If she kept up this sort of behavior, their honeymoon might turn out to be surprisingly amusing. "Our lodgings for the night. Come along now."

She blinked again, shook her head slightly as if to clear it, then squinted at him. "Your Grace?"

"Yes?"

"Pray tell, what is my name?"

His lips quirked. "Your name? Perhaps I shouldn't have let you sleep so long, after all. What do imagine your name to be?"

She scuttled her fair brow. "Why don't you tell me first, then I'll decide if we agree."

Adrian played along. "All right. Your name is Jeannette Brantford Winter, Duchess of Raeburn. Does that satisfy you, sleepyhead?"

A visible shiver raced through her. Then after a moment she planted a smile on her face that seemed almost forced in its brightness. "Of course. I just wanted to hear someone say it. It isn't every day a girl becomes a duchess, you know."

His own smile dimmed slightly at her prideful remark, but he decided to let it go. He stepped from the coach, turned to reach up a hand. "Come along, your Grace. The evening awaits us."

Silent, his new wife laid her hand in his and exited the coach.

They sat down to a light supper in a small but attractive dining room at the rear of the house. Silver candelabras filled with lighted beeswax candles were arranged to dispel the darkness. From the quaint English garden that lay just beyond the half-opened windows, the heady scent of roses drifted in to gently perfume the air. The mellow sound of night creatures added a soothing natural music.

Violet stared into her bowl of cold cucumber soup, tension straining her nerves so that she was barely aware of the pleasant atmosphere surrounding her.

It was her wedding night.

She squeezed her eyes closed for a second at the thought. She had little idea what to expect, little idea what Adrian would expect. The intimate acts of men and women remained largely a mystery to her. Although she had over the years read certain intriguing passages in ancient texts of Greek and Latin—texts to which gently bred females were not supposed to have access—that had spurred the baser elements of her imagination. Mostly, though, the books had left her with more questions than answers.

Certainly her mother had told her nothing of such delicate matters. Not in the past or today, a day neither one of them had realized would be her wedding day. Emotionally, she was, as she had so often been throughout her life, on her own.

After a moment of silent self-chastisement, Violet willed her hand, the one holding the soup spoon, not to shake as she lifted a bite of soup to her mouth. The liquid sat like paste against her tongue before she managed to swallow. It wasn't the cook's fault, she realized, or the soup's. She simply had no appetite. She ate one more bite out of politeness before setting her spoon aside.

She knew she ought to say something to Adrian, smile and interject some fascinating conversational tidbit. Jeannette would surely have been rambling away by now, regaling him with one of her witty stories or the latest bon mot. But hard as she tried, Violet could think of nothing even remotely interesting to say and feared the best she might manage would be a few stumbling, awkward phrases. She decided it would be safest to simply keep her mouth closed.

Adrian finished his soup, signaled permission to a nearby footman to clear, then serve the next course.

A lovely poached whitefish accompanied by a creamy dill sauce and a selection of tender summer vegetables was offered. Violet accepted servings of each, then stared down at her plate as if it might somehow infuse her with the courage she needed. Why couldn't she be at ease like Jeannette? she bemoaned. Why was it so hard for her to do what came so easily to most of the human race?

"Perhaps the turbot will be more to your liking than the soup," Adrian said.

Her gaze flew upward to meet his. She cursed inwardly as she felt a flush of color rise in her cheeks. "Oh, the soup was fine. D-delicious, in fact."

"Ah, so delicious I noted you took all of two bites." Humor softened his tone.

She flushed again. "I don't seem to have much appetite tonight, I confess."

"Shall I confess something to you as well?"

She nodded.

"I am not terribly hungry either. Still, I believe both of us ought to try to consume a little of this excellent fare Armitage's cook has labored to provide. Otherwise I fear we'll find ourselves in the bad graces of the kitchen staff come morning."

Her eyes widened. So astonished by the notion that some of her nerves melted away without her realizing. Of course, Jeannette would never have tolerated such insolence from servants, much less worried about their feelings. But Adrian seemed to consider such matters understandable, even important, so perhaps he wouldn't think it odd if his new wife did as well.

"You believe Cook might serve us cold tea?" she ventured.

"Oh, most definitely. And burned scones as well unless we take precautions now to ensure her pleasure."

Violet considered his statement, then picked up her fork. "We had best give this a try, then, before it turns cold."

Adrian lifted his own fork. "Right you are."

She managed to eat most of the food on her plate. The first actual meal she had consumed since early morning. She had eaten nothing at the reception other than a single bite of cake forced upon her by the requirements of tradition. Meanwhile, Adrian engaged her in light, undemanding conversation. She found to her surprise that she was able to keep up, even volunteer a comment or two of her own. For a short while, she forgot her earlier trepidation and simply enjoyed being in his presence.

Plates were cleared. Coffee served. Along with a snifter of brandy for Adrian. Both of them refused the very luscious-looking dessert that was offered.

The room grew quiet as their conversation wound down of its own accord. Adrian relaxed back in his chair, observing her out of suddenly pensive eyes.

They would muddle along together well enough, he decided, a swallow of liquor warming his throat. He did not love her, he admitted. Nor did he expect her to love him. But that was all right. Love was ridiculous; a self-serving, destructive emotion better left to fools and half-mad poets. Hadn't his own parents been perfect examples of that?

Married for love, they had spent the twenty years of their wedded life at each other's throats, bickering like fishwives over every slight and slur—real or imagined—until his father's untimely death in a riding accident when Adrian was only nineteen.

During his youth, his mother had complained constantly to him about his father's indiscreet affairs and hurtful infidelities. His father had grumbled that his mother was cold and heartless, that he would get more response out of a stone. What else was a man to do but look elsewhere for comfort? his father had defended. Yet somehow his parents had managed to produce six children: himself, his four sisters and lastly his brother, Christopher.

All of his sisters were married. Whether happily or not he couldn't say. They certainly gave every evidence of preferring the married state. Haranguing him mercilessly over the last few years about how it was well past time he found a wife and set up his nursery. At thirty-two, he finally had conceded the fight. If his parents could produce heirs while detesting each other the way they had, then he supposed he could do his duty as well, with love or without it.

Jeannette was beautiful, of that there was no doubt. He studied her as she sat glowing and golden in the candlelight. The well-bred daughter of the Earl of Wightbridge, whose pedigree traced back to the Conquerer himself. Strictly speaking, her bloodlines were better than his own. His mother was French. No more than the daughter of a lesser count who had had the wisdom to abandon France a few years prior to the Revolution.

Jeannette had been the unattainable prize every man had desired for the past two Seasons, despite her family's lack of fortune. He'd wanted her, had won her. Physical desire would be enough, Adrian assured himself. It was enough for most people of his class, he knew. And once she had given him an heir and a spare, as the saying went, she could go her own way, discreetly, if that was her wish. And he would go his.

In the meantime, he feared he might be in for a devil of a ride. His bride, he was coming to realize, could be as willful and unpredictable as a lightning storm. What was the purpose of her uncharacteristic reserve tonight, for instance? She was behaving more like her twin than herself. Perhaps he should have done himself a favor and married the other sister instead.

Now, where had that idea come from? he wondered in surprise.

Violet, a quaint name that matched the shy, unassuming young woman who bore it. She was every bit as beautiful as her twin sister behind the concealing spectacles she wore. But so awkward and reserved she could barely speak a sensible greeting to him half of the time.

He had come to know her a little during his engagement to Jeannette. Had drawn her out slightly on one or two rare occasions. She had an intelligent mind, he'd discovered, and a kind heart. He had found her down by the river that bordered her parents' country estate one afternoon late last spring, crying over a sack of drowned kittens. She had been trying to breathe life into one that lingered, puffing air into its tiny mouth and cold pink nose by covering both with her own lips. The scene had squeezed at his heart; he abhorred cruelty of any kind, particularly when done to animals or children. The poor kitten died a short while later. He had helped Violet bury it and its siblings beneath a nearby tree, had given his handkerchief to her to dry her tears afterward. In silent understanding, they had walked together back to the house.

In that moment he had liked her, liked her very much. But even if he had not already been engaged, marrying her would never have done. He needed a woman who was confident and secure. Poised in company. Unafraid to assume command, of herself or of others. He needed a woman who could stand as his duchess, not hide away in fright. No, Violet Brantford, sweet as she might be, was simply not duchess material.

He looked across at Jeannette, his bride. She smiled back, looking fully herself. He had made the best choice, he decided, reservations or no. He chastised himself for his wayward thoughts. What had he been doing, wool-gathering over her sister? He had absolutely no business thinking about Violet in any but a fraternal manner. They were brother and sister now. In future, he would make certain his mind never strayed in such a direction again.

Jeannette covered a small yawn with her palm. "Forgive me."

"No, it is quite all right, my dear. This has been a long, eventful day. Why don't you retire for the evening. I will remain here and finish my brandy." He lifted his glass, swirled the dark amber liquid inside, his eyes hooded and intense. "I will join you after a while."

Violet's nerves roared back to life with a sudden sharp ping as if they were harp strings and he had reached out and plucked one, letting it resonate within her. If she had had any doubts as to where Adrian planned to sleep tonight, she didn't any longer. Of course, it wasn't the sleeping part that actually concerned her. It was that mysterious "other" that made her quiver. Still, she loved him, so how bad could it be?

On shaky legs she climbed to her feet, quietly made her excuses and walked from the room.

Chapter Four

Half an hour later Violet sat in front of a small, mirrored dressing table in a cheerful green-and-white-striped bedchamber. Her long hair was neatly brushed and had been left to trail down her back, its heavy weight tied away from her face by a plain white ribbon. Her nightgown was white as well. But if the seamstress had meant the garment to be virginal, the woman was in even more profound need of eyeglasses than she was herself.

Made of a diaphanous silk, the sleeveless gown hung to her ankles but concealed little on its way down. The bodice was the most revealing of all, formed of a delicate Irish lace that clung to her bare breasts, soft and transparent as early-morning light. Violet couldn't believe Jeannette had purchased such a scandalous garment or that their mother had let her.

Instant mortification was her first reaction when her maid, Agnes, held the gown up for her to slip on and Violet realized she could see through the material to the maidservant standing on the other side. She nearly refused to put it on. Then common sense reasserted itself. If she balked at donning the night rail, her missish reaction might cast undue attention upon her. She knew the way servants liked to gossip. Curious, they might begin to notice other little things about her. Things that would distinguish her from her sister, and before she knew it, her secret would be revealed.

Luckily Agnes was new. Adrian's staff would be new to her as well, and she to them. Still, everyone needed to believe she was Jeannette, from his majordomo to his newest, youngest tenant. And making a fuss on her wedding night by refusing to wear the nightgown she had supposedly chosen herself was not the best way to begin.

So while Agnes waited, ready to assist her into the embarrassing night rail, Violet put aside her objections and obediently raised her arms. Once dressed—if one could call it that—she sat and let Agnes brush and arrange her hair. A few minutes later, the maid let herself out of the room, the door giving a soft fatalistic click at her back.

Violet began to pace. How could she allow Adrian to see her this way? What would he think? Might he not be as scandalized as she? Surely even a lightskirt would refuse to be seen in such a garment. Then again, she didn't know much about lightskirts. Perhaps when such women were with men they wore no clothing at all. Flaming color scalded her cheeks, burning there at the shocking idea. Violet paced faster.

At least the outfit came with a robe, she thought. Not that the outer garment—cut from the same revealing material as the nightgown—was all that much of an improvement. But at least it had long sleeves and buttons. Then a new thought occurred to her. More than one nightgown must have been packed for Jeannette. Maybe one of the others was more modestly sewn. A nice opaque cotton lawn like the sort she was used to wearing to bed.

A quick search of the trunk, though, dashed her hopes, the nightgowns she discovered inside every bit as bad as the one she was presently wearing. And in one particular case, worse—made with more lace, less silk, and dyed a shade of red the devil himself would have blushed to see.

Tugging the robe more tightly around her body, Violet glanced around the room. Her eyes settled uneasily upon the large tester bed that stood to her right, covers folded down in invitation. Should she climb in and wait for Adrian there? Would such an action seem too forward? Or should she sit on the small sofa near the fireplace, try for a casual pose? Neither choice seemed satisfactory. Who did she think she was, after all, Caro Lamb to Adrian's Lord Byron?

Normally she would have read a book until she grew sleepy. But she had left her copy of the novel she was reading on her nightstand at home, half finished. What a shame. Likely she would never find out how the story ended—another very entertaining tale told by the clever author Jane Austen. It was a foregone conclusion that Jeannette would care nothing for the book. In all likelihood, her sister would lose Violet's copy somewhere between Portsmouth and Rome, a convenient prop she would carry with her, then absentmindedly leave behind on a table or a coach seat.

Violet trod forward and back, forward and back across the pliant wool rug under her slippered feet. What had she done? How would she ever be able to keep up this charade? Would Adrian know tonight when he saw her that she was a fraud? When he kissed her? Would he sense she was not the woman he believed he had wed? Would he realize she was not Jeannette?

That was her true fear. The real reason she trembled even now. She wasn't so much afraid of what Adrian would do with her tonight in the bed—although that was a definite consideration—but more she trembled for fear of what he might find out.

A light rap sounded upon a connecting door she had

failed to notice earlier. It opened on silent hinges and Adrian stepped through.

Her time of solitary reflection was at an end.

Breath caught in her throat as she watched him shut the door then turn her way. Dressed in a long robe of dark brown velvet, whose color nearly matched his eyes, he stood tall and powerful, magnificent as a Greek statue. His thick, short black hair was freshly brushed, and damp on the ends from washing. His face newly shaven for the third time that day. Just looking at him made her ache, he was so painfully handsome.

She lowered her gaze toward the floor and was startled to see his feet were bare. Long and well shaped with neatly trimmed nails, a few fine black hairs sprinkled across the tops and on his big toes, his were the first adult male feet she had ever viewed. Not even her brother and father walked around barefoot, always clad in stockings or slippers or shoes. Seeing Adrian's feet, so masculine, so naked, sparked a fluttery sense of awareness inside her, together with a peculiar sensation of intimacy.

She swallowed hard and linked her hands before her. Then crossed her arms over her breasts a moment later, remembering the scanty state of her attire. She shifted uncomfortably and prayed he wouldn't notice the gown's indecent thinness.

"Jeannette," he said, holding out a hand. "Come here."

His tone was soft, gentle, the sort a man might use to coax a timid wild creature. Did he know she was frightened? Was her innate shyness about to give away her secrets? She doubted the real Jeannette would be this hesitant. Then again, she didn't know how her sister would behave alone with a man for the first time.

Would tonight have been Jeannette's first time? Violet shied away from the dishonorable thought but she couldn't help it. Especially in light of her twin's request earlier today, asking that she intercept notes from a certain individual named Kaye. If Kaye was indeed a man—and Violet would bet a year's allowance he was—she knew this was not the first secret flirtation in which Jeannette had engaged.

Putting her suspicions aside, she stepped close, laid her small cool hand into his large warm one.

He raised her palm to his lips, pressed a kiss into it, then upon the inside of her wrist as he had once before that day. "You are trembling," he said.

"Yes," she admitted, hearing the catch in her voice as she said the word. Her eyes focused on the vee of skin exposed above the collar of his robe, and the few dark hairs that peeked out where the lapels met. Was there more of that same hair hidden lower beneath the robe? What else did he have hidden under there? She flushed at the thought. *Oh, my.*

"There is no need to be so nervous. Everything will be fine." He paused and caressed her hand, dropping a leisurely kiss upon her knuckles that did nothing to lessen her trembling. Having him this close made her weak, shivery. He smelled so delicious, of bayberry and something else, something darkly male and uniquely him. Her toes curled inside her slippers.

"I wondered if there might be something you would like to tell me," he continued.

She frowned, puzzled. "No. I . . . I don't know what you could mean."

"Come now, you must have an idea. Isn't that the real reason for all this innocent shyness of yours? These unexpected attacks of bridal nerves you've suffered throughout the day?"

Panic squeezed sharply in her chest at his words. Oh, Lord, so he did know. But how? And for how long? And if he did, why wait? Why the charade, pretending to accept her as his wife? Why this intimate interlude between them now?

Had he decided to take his revenge upon her tonight? To punish her in some physical manner? Had he—oh, heavens, what a thought—decided to taunt her, then take her in place of her twin? Discard her come morning, to be sent home in ruin and disgrace?

Such a dishonorable plan as that did not seem in Adrian's nature, no matter how angry he might be. If he knew for certain who she was, wouldn't he simply confront her in a forthright manner instead of playing games, like a great cat toying with a shy mouse? Perhaps he was not positive in his suspicions and merely waited for her to offer up an admission of her guilt voluntarily.

He cupped her cheek in one hand, settled his lips over hers in gentle possession and persuasion. She whimpered, reached up to steady herself by clasping her hand around his wrist, solid and strong beneath her touch.

When he broke away, he pulled back only enough to speak, his breath fanning sweet warmth against her face, his eyes locked with her own. "You might as well be honest," he warned, low and silky. "I am willing to forgive whatever indiscretions there may have been in the past so long as you reveal them to me now."

"I-indiscretions?" She felt her eyes widen.

"Do not try to convince me you are untouched. I've heard talk, disturbing talk, and I will have the truth from you tonight, madam. One way or the other, I will know the truth. Whether it comes from your pretty lips, or I have to wait and find out when I take you to that bed. I would, however, prefer to hear it from you."

She nearly sagged with relief. He thought she wasn't a virgin—or rather, he thought Jeannette was not. Adrian still did not realize who she actually was. For now her true identity was safe.

But the sensation of relief was short-lived as his hand

lowered, easing gently around her neck, his thumb teasing across her collarbone. "Tell me," he repeated. His tone brooked no defiance.

"H-honestly, your Grace, there is nothing to tell. There have been no indiscretions, whatever you may have heard." None that she, Violet, had committed anyway.

He didn't believe her. She could read it in his eyes.

"There has been no one," she stated, trying to don a mantle of affronted pride and hurt the way Jeannette would have done. "I don't know who could have spread such vicious lies about me. I don't know how you could believe such blatant falsehoods."

He raised a brow. "So, you persist in this act, do you? Insist in the purity of your maidenly innocence?"

She stood her ground, swallowed her trepidation. "Yes."

"Don't think you can fool me with tricks," he said with a fierce scowl. "They won't succeed and I'll know what you've done. Now, one last chance. I promise I won't be angry so long as you are truthful."

She stiffened her shoulders, though she felt more like slinking away. "I have been truthful. I swear to you, your Grace, there is no one. No man has ever touched me. Only you."

His eyes hardened. "Very well. We shall have to resort to the direct approach, I see. Let us begin."

Adrian reached out, and without further niceties freed the buttons on her robe, slipping them loose, one after another after another. She kept her head high as she stood acquiescent beneath his touch, forcing herself not to quiver. He stripped her robe aside, flung it carelessly to the floor. She stared just beyond his shoulder as he raked his eyes over her body and the nearly transparent gown, shamed by what she knew he must be seeing.

Adrian sucked in a harsh breath at the ripe beauty

he'd uncovered, desire striking him a blow that settled hard between his thighs. Dear Lord, she looked like fair temptation herself. A sensual spirit brought to life. White lace hugged her breasts like an exotic second skin. Round pink nipples peeked out from beneath to tease and attract. The diaphanous skirt below, a misty veil that flowed over belly and hip, across long curvaceous legs, over the enticing, half-hidden vee of golden curls that lay between.

Seeing her so splendidly and effectively displayed only fueled his ire. Increased his need to rip through the false act she insisted on portraying. Innocent? Hah, she was no more innocent than he.

He hadn't planned to confront her. What was done was done. Women were human, he had counseled himself, subject to the same carnal cravings as men. They could make mistakes. Fall prey to temptations of the flesh, inside or outside the sanctity of marriage.

Yet as he had sat downstairs, sipping his brandy, left to his own idle reflections, he kept remembering her reticence throughout the day. Her quiet reserve over dinner. The shy, half-anxious glances she had thrown him. Her subdued conversation. The obvious case of bridal jitters that sprang to life when he had reminded her he would be joining her for the night. That was when his irritation developed, growing, together with his dark suspicions.

What if there was an underlying reason for her shy behavior? An ulterior motive for her uncharacteristic timidity? A reason she felt she must prove her innocence? True, it could simply be guilt; a well-bred woman was supposed to come to her marriage bed a virgin. She might be embarrassed. Then again, mayhap it was something more, something infamous.

Was she pregnant?

The idea made him half sick. He certainly didn't want

some other man's bastard whelp for his heir. He could always refuse to touch her, of course. Wait a few months to make certain she was not with child. But if he did that there would be talk. Word would leak out of their estrangement no matter how he might try to conceal it. Then, of course, there was basic math. Anyone could figure out the meaning of a healthy, robust baby born after only six or seven months of marriage.

And in the end, no matter what, she would still be his wife. If he discovered she had proved him false, he would have to divorce her. Drag the whole sordid affair out before the courts, his peers, the world.

No, he would find out the truth for himself tonight. The full truth. Then he would take whatever steps were necessary.

Features grim, he watched her. Wished she weren't quite so beautiful, quite so desirable. "Never been touched. That *is* what you said, is it not?"

She looked startled by his question, then she nodded. "No, never."

"Then you are bound to be shocked, my dear, but do not worry. I promise I will not hurt you . . ." slowly, deliberately, he slipped the white ribbon from her hair, let her tresses swing free over her shoulders ". . . any more than I must."

Her eyes widened at his implication. Silently, she cursed her twin for leaving her in such straits. Leaving her to accept the consequences for actions she herself had not taken. She wanted Adrian. But not in anger, not in falsehood and disillusionment. Then she didn't have time to think anymore as his mouth came down upon her own, smothering any protest or resistance.

Like being plunged headfirst into a deep whirlpool from which there was no escape, he crushed her lips to his. Passionate, impatient, without concern for her supposed maidenly sensibilities. She quivered and gave herself over to the storm. Letting him take as he wished. Letting him fit her close against his firm body, his arms locked behind her back like a pair of iron bars.

"Open your mouth," he demanded, pulling away enough to speak.

Senses swimming, she blindly obeyed, having no idea why he had asked such a thing of her. She gasped when his tongue thrust fervently between her lips. Hot and wet, he played with her own tongue in a way that left a warm, red haze rushing through her veins. She gasped again, then shuddered with pleasure when his hand moved low, curved over her left breast. He kneaded her flesh. Massaged it. Stroking his thumb across her nipple through the lace bodice. Back and forth, back and forth, until the sensitized nub stiffened to a rigid, aching peak.

"Kiss me back," he said. "Stop pretending you don't know how."

But Violet was beyond the point of pretending to be anything or anyone other than who she really was, and could only answer him with the truth. "I am not pretending," she whispered.

His eyes flashed, in irritation or hunger she could not tell. He slid a hand up into her hair, held her head steady for his delectation. Slower, with increased deliberation, he angled his head, tipped her jaw to one side. Softly at first, his lips grazed hers, plucking and nibbling. Playing with her, on her, in her mouth. Easing her into a dance he believed she knew but which she was only beginning to learn.

He kissed her in myriad ways. Hard then soft. Slow then fast. Sweet then sharp. Waiting between each touch for her to match his move, imitate his technique. Thinking became impossible as she acted purely on instinct. As she learned to simply enjoy and be enjoyed. And for a small span of time she forgot everything. Aware of nothing but the two of them, as he drew her into a drugged mating of lips and teeth and tongues that seemed to stretch into forever. Each of them taking from the other in long, pleasurable draughts of hot, wet wanting.

He pulled away suddenly and shocked her anew by bending to take the breast he had so thoroughly handled into his mouth. She could barely breathe as he licked and suckled her flesh through the thin barrier of lace that still lay between her skin and his lips. A patch of damp spread across the material.

She had never imagined such an act. Never dreamed such delicious, stunning pleasure might exist. A dark need she didn't understand began to crawl through her veins. An insistent ache forming between her legs that urged her on, demanding more. *More what?* she wondered in a daze.

Her eyes fell shut as she squeezed her fingers into the fabric of his robe. Sensation pounded through her in forbidden waves, roaring up, crashing over. She shuddered and strained for breath. Her lungs pumping as a thin, high sound she didn't recognize as her own issued from her throat. Then he bit her, a small pinch of teeth on her sensitized nipple.

"Oh," she cried out, body stiffening in astonishment. She took an abrupt step backward.

He looked up into her flushed face, into aqua eyes dilated with shock and dawning carnal awakening.

If he didn't know better he would think she was genuinely astonished by his last act. As if no man had ever touched her in such a manner. Had he made an error in his judgment of her? Was she actually innocent, or just a damned fine actress?

She was passionate, that was for certain. Yet somehow untried. Her kisses untutored in their hesitancy and eagerness to please. He could sense the raw need that lay coiled within her, waiting to be freed.

Already she made him throb like an inexperienced

youth ripe to couple with his first woman. It wouldn't do for him to lose control of the game now. No, it wouldn't do at all if he gave himself over to mindless animal instinct and forgot where his true purpose lay. After all, that was what she would want if she was playing him false. For him to begin to need beyond all other considerations, to forget her lies.

Enough with the preliminaries, he decided. He would know the truth, one way or the other.

He swept her into his arms and carried her to the bed. He removed his robe, tossed it across a nearby armchair, exposing his aroused, naked body to the warmth of the room. When he turned back, her eyes were wide as saucers. Her expression one akin to horror.

He was so big, Violet thought. So male. So completely different from her. She had never seen a naked man before. She had had no idea what to expect. He was . . . stunning, magnificent, his long limbs hard and sinewy with muscle, sleek arms, powerful thighs, narrow hips. As she had suspected, there was more of the same dark hair she had glimpsed earlier dusted over his body. It lay in flat, black curls across his firm chest, narrowed into a slender line that nearly disappeared as it ran over his taut stomach. Then the hair grew heavier again, circling down low around his . . . male parts.

She didn't know what else to call that portion of his anatomy. Seeing him unabashedly draped in nothing more than candlelight, her heart skipped a single, hard beat. She tried, yet somehow couldn't look away. Her mind scrambled frantically as a startling idea appeared in her head. Surely he didn't intend to . . . to put *that* inside her? For one thing, it would never fit; he would surely split her right in two with the attempt. For another . . . well, she didn't have time to think of another reason, she just knew she needed to get away.

She gulped visibly and scooted on her haunches toward the opposite side of the bed.

He reached out, snagged an ankle to stop her, then came down beside her. His long length, his great power overwhelming in its intensity. "Going somewhere?" he asked.

She shook her head, fatalistically accepting the fact that there was nowhere for her to go. Knowing she was well and truly trapped. Desperately she reminded herself who he was—Adrian, the man she loved, the man who was her husband. She gazed up into his eyes and told herself it would be all right. Whatever he planned to do to her, she would be fine. Wouldn't she?

He took her chin between his fingers. "Have you had a change of heart? Would you like to admit the truth now before we proceed?"

Violet shivered, wishing suddenly she could tell him what he wanted to hear. It would be so much easier. But she refused to lie. Not about this. Her integrity, her innocence, her honor. He had said he would know whether or not she was untouched. Soon, then, she supposed, he would realize she spoke the truth. If only she didn't fear what he must do first to find out.

She shook her head, silent, her eyes speaking the truth that she could not say.

His face hardened. He reached for the hem of her nightgown, pushed his hand underneath, stroking his fingers up along the skin of her thigh. Instinctively, she tightened her legs against his advance. He paused. "Open up."

When she didn't immediately comply, he gave the order again, this time in far more graphic terms. "Spread your thighs."

She trembled anew, then squeezed her eyes shut and forced herself to do as he bid.

"Don't be afraid, my dear," he said, dropping a kiss

upon her lips. "You know it won't hurt. And I'll take care to see you find your pleasure."

Then Adrian thrust a pair of fingers inside her where she was hot and wet and tight. Far tighter than he had expected. But that didn't necessarily mean anything. She was a small woman. Perhaps her previous experience had been with small men.

Before she could voice any objection, he began to work inside her. Stroking, rubbing, moving his fingers in a nimble rhythm he soon planned to repeat with another portion of his body. He looked up, watched her wide, open eyes begin to glaze over. Her fingers curling at her sides, clutching tight at the coverlet beneath her.

He'd have her panting before he was done, he promised himself. He'd have her writhing with desire.

Her breasts heaved. He watched them, her nipples puckered, pink as flower petals beneath their fine lace covering. He tugged at the material. Then he tore it, ripping it away to get at her bare flesh. He clamped his mouth around one nipple, drew deeply upon it as he pushed his fingers deeper still.

Violet's hips arched up off the mattress. Straining, grasping for something she did not understand but wanted irregardless. It was as though he had taken possession of her body. Literally reached inside and assumed control. Her fear vanished, falling away like leaves scattered from a windswept tree.

He had spoken of pleasure. And oh, he was giving it to her. Great heavy waves of pleasure. Delight such as she had never known. The sounds. The scents. Fresh sweat and other odors, unfamiliar odors, both sexual and forbidden. She should be embarrassed. But she was not, too caught up in the wanting to consider such things.

When he transferred his mouth to her other breast, to indulge it with the same treatment he'd given the first, she lifted a hand. Threaded it into the black silk of his hair.

He groaned and murmured against her flesh, "Touch me. Touch me."

Obediently, wanting to please him as he was pleasing her, she raised her other hand and stroked. First his shoulder, then down, over his smooth, naked back. He shuddered, groaned anew. She rolled her head from side to side. Mindlessly she opened her legs wider to permit more of his compelling touch.

Then abruptly he withdrew, taking away his lips and hands as he moved to rise over her. He planted his knees between her thighs, steadied her hips in his hands. She was ready, he knew. Wet and throbbing, trembling on the very brink of completion.

Now, he thought, now he would make her cry out in ecstasy.

And cry out she did. Only not in the way he had planned. Hers an exclamation of true anguish as he thrust inside with a single, firm stroke.

Adrian froze, not wanting to believe what his body was telling him. What his senses were shouting.

A virgin! Sweet Jesus, she was a *virgin*.

Chapter Five

Adrian trembled as his body hung suspended over hers.

She'd told him. Time after time. Only he had not listened, had not believed. *A virgin.* How could he have been so wrong?

What of the talk he had heard, the confidences shared? Were they all nothing more than scurrilous lies? Apparently so. He had no doubt now, remembering how he had torn through her maidenhead only seconds ago when he had forced himself inside. Even now he was not yet fully sheathed inside her, her passage so narrow.

A tear leaked from the corner of Violet's eye. Maybe if she didn't move, she thought, the pain would cease. Maybe if she stayed still, he would go away. Surely it couldn't be any worse?

"Jeannette, I—I'm sorry."

And then she knew it could be, his words hurting far more than the physical pain. Hearing him speak her sister's name at such a moment, with him lying over her, inside her like this. It was unbearable. Only, he didn't know who she really was.

Her fault.

Just as he hadn't known about the innocence that had been hers alone to give. Her fault again, she supposed. She turned her face aside, another tear sliding over her cheek.

He kissed it away, lips tender against her flushed skin.

His body held in the grip of a fierce, unsatiated desire. Poised halfway between heaven and hell. He should probably withdraw, he thought, leave her alone. Only, he couldn't quite bring himself to. Not now. Not when it felt so extraordinarily exquisite. Not when he knew it could feel even better still.

She was his wife, he told himself. He had a right. The thought made his body harden further. Besides, if he let her go now, he might never get her into bed again. Not without force. And that he did not want. All she knew now was the pain. He needed to show her there was more. Needed to show her there could be pleasure too.

"Relax and it will be better," he said.

She made a small sound like a squeak.

He reached down a hand to reposition her hips, then gently eased himself the rest of the way inside.

She whimpered.

"Wrap your legs around me," he urged.

Violet didn't think she could. But if it would satisfy him, get him to finish whatever it was he intended to do, then she supposed she would comply.

She raised her legs, hooked them around his hips. Moments later, he began to thrust. Shallow strokes at first, then longer ones. She sensed his restraint, as if he was denying his own urgings in favor of her own.

She held on to him, sliding her arms over his shoulders. Then stroked her palms across the fine, warm skin of his back. She reveled in the fluid texture she found, the tensile strength.

Yearning swept over her again. That same lovely rush she had experienced before when he had touched her with his hands. Building, swelling, leaving her body literally weeping for relief. Ripples of exquisite need pulsed through her system. Tingling in her toes. Exploding in her brain. Aching in her deepest depths.

She moaned.

Not from pain this time but from desire. Wanton, willing and ripe. A high, thin thread of sound that floated upward into the room.

Adrian's breath sang warm and heavy in her ear as he continued to move within her. Suddenly his body stiffened and shook. His head arched back, a look of intense, almost feral satisfaction etched on his features. A wet warmth filled her before he collapsed upon her. Lungs pumping for air. His face cradled against her neck.

She waited. Was it over? Was that all? It seemed to her there should have been something more.

As if sensing her thoughts, he levered himself onto his elbows. Took most of his great weight off her small frame. "I couldn't wait. Next time will be better, I promise."

He rolled away from her. Less than a minute later, he climbed from the bed.

She tugged the coverlet up over herself, high under her chin.

Was he leaving?

There came the unmistakable sound of water being poured, followed by a soft hush of movement. Next, the light clink of porcelain on porcelain. Old water dumped in the waste basin, exchanged for fresh. With his feet all but silent on the carpeting, he crossed back to her, a china washbasin painted with cheery yellow flowers held in one hand.

He stopped beside her, naked and completely unashamed. The skin along his thighs, and that other unmentionable part of him, damp from where he had obviously bathed. After a hasty look, she turned her eyes away.

"Would you prefer I put on my robe?"

She didn't answer, couldn't answer.

Setting the basin on the side table, he took up a spot next to her on the bed.

She didn't react until he reached out to pull back the covers. She clutched them to her, fought a silent tug-o'war.

"Let me," he urged, his tone gentle. He dunked a clean washcloth in the basin, rang out the excess water. "You'll be more comfortable."

Did he mean to wash her, down there?

Heat flooded into her cheeks, embarrassed afresh even after the intimacy they had just shared. "I—I'll do it myself, later."

"It will be easier if I assist you now. Let loose, my dear." He gave the covers another tug. "I've already seen you, you know. There is no need for this sort of modesty."

He was right, she supposed. He had seen her. And touched her in ways she had never envisioned. Jeannette would not have been modest. By now she would probably have been lounging beside him, relaxed as a kitten. And as much as she hated the necessity of it, she was, after all, supposed to be Jeannette.

Damn, she didn't want to think about her twin. Not now. Not here like this with him.

She released her hold on the bedclothes, let him fold them down. Shock rippled through her when she saw the blood smeared over her thighs, across the sheets, staining her nightgown. She had not realized she would bleed like this. No wonder losing her innocence had been so painful.

The wet cloth was cool. But not unpleasantly so when he laid it against her flesh to wipe away the evidence of their coupling. She closed her eyes while he ministered to her. His touch efficient, calm, tender as a nursemaid tending a beloved babe.

"Shall I bring you a fresh nightgown?" he asked

when he had finished. He discarded the washcloth into the basin of water.

She glanced down at herself. Noted the ripped bodice, bloodstained skirts, and realized she would be more comfortable in another garment. Until she remembered the choice of gowns available inside her trunk.

She shook her head. "My robe, perhaps."

It wouldn't cover a great deal, she knew, but it was better than any of the other possibilities.

He went to retrieve it.

He took a moment first to slip into his own robe, then walked to the center of the room, bent to collect her garment. Wordlessly, he laid her robe across the foot of the bed. Then he picked up the washbowl with its pink-tinged water, crossed to the commode to toss it away.

Taking advantage of his discreetly turned back, Violet stripped off her ruined night attire and slipped on the thin robe. She buttoned every button—all five of them—before climbing back into the bed.

Adrian soon returned, pulled the covers up to her chin, tucked her in tight. He brushed a lock of hair away from her cheek. "I should have listened to you, my dear. Should not have doubted your word. I will not do so again. You have my promise."

Now it was her turn to feel guilty. He was apologizing for assuming she had lied, then finding out she hadn't, when her very presence here was a lie. He believed she was another woman. She was letting him believe she was another woman. If Jeannette had been here tonight, Violet was sure Adrian would not have been apologizing. He wouldn't have had any reason to apologize, for anything.

"Would you rather I slept in the adjoining room for the rest of the night?" he asked.

No doubt Jeannette would have bid him good night

and turned her back. Likely she would have preferred to sleep alone.

Violet raised her eyes to his. Saw the man she still loved. The man she still wanted no matter what may have transpired between them. Reaching over, she folded down the bedclothes on the empty half of the bed.

He hesitated, then walked slowly around the bed. She snuggled down, the feather pillow comfortable beneath her head.

Adrian gutted the few candles still burning and plunged the room to black. She heard him slip out of his robe, then climb into the bed. The mattress gave beneath his weight.

They lay there on their backs. Each of them staring upward toward the bed canopy, which could not be seen in the dark.

After a time, Violet heard him take a deep breath.

"I am sorry for hurting you, my dear," he said. "I am sorry I was not more gentle when I could have been. When I should have been. I hope tomorrow we might begin anew."

She swallowed against the lump in her throat then turned on her side, scooting closer to lie against him. She wrapped her hand around his upper arm, pressed her cheek against his shoulder. "Go to sleep. It is late," she murmured.

He raised his arm to snuggle her more tightly to him, her face pillowed against the smooth warmth of his chest. His heart beat steadily beneath her ear. She listened, finding its rhythm soothing and uniquely relaxing.

She closed her eyes and let sleep take her.

Her maid, Agnes, awakened her the next morning when she drew back the curtains. Crisp yellow sunlight streamed through the windows like a sunny pair of hands to shake Violet from her rest. She grumbled and rolled over, buried her head deeper into the nearest pillow.

It smelled of Adrian, male and a little musky.

Delicious.

Her eyes opened fully this time as memories of the night past flooded into her consciousness. She was alone in the bed. She wondered how long ago Adrian had left.

"Good morning, your Grace," Agnes said. "I am sorry to wake you so early. But his Grace said he wants to be on the road no later than eight-o'-the-clock."

Violet sat up, brushed her tousled hair away from her face. "Hmm."

The girl gave her a look as if she half expected Violet to pitch a rebellion. Likely Jeannette would have done that very thing. She could imagine her flopping back into bed after delivering the message that the duke could be on the road any time he bloody well liked, but she was going to sleep in.

Violet didn't have the energy for any early-morning rebellion pitching, however. Her sister's juvenile temper tantrums had always been a sore spot with her. Pretending to be Jeannette notwithstanding, Violet decided she would curb that particular character trait starting this morning. Let the servants believe marriage had changed her, matured her. In this one respect, Violet was certain they would feel nothing but profound relief.

"I have your breakfast, your Grace. Would you like to take it in bed?"

Violet would have preferred to dine at the small table near the window. But she knew Jeannette never did anything—not even get out of bed—until she had drunk her first cup of tea.

"Here would be fine, Agnes."

After arranging the pillows at her mistress's back so

that Violet could sit comfortably upright, Agnes placed the tray onto her lap. The maid said not a single word about the fact that Violet wore nothing but her robe. Nor did she comment on the condition of the torn, bloodied night rail. She merely removed the soiled garment from the chair where Violet had tossed it last night, then carried it away.

"I've unpacked your blue traveling dress, your Grace. Will that be satisfactory?"

Violet looked up from the slice of toast she had been smothering with lemon curd—her favorite—to give Agnes a blank stare. She knew absolutely nothing about fashion. And even less about the contents of her twin's wardrobe. Ask her to quote Shakespeare or debate a point of historical fact and she would have been perfectly at ease. But clothes? For a split second, panic set in. Seconds passed as she got hold of herself once more, reined the emotion back in.

"Yes, the blue will be fine, thank you. Now, I should like to finish my morning repast, if you don't mind."

"Oh, of course, your Grace." Agnes bobbed a curtsey. "I will return in a few minutes to help you dress."

Violet nodded, reminding herself to behave like her sister, then lifted the teapot to pour herself a steaming cup. As soon as the door clicked shut, she set the teapot down, closed her eyes in relief.

How was she ever going to keep up this pretense?

One day at a time, she told herself. One moment at a time, actually.

Nearly two hours later, Violet strolled down the main staircase, garbed in the elegant periwinkle traveling dress Agnes had selected. Matching accessories of hat, gloves and small high-heeled shoes made from the softest kid leather completed the outfit. Affecting an air of nonchalance that she in no way felt, Violet acted as if her tardy arrival was of no concern.

Jeannette was rarely on time.

A prompt appearance—particularly this morning—would have been tantamount to admitting she was impersonating her sister.

Adrian waited in the hall, ready to depart. It was nearly nine o'clock.

She caught the briefest hint of a frown on his face just before he saw her.

The look cleared and he smiled, coming forward to take her hand. "Good morning, my dear." He dropped a kiss on the inside of her wrist in the spot he favored. "I trust you slept well?"

The usual tingle raced over her skin at his touch, heightened as her body recalled all of the other places he had kissed and caressed last night. It took every ounce of her determination to stem the blush that threatened to spread like a rash over her cheeks.

"Yes, quite well," she replied. "And you?"

"Quite well."

Their eyes met in a long speaking glance, each of them remembering the way it had felt to lie in the other's arms through the quiet hours of the night. Soon, Adrian dropped her hand, crossed to a small table and picked up a pair of tan leather gloves.

Dressed for riding, he was a picture of casual masculine elegance. Snowy white shirt, buff breeches, black-and-white striped waistcoat, his Hessian boots polished to a gleam. His snug, dun-colored coat showed off every inch of his sturdy, broad shoulders.

"I take it you mean to ride out?" she said, stating the obvious.

"You don't mind, do you?"

"Not at all," she denied.

With no book to read and no company, the hours ahead were bound to be long and boring. She wouldn't even be able to enjoy the passing scenery. Not without her spectacles. But perhaps traveling solo would be for the best. Alone, she wouldn't be forced to constantly keep up the pretense.

Adrian drew on his gloves. "Ready?"

She lifted her chin in a gesture she knew Jeannette would have used. "Quite ready."

Morning crept into afternoon as their party made its way toward Dorset and England's southern coast. Guilt crept upon Adrian for taking the coward's way out, riding instead of passing the time with his new wife inside the coach. But after last night he felt in need of some solitude. Perhaps she did as well.

How could he have been so completely mistaken in his judgment of her? He had been convinced he knew the truth. Gleaned in large measure from the confidences related to him by his friend Theodore "Toddy" Markham, a man who had a unique ability to learn things about people they might prefer others didn't know.

Most considered Toddy a harmless fop who spent far too much money on his clothing and horses and far too little time on other more sensible pursuits. Little did they realize he had served as one of Britain's top spies during the war, gathering information on the home front and abroad and passing it along to the highest levels inside the British War Office. Adrian had been one of the select few chosen to serve as a contact to receive that vital information.

After suffering a nearly fatal wound at the first Siege of Badajoz in 1811, Adrian had been forced to resign his commission and take a less obvious role in the war effort. He'd traded the heat and gore of the battlefield for the cool anonymity of clandestine alleyways and dark smoky pubs. In such places he made contact with a variety of informants, some of an admittedly unsavory character, who were willing to trade information in exchange for money or favor or, upon occasion, for nothing more than the glory of pure patriotism. Toddy was one of the noble few, content merely to be of service to his nation.

Over the years, he and Toddy had developed a deep respect and affection for each other. Which is why Adrian had believed him when his friend reluctantly confided reports of some unsettling rumors he had heard about Adrian's intended bride. Although Toddy's warnings had come a bit too late, Adrian assured him he could handle the situation, whatever it might be.

Well, he'd certainly handled it last night, Adrian thought with a rueful grimace. How could he, and Toddy's information, have been so drastically wrong?

Mercury, his big gray gelding, danced a few steps sideways on the gravel turnpike, spooked by a covey of wood pigeons flushed from some nearby brush. Without the faintest break in concentration, Adrian reined his mount back under control, the gentle pressure of his knees against Mercury's side enough to reassure the steed and return him to his proper forward path.

He caught Jeannette observing the tableau through the coach window. He raised a hand in greeting. She nodded in reply then lowered her eyes and turned away.

Still annoyed, he supposed, about his choice of destination. Another black mark on his slate. Though thinking upon it, he couldn't recall her voicing a single derogatory word since the wedding about spending their honeymoon in Dorset. Odd that. Up until that point, she had done little but complain and mope. He sighed to remember her behavior. As though the canceled trip to the Continent had cast a permanent blight upon her life.

Since the wedding, however, a change seemed to have swept over her, one of unexpected serenity and acceptance. Mayhap her father had sat her down for a meaningful talk on her wedding eve. Although knowing what he did of the earl, it seemed unlikely. Wightbridge took little interest in anything other than his club, gambling and sport—the Hunt his favorite pastime. The man had never struck Adrian as a terribly involved parent. Then again, perhaps he was mistaken in that as well.

He observed Jeannette again out of the corner of his eye, watching the pretty feather that decorated her bonnet bounce as the coach rolled over a rough patch of road.

Tonight would be different, he promised himself. He would use a gentler hand with her. Try to regain some of the trust he had abused last night. She would know nothing but pleasure and fulfillment when he took her to his bed tonight.

Mortifying as it was to admit, he'd lost his usual control last night, there at the very end, in a way he had not done since he had been an innocent sprig. She had an effect upon him he could not explain. A disturbing effect. Although he had longed to awaken her with kisses this morning at dawn, to show her his reputation as an experienced, considerate lover was not an exaggeration after all, he'd known she needed to sleep more.

A virgin. He still could not believe it.

A fist of primal satisfaction clenched inside him at the knowledge, spread in a hot wash through his belly. It should not matter, such things never had before. Yet knowing he was the only man she had ever lain with made him hunger for her all the more.

And she wanted him as well. Even in her innocence, there was no disguising the passion that ran deep inside her fiery core. He would tap that heat. Coax it. Coax her. Teach her everything she needed to know and more. He smiled, greatly looking forward to the instruction to come.

His prurient thoughts had him shifting uncomfortably in the saddle, rolling his shoulders to dispel the sudden strain. He frowned and forced himself to think about something else. Something dull and tedious. Or something worrisome, such as the recent unfortunate incidents on his estate.

The unusually cool spring and wet summer they'd had in Derbyshire was causing the rivers and streams to swell and overflow their banks. Several tenant homes had been damaged in the floods, forcing families to flee and seek shelter with their more fortunate neighbors and friends. Three of his farmers had been made to look on, helpless, as their homes were swept completely away in the raging waters. Those families, with his assistance, were even now working to rebuild.

The crops in the fields suffered as well, leaving many fearful of a poor harvest come fall. Hopefully, the clear skies many were praying for would arrive soon. If not, he would see to the welfare of his people this winter. Even if he was forced to import grain to make up the shortfall.

Given that, he hadn't felt comfortable traipsing off to the Continent, not even for his honeymoon. Jeannette would simply have to understand his responsibilities. Hers now as well since she was his duchess. They would embark on a grand tour next year. Visit all the places she most longed to see and a few more too. Until then she would have to be patient.

He rode on, their party stopping at an inn a short time later to change horses and enjoy a hearty midday meal.

Violet climbed from the coach into the bustling yard, relieved to stretch her legs and have something of a more active nature to occupy her mind. A pair of hostlers ran up to see to the horses, exchanging greetings and instructions with the coachman and footmen, who jumped to the ground.

She had been bored senseless with nothing to do but watch the blurry scenery roll past and think her own dreary thoughts. Even watching Adrian hadn't proved as entertaining as she might have hoped. He had ridden ahead of the coach most of the journey. Nearly out of sight—especially her sight, impaired as it was. Her stomach grumbled, her breakfast of toast and tea long since gone. She would be glad of a meal.

Aware Quality had arrived, the innkeeper hustled out the front door. A beaming smile of welcome creased his spare cheeks. Tall and thin as a maypole, his bar apron wrapped double around his narrow waist over the thick leather jerkin he wore. On his head, a thatch of rust-colored hair that looked bright enough to light a fire.

"Good day to you, your Grace," the innkeeper said. "And to your lady. Welcome to my humble establishment. I hope your journey has been a fair one so far."

"Thank you, it has. You have a private room, as requested, do you not?"

"Of course, of course. All is ready. If you will come this way—"

At that instant, a loud crash sounded, followed by a thunderous bellow of pure rage. From the rear of the inn charged a huge black and white dog. Running fast behind him came a large man, red in the face and waving a cane. The dog would have outrun the man for sure if the animal hadn't had the misfortune to skid on a slick patch of muddy earth at just the wrong moment. His legs slid out from under him, long enough for the man to reach out and grab his collar.

The cane came down upon the dog's flesh with a horrifying thud. The dog let out a painful howl, shivering and cowering even as he struggled to get away. Violet didn't pause to think, acting wholly on instinct as she raced forward. Her only thought was to prevent the abuse she saw unfolding before her. "Stop that! Stop that this instant," she demanded.

The man ignored her and struck the dog another blow. The animal yelped, then issued a series of furious barks, showing his teeth and snapping at the hand wielding the cane.

"Try to bite me, will you?" The man raised his cane high into the air.

Oblivious to the danger, Violet reached out and wrapped a gloved hand around the base of the cane. "I said, stop."

He turned, his eyes flashing cold as night at the unexpected interference. He shook her off as easily as a gnat. "Who the hell are you?" he roared. "Leave off. This is no concern of yours."

He was a beefy brute of a man, the kind who likely beat women as well as animals. Fear clutched in her belly. She shivered but stood her ground, spine straight, her outrage too great for caution. "I am making it my concern. Release that dog."

"This here bastard stole my supper, and I'll be givin' him exactly what he deserves, without any sass from the likes o' you."

"If he weren't starving, I am sure he would not have stolen anything." Even Violet with her less than perfect eyesight could see the terrible condition the dog was in. Sharp bones covered in taut black and white fur, painful to witness.

"He's a thieving beast, that's what he is. And I'll thank you to mind your own business, woman." He shook the cane again, waving it in her direction this time.

"And will you thank me as well?" a voice interceded, smooth and deadly as a silk-covered fist.

Chapter Six

Adrian towered over the trio of man, woman and dog, magnificent as an avenging archangel. Even the dog stopped his impassioned barking and fell quiet.

The man had the good sense to gulp. He bobbed his head. "Sorry, guv'nor, didn't mean to offend."

Adrian stared down the length of his nose as if he were viewing a particularly disgusting insect. "Your very existence offends. Apologize to my wife."

The man swallowed tightly. "Your pardon, missus."

"Your pardon, *your Grace*," Adrian corrected in a frigid tone.

The man's eyes widened, protruding as though they might pop right out of his head. He now sensed the importance of the personage with whom he dealt. "Your pardon, your Grace."

"Now release that poor, unfortunate animal," Adrian ordered.

The man hesitated for the briefest of instants, as if working up the nerve to refuse. Then, with a small pugnacious curl to his upper lip he couldn't quite hide, he did as Adrian demanded.

The dog raced away.

"Now your cane," Adrian said.

"My cane? What do you want with me cane?"

"Hand it over and I shall instruct you."

Reluctantly, the man passed the cane into Adrian's hands.

Without revealing so much as a hint of his intentions, Adrian took the cane and snapped it smartly in two over his raised knee.

The man gasped.

Jeannette goggled.

Nonchalantly, Adrian passed back the pieces. "I hope this will serve to remind you that a cane is not a weapon. Certainly not one to be used on the defenseless."

"You broke me cane. That there cost me ten quid."

"Far less, I suspect, than it will cost you should I decide to press charges and have you sent to the local gaol. If you say even one more word, I might change my mind and do that very thing."

"For what? Beatin' a dumb beast?"

"For threatening the safety of the Duchess of Raeburn. Although I would press the matter of the dog as well, if I believed the law would punish you sufficiently. Now be gone, and don't show your face around here again."

The man flushed and opened his mouth as if he might offer a further protest. Then he seemed to think better of it, turned on his heel and stalked away.

The innkeeper rushed forward, wringing his hands. "Oh, your Grace, I am most profoundly sorry for this unfortunate incident. Nothing of this sort has ever happened before at my establishment. I'll see to it he receives no additional service from me."

Adrian inclined his head.

"The man's trouble," the innkeeper continued. "A soldier, from what I hear, recently sold out. Has a mean temper. I suppose the war turned him hard."

"Perhaps." The brutality of war could damage even the best of men. Adrian had seen it firsthand, seen men's minds twist and crack beneath the grim, unrelenting horror of battle. Even he'd suffered through his own share of nightmares and troubled memories over the years.

"Still," he stated aloud, "it's no excuse for whipping a defenseless animal, no matter what the man's difficulties may be."

"No indeed," the innkeeper agreed.

Adrian turned, intending to speak to his wife. Only she was no longer beside him. Surprised and not a little concerned, he set his hands on his hips and scanned the yard. *What sort of danger has she decided to thrust herself into now?*

He found her easily enough, near the stables, where the dog had taken refuge. One of the stable boys—a lad of eleven, perhaps twelve—was trying to prod the animal out from behind a hay cart using the bristle end of a broom. The dog, hunched into a defensive, cowering ball, was having none of it.

"I'll get him, milady," the stable lad chirped in an eager voice.

"Please, stop. You're only scaring him more than he already is." She bent down, showing an unexpected disregard for any ruin that might come to her elegant attire, apparently interested only in reaching the terrified animal. She murmured soft words, low and soothing. "It's all right now, love. No one is going to hurt you. No, no, they are not going to hurt you anymore."

The dog didn't move but he did stop trembling. His amber eyes moved upward to meet her own.

"That's right. Come now. Come to me, boy. You'll be fine."

"Jeannette," Adrian said, his voice quiet, even, yet carrying an underlying edge of steel. "What do you think you are doing? That dog is injured, abused. If you are not careful, he will bite you."

"Oh, he won't bite me. He is a sweet dog. Are you

not a sweet dog?" she crooned to the animal. "Yes, you are." She stretched out a hand, fingers curled to show the canine she posed no threat.

"Jeannette!" Adrian moved to pull her away but she evaded him, leaning farther in.

The dog sniffed, catching her scent. Slowly, he snaked out a warm, pink tongue and licked the top of her hand.

"See," she said, "he's fine. He's a good boy."

The dog's tail thumped in a friendly wave. Up and down against the hard, dusty ground beneath him. He continued to bathe her hand, nuzzling his cold black nose into her relaxed, open palm. Then slowly he rose to his feet, slender dappled tail wagging like a black and white flag of truce. He walked out from behind the cart to huddle against Jeannette's skirts.

"Would you look at that," the stable boy marveled.

"Yes, would you." Adrian relaxed, seeing the dog posed no threat to his wife, no matter how big a brute he might be.

Though whipcord thin from starvation, the animal was still massive. His jaws were big enough to eat Jeannette's entire delicate hand in a single gulp if that had been his wish. His canine head easily reached past her waist. Great Dane derivation, Adrian imagined, and sporting a collar as well. He must belong to someone, but who? And where were they?

As if the boy had heard Adrian's musings, he began to tell them about the dog. "He's a stray. Been hanging around these parts since spring. Wouldn't let nobody get close to him till now. Been eatin' scraps and such. Drivin' my boss, Mr. Timmons, crazy with the mess he leaves from trolling through the garbage at night. Looks like today he got bold, stole that bloke's pie from right off the dining table."

"Well, I think he is a very brave dog," Jeannette declared, petting the animal's head, stroking his pointed ears. The dog's eyes fell closed in obvious rapture at her touch. After spending a night in Jeannette's arms, Adrian knew exactly how the dog must feel.

"You are certain he has no master, then?" Adrian questioned.

"No, milord. Leastways, none that I know of. If you want him, he's yours to keep."

"Oh, yes, Adrian, let us keep him." She turned her luminous aqua eyes his way. Eyes against whose power, he discovered, he was hardly immune. They tugged at him with an almost magical pull.

"What a great lummox he is," Adrian observed. "Whatever would you do with him?"

She smiled. "Fatten him up, for one, and give him a bath. He smells a bit of the barnyard, don't you think?" She wrinkled her pretty nose in emphasis of her comment. "I am certain he will be a splendid beauty once he is restored to health. All he needs is love and care."

"I should have thought a lapdog would be more to your taste. A spaniel or toy poodle, perhaps."

She paused, as if debating her answer, then shrugged. "Well, no doubt you are right, were I choosing a dog. But he is here and he needs a home, no matter his size. We cannot abandon him now. After all, that villain might return and do him a dreadful turn. I shouldn't be able to sleep for worrying over him if we left him behind."

"Perhaps a family in the village might be persuaded to take him in," Adrian suggested.

"You heard the boy. He has been a stray for months. If a family here wanted him, they would have adopted him already."

"The lady's right, milord," the stable boy interjected. "Folks round here figure a big 'un like him would eat 'em out of house and home. Worse than being saddled with a set of ten-pound twin boys."

Adrian's lips twitched at the lad's colorful way of speaking. His expression sobered as he turned to his wife. He had never before known Jeannette to demonstrate a particular affinity for animals. That specific trait seemed more in keeping with her sister, Violet, whose love of lesser creatures was apparent for all to see. Yet maybe he had underestimated his wife again. Perhaps she shared more in common with her twin than he imagined. After last night, he was loath to prejudge anything about her.

"Would you truly like him?" he asked.

Her face brightened. "Oh, yes, indeed I would."

"It seems, then, my dear, that you have a dog."

"Oh, Adrian." She closed the distance between them, threw her arms around his waist.

He hugged her to him, gazed down into her radiant eyes. "Does this mean that I am forgiven?" he inquired in a gentle, intimate voice.

"Forgiven?" Her eyes widened, a wash of color pinking her cheeks.

He knew she must be thinking about the night past. His next words corrected her. "Hmm, for dragging you into the countryside for our honeymoon trip."

She relaxed, settling more comfortably against him. "Well," she said slowly, "that is a great deal to ask, for I am still sorely vexed with you over the matter. But I suppose under the circumstances, I must make the best of our situation. Yes, your Grace, you are forgiven."

He smiled, watched her lips part in reply and nearly bent to cover them with his own. Then he remembered they had an audience. A rather large audience, considering they were standing in an inn yard. Had it been solely his choice, Adrian would have tossed the proprieties aside and kissed her as he wished. But he didn't know how his new bride would feel about him taking such liberties in public.

Reluctantly, he released her and extended his arm. "Shall we adjourn inside to partake of a meal?"

"Yes, that would be lovely. I am rather hungry. But what of Horatio?"

"Horatio?"

"Our dog. Horatio is what I should like to call him. It seems such a fine, brave name. And I think he deserves that much after everything he has suffered."

Adrian smothered a smile. "Horatio it is, my dear. But you are right, we can't simply leave him here." He motioned to the stable lad. "Boy, fetch us a rope or some such to use as a leash."

"Right away, milord."

"That's 'your Grace,' Robby," Mr. Timmons corrected, bustling back into view. "This gentleman and lady are the Duke and Duchess of Raeburn, and you'll address them properly."

Robby gulped. "Sorry, milord, milady. I . . . I mean, your Grace, your Graces. I'll get that rope now." Executing a quick bow, Robby bounded off into the stable.

Adrian made a mental note to leave the lad a nice wage for his efforts.

"And some food, Mr. Timmons," Adrian said, turning toward the innkeeper. "For the dog. A joint of beef or perhaps one of the pies that caused all the commotion. It seems he favors them."

They arrived near the Dorset coast early that evening as the sun crested to its highest peak. Beyond, on the horizon, broad cliffs dropped off in a great hard tumble of rock that angled down toward the ocean. The water itself was a patchwork of blues and grays. Sunlight winking and glittering off the white-capped waves as they rolled to shore. The English Channel in all her majesty and glory.

Breathtaking.

Even without her glasses, Violet could tell how beautiful the landscape was as the coach passed along the coast road that led toward Adrian's estate. The inland fields were vivid green with bushy clumps of waving grass. Songbirds dived in a merry game from tree to tree, a few trading pretty calls as they filled their bellies with the last grain of the evening. While out across the ocean, their sea-loving cousins keened for fish. Gulls whirling in lazy, sweeping circles, feathery flashes of white against the piercing azure sky.

Horatio perked up, moving from open window to open window on both sides of the coach, pausing in between to hang out his massive head, mouth agape, and watch. Violet was little better herself. Delighted as a child, she thrilled to the invigorating tang of salt air, its scent sweet-crisp in her nostrils.

Violet had been to the seaside only once before, on a visit to her mother's cousins, the Chesters, the summer she turned eight. She remembered it particularly because Jeannette had not been along on the trip, confined to her bed with the influenza. One sick child in the house, their fretful mother had pronounced, was more than sufficient.

So Violet had been shuffled off to Kent. Instead of being homesick, she had reveled in the adventure. She could still remember the way she had felt then. The freedom, the fun of being allowed to run wild in the surf with the Chester children, Jeff and Sarah. The three of them coming home after long, long hours, sunbaked, clothes stained and dripping, feet and legs caked with sand. The Chesters had not scolded them. Just shaken their heads and sent them off with the nanny for baths and dinner. Even now, the memory of those few short weeks remained one of her very favorites, a place to escape in lazy afternoon daydreams.

Jeannette had been very put out after Violet's return, decreeing she never wanted to hear another word about the English seashore again. Perhaps that was why she had been so distressed when Adrian informed her they would be spending their honeymoon on the southern coast.

But Violet knew this week away was going to be a rare treat. Even if she would not be able to romp in the waves as she had done as a girl. For that reason, she would have to be very strict with herself, watching every reaction so she didn't reveal her true self by accident. It wouldn't do for her to admire her surroundings too excessively. "Jeannette" may have forgiven Adrian his choice of honeymoon locale, but it did not follow she would fall in love with the place.

For the same reason, she would need to dampen a little of her enthusiasm for Horatio. She feared she had nearly given herself away back at the inn. Her twin tolerated animals so long as they did not make a nuisance of themselves, but she would never have fought for an animal the way she herself had done despite Jeannette's natural abhorrence of such abuse.

Violet reached out and stroked Horatio's velvety head. He turned his expressive eyes her way and gave her a doggy smile of pure contentment, pink tongue lolling. She smiled back at the animal, her heart lighter despite the weight of her worries.

The coach rolled up a long shell and pebble drive, stopping before a stately Georgian house made of mellow golden stone rising three stories high. Adrian had merely said they would be staying at one of his family's many country houses. His description had not done the residence justice.

For one, it was huge, forty rooms at least. Sprawled out over the land like a hulking giant. Pane after pane of sparkling window glass glinting in the well-ripened sunshine. The servants' entrance stood at ground level. A set of elegant double stairs led up around it to the main portico, finished in the Palladian style, complete with columns.

Yet all that faded into insignificance compared to the roses. Hundreds of them clinging to the far side of the house, pink and lush, climbing skyward on tall white trellises as if they meant to touch heaven itself.

Oh, and the fragrance. It was like being bathed in a bottle of the most luxurious perfume ever created. Violet drew in a deep breath and closed her eyes, savoring the experience.

It was quite simply the most beautiful, most romantic setting she had ever seen.

Her twin, she thought, was a fool. And not for the first time, Violet had to admit she was glad of the switch.

The coach door opened. Horatio bounded out, releasing a series of joyous barks as he loped to and fro on the drive. She proceeded at a more sedate pace, allowing Adrian to reach in a hand to assist her down the small steps to the ground, swinging her the last few inches with an arm effortlessly looped around her waist.

"Finally here," he commented after she was settled. "It has been a long day's travel." He paused at her silence, as if afraid to voice his next question. "So what do you think, my dear?"

She knew she should not reveal her delight. Her twin would not have been overly impressed with the display of natural beauty. Such things mattered little to Jeannette. But in that moment, Violet could not contain her true feelings. "I think it is simply enchanting."

His eyes warmed, tiny lines fanning in the corners as he smiled. A dimple popped to life in his right cheek. She fought the urge to trace her finger over it, her heart hitching inside her breast. Love washed through her, crashed like the rough ocean waves she could hear sounding in the distance.

She had lied to him. Her very presence here was a hideous deceit for which she would someday surely pay. But right now she had not a single regret. Right now, he was her husband and he belonged to her.

The look in his eyes changed, lids drooping with sudden desire. She waited to see if he would kiss her, right here in front of the line of servants that had formed at the foot of the main staircase. Over a dozen people waiting to welcome the master and mistress home.

She wished they would all vanish. She wished she and Adrian were alone.

Horatio raced up, inserted his large body between them in an exuberant canine wiggle. He shattered the mood as effectively as a scolding duenna.

Adrian arched a brow of amused resignation. "Shall we, my dear?"

She accepted the arm he extended and let him lead the way.

Adrian introduced her first to the regular caretakers of the estate. The Grimms, an older couple who were the exact opposite of their name, smiling and full of good local cheer. Mr. Grimm oversaw the grounds and upkeep on the property with the aid of two assistant gardeners and groundsmen. Mrs. Grimm served as housekeeper and cook, with her own staff of two: a parlor maid, Susie, who was too shy to do more than squeak out a greeting, and Cynthia, the kitchen maid, as round and pretty as a freshly picked apple. The remainder of the servants were from Winterlea. Josephs, the coachman. Robert and Harry, the footmen. Mr. Wilcox, Adrian's valet. Agnes, her lady's maid. And three additional maidservants brought to lend a hand wherever they might be needed: Tina, Nancy and Leah.

Violet forced down her natural shyness. It wouldn't

do to appear frightened in front of the servants. Yet she could not bring herself to don the regal cloak of authority she was certain Jeannette would have slipped on.

Despite her rank, Violet realized servants were people with lives and needs, hopes and aspirations quite separate from her own. At home she had been close to many of the servants, receiving from them the kind of tolerant acceptance and understanding she had failed to receive from her own family. The servants never complained of her quiet, studious ways, never criticized or ridiculed her interest in intellectual matters such as history and languages. They accepted her for the person she was, and in return she had always tried to do the same for them.

Respecting that, respecting her new position as duchess, she did her best to greet each one of them with warmth and appreciation. She accepted their good wishes on her marriage, nodding graciously and smiling.

It soon became obvious they adored Adrian and would do anything within their power to please him. He was relaxed, friendly, yet still in command in a way her father never was with his own people. She knew Adrian had been in the military during the war. A decorated war hero, although he preferred not to speak of it. She wondered if this was how he had treated the men under his command. If they had revered him this much. She suspected they had. Suspected they had been willing to do anything—including offering up their own lives—for him and their cause.

Introductions complete, Horatio made to follow them as she and Adrian started toward the stairs. She turned back, her heart pained when she realized she could not bring him inside. At least not in his present unkempt condition.

"Would one of you see to my dog?" she asked the servants. "He is in need of a bath and a good meal. Then a walk afterward."

A long moment of silence commenced as all eyes turned to the canine behemoth standing next to the duchess. Each of them calculated the odds of their success in dealing with the beast.

Then Robert stepped forward. A wiry, earnest young man with hazel eyes and close-cropped brown hair. "I'll see to him, your Grace. I like dogs. We had four big 'uns when I was growing up. Though not as big as him." He nodded toward Horatio. "Him and me will do, though."

"Thank you, Robert."

The footman stepped forward, taking Horatio's collar in hand. The dog stood, unmoving, obviously reluctant to be parted from her.

She leaned down, smoothed a hand over the dog's ears. "Go with Robert. You have nothing to fear. You will be cleaned and fed and rested, and I shall see you in the morning."

Horatio whimpered as if he understood every word she said, unhappy at being separated from his savior. Another long moment passed, then tail down, he acquiesced, let Robert lead him away.

She drew herself up, suddenly aware of what she'd just done. Gushing again over the animal. Had Adrian noticed her rather un-Jeannette-like behavior? She raised her eyes, found him waiting, watching, no outward sign of suspicion on his face.

She raised her chin. "I should like the same," she announced. "A bath and dinner as soon as it might be arranged. I feel quite travel-weary."

Mrs. Grimm swung forward, all business, quick despite her wide hips. "Of course, your Grace. All will be to your liking. Allow me to show you to your rooms."

The housekeeper ascended the stairs. The duke and duchess followed.

Violet had her bath, then let Agnes assist her into a gown suitable for a quiet, at-home meal. The dress was comfortable, a spotted muslin in pale yellow with an overskirt of sea green that her maid declared made her eyes sparkle like jewels.

She joined Adrian, finding him splendidly attired and looking quite elegant in his black evening clothes, worn in spite of the country setting. They shared a few moments of desultory conversation in the parlor before proceeding into the dining room.

Mrs. Grimm had gone out of her way preparing the evening meal, Violet noticed, as one sumptuous course after another was presented for their delectation. Tender roast squab with raspberry sauce. Chicken and mushrooms in a delicate puff pastry. Roast beef and creamed baby leeks. Braised whitefish with lemon, capers and dill. Each successive course was served with a lengthy selection of accompaniments, including a cheese herb soufflé and stuffed baby eggplants. There were salads, relishes and breads as well. And for dessert Mrs. Grimm had chosen wisely, presenting a simple selection of cheeses and fresh fruit.

Unlike the evening before, Violet ate with a hearty appetite. Consuming more than she usually did mainly because she was so hungry, but also, in part, as an effort to show her appreciation for the culinary effort and skill put forth for her and Adrian's pleasure. She did her best to sample a selection of as many dishes as she could comfortably manage, finding them all equally delicious.

"Wherever did you find Mrs. Grimm?" she inquired, accepting an after-dinner cup of coffee in a delicate china cup. "She is an exceptional cook."

Adrian ate a piece of Stilton cheddar and a wafer-thin slice of pear. "Actually, she found me," he explained after he swallowed. "When I purchased this property about four years ago, the Grimms came with it. A fortuitous event, I have always believed."

"I'm curious, why did you buy this house? It's not in a likely location for a vacation residence."

He arched a brow, ate another bite of pear. "Likely for some, unlikely for others. Truth be told, location is precisely the reason I bought it. I suppose there's no harm in telling you, now that the war is over. I used to do some work, confidential work, for the War Office. Owning a house that looks straight out over the Channel toward France offers several distinct advantages. The beach is private and very isolated. It makes for an unparalleled rendezvous point on quiet, moonless nights."

Violet felt her eyes widen. Was he saying he'd been a spy? How extraordinary, she thought, her mind filling with images of secret messages and clandestine meetings. British spies coming and going by way of Adrian's beach, probably bearing news vital to the war effort. Adrian's mother was French. Likely he spoke the language like a native. What a perfect choice he must have been. A trusted, respected ex-officer. An aristocrat who just happened to own a house on the seashore.

She was still digesting the intriguing revelation when he abruptly changed the subject.

"Are you certain I cannot interest you in a bite of this delicious dessert?" he asked.

"No, no, I have eaten far too much tonight as it is. If I consume any more, I fear I will be unable to lift myself out of this chair."

"Don't worry. If you find yourself stuck, I will come round and help heave you out."

"Heave me out? Are you implying I am fat, your Grace?"

"Heavens, no. If anything, you could do with an extra bit of flesh on your bones, comely as they are."

The relaxed atmosphere, the enjoyable meal and the role she was performing combined to make her bold.

"So you would not mind if I increased my girth?" She waited, finding herself suddenly anxious to see how he would reply.

"If you got as round and wide as our esteemed cook, it would simply provide me with more of your beauty to admire." He smiled, lips curving with slow warmth.

Her own curved in reply, pulse quickening in an unsteady beat. "Be careful," she murmured. "You know it would only give me reason to shop for an entirely new wardrobe."

Adrian tossed back his head, roared with laughter.

Coffee consumed, plates cleared, candles snuffed, the evening progressed until soon it was time for bed. They parted at the base of the main staircase, Violet too shy to inquire when or if he might join her. Forcing aside a blush, she retreated up the stairs.

Agnes dressed her in yet another of the scandalous nightgowns. Pink this time, with a scallop-shell hem and no lace, just diaphanously thin. She waited in the sitting room that adjoined her bedchamber, perched on a settee covered in watered apricot silk. Ordinarily she would have found the color charming. Enjoyed the ambience of the room decorated in soothing tones of peach and cream. Tonight her mind was preoccupied with other matters.

Would he come? Did she want him to?

She was still struggling to find an answer when Adrian arrived half an hour later, dressed in the same robe he had worn the night before.

A memory swept upon her. How rich the texture of the brown velvet beneath her hands. How warm and sleek his skin to her touch after he had removed the garment.

She lowered her eyes and held her breath as he drew near.

"Would you care for a game of cards?" he inquired.

Her gaze flew upward. Surely she had heard him wrong? "Cards?"

"Hmm." He held up the deck in his hand. "It is early yet. I thought you might enjoy the diversion."

"You wish to play cards," she repeated, nonplussed.

"Mmm-hmm. Your choice. Hearts or two-handed whist?"

"I . . . I . . . Hearts, I suppose."

"Excellent choice." He removed a vase of flowers from a round cherrywood tea table that stood near the unlighted fireplace, set the arrangement high on the mantel. He drew up a pair of side chairs, took a seat and began to shuffle the cards. "Come on," he urged when she failed to move from the settee.

Utterly confused, she masked the unexpected twinge of disappointment that swept through her. Then rose and accepted the seat across from him. She picked up her hand, blinked in dismay at the card's blurry appearance.

Her spectacles. How could she have forgotten she would need them? He had caught her completely out. If she squinted a little, though, she believed, she could just make out the numbers. At least she had no trouble distinguishing the colors, red from black. She only prayed she didn't mix up the suits.

"Anything wrong?" He lifted a single dark eyebrow.

"No, simply studying my cards." *Studying them hard,* she thought.

Somehow she managed to compensate, the game falling into an odd rhythm, of sorts. Although he won the first two hands, she trounced him on the third, relaxing enough to forget most of her difficulties as she chuckled over a very droll story he told concerning a wagonload of apples and a farmer trying to escort his hungry pigs to market.

"My game," she declared, grinning in triumph as she spread her cards faceup on the table.

"So it is." Adrian tossed down his hand, tallied the points. "By my calculation, you're twenty points ahead. I demand another chance at victory."

"Very well."

"A drink first, however. What would you care for, my dear?"

"Thank you, nothing for me."

"You must have a little something. Drinking alone is never any good."

"Well, all right, if you insist."

Adrian disappeared through the connecting door that joined her suite to his. He returned in a short while carrying a pair of bowl-shaped snifters. He set one in front of her.

She eyed the amber liquid with suspicion. "What is that?"

"Brandy." He sipped from his glass, then resumed his seat.

"I have never had brandy. I am not in the habit of drinking hard spirits, you know."

"I did not think you were. But it seemed to me you might enjoy indulging in a little experimentation."

He was right. Jeannette would enjoy just such a thing. She was always ripe to try the unusual or the forbidden. Violet raised the glass, gave it a tentative sniff. The scent was sweet yet tangy.

"You are not trying to get me drunk, are you?" she asked.

"There is barely a splash in that glass. Hardly enough to get drunk on. Besides, what use would I have for plying you with liquor?"

"To help you win the next game, perhaps."

Adrian laughed, flashing her a devastating grin. He drank another swallow of his brandy, then set his glass aside and began shuffling the cards.

She sniffed at her glass and swirled the alcohol,

watching it run in rivulets inside the snifter. Her twin would try it, she knew. And she was supposed to be her twin, after all. She was also a married woman now. What could be the harm, as he said, in a little experimentation?

She took a drink and choked, her throat burning as if a fierce hand had wrapped around it and squeezed. She sputtered and coughed, fighting to catch her breath.

Adrian reached out, rubbed his palm over her back. "There now, not so much at once."

"That is vile," she gasped as soon as she could speak, coughing a few more times. "Why on earth do you drink it?"

"It's not so bad. You merely have to acquire a taste for it. Takes practice."

"Hah. Well, I believe I will leave the practicing to you."

He arranged the cards he had dealt for himself, pierced her with an eye of mock condemnation. "I will have you know that is some of the finest brandy to be found anywhere. Liberated from Napoleon's own cellars."

"All I can conclude, then, is that you and the Emperor have atrocious taste."

Adrian smiled, drew a card to start the next game.

Violet won the first round and extended her lead. Adrian claimed the next two, placing him a few points ahead. As a kind of challenge to herself, and to Adrian, she took a small sip of her brandy. The liquor spread like a comfortable fire inside her, warming her blood, relaxing her muscles. She still didn't like the taste, but perhaps the stuff was not as bad as she had originally thought. She swallowed another tiny sip before setting it aside.

Her turn, she took the top card off the deck.

"What did you draw? You look like a cat who has been in the cream."

"I'll never tell," she taunted.

He drew a card, discarded a four of clubs. Reaching out, he covered the hand she had left on the table, toyed with her fingers. Her skin tingled where he touched her.

She swallowed and tried to concentrate on the play. She picked a card, ended up discarding one she should have kept. "I believe you are trying to distract me."

"Really," he drawled. "Is it working?"

"Not a bit."

But it was. Her play began to suffer despite her best attempts to ignore his overtures.

He found her hand again the next time she set it on the table and tugged it slowly upward to press a kiss into her palm. Instead of pulling away, her fingers moved as if of their own accord. She stroked the supple, clean-shaven skin of his chin and cheek. He nuzzled against her, drawing one of her fingers into his mouth.

Her breath caught, knees turning gooey when he swirled his tongue around the digit. His eyes locked upon her own and held her mesmerized. Helpless, she let him do the same with her next finger. And the next. She shivered as he pressed warm kisses onto her palm in between. The sensations were devastating. As if he were touching her intimately, not just her hand but everywhere, all at once.

Bewitched and breathless, she felt her whole body tingle. The cards in her other hand tumbled to the table, forgotten.

"Shall we finish the game?" he asked, voice husky. He ran the tip of his tongue across her palm, ended by planting a drawing kiss against the inside of her wrist. Her fingers quivered and convulsed.

"What game?" she sighed.

"Come here."

Chapter Seven

Adrian pulled Violet up and out of her chair, her legs shaking as he settled her onto his lap.

"Kiss me, my dear," he urged. "Kiss me."

He wrapped a steadying arm low around her back, held her and waited.

She blinked, surprised and uncertain. She'd expected *him* to kiss *her*. Apparently he was leaving the matter quite literally in her hands, despite his obvious need, pressing as it was against her hip. Last night she might have found his physical response unsettling. Tonight, resting warm and relaxed in his arms, brandy buzzing pleasantly in her head, she only wanted to lean closer. To touch him, taste him, pleased by her blossoming knowledge that he desired her.

She gazed at his beautiful face, into his dark, compelling eyes. Her lashes fluttered downward as she studied his lips. So strong and masculine, parted in anticipation of her touch.

Tentative, hesitant, she placed her mouth against his. Soft as a butterfly's wings, she moved her lips, brushing, gliding, absorbing the tiny shock waves that pinged like firefly lights through her system.

He remained acquiescent, resting his head against the chair back to let her explore, at her own pace, in her own way. Somehow, she forgot to be afraid. Forgot all the reasons why she might be reluctant to let things progress between them.

Needing the contact, she slid her fingers into his hair. It curled against her flesh. Silky, springy, luxurious. She closed her eyes, parted her lips and pressed them more insistently against his own. She waited, expecting him to take over, to drag her into the maelstrom the way he had last night, to control her, command her.

When he didn't, when he went no further than the dictates of her own uncertain touch, she pulled away. "Why aren't you kissing me back?"

"I am kissing you back."

"No," she whispered. "I mean, why aren't you kissing me the way you did last night?"

"Is that what you want? If you do, you must tell me. I am completely at your disposal this evening, my dear. It's up to you to lead the way, set the pace. If you want to take it slowly, we'll go slowly. If you want to take it fast, we'll go fast. You must tell me everything you desire, everything you like."

"And if I don't know what I like? What I desire?"

"Then use your instincts. You'll find they're rarely wrong."

She gulped down a breath and tried to banish the pesky nerves that threatened to halt her. "Kiss me," she commanded this time.

He feathered his lips over hers, slowly, softly.

"No, harder," she breathed.

He kissed her harder.

"Openmouthed, like you did last night."

He did as she asked and sent her senses reeling. Remembering he was waiting for her, she forced herself to make the next move, touching her tongue to his. Timidly at first, then with increasing boldness, tangling her flesh with his own in a dance both wet and wild. He met her movements, matched them, lips and teeth and tongues mating in an imitation of the most intimate act of all. She drew upon him. He drew upon her until she was left gasping, quaking. Her lungs were screaming for air when she broke away. She rested her forehead against his cheek.

"What else?" he panted, his breath warm in her ear. "What else would you enjoy?"

Images popped into her mind. Carnal images that should have made her blush from shame but didn't. She shifted against him, restless, aching. "Touch me," she whispered.

"Where?"

She knew where, but she couldn't say the words, not yet, certainly not out loud. But she could show him. Her body yearned, urging her on.

With eyes closed, she found his hand, placed it over her breast. "Here," she whispered. "Touch me here."

He cupped her flesh, molded it as if it had been formed exclusively for his touch. He stroked. He fondled. He caressed. Passion grew, blossoming within her, lush as the roses that flourished on the walls outside the house. A fragrant heat ripened between them, rich with pleasure, dark and forbidden in its intimacy.

He unbuttoned her robe, peeled it off her shoulders, down her arms, leaving it to drape onto the floor. Skimming a finger under the slender strap that held up her gown, he eased the narrow bit of material downward. "Yes?" he confirmed.

"Yes," she agreed.

She moaned when his warm fingers touched her bare breast, tracing a path across her skin. He kissed her, nibbling and plucking. Teasing her. Tempting her. His scent swam in her brain, a dizzying joy. He pulled away after a time, measured the weight of the breast cupped in his palm. He finessed a thumb over her taut nipple. "Yes?"

She understood what he meant. Did she want him to

kiss her there? She nodded, realizing she wanted it very badly.

He eased her slightly back and away before arching her over the firm safety of his arm. He took her flesh into his mouth, loving her with his tongue and teeth and lips. Violet whimpered, panting at the volatile pleasure, her body drowning beneath relentless waves of heat and delight. She tried to raise her hand. She needed to touch him, but the nightgown strap at her elbow prevented her.

Sensing her desire, her frustration, Adrian reached up, tore the strap loose, then ripped the other one aside as well. He moved back from her long enough for the bodice to drop to her waist, baring her fully to his eyes, his touch.

Violet gasped. Then she laughed. Seconds later, she was groaning, her eyelids fluttering shut as he bent his head to her other breast.

Her hands free, she stroked his head, caressed his neck, traced the outer curve of his ear, unconsciously urging him to take even greater liberties. He reached down, grasped the hem of her nightgown and insinuated his hand beneath. When she stiffened, he stopped, raised his heated gaze to meet her own.

"Too soon?" he asked. Gliding, he smoothed his hand upward over her knee. He paused and began to draw lazy circles there, first above the joint, then below. Above and below in a belly-clenching figure eight.

She trembled and hung her head. "I don't know. Yes," she whispered. She kissed his cheek, tasted his lips. *So sweet, so sweet,* she thought, her mind spinning. "I mean no. It's not too soon." She sighed in longing and surrender. "I mean all right."

A small answering shudder ran through his body. He crushed his lips to hers, drinking from her, plunging them fast and deep into a world where only they two existed. Where she forgot everything but the exquisite way he made her feel.

His hand moved, gliding higher this time as he dotted random, leisurely kisses over her face and neck and shoulders. He coaxed her thighs open, threading his fingers through the nest of short curls above, then onward, parting her moist flesh for his exploration. And she let him, burying her face against his neck, floating, abruptly helpless.

Beyond speech, she hung suspended, trapped inside the glorious sensations he was igniting. Her body burned. Hot. So hot, it seemed she might be consumed by the flames, reduced to cinders. She gasped as a rough, edgy storm clawed her. An urgency she barely understood driving her, making her arch and open to him. She clutched his robe in her fists as he sent her spiraling upward, her entire existence suddenly poised on the brink. The brink of what? she wondered. Then he flicked his fingers and gave her the stunning answer, sending her plummeting wildly over the edge.

She cried out as convulsive pleasure swamped her. Yanking her downward into a merciless undertow that threatened to drown her before flinging her upward again, to toss her whole and safe once more onto dry land.

Panting, replete, she curled against him, little electrical hums jangling every nerve ending in her body. Yet before she had a chance to regain her senses, he was urging her upward again. Driving her body to hunger anew, greedy and unrelenting in its need.

"I can't," she cried, shocked by the response of her body.

"You can," he insisted, threading his hand into her hair. He steadied her head, savaged her mouth and thrust his tongue deep, at the same instant caressing her down low with a wicked, wild stroke.

She shattered, screaming her release.

Adrian swallowed the sound, reveling in it, knowing he had brought her successfully to peak. Not once, but twice. She collapsed against him, breasts heaving. He cupped one, traced her pretty nipple and a pale blue vein that ran just underneath her milky skin. He could wait, he told himself, a little while longer anyway.

They were only getting started.

He let her have a minute or two to recover, then stood her on her feet. He kept a strong hand at her waist to make certain she didn't crumple to the floor. Her nightgown hung bunched around her hips, barely clinging. He gave it a slight nudge, watched it whisper into a silken pool at her feet.

Adrian stood and placed Violet's hands on the belt looped at his waist. "Will you help me untie it?"

She quivered, hesitated, then tugged at the tie, ineffectually at first but gaining confidence with additional effort. She slipped the belt free of its knot. The folds of his robe opened, partially exposing him to her gaze.

"Help me with the rest," he invited.

She surprised him by skimming her hands up over his chest, along his shoulders, down his arms. His robe joined her nightgown on the floor. Taking her hand, he led her to the bed, tumbled them down upon it onto their sides.

He skimmed his knuckles over her cheek, dusted a few kisses across her lips. Then he groaned and rolled onto his back.

Violet lay next to him, confused. Why wasn't he kissing her? Touching her? Why wasn't he taking her as he had done last night? Surely he was not yet satisfied. She could tell from the rampant condition of his body that he was not.

She leaned up on an elbow. "Adrian?"

He reached up, played with the ends of her hair. "Hmm?"

"Aren't you . . . aren't you going to . . ."

"To what?"

"You know. You must want to take your pleasure too."

"Did I pleasure you, my sweet?"

She didn't see how it was possible to blush at such a moment, lying utterly naked next to him, but she did. She lowered her eyes. "Yes, you know you did."

He smiled. "Good."

"But what of you?"

"I told you, tonight is for you."

"But I cannot . . . well . . . leave you like that." She gestured toward his unmistakable erection. "Isn't it uncomfortable?" she whispered.

"Hmm, but I will manage." He paused. "Unless you'd like to help."

"Help?"

"Yes, make love to me, my dear. Touch me, kiss me, anything you wish. I leave myself to your tender mercies. My comfort, as you called it, is quite literally in your hands." He closed his eyes.

Violet stared, nonplussed by his actions for the second time that evening. There was no understanding the man tonight. Touch him? Kiss him? She'd assumed he would keep doing those things to her. And such things. Her inner muscles clenched at the memories, a fresh wave of desire crashing through her. She hadn't known such delights were possible, had never even imagined. Did it feel that wonderful for him when he was touched? Could she please him as he had pleased her despite her lack of experience?

Adrian waited in a torment of need. He feared he might die if she didn't accept his offer and take the initiative. Merciful heaven, what if she decided to curl up next to him and go to sleep? He clenched his teeth in an agony of frustration at the idea.

Then his prayers were answered, her small cool hands skimming experimentally over his chest, arms, shoulders. He forced himself to lie still as the inferno of want inside him raged hotter, his body thrumming under her untutored caresses. Down his stomach and sides, over his hips and thighs, knees, calves and ankles. She even stroked his feet. She touched him everywhere. Everywhere, that is, but the one place that ached the most for her attention.

He slung an arm over his face and steeled himself to endure more of her exquisite embrace.

"Are you all right?" she asked, her words husky, quiet. "Do you like it?"

"If I liked it any more I fear I'd unman myself here on the sheets." Peeking out from under his arm, he caught her look, realized she didn't fully understand, not even now. "Yes, I like it," he grated out in a strangled tone.

"Then I am doing it correctly?"

He nearly laughed. She could have given lessons to trained courtesans, her touch was so delicious. "Yes."

"Shall I kiss you?"

"Please," he said, his tone rough as gravel.

But she didn't begin where he expected, her long hair brushing his chest before she parted her lips over one of his nipples. She feathered the taut nub, his muscles jumping when her tongue reached out to circle and flick.

He sensed her confidence begin to increase as she leaned upward to scatter kisses across his chin and cheeks, his throat and collarbone, before moving back to pleasure his chest once more.

He purred low in the back of his throat as she kissed her way down his stomach. Groaned when she reached his thighs. Shuddered when she licked the backs of his knees.

Then she touched the most male part of him. His arm came away from his face, his eyes flashing open as her small fingers curled in a loose clasp around his arousal.

"Oh, you are so very warm," she whispered in a sort of awe. "Hard yet smooth, like velvet."

A harsh, guttural moan rumbled from his throat.

She released him. "Did I hurt you?"

"No. God, no."

Their eyes met. He reached down, took her hand and returned it to his willing flesh. Her eyes widened in astonishment and wonder, her eyelids drooping as he gently demonstrated to her how he longed to be touched.

An agile learner, she caught on quickly.

When he didn't think he could stand any more, he pulled her hand away and rolled her over on the bed so that he lay on top. He captured her lips in a ravenous kiss, feverish with want, fervent with need. His hands raced over her lithe frame, cajoling, caressing, inciting her to riot.

And all the while, she touched him. Surrounding him with her scent. Beguiling him with her sinuous moves and fiery embrace until he could barely remember his own name.

Violet let him take her into the storm, her senses drugged on a surfeit of passion. Blood drummed a heated rhythm behind her closed eyelids. Pulse points throbbed in every extremity of her body. She ached, empty in a way she had never been empty before. As if the heart of her needed to be filled, needed to be claimed.

By him. Only by him.

Yet when the moment arrived, when she sensed his need to join with her, she balked, stiffening despite her undeniable ardor.

He leaned over her, trembling and ready. Then he

stopped, noticing her sudden reluctance. He cupped her cheek in his hand, gazed into her eyes.

"What? What is it?"

But even as the words left his mouth, he knew. She was afraid, remembering the pain of his entry. The first, the only time she had ever made love.

In sudden decision, he tumbled them over the sheets, flipping onto his back so she rose above him. He should not have forgotten, he reminded himself, tonight was for her.

"It won't hurt this time," he told her. He traced a single fingertip along her breastbone to her stomach. Then spread his palm flat on her skin, just above the juncture where her body wept for him.

"How you felt earlier when I touched you here?" He slid his fingers between her legs, stroked her slowly, intimately. "Having me inside you will feel even better, I promise."

Her body quavered beneath his nimble hands, then he drew them away. "You take me tonight."

"Take you? I don't understand."

"Yes you do. Here." He caught hold of her hips, positioned her legs so she straddled him, his tip poised against her entrance. He caught hold of her hands, drew them forward to rest them on his chest. "Leverage."

Leverage? She nearly laughed, stunned by the concept. Then she trembled, caught in an agony of longing and uncertainty.

"If it hurts," he said reassuringly, "you can always stop."

Buoyed by the idea, Violet hesitated only a second more before she sank downward, the full, powerful stretch of him filling her, almost too full, too big. But he was right, there was no pain. Only a deep, compelling ache of desire. She moved her hips, took more, as much of him as she could handle.

"Now what?" she panted.

"Now you move. Up and down, over and over again until the exhilaration sweeps you away."

And doing as he instructed, she soon understood why he craved this. How their bodies were perfectly formed to feed each other's mutual needs, to satisfy each other's hunger. She sank onto him, catching a rhythm, riding the dark waves as they thundered through her. Her thinking mind ceased to function as her body took control. She heard her gasping cries but barely recognized them as her own. She heard his choked exclamations but found nothing shameful in them.

Then, lungs pumping for air, muscles quaking from the strain, the crisis hit her once again. She shook all over, stars and moons sailing through her head as ecstasy flooded her system.

Exhausted, replete, she collapsed over him.

Adrian rolled her onto her back and plunged deep, as deep as he could go. Clasping her hips in his hands, he raced to find his own release. It seized him in its grasp moments later, so strong he shouted against the force.

Floating in a haven of warm bliss, he buried his face in the damp curve of her neck and waited for the shock waves to subside. Only when his brain quit spinning did he realize she'd fallen asleep.

Violet surfaced slowly, curving her arms up over her head as she stretched in pure, lazy contentment against the fine linen sheets. She reached out a hand for Adrian, and found nothing but cool empty space on his side of the bed.

From the amount of light in the room, she realized it must be full morning. How long ago had he arisen? she wondered. She wished he were still here. She missed him already. His pillow even now bore a slight indentation from where his head had lain. She tugged it into her arms and snuggled her face into the crease. Breathing him in, she remembered the night past with a well-satisfied smile.

After their first delectable bout of lovemaking, she had fallen into a heavy, dreamless slumber. He had roused her twice more during the night to make love, as if he couldn't get enough. He came into her the last time as dawn broke through the lightening sky in brilliant shades of pink and orange. By rights she should be exhausted. Yet she couldn't remember the last time she had felt so splendidly rested. She savored his scent on the pillow once again, then sat up.

The bedroom door opened a crack and Agnes peered inside. "Are you awake, your Grace?"

Violet quickly drew the sheet up to cover her naked breasts. "Yes, come in."

Agnes bustled through the door, closed it at her back. In her hands, she carried a large copper urn, several fluffy towels draped over her arms. "Good morning, your Grace. I hope you slept well. I've brought hot water." She set her burden down near the fireplace. "His Grace thought you might like a bath. Shall I ring for the tub?"

"Yes, a bath would be nice."

Agnes gave the bellpull a tug, then crossed to yank back the drapes. A flood of rich, warm sunlight crowded into the room.

"What time is it?" Violet inquired.

"Just past noon, your Grace."

"Noon! Oh, I never sleep so late."

Agnes paused, surprise plain on her face.

Violet realized what she had said and moved quickly to correct her error. "I mean, I never sleep so late in the country. Only in Town."

Agnes relaxed, nodded in understanding. She bustled

toward a massive walnut wardrobe ranged against the far wall. Opening its heavy double doors, she withdrew a dressing gown, carried it over to Violet. "His Grace said you were tired from the journey and to let you sleep in."

"How considerate of his Grace," Violet murmured. Obediently, she climbed from the bed to slip into the robe. The garment was gorgeous, cut from a length of cream-colored sateen, heavily embroidered with gaily-hued lilies, tulips and irises.

She observed that Adrian had also been considerate in another matter—her nightgown and robe laying neatly draped over one of the straight-backed side chairs. The brandy glasses and playing cards gone from the table. Violet hugged a small, secret smile to herself, remembering anew.

"His Grace is a lovely man," Agnes volunteered. "If you don't mind me saying so, your Grace. All the servants have nothing but praise for his kindness and generosity."

"You are right, Agnes. I am a very fortunate woman." Agnes had no idea how very fortunate, Violet thought, since but for a stroke of fate she would not be standing here right now. Her sister would.

Agnes had just finished pinning up Violet's hair when a knock sounded on the door.

"That must be the tub," Agnes said.

Violet loitered near the window as two of the servants, Robert and Harry, carried in the large metal bathtub. The men deposited their burden, then departed, returning shortly bearing four large buckets of steaming water. They poured it into the tub, turned to leave.

"Oh, Robert," Violet said. "Pray tell, how is my dog this morning?"

Robert turned, eyes lowered in deference to her relative state of undress. "Oh, he's doing well except for his needing to add a few pounds. He passed a fine night in the stables, your Grace. Wolfed down a hearty breakfast this morning and licked the bowl clean for good measure."

"Excellent." She smiled. "If you would bring him round after I dress and eat my breakfast, I shall meet both of you outside."

"Of course, your Grace. I'll have him ready. He'll be eager to see you, I'm sure."

"Have you seen the duke today, by chance?"

"Oh, yes, your Grace. He spent some time walking the estate with Mr. Grimm this morning. Then I believe he took Mercury out for a gallop."

"Well, thank you, both of you." She nodded to include the other footman. "That will be all for now."

The men bowed respectfully and left, shutting the door behind them.

"Robert is frightful brave, taking care of that great bounder of a dog." Agnes's eyes widened, realizing what she had said. "Oh, beg pardon, your Grace."

"Are you afraid of Horatio?" Violet asked, astonished at the idea. "You needn't be. He is quite large, I concede, but he is sweet underneath, with a good, true heart."

From the maid's expression, Violet could tell she was far from convinced.

"Actually," Violet mused as she approached the bathtub, "he reminds me of the duke in that respect."

"The duke?" Agnes gasped, then giggled. "Whatever can you mean, your Grace?"

"Well, they are both of them very large, fearsome creatures when threatened. Yet undeniably sweet on the inside. You said so yourself, the duke is a lovely man. A man with a pure, true heart, good as gold."

A good, true heart that she was deceiving.

Violet pushed aside the rush of guilt that claimed her,

slipped out of her morning gown and stepped into the warm bath. Leaning her head back against the side of the tub, she let the water lap around her in a soothing wave.

"See to my breakfast, will you?" she asked Agnes in a quiet voice. "For some reason, I'm utterly ravenous this morning."

Chapter Eight

Afternoon sunlight streamed downward, so brilliant Violet had to raise a hand against it as she exited the house an hour and a half later. Her shoes crunched noisily on the crushed-shell drive as she walked, a steady breeze blowing in off the nearby coastline easing what would otherwise have been a hot day. And in the air, tangy and strong, hung the scent of the sea, perfume-rich roses sweetening the mix.

She closed her eyes and drank it in. Relishing the moment as the wind enfolded her in gentle arms, mischievous airy fingers plucking at her hair and long skirts.

Moments later another pair of arms, real arms, slipped around her from behind. They pressed her back against a tall, firm, masculine body. A body she recognized immediately, having spent the past night curled snugly against it.

"Adrian." She sighed on a smile.

He bent his head, smoothed his lips over her neck and along the underside of her jaw. "Good afternoon, my sweet. Or perhaps it still seems like morning to you."

She laid her hands over his. "If it does, you are entirely to blame. You are the one who told Agnes to let me sleep in."

He tipped her head back, feathered kisses over her cheek and lips. "I thought it only fair, seeing how thoroughly I wore you out. You were sleeping as soundly as a child when I left."

She turned in his arms. "You should not have left. I missed you when I woke."

Heat flared in his eyes, his voice deep and intimate. "I feared if I stayed we might never leave the bed at all. I thought it best not to scandalize the servants."

Violet stroked a hand over his chest, peeking up at him from beneath her eyelashes. She surprised herself a moment later when she said, "A little scandal would not have hurt them, I think."

Adrian laughed, his white teeth flashing.

"You have been riding," she remarked, needing to distract her thoughts. "You have the scent of horse about you."

He drew back a few inches, stiffening slightly. "My apologies. I was just heading into the house when I saw you. Shall I go in and change?"

Jeannette would have insisted, she knew. Likely she would have followed him inside and changed her own clothing as well since they had been embracing. She supposed she ought to react exactly like her twin. Yet she abhorred the idea of putting any sort of distance between her and Adrian, especially over such a minor matter. Surely he wouldn't notice the difference.

She pulled him close again. "No. You are fine exactly as you are. Change or not as you wish, your Grace."

He paused, a pleased light entering his eyes before he bent to drop a tender kiss upon her mouth. He paused again, then returned for a second helping as if he couldn't bear to deny himself. The kiss heated, deepened, bodies quickly overruling minds.

Before anything too torrid could ignite, a series of loud, boisterous barks interrupted their embrace. They drew apart with rueful reluctance, a large blur of black and white streaking their way.

Horatio ran full tilt toward her, paws pounding across the drive. He slowed seconds before he reached her, rear leg muscles gathering to jump, his large wet tongue already extended, ready to bathe her face in canine kisses.

"Horatio, heel," Adrian said with forceful command.

Horatio broke stride, getting in only a single lick across Violet's cheek before he whimpered and settled onto his haunches.

An instant later, Robert rounded the side of the house at a dead run, skidded to a breathless halt when he saw the tableau already formed. "Oh, pardon me, your Graces," he panted, bending at the waist to draw breath. "I am sorry. He got away from me . . . slipped his leash."

Having been denied the delight of thoroughly licking her face, Horatio snuck a couple of wet swipes at her hand. She watched him surreptitiously peek at Adrian to see if his defiance had been observed.

It had.

She stroked his furry head, his tail wagging like a metronome. "That is all right, Robert," she said. "He is simply full of puppyish exuberance."

Robert and the duke exchanged a speaking look.

"He requires a long walk to wear off the worst of his pent-up energy, that is all, I am sure," she concluded, leaning over to thoroughly massage Horatio's ears. The dog closed his eyes in ecstasy.

"What he needs," Adrian said, "is lessons in deportment. He is an utter barbarian."

"He's no such thing. Don't be so severe on him. He just needs attention and loving care. Robert, I will take that leash, please." She held out an expectant hand.

The footman stepped forward, laid the leather strip over her palm. Without a smidgen of difficulty, Violet reattached the leash to Horatio's collar. The dog sat, utterly docile, apparent putty in her hands.

"Shall we go for a walk?" she cooed to the animal.

He stood, tail waving faster, back end wiggling in happy anticipation.

Violet turned to Adrian. "Your Grace, would you care to accompany us?"

"Yes, of course," he agreed, reaching out to take her elbow.

Horatio surprised them both by behaving like a perfect gentleman as the three of them set out at a leisurely pace. They strolled toward the ocean, its surface glistening in the distance like a flawless sapphire.

"I thought tomorrow you might enjoy taking an excursion." Adrian slipped an arm around her waist.

"What sort of excursion?"

"A day trip to an old ruin that is considered something of a tourist attraction around these parts. I thought we might pack a picnic luncheon, assuming the weather holds clear. Some of the views from Corfe Castle are quite splendid this time of year."

"Corfe Castle?" she blurted without thinking. "You mean the one King John once deemed his favorite residence, but which was razed centuries later by Parliamentarian forces during the Civil War? That Corfe Castle?"

Adrian stopped, eyebrows arched in high surprise. "Yes, the very same. How on earth do you come to know so much about the place?"

Yes, Violet thought, how did she come to know so much? Mentally she gave herself a good hard kick. Dumb, dumb. It was certain Jeannette took no particular interest in history, and she wouldn't have cared a jot about some old castle that had been destroyed nearly two hundred years ago. She doubted her twin even knew England had fought a civil war, let alone any of the sieges or battles involved. Unlike her, Jeannette had never been a good student. To Violet's knowledge, her sister hadn't cracked open a book in the three years since their lessons ended with their former governess, Miss Haverhaven.

So, how did she, posing as her sister, know about the castle? *Blast her imprudent tongue.*

"Well," she began, waving her hand in a gesture of casual dismissal, "it is not from any wish to know about it, I will tell you that. Mortimer Landsdowne, you know what a dreadful bore he can be, he fairly drummed the information into my brain during the reception. Cornered me to offer best wishes, and once he found out we were coming to Dorset for our honeymoon, I simply could not stop him from going on and on about the place. Said how affecting the castle ruins were, and that we must be sure to visit them while we were here. I was ready to raze *him* by the end of our conversation, I must say. Heavens."

Heavens indeed. She willed herself not to panic, praying Adrian had bought her Banbury tale. She peeked up at him from underneath her lashes. A full half minute of silence ticked past. A long, slow, agonizing half minute that seemed to last forever.

Finally, he drew a breath. "I am most sorry for your suffering, my dear." He turned her to resume their walk. "I hope he did not put you off the place entirely. We can always go elsewhere if you would like."

"Oh, no. I am certain if you think it worth the trip then it must be. Particularly if the vistas are pleasant. A picnic sounds an especially delightful idea. Perhaps Mrs. Grimm can be persuaded to include a few of those delicious biscuits she sent up with tea yesterday, after we first arrived."

"I am certain she can be convinced to include a batch,

since they are already an especial favorite of yours. How does roast chicken sound as an accompaniment?"

"Delectable."

He stopped again, pulled her close. "What about a kiss? Would you enjoy that as well, here with the wind whipping at our backs?"

Violet looped an arm around his waist, hugged him closer. "That sounds delectable too."

His mouth was on hers, taking her lips in a slow simmering kiss that quickly heated their passions. She closed her eyes and gave herself over to the crushing pleasure, letting the world around her melt away.

Their honeymoon week flashed by on hummingbirds' wings, a brief span of time both magical and intense. Each day an adventure. Each night a magnificent delight.

The outing to Corfe Castle proved a great success. Violet roamed the grounds with Adrian at her side, soaking up the history and the atmosphere without being compelled to reveal the true depths of her enjoyment. They lunched on a grassy knoll beneath the shade of a small oak tree. A gentle, luffing breeze cooled the air to a pleasant degree while they dined on tender roast chicken, succulent morsels of fruit, sweetmeats and Mrs. Grimm's delicious biscuits.

Afterward, Adrian stretched his long frame across the picnic blanket, nestled his head onto Violet's lap and fell asleep. She sat utterly content, watching him while dreams filled his mind. Occasionally, she would stroke a few locks of his thick, black hair. Fingering the ends that curled ever so slightly in the warm, humid coastal air. Slowly, he awakened, a look of slumberous desire glinting in his eyes. Her heart gave an answering leap as he drew her to him. Then he captured her lips in a fiery joining that would surely have caught the castle keep on fire had it not already fallen to ruin long ago.

The days to follow were wonderful, occupied by long walks and quiet conversations. Horatio accompanied them quite often. His manners and his health improved daily as he gained weight and began to trust. Violet was still his favorite, but he loved Adrian too; the dog's long skinny tail flashing a happy salute every time the duke drew near.

Violet and Adrian indulged themselves in two additional day excursions. One to see the spectacular, fossil-rich shale beds that formed the steep dark cliffs of Kimmeridge Bay. The other to the small village of Lulworth for a look at another castle, and the beautiful Lulworth Cove with its odd rock formations and impressive stone arch.

Little doubt, Jeannette would have yawned her way through every minute of their provincial sightseeing. But Violet adored it, grateful Adrian did not know her sister well enough to realize what Jeannette's real opinion would have been. Still, she was forever on her guard with him and the servants.

Night was the one time she felt truly free to be herself. She reveled in the dark quiet hours when Adrian came to her, came into her, allowing her to pour forth all the love and passion waiting inside. When they made love, he made love with *her*, with Violet. Every touch, *her* touch. Every kiss, *her* kiss. Each emotion, real and honest. Each cry of pleasure and delight cleaved from *her* body, drawn from *her* soul.

The only strain on an otherwise perfect union were the times when he would call out her sister's name, leaving a lump in her chest, an ache in her heart that she was helpless to dispel. She had chosen her path. Assumed her twin's identity. Now she must live with the consequences, be they joyful or filled with pain.

She wanted to tell him. Sometimes she had to bite her lip to keep the truth from tumbling out. In only a few days' time, she had come to know him as she had never thought she might. To understand him, at least in part. She knew he would be viciously hurt, violently angry, utterly betrayed if she told him the truth. He turned to her now in the night, held her in her sleep. She didn't think she could bear a day when he might turn away. When he might reject her, leave her.

So she kept her silence and her lies to herself. And tried to gather as much happiness as she could.

"Take off your shoes." Adrian shucked his boots and stockings, his bare feet sinking into the warm, soft sand. His attire was casual. A white linen shirt and plain waistcoat, and an old pair of black trousers he'd rolled up to his knees.

His wife crossed her arms, hugged them to her chest, her pretty pink skirts blowing in the warm afternoon breeze. "No, thank you. I am fine exactly as I am."

"You will only ruin them. They will be clogged with sand before you walk ten feet. Off with the shoes, Duchess."

She arched a proud brow. "That is right. I am a duchess and as such do not cavort around barefoot in public."

"Ah, but therein lies the speciousness of your argument. There is no public here; we are completely alone. As a duke, and your husband, I decree barefootedness to be perfectly proper attire for today's adventure."

"Barefootedness indeed," she repeated scornfully, shaking her head. Moments later, though, she did as commanded, rolling her stockings into two neat balls that she stuffed into her abandoned footwear.

Adrian extended his hand.

She took it, let him lead her forward.

The day was sunny and warm, the warmest they had had all week. A sandpiper with its stubby brown and white body raced ahead of the incoming surf, long toothpick legs flashing fast. The bird turned to chase a receding ocean wave. He paused, quickly thrusting his narrow beak into the wet sand in search of a moist sea worm or small crustacean. Adrian smiled when the bird raced and the wave chased, the two beginning their curious dance all over again.

He turned his head to look at Jeannette, walking in silent contentment beside him despite her protestations against coming here. Odd that, he thought. He couldn't count the number of times he'd caught her gazing out upon the sea over the past several days, noticeable pleasure alive in her eyes as she studied the rolling waves and the beauty of the winding shoreline.

In spite of her obvious enjoyment, she expressed no interest in exploring the beach. She would be hot, she'd say. She would get dirty. She would ruin her attire. Yet he sensed her protestations were halfhearted at best. That underneath them she longed to indulge her senses, to break free of the restraints she had imposed upon herself and simply explore.

At first, he'd worried she would be hopelessly bored without Society and its constant diversions. He'd experienced a few uncomfortable moments, doubting his decision to bury the two of them here in the country with nothing more exciting to do than tour the local sights. Yet she hadn't seemed bored at all. Quite the contrary. She'd had fun, he knew she had, her enjoyment in no way feigned. His own certainly hadn't been. He couldn't recall a better week, sorry their time here was nearly over.

She'd surprised him. Her moods were mercurial, hard to pin down, ranging from gentle to haughty, playful to prickly. He never knew what to expect of her. Strange, but at times she almost seemed like two women. The outgoing belle-of-the-ball he'd courted in London; the woman who loved parties and people, and took far too many pains with her appearance. And the shy innocent. The girl who put herself in harm's way to rescue a stray dog. Who seemed utterly content to hold hands and share a quiet evening of lazy talk. Who kissed him with such sweet, eager abandon he thought his heart might burst from the sheer glory of it.

Which woman would she be today?

"Let's wade," he urged suddenly. Grabbing her hand, he dragged her behind him and plunged them both into rushing waves.

"Oh, my dress. Look what you've done. It is quite ruined, you fiend." Her pink muslin gown swirled in the receding wave, wet sand clinging in a wide swathe along the bottom of the material as the water drained away.

"Don't fret. I'll buy you another. Watch out, here comes the next wave." The sea roared in, drenching them both up to the knees.

She pulled away, waded up onto dry land. Her sodden skirt was wet and heavy, and clung to her calves. She leaned over, squeezed as much water as she could from the hem. "Now what am I to do?" she demanded, holding her arms out to her sides to display her sad predicament.

"Take it off."

"I beg your pardon?"

"Take it off, the dress. Keep your petticoat on and tuck the skirt up between your legs so you can play in the waves."

Color stained her cheeks. "Adrian, I couldn't."

He stooped over to pick up a seashell, tossed it back when he found half of it eroded away. "Of course you can. No one will see you."

"What about the servants? Or the local villagers? Or sailors out there on the sea?" She motioned a hand toward the open water. "Who knows who might happen by."

"The servants won't come looking for us down here. The nearest village is two miles away, so there won't be any locals venturing in our direction. And as for sailors . . ." He raised a hand to shield his eyes, scanning the distant horizon. "Not a single boat in sight. Unless a Navy frigate cruises past and her captain has a very fine telescope, I believe your modesty has naught to fear."

"Does the Navy often sail in these waters?"

"Not so much since the war. Turn around. I'll help with the buttons."

A long moment passed before she acquiesced. "You are making me over into a complete wanton, you know that," she grumbled, presenting her back to him.

"Good," he murmured, leaning over to kiss her neck. "So long as you are *my* wanton and no one else's."

"There could be no one else. No one but you."

Their eyes met and held for a long, speaking moment. His heart tightened like a fist inside his chest, his throat squeezing closed as if he had swallowed wrong.

Mine, he thought. *She is all mine.*

And he would maim any man who tried to take her from him. The fierce rush of possessiveness surprised him, alarmed him, the emotion entirely foreign to his nature. He'd thought it didn't matter, her purity, her fidelity. But he found that now, after barely a week of marriage, it did.

Just as she mattered, in a way he had not thought she would.

Was he falling in love with her? The notion jarred him.

No, he decided as he forced his suddenly unsteady fingers to keep working at her buttons. That sort of emotion was impossible. He wanted her. He had no doubt of that. He'd taken her every night and most mornings since they'd arrived. Waking her in the black velvet darkness just before dawn. He loved hearing her sweet sighs ring in his ears as pale light seeped in from behind the bedroom curtains while birds trilled a chorus in the trees outside to welcome the new day.

Of course he wanted her. It was their honeymoon, after all. Still, it troubled him. The intensity of his feelings. The consuming depths of his need. But it would pass, he was certain. Passion was an ephemeral thing, and his desire for her would wane in time. If only he didn't want her so much. If only he didn't want her right now.

As if to prove to himself that he could resist her, he yanked his shirt over his head, bared his chest to the sun. "I have a sudden fancy for a swim. Come on."

"You didn't say anything about a swim," she squeaked.

"I'm saying it now. Come on, my dear. It will be fun." He raced into the waves.

At length, she followed.

Adrian was by far the stronger swimmer, traveling farther and faster, out away from shore, where the waves were nothing more than a gentle rolling of the water. She stayed in closer to shore, floating on her back.

Decadent, that's how she felt, the sun a warm kiss on her face and shoulders, her long hair floating behind her like a sleek cape. And shameless, clad in nothing but her undergarments. Drifting out in the open where anyone might happen upon her, despite Adrian's assurances to the contrary. She felt happy too, she realized, in a way she'd never been before. She smiled, glad Adrian had lured her here, where she had so wanted to be.

Something plucked playfully at her hair. Her eyes

sprang open, to find Adrian treading water next to her. His lips moved but she couldn't hear what he said.

"What?" She bobbed upright.

"I said I thought you had fallen asleep."

"No, just daydreaming. Did you enjoy your swim?"

He nodded. "Very much. Shall we go in closer now?"

At a relaxed pace, she swam beside him toward shore. By unspoken mutual consent, they stopped at the same moment, feet easily touching bottom. She faced him, watching salty droplets drip from his hair. Adrian slicked it back, muscled arms and broad shoulders flexing.

Her eyes moved to the puckered scar that rode high on his chest. The flesh was bone white and shaped like a guinea-sized starburst. She knew another scar—equally white, equally ragged—lay on his back.

She'd noticed the scars before. They were impossible to miss. Still, she had never asked him about them. She rarely touched them, not because they repelled her but because the damage and the story behind their cause struck her as intensely private.

She reached out, traced her fingertips over the small curve of wounded flesh, the skin unnaturally smooth and taut. "How horribly painful this must have been," she murmured.

He stood, acquiescent beneath her touch. "Having a bayonet point thrust through your back is rarely pleasant."

Her fingers paused. "I thought it was a bullet."

"Is that the story making the rounds in the salons these days?" She nodded. "A bullet's neater, I suppose," he continued, "less gory for the ladies. Likely I should have let you keep your illusions."

"No," she told him fiercely, "I only want the truth."

He caught her hand as her fingers began their tracing once more, pressed her palm flat against his chest. "I don't know how much of the truth I ought to tell you."

Dark shadows flickered inside his eyes. "War is a horrible, tragic business, not fit for discussion in polite company."

She raised her other hand to his cheek. "I am not polite company. I am your wife. You may tell me anything."

The shadows receded, a slow smile warming his lips. "Thank you, my dear. I shall keep that in mind."

"You are not going to tell me."

"Tell you what? About my wound? There is little enough to tell and likely you know most of it already. I was stabbed straight through with a French bayonet during the worst of the Siege of Badajoz. My wound was grievous enough, I was later informed, that the doctors quite gave me up for dead. By the grace of the Almighty, I pulled through. Once I had, my mother wrote to inform me that if I did not resign my commission at once and return home where I belonged, she planned to embark on the first ship available and drag me home herself. Hers was a threat even Wellington himself could not withstand."

She doubted anyone could force Adrian to do anything he did not wish to do, not even his passionate whirlwind of a mother. Stories told how he'd saved an entire squadron of men by ordering a retreat, then holding the front lines with a chosen few until the rest could reach safety. He'd been stabbed for his heroism, decorated for his bravery.

She wrapped her arms around his waist. "Well, in this instance, I must agree with your mother. You were lucky to survive. Tempting fate again would not have been wise."

He tipped up her chin with a finger. "So you are saying you would be sad if I had been killed?"

"I would never have known you, and for that I would have been quite sad indeed."

His pupils dilated with sudden emotion. "As would I.

How tragic never to have beheld a face as beguiling as yours. These splendid creamy cheeks . . ."

He leaned closer, kissed her right cheek, then her left.

"And this gorgeous chin . . ."

His lips pressed to her chin.

"This luscious neck . . ."

Her skin tingled as he dappled her throat with slow, sensuous brushes of his mouth.

"This delectable forehead . . ."

Her eyes closed and she sighed as he lavished his attention upon the spot.

"These glorious eyelids . . ."

She shuddered as he dusted butterfly kisses over her trembling lids.

"And of course your lips, the prettiest I have ever known."

Languid and lush, he captured her mouth, tasting her as though she were a rare delicacy presented for his delectation. There was no hurry, only mutual enjoyment, mutual delight.

Violet curved herself more fully against his hard, heated length, her arms wrapped tight around him. Their clothes clung like a wet second skin, seawater lapping against their hips, all else forgotten as they drowned in the pleasure they were creating together.

His hands slipped beneath the waves to cup her buttocks.

Violet did the same to him, feeling his surprise as well as his appreciation.

Hot sun beat down upon her head, desire turning her body ripe and willing. Long minutes passed as they indulged in a healthy mating of lips and teeth and tongues. He broke the kiss, his eyes smoldering. He took her hand and led her from the water.

She didn't say a word as they traversed the warm sand, drawing to a stop next to their discarded clothing.

She expected him to hand her dress to her to put on so they might return to the house, up to the privacy of their bedroom. Instead, he tossed the garment over his arm, retrieved his shirt, then clasped her hand to lead her farther along the beach. Away from the house.

They halted near a rough, oddly shaped curve of rock that jutted toward the sea. It provided shelter on three of its sides, creating a perfect location for a clandestine meeting or a lovers' tryst.

Inside the natural haven, Adrian shook out her dress, spread it flat over the sand. He did the same with his shirt, laying it just above the dress.

"Here?" she asked, gazing around her, out across the broad stretch of undulating blue waves, gulls riding high on the shifting air currents.

"Only if you want." He held out a hand.

She shivered, amazed at her own daring. She placed her hand into his. "I want."

He drew her down onto the makeshift pallet and began to love her with slow, deliberate care. The scents and sounds of the ocean surrounded them. The air played upon her skin, teasing and tantalizing in delicate, erotic strokes. Time slowed, inhibitions faded as Violet let him bare her flesh to the elements. Her hands roved over his body as if possessed, as if she were indeed some other woman. Not her sister but her own other self, a woman free of shyness and restrictions, able to express her feelings, her needs, without hesitation or regret.

And when he came into her, she gloried in the possession. She wished they could stay this way forever, only the two of them here in this place. Together and happy. Without demands or expectations, without obligations or duties or roles. Without anything but themselves and their passion. Here she could be fully herself with nothing to hide, no lies, no pretenses, only the raging depths of her love for him.

She closed her eyes and gave herself over to the moment, refusing to think about the difficulties that might come in the future. Then she couldn't think at all as the demands of her body engulfed her in a long, unrelenting cascade of ecstasy.

When she climaxed, the wind stole her cries of repletion. The birds were the only witnesses to her movements as she clutched Adrian in fierce arms and entwined legs, holding on tight even after he had found his own release inside her.

Violet watched the passing scenery as the coach rolled away from the house. She wished she could don her spectacles so she might fully appreciate its beauty before it faded from sight. After a week of viewing the world through a placid haze, she had adapted, or mostly adapted, to the limitations of her uncorrected vision. Still, those limitations proved quite vexing at times, such as now.

She sighed and rested a gloved hand on the seat between them.

He covered it with his own gloved palm, gave it a reassuring squeeze. "Don't be melancholy, my dear. We will return one of these days."

"I know." She forced a smile. "And I am not melancholy—or rather, I shall not let myself be. There is so much to look forward to, after all. We're traveling home to Winterlea."

His eyes warmed at the mention of his principal estate. "It will be good to be there again. I always miss it when I've been too long away. I hope you shall come to feel the same. Come to love it as I do, now that you are its duchess."

Duchess. The word shot a shudder of terror through her veins. How was she ever going to live up to the obligations her new status would require of her? Overseeing the domestic management of one of the grandest homes in all of England. She had been trained in housekeeping, of course, as any well-bred lady was expected to be. Yet never had she considered that one day she would be required to assume the weighty mantle of responsibility for an estate as vast as Winterlea.

She would simply have to put aside her qualms and adapt, she told herself. Perhaps if she looked upon it as a discpline to be mastered, it wouldn't prove to be so very dreadful. Teaching herself Greek, after all, had not been easy at first, nor come instantaneously, but she had applied herself and become proficient over time. With an optimistic attitude and a bit of determination, learning to be Winterlea's duchess could be the same.

Yet when they arrived three days later, weary from the journey and from being confined inside the coach for so long, she was no more ready to assume her duties than she had been when they'd left Dorset. Anxiety clutched a fist inside her stomach as the coach drove through the gates, down the mile-long corridor of giant oak trees that lined the entrance to the estate.

She had been to Adrian's principal residence once before. Invited along with her parents, her brother and Jeannette late last spring, during her twin's engagement. The grounds were extensive, covering over fifteen thousand acres that included within them: a park and vast woodlands; a deep, natural lake stocked with over twenty different species of fish; several bridged waterways and an orchard, which at the time had been ablaze with color and fragrance from hundreds of blossoming trees.

A series of elegant formal gardens led up to, and around, the house; landscaping that could keep a person wandering quite happily for hours. She vividly recalled the beauty of the Elizabethan garden near the oldest section of the house, built in the 1580's, if she remembered correctly. Columbine, cupid's dart, foxglove, woodbine, all had raised their sweet flower faces to the sun. Horse chestnut and maple trees, unfurling new coats of leaves, provided areas of shade and shelter for later in the season.

The house itself was immense, more along the lines of a palace. It boasted four wings done in three separate architectural styles and numbered 145 rooms, not including the servants' quarters found on the third story. The most recent and most major renovations to the house had been commissioned by the third Duke of Raeburn, beginning in 1763. His contribution had been the addition of the east and west wings, and the central facade of the U-shaped house, done in the Palladian style. Great stone steps led up to massive Ionic columns that held up a carved pedimented entryway.

The interior of the house was every bit as sumptuous as its exterior. The entrance hall glorious, with a central dome that cast natural sunlight down into the pink-marbled hallway before drawing the eye upward to witness a painting of an idyllic Venetian village scene by Robert Adams.

Only the finest furnishings and draperies were used. Each room containing at least one—and often two—well-tended fireplaces, capped by hand-carved marble mantels. Soft, hand-sewn Aubusson and Turkey carpets cushioned the floors. Antiques and priceless works of art, paintings, sculptures and friezes graced each and every corridor, hallway and room.

During her stay, Violet had been able to enjoy no more than a fraction of the beautiful art and architecture on display. As the new duchess, she would have ample time to study the objects at her leisure. If only the duties that went along with her new position didn't make her gulp in an agony of terror.

As the coach continued onward, she reacquainted herself with the grandeur of the house and its grounds. Her eyes widened at the spectacle of the servants lined up in rows, four deep, before the entrance.

She took a steadying breath and forced herself not to tremble. Greeting the servants at the house in Dorset had gone well. This would be no different, she assured herself.

Adrian assisted her from the coach. Horatio, who had been riding with them, leapt out immediately after, tail wagging with pleased enthusiasm as soon as his large paws hit the ground. Robert, the footman, came forward to take him in hand.

Adrian tucked Violet's arm into the crook of his, then led her forward. She scanned the mass of expectant faces. Oh, dear, there were so many of them. A hundred at least. This wasn't anything like Dorset!

March, the majordomo, stepped forward. He was an impressive figure with a ramrod-straight bearing and piercing blue eyes. "Welcome home, your Grace." He greeted Adrian first, then turned to acknowledge her. "Your Grace." He nodded respectfully. Violet inclined her head in reply. "I hope your journey was a pleasant one," he said.

"Quite pleasant," Adrian replied. "I see you have assembled the staff."

"Yes, your Grace. I took the liberty. May I speak for everyone by extending our most heartfelt congratulations to you and her Grace on your marriage. May the years to come be happy, fruitful ones."

"Thank you, March. Thank you all. It is good to be home."

Adrian and Violet smiled.

The small army of people smiled back.

Adrian introduced her to the senior staff, including the housekeeper, Mrs. Hardwick, a tall, thin bird of a woman with a bun of steel gray hair wrapped so tightly over her skull it seemed a wonder she could blink her eyes. And François, Adrian's French chef, who in his youth had worked as a kitchen's assistant at Versailles in service to King Louis XVI and Marie Antoinette. His hazel eyes twinkled when he told her he had made cream puffs in the shape of swans in honor of her and the duke's homecoming.

Thankfully she was not expected to say much. As a result, her nerves began to simmer down. She felt nearly relaxed by the time she and Adrian moved to enter the house.

Before they could, the majordomo discreetly drew Adrian's attention, speaking in a quiet aside. "Your Grace, a moment, if I might."

Adrian stopped, turned his head. "Yes, March? What is it?"

"I wanted to inform you that her Grace is in the drawing room. She arrived this morning from the dower house."

Violet's throat squeezed closed at the news.

Adrian's mother was here.

Chapter Nine

"Adrian, *ma chou,* finally you are arrived. Come and give me a kiss." From her place on the sofa that was upholstered in golden watered silk, the Dowager Duchess of Raeburn stretched her arms wide. She made no effort to rise, seated regally as a queen greeting her subjects.

"Hello, *Maman.*" Adrian bent, returned her embrace as he dusted his lips across his mother's flawless cheeks. "What a pleasant surprise to find you here." Humor lit his sable brown eyes.

"I am sure you do not find it pleasant at all," she retorted with blunt honesty, her French accent still very much in evidence despite her having lived in England for over thirty-five years. "Barging in on you, only just returned from your honeymoon. You must forgive me, but it could not be helped. See?" She gestured with a hand. "Jeannette, she will not even speak to me."

Violet stepped away from the doors where she had been hovering. She swallowed past the hard knot in her throat as she prepared to greet Adrian's mother.

Marguerite Le Richeaux Winter was like a Gallic whirlwind, passionate and highly unpredictable. During the engagement, the dowager duchess and Jeannette had been scrupulously polite to each other but far from bosom beaux. Violet knew she would need to tread lightly, at least in the beginning, around her new mother-in-law.

"You could not be more mistaken, your Grace." Violet came forward to clasp the dowager's hands. "Of course I will speak to you. You are most welcome here." She leaned down, brushed a kiss over the woman's perfumed cheek.

"Why, thank you, my child. How gracious you are. And you must call me *Maman,* now that we are mother and daughter."

"Of course, *Maman,*" Violet dutifully repeated.

The dowager released her hands. Violet crossed, sank gratefully into a wing chair opposite the sofa.

"I already rang for tea," Adrian's mother announced. "I hope you don't mind, my child." She lifted a single dark eyebrow in a gesture very reminiscent of one Adrian often used.

Violet paused, wondering how she ought to respond. Jeannette, she knew, would be anxious to establish her preeminence as the new duchess.

"I don't mind in the least." Violet smiled, pointedly gracious. "I shall be certain to do the same for you the next time you come to visit."

The dowager acknowledged the riposte with a slight tilt of her sensuous lips, another trait she had passed on to her son.

The resemblance between mother and son was quite strong, particularly around the eyes and mouth. It wasn't hard to see where Adrian got his dark, magnetic beauty. Barely into her fifties, the dowager duchess was still an extremely attractive woman. Only a few threads of silver glistened in her lustrous black hair. Her creamy white complexion was youthful as a girl's, the faintest fanning of lines visible at the corners of her eyes and in the slight creases that ran along either side of her nose.

Adrian strolled to the sideboard and poured himself a glass of wine from the decanter.

"How was your trip?" his mother asked. "I can see it

must have been pleasant. You both look positively refreshed."

Adrian took a sip from his glass. "Yes, it was quite pleasant." His eyes moved to Violet, passed over her in a long, slow, intimate sweep. "Quite tolerably pleasant indeed."

The tea arrived. The dowager duchess poured. Having forgone luncheon on the road, Violet and Adrian both accepted the plates of sandwiches and cakes the dowager passed. He refused the tea, however, preferring to keep his wine.

"How are all the family?" He sank into a wing chair that matched Violet's. "Still hale, I presume, since last we saw them at the wedding."

His mother patted her lips with her napkin, ignoring the amused sarcasm in his query. "Everyone is well," she began. "Though dear cousin Filbert was confined to his bed with a sprain for several days after the reception. Apparently he tripped on Lady Rankin's dress that evening while they were walking near the gardens. Took a tumble down a few steps, by all accounts."

No doubt the result of too much champagne and a well-deserved push from Lady Rankin, Adrian mused. Filbert was an inveterate, though mostly harmless, flirt who often misplaced his better judgment when he imbibed too freely. Lady Rankin, an attractive young widow, had presumably decided the word *no* was not having a sufficient effect and had resorted to a more physical means of refusal.

"I hope he did not suffer greatly?"

He and the dowager turned their eyes to Jeannette and her words of innocent concern. It was obvious his wife was unaware of cousin Filbert's notorious reputation. Surprising, Adrian thought. Stories about Filbert were a frequent source of amusement with the London set. Although perhaps not, it would seem, among respectable young ladies.

Each day she did something to surprise him anew, please him anew. Smiling softly, he ate one of the small sandwiches on his plate.

"Filbert is quite recovered," the dowager reassured. "However, Sylvia is not."

Adrian's attention piqued at mention of his eldest sister. "What is wrong with Sylvia?"

"She is enceinte, as you know, and Herbert is of absolutely no help to her at all."

Sylvia, Lady Bramley, was nearly six months pregnant with her fifth child, the first four boys. She and Herbert were trying again for the daughter Sylvia desperately wanted. Sons, she would complain, were all very well, but they had no use for dresses and parties and feminine pursuits. A woman was entitled to have a little girl to fuss and coo over, to send down the aisle when the time came. What if she never got to be mother of the bride? she often fretted. Every woman longed to plan her daughter's nuptials someday.

Everyone on both sides of the family was fervently praying this next baby would be a girl.

"Oh, that," he grunted.

"Yes, *that*," the dowager scolded. "It is very cruel of you to make light of your sister's discomfort. You know how sorry she was to miss your wedding."

"I am not making light of Sylvia's condition, and I am sorry if she feels unwell. But one would think by this time she would be well used to the complications that come from being in a family way."

"Each baby is different. She writes her ankles are quite dreadfully swollen. The reason for my impromptu visit today."

"To tell us about Sylvia's swollen ankles?"

"*Non,* do not be ridiculous. I have decided to go stay

with her for the rest of her confinement. Make sure she is healthy and well cared for."

"I am positive Bramley has retained the best physician available."

"*Certainement.* But a woman needs another woman at such a time, a daughter her *maman.* Besides, she says the boys are driving her quite mad. I shall go play *grand-mère* for a time. I am packed already. I leave tomorrow."

"Tomorrow? So soon? In that case, you must stay to dinner," he invited.

"Yes," Violet concurred softly, "of course, you must stay."

The dowager smiled, her face lighting up. "*Merci beaucoup,* I accept." She gave her daughter-in-law a probing look. "You are very quiet today, my child. Is anything wrong?"

Violet just barely kept herself from jumping. "Why, no . . . no, of course not. I'm . . . a bit fatigued from the journey, is all."

"*Naturellement.* And I am a selfish beast to keep you here. Do not think you must stay to entertain me." The dowager made a shooing motion with her hands. "Go on to your rooms. Lie down. I will bend my son's ear for a little while longer, *non?*"

"Thank you, your Grace. It would be most pleasant to refresh my attire," Violet said.

The dowager shook a reproving finger. "It is *Maman* now, remember."

"Yes, *Maman.*" Violet stood, gave her a smile. She turned, shared a more intimate smile with Adrian.

"March will have Mrs. Hardwick show you to your rooms." He stood, walked with her to the door. He drew a fingertip down her cheek. "Rest well, my dear. I shall see you at dinner."

"Until then, your Grace," she replied softly.

Adrian crossed back into the room, selected a tiny

wedge-shaped sandwich of herb cheese and ham from the silver serving tray. He popped it into his mouth, chewed and swallowed. "So what are you really doing here today, *Maman*?"

Feigning astonishment, the dowager raised a hand to her chest. "I told you, *ma mie*, I wanted a chance to see you before I leave for Herefordshire. I will be away until Martinmas at the very least."

"And Jeannette and I shall be quite bereft without your company until then. But that is not why you have come."

"Well, there is another small matter. Some repairs at the dower house that need attention. The drawing-room door squeaks like a little mouse every time it is opened or closed. And there is a draft in one of the upstairs maid's rooms. Obviously, the roof, it requires an inspection."

"Did you consult with McDougal?" Ewan McDougal was Adrian's chief steward with oversight of Winterlea, its grounds, tenant houses, outbuildings and the dower house.

"*Non*, I am consulting with you."

He gave a half smile, well used to her ways. She never liked to speak directly with Mr. McDougal. She said she could understand only half of what the Scot said.

"I will have the repairs seen to while you are away." Adrian carried his glass to the sideboard, poured himself more wine. "So, will you tell me?"

"Tell you what?"

He gave her a speaking glance.

"Oh, that." She pursed her lips, finally relenting when it became clear he would not be put off. "I did not wish you to think I was interfering, but I wanted to see how you are getting on. I was concerned. I sensed some tension between you and your bride before the wedding. Do not tell me I am mistaken."

He returned to his chair, swallowed a mouthful of wine, set the glass aside. "No, you were not mistaken, but all is well now. The trip to the coast was very good for us both."

"She forgave you for your change of plans?" His mother knew about Jeannette's less than enthusiastic re-action to their canceled tour of the Continent.

"She was upset at first, but it was all forgotten once we arrived in Dorset."

"And you are happy," his mother stated. "I can see by the way you look at her that you are."

Did he look at Jeannette in a particular way? he thought, surprised. Yes, he supposed he did. "I am well contented with my marriage." And he was. More so than he had ever expected to be.

"Then I can visit your sister with an easy heart," the dowager said. "I did not like to think of going away, leaving you troubled and unhappy."

"I am a grown man, *Maman*. I appreciate the con-cern, but I am well able to look after myself these days, you know."

"Bah! You may be a man, but you are still my son. That and my love for you will never change, no matter how old you become."

"I love you too, *Maman*."

She beamed a happy smile at him.

"Now, what is this I hear about George Finchley?" Adrian said, indulging his mother's love of scandal broth. "Did he really agree to marry Grenton's eldest chit?"

The duchess poured herself another cup of tea and launched into the tale.

Upstairs in her bedchamber, Violet woke, surprised to discover she had fallen deeply asleep.

Agnes, bless her heart, bustled in moments later to help her dress for dinner. She assisted her into a lovely gown of spotted primrose India muslin with short sleeves and a scoop-necked bodice. Then the maid brushed and repinned her hair, hooking a creamy strand of pearls around her throat.

Thanks to a good sense of direction, Violet managed to find the second-floor drawing room after taking only a single wrong turn. Adrian was already inside, along with another gentleman. Introductions were made. Mr. James Dalton, Adrian's private secretary, would, it seemed, be joining them for dinner tonight.

As a rule Violet found strangers utterly intimidating. But Mr. Dalton with his crooked smile and ruddy cheeks was so thoroughly pleasant, so thoroughly polite, she felt relaxed and at ease in his presence in no time at all.

She learned that Mr. Dalton was a great dog lover and had already acquainted himself with Horatio. A fine specimen of canine grace, he declared, winning her over completely. They were eagerly comparing notes on the most even-tempered breeds, Adrian listening on with an amused tilt to his upper lip, when the dowager duchess entered the room.

Violet did her best not to tense up and fall silent. It was vital she maintain her ruse and do nothing out of character for her sister. She knew it would not do for her to rely upon the excuse of tiredness for a second time that day. Unknowingly, Mr. Dalton came to her aid, drawing Adrian's mother into the conversation as if she had been there the entire time. To Violet's utter relief, her own occasional lengthy silences seemed to go by without notice.

Dinner was served in the family dining room, small by ducal standards, only large enough to seat fifteen to twenty people. A center leaf had been removed from the long, polished pecan table. That way the four of them would be able to dine in comfortable intimacy, and not be forced to raise their voices to be heard.

Adrian sat at one end, Violet at the other, in the place reserved for the hostess. How odd it was, Violet thought, to act as hostess. Even odder to do so while pretending to be her sister. By some sheer miracle, she managed. Silently she directed the staff while she ate and talked, forcing herself to carry her share of the conversation as each new topic was introduced.

Profound relief swept through her when the coffee was poured and dessert laid. The beautiful puff pastry swans Chef had promised glided—one on each plate—in a small, delicious lake of melted dark chocolate, serving as the final conversation piece.

Her relief was short-lived, however.

Once the meal was concluded, the men excused themselves to discuss a pressing matter of estate business. Violet was left to return to the drawing room with the dowager. She had no idea what to say. Oh, why had Adrian had to abandon her? Drat the man.

His mother seated herself on one end of the comfortable sofa. Violet settled into the spot on the other end while she racked her brain for a suitable subject. Perhaps some mention of the weather. Generally it was considered a safe subject.

"The day looks to be most pleasant for your journey tomorrow," she ventured.

"Hmm," the dowager replied. "Though sudden storms often erupt in the afternoon this time of year. It may turn out to be quite inclement."

Violet kept herself from rolling her eyes. So much for the weather, she thought. She drew in a bracing lungful of air and tried again. "You lived here at Winterlea for quite a long number of years . . ."

The dowager turned her refined face toward her, one eyebrow elevated.

Dear heavens, Violet fretted, had she just inadvertently insinuated that the dowager was old? She rushed on. "Perhaps you could tell me something of the families who live in the neighborhood."

Her mother-in-law pinned her with a long probing stare, then relented. "There are several fine families in the area, though none to compare in wealth or status with our own. A Winter has been the leading peer and landholder in this part of Derbyshire for nearly three hundred years. Ever since King Henry VIII granted the land to the first Earl of Exeford in 1545."

Violet remembered a small smattering of family history from her original visit to Winterlea. If she recalled correctly, Adrian was, in addition to being the sixth Duke of Raeburn, also the tenth Earl of Exeford, Viscounts Trentworth and Faynehill, Lord Leighton and Baron Crofton. He held a few other assorted minor titles that she couldn't easily recall. One other that she did recollect clearly was the Marquis of Ashton. Their firstborn son would become the ninth marquis, should she and Adrian ever have a son.

A tingle ran through her at the thought.

"Lord and Lady Carter own Cresthaven, some miles distant," her mother-in-law continued. "Very genteel people. The Miltons and the Lyles, they are fine people too. And, of course, Vicar Thompkins and his wife. They have the living here and reside very near the village. *Certainement,* they shall call upon you after a reasonable period."

Call upon her? Violet shuddered imperceptibly. She hadn't considered having to receive her neighbors. But of course she would, politeness would dictate that she must. How stupid of her not to have considered. She twisted her hands together and forced herself not to scowl.

"You will get along well in the area so long as you

provide a few entertainments here and there. People expect others to keep the boredom away. But that should not be a problem for you, since you have such an honest love of Society."

Violet smiled, the delicious meal she had so recently consumed burning uncomfortably inside her stomach.

"I expect you shall spend a fair amount of time in London. It is good," Adrian's mother declared, "you have established already so many connections there. Your polish and easy ways will be a great boon to my son's career, *n'est-ce pas?*"

"What do you mean?"

"Up to now, he has taken only casual interest in his duties in the House of Lords. But now that he is married, I am sure he will take a more active roll in government. The Dukes of Raeburn have always been leaders. Even his father, and I shall say no more on *that* subject, was very active politically. Adrian is no different. He is bound for greatness, by birth as well as inclination. It is only a matter of time."

Violet stared. Did Adrian have political aspirations? He had never mentioned anything about it to her. But then, why should he have? They had only been wed for a little over a week, and men did not always discuss such things with their wives. They simply went out and did as they chose. At least, that is how her father behaved. He did as he wished and let her mother cry and complain about it later if it turned out to be something she did not like.

"You will be a wonderful asset to him." The dowager reached out, patted her hand. "A skilled hostess, she can be every bit as essential to a man as his abilities and convictions. I am depending upon you to aid him in all his future successes."

"Yes, of course," Violet said, falsely cheerful. "I would want nothing else."

"I love my son. I would be greatly distressed to hear that Adrian was in any way discontented."

Violet's back stiffened, her chin coming up of its own accord. "As would I. You are not the only one who loves him."

Something softened in her mother-in-law's eyes. The dowager nodded once, then moved on to another subject.

Adrian and Mr. Dalton joined them a few minutes later.

A distant clock sounded the time, two mellow strokes that echoed in the buttery softness of the night.

Violet lay awake, gazing into the darkness, Adrian asleep beside her.

Her conversation with the dowager kept playing in her mind, words repeating themselves over and over again in a loop that had become a diabolical sort of torture.

Your polish and easy ways will be a great boon to my son's career.

What polish and easy ways?

The Dukes of Raeburn have always been leaders . . . He is bound for greatness.

Unless she committed some grievous mistake and spoiled everything for him.

You will be a wonderful asset to him.

Oh, but she wouldn't, Violet moaned to herself. She knew little of Society and even less about being a political hostess. If Adrian's mother was correct, if he wanted to take a prominent role in leading the nation, she was the last person to whom he should turn. She was floundering around as it was, clutching at any likely straws just to get through each day. Pretending to be her sister among her new family was difficult enough. How on earth could she hope to dazzle the world at something she was not certain even Jeannette could pull off? Jeannette was about as political as a brown mouse. Then again, she had a way with people. Perhaps that's all it took.

Dear God, why had she ever agreed to this deception?

She would be Adrian's ruination, and her own as well.

I would be greatly distressed to hear Adrian was in any way discontented.

The words stabbed at her. Violet rolled to her side and squeezed her eyes shut. She loved him. The last thing she wanted to do was hold him back. Panic hummed in her veins, her heart thumping a rapid staccato inside her breast.

"Jeannette?" Adrian murmured, waking at her movement. He slid a hand over her shoulder.

She stiffened, recoiling to hear her sister's name. *No,* she thought, *I am Violet. I am Violet.*

"Is anything wrong?"

She had to answer him. "Nothing. I can't sleep," she said.

"Bad dreams?"

Bad dreams, troubled thoughts. "Mmm-hmm."

"Would it help to talk about it?"

If only she could talk about it. Turn to him, tell him what his mother had said, ask if he really did have serious political aspirations. But what if it was true and he had already discussed his plans with Jeannette during their engagement? It would seem awfully odd for her to be inquiring again now. She couldn't take the risk.

"No. I scarcely remember what I was dreaming," she said.

"Well, maybe I can think of a way to lull you back to sleep. Come here." Gently, he turned her into his arms, his lips meeting her own in tender warmth.

She threaded her fingers into his hair, loving its silky texture, warm and mussed from sleep. His cheeks were rough with nighttime whiskers. She didn't mind, kissing him harder, suddenly desperate to lose herself in his lovemaking.

"Yes," she whispered, wrapping her arms fully around him. "Take me away. Make me forget everything but you."

Chapter Ten

"Those are the last of the linen wardrobes, your Grace. Would you care to inspect the china cupboards next?" Mrs. Hardwick shut and locked a set of tall double doors that lined one section of hallway in the east wing. Once finished, she turned inquiring eyes upon the new duchess.

Violet stifled a weary sigh. In the past four hours she and the housekeeper had walked what must have been a mile at least of hallways and staircases. Striding into rooms and back out again as the older woman acquainted her with Winterlea's current domestic arrangements. The torture had commenced promptly after breakfast with an inspection of the wine cellars, then gradually moved upward through the house. They were now on the second floor.

"Not at present, Mrs. Hardwick," Violet declared, forcing herself to be pleasant but firm. "I am sure they are in the same excellent order as were the contents of all of the other cabinets and closets we've inspected this morning. I thank you for a most thorough tour, but now I must return to my rooms to change for luncheon. The duke will be quite cross if I am late arriving at table."

Mrs. Hardwick frowned as if she meant to disagree. In a precise imitation of her twin, Violet gave a perfunctory nod then turned away.

Mrs. Hardwick, however, was not ready to be dismissed. "If your Grace has time this afternoon, there are next week's menus to approve. Chef is most insistent about knowing beforehand what meals he is to serve."

That's right, Violet thought, *shift the blame onto Chef.* "Who has been in charge of approving the meals up to now?" she asked.

The housekeeper straightened her scrawny shoulders, crowlike in her black bombazine dress. "Prior to your Grace's arrival, that duty has fallen to me."

Violet knew decisions concerning meals, table arrangements and such fell under her purview as duchess. But the thought of being troubled over such mundane details left her less than enthusiastic. Jeannette would likely have reveled in such domestic authority. For Violet's part, she could think of a hundred and one more interesting ways to spend her time. She wished she could simply chuck it all, but she was the Duchess of Raeburn now. She had responsibilities. She did not want to disappoint Adrian.

"Yes, very well," Violet said, watching the other woman's eyes ignite with a subtle gleam of triumph. The look, and the knowledge that her sister would never cavil to a servant, gave Violet the courage to rebel just a little. "But not today," she stated. "Tomorrow is soon enough. Ten o'clock, in my study. I shall see you there."

The gleam dimmed, the housekeeper's mouth opening and closing for a long moment while she decided whether or not to argue. Then she lowered her eyes and curtseyed, stepping aside to let Violet pass. "As you wish, your Grace."

"Good day, Mrs. Hardwick." Violet swept past, allowing herself to tremble only after she rounded a corner in the corridor beyond.

In Violet's bedroom, Agnes had set out a comfortable green-and-white-striped muslin day dress and green slippers to match. After bathing her face and hands, Violet

let her maid assist her into the new outfit. Then she made her way through several long hallways to the family dining room.

Adrian arrived ten minutes later, striding in at a brisk pace. "Forgive my tardiness, my dear. Reams of correspondence cluttering my office. I left Dalton scribbling away. He claims he is content to catch a bite at his desk. That's what comes from having your attention focused on other pursuits, too much work."

He bent down, dusted his lips across her forehead, then crossed to assume his place at the head of the table. He spread his napkin onto his lap. "But I am sure you don't wish to hear a lot of boring business talk. How was your morning?"

His business talk was not boring, she wanted to tell him. She would far rather hear about his day than discuss her own. After all, what could be more tedious than inspecting kitchen stores, bottles of wine and stacks of linens? Jeannette, however, would likely have shown little interest in the affairs of business, especially those of her own husband.

Doing her best to make her morning's plight amusing, Violet launched into an abridged account of her explorations of Winterlea. She left out her misgivings concerning Mrs. Hardwick.

The woman made her uncomfortable. For a brief moment she considered telling Adrian, then dismissed the urge. It wasn't as if the housekeeper had actually done anything wrong. She was very efficient, *too* efficient really. Perhaps that was the problem. The woman left Violet feeling as if she were an intruder in her new home. As if *she* were the servant and her abilities had been found distinctly lacking.

Perhaps it was her own sense of insecurity that made her feel that way. Jeannette certainly wouldn't have had this problem. Pity was, she wasn't Jeannette. She ate another mouthful of Chef's delicious steak-and-kidney pie and kept her worries to herself.

"I do not mean to seem as if I am neglecting you, my dear," Adrian said when the meal was concluded, the plates cleared away. "But I have some pressing matters that cannot wait. Would you be terribly distressed if we skipped the ride we'd planned for this afternoon? I promise I'll make it up to you tomorrow. We'll spend the entire day together, if you like. Ride out and have a picnic. What do you think?"

He waited as if anticipating an argument.

From Jeannette he would likely have gotten one.

"I can't claim not to be disappointed," she said truthfully, "but I understand that you are quite busy. Therefore, I shall endeavor to occupy myself this afternoon."

He relaxed, looking relieved. "Are you certain?"

"Of course I'm certain. You needn't dance attendance upon me twenty-four hours a day. I am your wife now. I have duties too."

After she had made her selfless statement, Violet wondered if she should have. In Jeannette's mind, business might always be put off for later when there was pleasure to be had. Yet Violet could not regret her words. She did not want Adrian to think her overly demanding, regardless of how her sister might have behaved.

"But don't imagine I won't hold you to your promises about tomorrow. I shall be quite cross if you renege."

Adrian rose, strode to her. All the footmen had withdrawn, leaving them alone in the room. He rested his hands on the arms of her chair and leaned close. "Never fear. I won't renege."

He kissed her, a leisurely blending of lips and tongues, gentle and sweet as a warm spring morning. "I believe, my dear, that I am a very lucky man. A very lucky man indeed to have a wife such as you."

After he departed, Violet sat for a time, absorbing what he had said, how he had acted, the memory of his kiss still tingling upon her lips. Was he coming to love her? The word was never spoken between them, and yet . . . Her heart swelled with the joyous hope of it. Her next thought, however, plunged her painfully back to earth. Was it she he was falling in love with? Or only the woman he believed her to be?

Gloomy, she rose from the table.

That's when she remembered the library and brightened a bit. Perhaps the afternoon wouldn't be utterly dismal, after all.

Violet had never seen so many books assembled in one room in her entire life. The elegant leather-bound volumes ranged all four walls, climbing in two tiers to the very top of the twenty-five-foot-high ceiling. For a book lover such as herself, the effect was a truly monumental experience. Of course, she had viewed the library at Winterlea before, but this was the first opportunity she had had to explore its contents at her leisure.

Glancing over her shoulder to confirm she was alone, she withdrew from her pocket the spectacles she kept hidden in her keepsake box upstairs and slid them onto her nose. *Hallelujah,* she thought, as the world came once more into sharp focus. She could see. She blinked a couple of times to get used to the enhanced clarity, then began to scrutinize the selection of available books.

There were so many of them she could literally have spent hours doing nothing more than reading the titles. The classics were well represented: Euripides, Homer, Socrates and Plato. Violet considered taking down *Plutarch's Lives,* but decided she wasn't in the mood for such heavy reading. There were the collected works of William Shakespeare and a few volumes written by his contemporary, and supposed mentor, Christopher Marlowe.

Molière, Voltaire and Descartes were present in both the original French and the English translations. And there were several volumes of essays from such notable authors as Adam Smith, John Milton, Francis Bacon and Edmund Burke.

Concerned she was dawdling, she plucked down a volume of poetry by Robert Burns—romantic, relaxing and easily interrupted should she find herself in need of a quick retreat. She would have to be careful of her time, careful as well to make sure no one actually saw her reading in the library.

Luckily, the room possessed several splendid nooks, including one with a deep window seat. Arranging herself inside against a comfortable, plush blue cushion, she drew the draperies closed and shut herself into her own private little world. With a pleased smile flirting over her lips, she opened her book and began to read.

Three weeks later, Violet was arranging cut flowers into a vase in one of the downstairs drawing rooms when March gave a light tap upon the door. She bid him to enter.

"Good afternoon, your Grace." He walked forward, a silver salver in hand. "Some correspondence has arrived for your attention."

She slipped a peach-faced zinnia in amongst several tall hollyhocks whose sunny yellow petals burst like fairy puffs upon each long stalk. "Oh, thank you, March. Would you be so kind as to place them on the escritoire, please?" She reached for another zinnia, a crimson one this time.

The majordomo bowed. "My pleasure, your Grace."

"March?"

He paused, waited politely. "Yes, your Grace?"

She took a step back, angled her head to one side. "What do you think?"

"Think, your Grace?" he repeated.

"Yes." She nodded toward the vase of flowers. "What do you think of my arrangement?"

"It wouldn't be my place to say."

"Whyever not? You have eyes, do you not?"

"Well, yes, your Grace, but—"

"Please. I should value your opinion. You have a fine aesthetic sense. You never set anything but a perfect table and everything under your direction here in the house is done in the finest of taste." She gazed again at the vase of flowers and sighed. "I fear I am not much of a hand at arrangements."

Warmed by her words of praise, March let some of his usual stiff formality slip away. He studied the flowers, a riot of bold color and haphazard shape—stems, leaves and petals squeezed in so tightly, the vase seemed in imminent danger of exploding.

She caught his look. "I should prefer you to be honest."

He paused for a long moment as he gathered his thoughts. "Your choice of color and flower type is delightful. Pastels cheerfully intermixed with a few bold primaries lend the arrangement visual interest. Tall and short stalks to give it movement. But if I might suggest, your design could be improved by using fewer flowers. Perhaps you could intersperse the taller ones throughout the design instead of clumping them all in the back." He fell suddenly silent, fearing for an instant that he had voiced far too much of an opinion.

Yet the duchess did not seem angered. Squinting at the arrangement, she tipped her head in the opposite direction from before. "You know, I believe you are right." She stepped close, yanked out nearly a dozen dripping stems. Putting them aside, she rearranged the others so that the long hollyhocks were more uniformly distributed.

She moved back again, hands clasped beneath her chin. She smiled. "Oh, that is exactly what it needed. Thank you, March. Thank you very much indeed."

A slight wave of color stole into his cheeks, leaving him uncommonly discomposed. He hadn't blushed in nearly forty years, he realized, not since he'd been a small lad enduring a scold. He cleared his throat. "You are most welcome, your Grace. I am pleased I was able to be of assistance."

She smiled again, straight at him. Unable to repress the impulse, he smiled back.

Since the duke and his new bride had taken up residence, she had captivated them all. Showing surprisingly little resemblance to the spoiled girl who had visited Winterlea for a week last spring during the engagement period, this young woman was a pure delight. Warm, kind and thoughtful. Clearly marriage suited her.

They idolized the duke, respected and admired him. He was very good to them all. But they adored the duchess, every one of them her devotee.

Everyone except Mrs. Hardwick.

The duchess gathered up the flowers she'd removed from the vase and handed them to March. "I won't be needing these. Do you think the staff would enjoy them? I believe they would brighten the belowstairs dining tables for this evening's meal."

March accepted the flowers, inclined his head. "Most kind, your Grace. It will be a cheerful addition indeed."

A brief frown creased her forehead. "Oh, but there are not nearly enough. Please instruct Dobbins and the gardening staff to cut as many more as you need so that everyone may enjoy them."

March nodded again, full dignity restored. "It shall be done as you wish." He bowed, departed the room.

Alone, Violet studied the finished flower arrangement with justifiable pride. Even Jeannette could not have done better. She carried her floral work of art across to a wide, marble-topped table where she knew it would look good and carefully set it down. She admired it a moment more then turned away. She sighed as she caught sight of the small stack of correspondence March had brought in.

More invitations, she supposed. They'd started arriving a little less than a week ago, right after their neighbors began to call. The Miltons had been the first to arrive, a friendly older couple whose six children were all grown and married. Their eldest son was a barrister who now resided in London.

Squire Lyle and his wife, Joan, came next, their two eldest daughters in tow. Pretty, apple-cheeked girls of fifteen and sixteen years, the Lyle children had sat in wide-eyed silence while the adults talked. The only outburst came when the girls had fallen into a paroxysm of high-pitched giggling over a naked Greek figurine that stood in one of the hallway alcoves.

Vicar Thompkins, tall and solemn in black, arrived soon after with his wife, Emeline. A tiny, pale doe of a woman, Mrs. Thompkins only came up to her husband's shoulder and spoke in a breathless sort of whisper one had to strain to hear.

And then there had been Lord and Lady Carter, the only couple with whom she and Jeannette had a prior acquaintance. Unlike the other neighbors, who knew her not at all, she'd had to be most on her guard with the Carters, striving to be as genial and lively as possible.

She'd nearly muffed it by splashing tea all over her skirt while she had been nervously pouring. Luckily, she'd caught herself just as the first drop was about to spill. Through sheer force of will, she'd made it through the rest of the visit without giving herself away.

She crossed now to the writing desk, and aware she was alone, pulled her spectacles out of her dress pocket. She balanced them on her nose, savoring her improved eyesight.

The first two items of correspondence were indeed invitations. She set them aside for later consideration.

The third was a letter posted from London, her title written across the heavy cream-colored vellum in a broad, dark hand. She broke the seal, her eyes widening as she began to read.

My dearest love,
   You know not the torments I have suffered since your marriage . . .

She gasped.

A love letter.

My God, she had completely forgotten Jeannette's admonition that letters of this sort might arrive. And if she'd had any doubt as to the sex of the mysterious "Kaye," she didn't any longer. Only he wasn't "Kaye," as she'd assumed. He was "K," the single initial scrawled at the base of the missive.

Hastily, Violet snapped the letter shut.

What to do? Jeannette had told her to forward them on to her immediately. But should she? Did she have any right not to?

Unable to resist, she opened the letter again and read a little farther. It wasn't a long note. But, oh my, the passion that leapt off the page with each and every word.

Who was this man her sister was involved with? What sort of person must he be to pursue a woman he thought married to another? A man desperately in love, she decided, the depth of his ardor unmistakable, as imprudent as it might be.

And what of Jeannette, did she return his regard?

Oh, heavens, Violet sighed, what a tangle each of them had woven for the other.

To date, she had received only one letter from Jeannette. A brief, hastily scribbled missive typical of her twin's careless style. Jeannette had assured her all was well, giving her current direction in Italy. She and Great-aunt Agatha were having a splendid time, she'd written, attending many elegant parties and meeting dozens of fascinating people. "Violet," it seemed, was beginning to come out of her shell, much to the amazed approval of their aunt.

Violet prayed Jeannette was not overdoing it, would not end up revealing their deception. But her twin was clever. It wasn't likely she'd give herself away.

They planned to stay in Naples through the last week of August, then journey south to Florence, where they would remain for at least a month. Jeannette had said she would write again with news and the location of their new accommodations after they arrived. Violet had yet to receive another letter from her twin.

She tapped the illicit billet-doux against her hand, supposing she ought to send the blighted thing on to Italy. The wisest course of action, though, would be to destroy it. It was all very well for her to know to whom the letters really belonged, but if anyone else should see? If Adrian should ever read . . . she couldn't bear to contemplate the horrendous outcome of that.

No, the letters must stop.

Yet Jeannette would never forgive her if she destroyed the thing. And there was another problem besides. No matter what action she took, what was to prevent K from sending another letter, even if she did succeed in getting rid of this one?

She would have to write Jeannette. Make her agree to sever the connection with this mystery man. What other solution could there be? Perhaps in time he might develop a tendre for "Violet" and all could be well. Assuming her sister truly had feelings for this K person and wished a future with him.

Violet slipped the letter into her pocket, then seated herself at the desk. She reached for a fresh sheet of writing paper. Totally engrossed, she did not immediately hear the footsteps behind her. When she did, she flicked a glance over her shoulder and dropped her pen.

Chapter Eleven

Violet's breath squeezed hard in her lungs as Adrian approached. Powerfully aware of the spectacles perched on her face, she whipped them off, clutched them inside her palm. As casually as possible, she lowered her hand and the incriminating eyewear, concealing both within the folds of her skirt.

Oh, Lord, had he seen them?

Her gaze fell upon the letter she'd been writing, her heart jackknifing up into her throat. She couldn't let him see *that* either, and he was almost upon her.

She edged a sheet of plain paper over the one upon which she had been writing, then pivoted abruptly in her chair.

"Adrian," she greeted, flashing him a wide smile. "What a happy surprise. Are you returned already? I thought you said your appointment with Mr. McDougal would last the entire afternoon."

He stopped, gave her a curious smile. "Our business took less time than expected." He glanced over at the desk, then looked slowly back. "What have you been doing, madam? Writing letters?"

She stood, careful to face him as she deliberately moved away from the desk. She angled the hand holding her spectacles behind her back.

"Yes," she said. "We received two more invitations, though I haven't had a chance to review them yet. I was composing a letter to . . . umm, Violet. She is due to leave for Florence soon and I did not want to miss her before she departed on the next leg of her journey."

"How is your sister?"

"Very well, last she wrote. Italy agrees with her, it would seem."

"Jealous of her adventures?" he questioned.

"Of course," she replied with the kind of breezy candor she knew Jeannette might have employed. "But I console myself with the surety that one day you shall take me there. You have promised, have you not?"

"Yes. One day we shall visit the Continent, Italy included."

She smiled.

He smiled in return. "Well, are you going to tell me?"

"Tell you what?"

He nodded toward her concealed hand. "Whatever it is you are trying so desperately to hide behind your back."

Blast. And she had thought he had not noticed. What to do? Her heart pounded furiously, realizing there was no hiding them, not now, not anymore. Unless she could brazen her way out.

Going on the defensive, she said, "It is nothing. If I wanted you to know, I would tell you."

He took a step forward, idly clasped his hands at his back. "Why don't you wish to tell me?"

Violet raised her chin in a haughty tilt. "It is a private matter."

"A private matter? Here in the downstairs drawing room?" He arched an eyebrow.

"Yes, and I would thank you not to inquire further."

For a hopeful moment she thought he was going to desist. Then he swung his arms free, took another step forward. "That tactic may work on everyone else of your acquaintance, but it won't wash with me." He held out an insistent hand. "Let's see."

Her shoulders dropped, together with her defiant posture. "Adrian, please. It's nothing important. Let it be."

But his curiosity was roused and once Adrian was curious about something, there was no stopping him. "Show me or I fear I shall be forced to resort to stronger methods."

He reached out before she could step away, snagged her wrist and brought it forward. He unfolded her clenched fist.

"Spectacles?"

Violet tried not to let her worry show. "I need them to read, if you must know."

Surprise showed plainly upon his face. "I had no idea. And you've been hiding your glasses from me all this time?"

She lowered her eyes. "Imperfect eyesight is an affliction I share with my sister. But unlike her, I do not choose to broadcast the impairment to the world. A woman never shows to advantage wearing eyeglasses, you know." She expressed the sentiments easily, repeating the same phrases her sister and mother had said to her a thousand times over.

"They cannot look so very bad," Adrian insisted gently.

"You never said they looked good on my twin." The words were out of her mouth before she could prevent them.

"The question did not arise. But I never thought your sister looked plain in her spectacles, if that is what you mean."

An inexplicable breathlessness stole over her. "Did you not?"

"You are both beautiful women. You are twins, after all. Put on the glasses."

"No! I couldn't."

"Put them on," he urged in a gentle voice.

She stood mute. Trembling, and trying not to show it, she realized she had no choice. She was well and truly trapped. With great reluctance, she slid the spectacles onto her nose, then looked up at him through the glass lenses, his dear face for once in clear, sharp focus. She waited, hands clutched, heart thumping rabbit fast. He would see the truth now, wouldn't he? Know who she really was?

Her stomach seized at the thought.

"You look exactly like her," he murmured after a long moment of study. "I know the two of you are identical, but it is truly uncanny."

Violet blinked.

He didn't realize the truth. Relief swept through her, followed by an odd sense of disappointment. A deflated, bitter aftertaste she knew she should not feel. Did she want him to find out?

Of course not, she scolded herself.

Still, what would it be like to have him gaze at her with an expression of caring in his eyes and to know it was meant for her? The real her. What would it be like for him to kiss her as Violet and know he wanted her regardless? To hear him speak her true name—*Violet*—a passionate whisper on his lips, a murmur of ecstasy uttered in the dark, cool hours of the night or beneath the fresh warmth of a morning sun.

But such thoughts were pure insanity. Such a circumstance could never be. Abruptly melancholy, she reached up to remove her glasses, not trusting her luck to last.

"No," he said, stopping her. "Leave them on."

She frowned.

"I understand that you do not wish to wear your

spectacles in public," he continued, "but here at home you must use them as much and as often as you need." He took her hand, raised it to his lips. "I assure you, my dear, your radiance is in no way diminished by the addition."

She should refuse. It was too great a risk even now. Yet what a relief it would be to see normally again. What a delight to read and write without having to sneak peeks through her glasses when she thought she was not being observed.

His suggestion was a temptation not to be denied.

"Very well," she said, acquiescing as if his request were a great burden. "I shall wear them if my need is great. But *only* here in the house and only in private."

"Now that that is settled, I stopped by to inquire whether or not you would like to go rowing on the lake. 'Tis a fine day, far too beautiful to stay cooped up indoors. I'll ask François to pack us a light afternoon repast, and we could dine on the small island at the lake's center. My siblings and I used to play and swim there in the summer. I know of a comfortable, secluded spot just perfect for a picnic. I've been wanting to introduce you to it for some while."

Violet caught the wicked gleam in his dark eyes and knew he had more than boating and dining in mind. Her body warmed at the notion. "I have my letter to finish, but I suppose it can wait. I should change into something more appropriate for the out-of-doors before we leave."

"Very well." He feathered a pair of kisses over her lips, a taste of more to come. "I shall go speak to François about our meal. A half an hour, shall we say?"

"A half an hour it is." She smiled.

She waited until he left the room, then gathered up the pages of the letter she had been writing to Jeannette. She locked them, together with the letter from her sister's lover, into a small, recessed drawer in the writing table. She would finish the letter and have it posted on the morrow.

Pocketing the key, she went upstairs to change.

The last of summer faded, the heat of August melting into September. October dawned, treating area inhabitants to chill, frosty mornings, mild afternoons and crisp, clear evenings. Bright as newly minted coins, the leaves glinted on the trees in festive colors: ruby, copper and gold. Bushy-tailed squirrels, badger and deer busied themselves making their woodland homes ready for the winter to come. Inside, people lighted fires, exchanged cool cottons for woolen warmth, drank mulled cider and ate hot soups in place of cooler, lighter fare.

At Winterlea, it was much the same.

Erin, one of the downstairs maids, tended the fire in the duchess's study. Violet thanked her when she finished, exchanging smiles with the winsome girl, who couldn't have been a day over fifteen. The maid gave a shy curtsey and departed, ash pail and fireplace brush in hand.

The room was a comfortable one, smaller than many others in the huge house. Over the past few weeks, Violet had quite made it her own.

Set at the rear west corner of the house, it overlooked one of the gardens, which was bedecked for fall with lush sprays of goldenrod and sunny-faced chrysanthemums. Peaceful and quiet, the room exuded a gentle, soothing hush that Violet loved. On afternoons when Adrian was occupied with business and there were no tenants to visit, no neighbors come to call, she would curl up in one of the room's snug armchairs and lose herself inside a book.

Reveling in a greater sense of freedom now that she

could wear her glasses without fear of discovery, she indulged herself by reading here in the study whenever she could manage. She kept a piece of embroidery near at hand just in case she was interrupted. She didn't want anyone, especially Adrian, to realize she was spending her afternoons happily buried in a book.

Horatio snuffled, snoring gently where he lay near her feet, dreaming his doggy dreams. Violet resumed her reading and was deeply engrossed many minutes later when a light scratch came at the door. Acting fast, she hid the book between her hip and the seat cushion, pulled the embroidery frame a few inches closer so it appeared as though she was sewing. Only then did she bid the person to enter.

March stood in the doorway. "Pardon the intrusion, your Grace, but I thought I should inform you Lord Christopher has arrived."

Violet's eyebrows shot upward at the news. Adrian's younger brother, here? Now? He had written nothing about a visit in the letter Adrian had had from him only last week. To her knowledge, he was supposed to be at University, studying for mid-term exams.

"Lord Christopher has gone up to his rooms to change," March supplied. "He asked after his Grace upon his arrival. When I explained that his Grace is not home at present but that you were receiving, he said not to trouble you. He then requested a meal and went upstairs."

She could tell from March's tone and his actions that he disapproved of her brother-in-law failing to stop and immediately pay his regards to her. On the few brief occasions they had met, Lord Christopher—or Kit, as he was known to his intimates—had never been anything but unfailingly polite and friendly to Jeannette and Violet both. She didn't know him well, but given his unusual behavior, it seemed something must be amiss.

"Did he look well?" she asked.

"His lordship gave every appearance of enjoying robust good health, your Grace."

"Hmm. Well, since he is arrived, please inform Chef there will be three of us for dinner this evening. And have a tea tray sent up to the family drawing room. Unless Lord Christopher has an objection, ask him to join me there in half an hour's time."

"Very good, your Grace." Approval showed in March's wizened eyes. He bowed and closed the door behind him.

She sighed. So much for reading this afternoon. She hoped she'd done the right thing asking Kit to take tea with her. Perhaps she should have left him to his own devices since he clearly did not wish for company. But they were related now and it would be best if they could develop a cordial relationship right from the start.

Of course, she had no true idea how Jeannette had gotten on with him in the past. She would simply have to muddle through just as she had been doing all these weeks. She slipped her book into its hiding place underneath the thick cushion of her seat, then left the sanctuary of her room, Horatio trailing in her wake.

"If you must know, I've been sacked. Sent down. Banished."

Kit made his dramatic statement, then stuffed a tea sandwich into his mouth, chewing as if he was in need of vital replenishment after issuing such a vivid declaration.

He swallowed and immediately reached for another sandwich. "Adrian's going to murder me when he finds out I've been expelled. He'll likely set me to digging drainage ditches on one of his farms as punishment."

"Surely not," Violet said, unable to prevent her sympathetic nature from coming to the fore. "Mayhap it will not be as dreadful as you imagine."

"No, it will be worse." He drank some tea, his long, lean frame slumped in his seat. He reminded Violet of a sparer, younger version of his brother.

"When will he be back, do you know?" Kit mumbled in a mournful tone.

"Anytime, I should imagine."

Kit stared at the red raspberry jam tart on his plate, his expression as doleful as a condemned man awaiting the final hour of his execution. After long contemplation, he ate the sweet in one bite.

"I would have gone to Town, but my quarter's allowance is spent already. Won't get another till the new year."

"Was it gaming or women, then, that did the damage?" A couple of months ago she wouldn't have had the nerve to ask such an impertinent question. But pretending to be her twin seemed to be lending her an extra measure of bravado as of late.

He studied her for a long minute out of deep-set hazel eyes, then shrugged. "If you must know, it was neither women nor gambling. It was a foot race."

"A foot race? Where could the harm be in that?"

Having the grace to look slightly chagrined, he crossed his well-shod feet and lowered his eyes. "A naked foot race."

She gasped, unable to hide her astonishment. Startling images flickered through her mind. Realizing her mouth was hanging open, she forced it closed.

"It seemed like jolly good fun at the time," he mused. "Three laps around the University commons before the clock strikes midnight, best man wins and all that. Of course, the lot of us were sadly in our cups when we hatched the fool plan. Who knew Dean Musgrove would pick that particular evening to take his wife up to the roof for a late-night astronomical survey of the heavens?"

He paused, a naughty grin creeping over his lips. "Guess she ended up seeing a great deal more than stars."

The humor of the situation bubbled up inside her. "Then it *was* wagering, after all," she accused. A small burst of laughter escaped, completely ruining the effect of her stern words.

"More of a dare really. We had been discussing past house initiation capers and, well, it all sort of escalated from there. Brentholden is a champion runner. I said I could best him."

"So it was only you and this one other man?"

"The rest of our crowd were there cheering us on, but they were too pusillanimous to take part in the actual race."

"What happened to Mr. Brentholden?"

"He's out, but only for the rest of this semester. If he keeps his record clean, he'll be back in without blemish."

"And you will not," she said as a statement, not a question.

A mixture of bitter dejection settled over his features. "It was not my first infraction."

She considered his words, thinking of her scapegrace brother. Darrin had spent his life embroiled in one peccadillo after another, several far more serious than this. Last year he'd run up a debt of nearly five thousand pounds playing dice and cards. Then turned up on their father's doorstep, pockets completely to let, begging for the funds to cover his losses. Seemed the bone-crackers would be after him otherwise. Worse, he had nearly caused a public scandal by having an affair with the wife of one of his professors at Cambridge. The professor had wanted to run him through. Instead he'd been forced to settle for Darrin's apology and his promise to leave school and never set foot in the town of Cambridge again.

Seen in that light, Kit's indiscretion was rather insignificant. Certainly not worthy of expulsion. Leaving out mention of Darrin, Violet stated her opinion to her new brother-in-law.

He shrugged, cast once more into the doldrums. "Sadly, the University board did not see it that way. I was informed by that hidebound body politic that I may apply again next term for readmittance in the fall, which may or may not be granted. As far as I am concerned, they can keep their benighted school. Unfortunately, my brother doesn't agree. I am to have an education whether I wish to have one or not."

"What would you do if you were not at University?"

He paused, a surprised look on his face as if no one had ever thought to ask him such a question before. He reached for another raspberry tart, ate while he considered his response.

"Travel, I believe," he mused. "There are so many intriguing places in the world: India, China, the South Seas, the Americas. I hear they have herds of monstrous beasts, great shaggy brown creatures that run wild throughout the unexplored regions of their western lands. Buffalo, I believe they are called."

Fascinated, she wanted to ask him more. Instead she refreshed her tea and buried her interest inside the cup. Jeannette would have found nothing the least bit absorbing in hearing about buffalo, even if she did long to travel abroad.

"Well," she responded, forcing herself more firmly into the role she had agreed to portray, "the Continent is adventurous enough for me. Assuming your brother ever agrees to take me. This wearisome business of his seems never to have an end."

She watched a nascent light of interest sputter out in Kit's eyes. "Yes, well, he has much responsibility on his shoulders."

"As do we all. Chef is making medallions of beef tonight for dinner. I have asked that an extra place be set for you, of course."

"My thanks, but it may be pleasanter for us all if I do not join you this evening." He set his teacup and plate aside.

"As you wish, but I hope you will reconsider. He may be angry now but this will pass, likely sooner than you imagine. You are his brother and he loves you dearly. Nothing can change that."

Before Kit had an opportunity to reply, Adrian strode into the room.

The duke shot a frowning look at his sibling. "March told me you were here. What has occurred?"

"Is that any way to greet your brother?" Violet reproached in a soft voice. "Come sit and have some tea." She patted the sofa cushion next to her. "You must be famished after your long day. How did it go?"

Kit waited, expecting his brother to make some curt, dismissive remark to her suggestion, then have directly at him. Instead Adrian shelved the interrogation and did as his wife asked, moving to take a seat beside her.

He let her serve him hot tea from a fresh pot one of the maids brought in, along with a plate of assorted sandwiches and scones. She added an extra dollop of clotted cream on the side just the way he preferred it.

Allowing her to draw him out, Adrian gave them an accounting of his day's business. At length, Adrian turned to his wife. "My dear, thank you for the delicious repast. If you will excuse us, my brother and I have some things I believe need discussing. Kit, shall we adjourn to my office?" Adrian stood, moved to the door, his suggestion a command.

Stealing himself with a deep breath, Kit levered up out of his chair. He paused to make a short, polite bow to his sister-in-law.

"You never told me," she murmured in a voice too low to reach Adrian's ears. "Who won the race?"

Kit's eyebrows shot skyward, a small grin erasing a trace of the dejection from his face. "I did."

Contrary to Kit's glum prediction, Adrian did not force him to perform manual labor as penance for his foolish indiscretion. Nor was he confined to his room on a diet of bread and water or banished to the family's remotest estate on Scotland's Orkney Islands.

No, what Adrian did was far, far worse. At least to Kit's way of thinking.

His brother set him upon an intense course of study with Vicar Dittlesby. A retired clergyman, the man was so old he could actually recall the birth of Mad King George. With a fashion sense stuck in the last century, Dittlesby still wore a curled white wig upon his head and favored long frock coats. Almost deaf, he carried a small metal horn that he would lift to his ear to hear. Despite its use, Kit often had to raise his voice to a near shout.

Age and infirmity aside, the vicar's mind was tack sharp. A learned scholar, he knew Greek and Latin and all the classic texts so well, he might have penned them himself. Nothing got by Vicar Dittlesby.

Adrian certainly knew how to turn the thumbscrews when it suited him, Kit decided. His plan—laid out in a frigid voice during that first agonizing meeting—was to discuss Kit's status with University officials and get him reinstated. Meanwhile, Kit was to complete all the work he was currently missing so that he might sit for exams at the end of term and not fall behin l. There were to be no more infractions. He would be as circumspect as a monk. And he would willingly study with Vicar Dittlesby, no matter how much it might pain him to do so.

Adrian set down the law and Kit obeyed.

Yet there was only so much misery a man could endure. Which was why, after nearly two weeks of study, Kit sought refuge in the one place he hoped he could elude detection.

His sister-in-law's study.

He knew she disappeared most afternoons for a few hours. At first he thought she was slipping off to nap or pen letters to friends, or walk that behemoth dog of hers. Then he realized she was not engaged in any of those activities. He asked one of the housemaids, a pretty little armful who giggled every time he got within ten feet, where her Grace disappeared to each day. The answer—her study in the rear of the house.

His brain ached after a day spent ciphering calculus equations and translating passage after endless passage of Greek and Latin. He knocked on the door to Jeannette's study, letting himself in a brief second after she gave her assent. He closed the door and pressed his back flat against it, fully aware he must look like a fox fleeing from a pack of slavering hounds.

His sister-in-law gave him an inquiring look. "Is something amiss, Kit?"

He forced himself to relax, move into the room. "No, not at all. Do you mind if I sit in here for a bit? I promise not to interrupt whatever it is you're doing."

Eyes shrewd, she waved him toward a matching armchair located on the opposite side of the fireplace. "Desperate for a break from the vicar, I take it."

He sank into the seat, relief washing over him. "Yes, rather." His lips curved into a sheepish smile. "He was preparing to launch into a comparative analysis of Socrates and the great Roman Stoics when he excused himself for a few minutes—nature's call, I believe. I fear I took advantage of his absence and slipped out of the room."

"If you are not careful," she teased, "he may call out a search party. But you are welcome to remain here as long as you like. I was just . . ." she paused, sliding the sewing frame at her elbow several inches closer ". . . embroidering."

"I brought a book with me." He held up a thick tome bound in dark leather. "That way if I am found I can claim I misunderstood what the vicar said and came in here to study. He only hears about half of what I say as it is, and always when I've made some foolish error." He ran a hand through his short black curls. "Adrian is a devil to have sicced him on me."

She smiled gently. "I am sure he had a good reason for his choice."

"Torture. That was his reason." He leaned forward, angling his head. "Are my ears bleeding yet? I wasn't subjected to so many hours of lecture at University. I may soon go as deaf as that old man. And my eyes. Are they as red as I suspect? I fear they will fall out from all the reading."

She shook her head at his exaggerated humor, squinting slightly as she traced her fingertips over the surface of her embroidery. She jumped suddenly and stuck a finger in her mouth.

"Are you all right?" he asked.

She nodded. "Pricked my finger on the needle. Stupid of me."

"Mayhap you should find a duller sewing implement."

"Yes, mayhap," she murmured.

A knock came at the door. Kit stiffened. Had his hiding spot been discovered already?

March stepped into the room, barely giving him a

glance. "Your Grace," the majordomo said, "I am sorry to interrupt, but there has been an accident in the kitchens. One of the maids dropped a heavy pot of boiling wash water and has sustained several burns. I thought you would wish to be notified."

Instantly alarmed, she straightened. "Of course I do. Has a physician been called?"

"A boy was dispatched to summon the local healer."

"No, no, you must have Dr. Montgomery come." Dr. Montgomery was the duke's personal physician, a young London-trained doctor whom Adrian had convinced to come to the area two years before. "He will know what to do."

"Yes, your Grace."

"Was it Sarah?" she asked.

"No. Brenna, the one from the north country."

"Oh, poor girl." She stood, turned to Kit. "You will have to excuse me. I must go see if there is anything I can do for her."

Kit stood, as good manners dictated. "Of course. You must let me know how she fares."

March and the duchess left the room. Kit closed the door behind them and turned to resume his seat. With all the hubbub, he might be able to elude detection for some time. That being the case, he decided to indulge himself in a short nap while he had the opportunity.

His gaze alighted upon his sister-in-law's chair and the corner of what looked to be a book, poking out from between the chair's side and the seat cushion. Curious, he walked closer, tugged the volume from its hiding place.

The *Aeneid*.

He blinked, stared at the spine. How very singular, he thought. What on earth was such a bloody literary bore doing in Jeannette's chair, of all places? Surely she had noticed the wretched thing digging a hole into her hip when she'd sat?

Just holding it gave him shudders.

He flipped open the front cover, eyes glazing when he saw it was written in the original Latin. For a fleeting instant, he'd hoped it would be a translation. He might have gotten some use out of that; Dittlesby adored plaguing him with passages from Virgil. But Adrian, crafty bastard that he was, had seen to it that all the English versions of the books Kit was studying had been removed from the library shortly after his arrival. He was going to have to have a chat with his older brother soon. This blatant harassment must end, even if he had brought most of it down upon his own head.

So what was he to make of finding this book in Jeannette's chair? She wasn't exactly the scholarly type. He doubted she ever cracked open a book. It was certain she hadn't been reading this one. Lord, he couldn't read it, even if he wished to. Perhaps Adrian had carried it into the room—he was, wouldn't you know, fluent in Latin—and had forgotten it on the chair. Wasn't like big brother to be careless with a book, though. Adrian was never careless with anything. It was, Kit concluded, a confounded great mystery.

He pondered it for a few moments more, then decided he really should get moving on that nap business while the chance was ripe. Returning the book to the place he had found it, he added a log to the fire, stretched out comfortably in his chair and closed his eyes.

Chapter Twelve

Another letter for Jeannette arrived the next morning.

As with the first, Violet didn't immediately recognize its significance. All innocence, she lifted the missive from the silver salver March placed at her elbow and broke the seal. The scandalous words leapt off the page, smacking her hard between the eyes.

My dearest darling. How I ache for want of you . . .

Hastily she refolded the letter, clutched it in her suddenly damp palm. Blast Jeannette. Obviously she hadn't written to discourage her lover. She probably hadn't even tried.

Violet contemplated the fire burning in the grate. Such a simple thing to toss the letter in and watch it blacken to ash. Yet ultimately the small act of cowardice would solve nothing, give her little more than a temporary respite. And there was her conscience to consider—annoying thing that it was—chiding her to remember the letter was not hers to destroy.

She would have to write Jeannette again, she decided. Stress most emphatically that this dangerous correspondence between her twin and her mystery lover must end.

With that in mind, she crossed to the fire. Heating the metal letter opener in the flames, she used a skillful hand to repair the wax seal. Satisfied with the result, she found ink and pen and began to compose her letter.

A completely different sort of letter arrived from Adrian's mother a couple of days later. Deciding there was no point in delaying a response, Violet went to the first-floor drawing room to draft her reply.

Kit and Vicar Dittlesby were already there, working hard, as they generally did in the afternoons. Although there were other places she could have sought out pen and paper, the drawing-room writing desk was the most convenient. Her plan was to slip in, barely noticed—it was, after all, a very spacious room—and quietly compose her message.

Both men rose to their feet at her entrance.

She waved them back into their chairs. "Please do not trouble yourselves over me. I have come to write a few letters. I shall be ever so quiet. Forget I am even here."

"Good afternoon, Duchess." The vicar bowed, sending the puffed white wig on his head into a perilous quiver that threatened to topple it to the floor. "Are we disturbing you?"

He raised his tin listening horn to his ear, all attention.

"No, no, I fear I am the one guilty of causing a disruption," she said. "Pray continue with your lesson."

The vicar nodded, his voice loud. "Yes, we are having a lesson. We can work elsewhere if you would prefer that we withdraw."

She met Kit's eyes, which glittered with resigned humor. "Sister," he greeted.

"Kit." She nodded, then turned back to the vicar. She modulated her voice in hopes of being better understood this time. "Do not leave. Pray sit." She motioned him down with her hands. "Continue your work and pay no mind to me. I shall be at my desk, composing a few letters."

"Letters? No, we are presently reviewing the conjugation of irregular Latin verbs. Your attention to such matters does you credit. You are a most refined and gracious lady."

She goggled at him for a moment. "Yes, well, thank you. Carry on. As I said, I shall be writing a few letters." She smiled, pantomiming the act. Understanding lighted suddenly in the old man's eyes. He nodded, bowed again.

She shared another amused look with Kit, stifled a smirk and retreated to the escritoire. The men resumed their lesson.

With a quick glance around to make certain they were occupied, she donned her glasses, angling her head so her face could not be easily seen.

She began the letter to her mother-in-law by inquiring after the dowager's health, and that of Adrian's sister Sylvia and her family. Last Violet had heard, Sylvia's pregnancy was progressing well. Although her sister-in-law had recently taken to her bed for several days after an unfortunate incident involving her five-year-old son, an afternoon tea party and a jar full of frogs.

She smiled, chuckling softly at the recollection of the droll story as she continued her letter. She listened with half an ear to the progress being made behind her. Poor Kit, she thought, he was having a dreadful time of it, struggling over a subject he so obviously detested.

Personally, she enjoyed Latin. Women generally were not exposed to such disciplines, concentrating instead on proper female pursuits: needlework, watercolor painting, geography, French, maybe a little Italian. And had it not been for language lessons, she might never have learned Latin either. But the tutor hired to teach her and Jeannette Italian had also been hired to instruct her brother in the classics. The similarities between the old and new languages sparked her initial interest. Helping Darrin complete his translations did the rest. By the time she was fourteen, she was accomplished enough to read Latin on her own.

"That is incorrect, your lordship." The vicar sighed in obvious frustration. "You should have mastered this long, long ago. You must memorize. Only then will the translations go smoothly. Please recite all tenses of the imperfect subjunctive of *ire*."

She listened, silently repeating them with him. She willed him to find the correct answer through each long, painful pause as he fought to find the words.

Finally, they moved on to the next. "*Nolle*, your lordship, pluperfect active."

She murmured them to herself as she wrote another sentence of her letter. "*Nolueram, nolueras, noluerat, nolueramus, nolueratis, noluerant.*"

Kit muddled his way through with only one mistake in third-person singular.

"*Nolle* again, your lordship, pluperfect subjunctive."

Barely aware she was doing it, she muttered the answers, forgetting to keep her voice as low as she should have.

She didn't see Kit's head shift in her direction.

"Continue. Second person, your lordship," the vicar stated.

"*Noluisses,*" she said quietly.

Kit repeated the word.

"Good, good, continue," the vicar encouraged.

"*Noluisset,*" she murmured.

He repeated what she'd said.

"Excellent. And the rest?"

"*Noluissemus, noluissetis, noluissent.*"

Kit listened to her, incredulous, scarcely able to comprehend what he was hearing. Jeannette knew Latin!

How was that possible? Stunned, he'd listened while she said the answers, repeating them back to the vicar in a kind of amazed awe. Jeannette knew the answers. She'd gotten every single one of them right. He stared at her as she bent over her writing. If she'd suddenly sprouted wings and levitated into the air, he could not have been more surprised.

He remembered the book by Virgil that he had found in her study several days ago. At the time, he'd told himself it belonged to Adrian. Now he wasn't so sure.

"Very well done, my lord. I believe you are improving. Let us try a translation." The vicar scratched a quotation onto the slate he had set up earlier.

Kit forced his attention toward the board, his mind awhirl from what he had just learned. He struggled to decipher the words. "Patient and stubborn, hurt will be of use?"

"No, my lord," the vicar said in disappointment. "It begins, 'Be patient and tough.' You attempt the rest."

"Be patient and tough . . ." he repeated, his brow furrowed.

Jeannette giggled ever so softly. He looked her way and that was when he saw her, *really* saw her, as she peeked over her shoulder to read the indecipherable words on the slate.

She had on eyeglasses.

Jeannette didn't wear eyeglasses. She had told him once at a party that ladies who cared about their looks found ways to do without spectacles. Lucky for her she'd never had to worry since she was blessed with perfect eyesight.

"My lord," the vicar encouraged. "Be patient and tough . . ."

Then he heard her murmur the rest of the saying under her breath before she turned back to her writing.

"For one day this pain will be useful to you."

Ordinarily he would have chaffed under the vicar's little dig. But right now he didn't have time to care about the quotation because he'd discovered a most astonishing truth.

His sister-in-law was an imposter.

The following day at luncheon, while they were dining on a splendid braised veal with tiny button mushrooms, Violet began to notice a difference in Kit. The change was nothing overt. A few longer-than-usual glances her way. An odd glint in his green-gold eyes whenever he addressed a question or comment to her.

At first, she shrugged it off. Overactive imagination, no doubt, brought on by a lack of sleep. Adrian had been in a particularly amorous mood last night. He'd kept her awake until the wee hours, waking her to make love a final time shortly after dawn, much to her sleepy delight. Now she was paying the price for their carnal indulgence, tired and imagining things.

Adrian, she noted, seemed disgustingly well rested and content. He grinned at her after eating a forkful of carrots, then continued his discussion of Gothic architecture with the vicar and Mr. Dalton, who had accepted an invitation to dine.

She raised a hand to her mouth to cover a delicate yawn, and once again caught her brother-in-law staring. She tossed him an inquiring gaze, arched a single upward eyebrow. He met her look with an inscrutable one of his own, then lowered his eyes and continued his meal.

She wanted to question him over his uncharacteristic behavior, but couldn't, not with the other men present in the room. And afterward, there was no time.

Kit excused himself as soon as the meal was concluded, the vicar shuffling in his wake, eager to continue their studies. Adrian and Mr. Dalton begged her permission to withdraw as well; more business that required their attention.

Leaving the servants to tidy up, she consigned thoughts of Kit and his odd watchfulness to the back of her mind and went to the conservatory. Horatio padded beside her, his nails tapping musically against the flagstone floors.

The vast glass-enclosed room was a marvel of light and air, warm and tranquil even on chill, dreary days such as today. Raindrops pattered against the multitudinous panes, merging into thin watery lines that spiraled and squiggled their way toward the earth.

Flora thrived in a lush abundance of green, packing the space full of color and life. Several varieties of flowers were in bloom, including the roses she had come to snip. On her way toward them, she passed a pair of orange trees, tall and thriving in immense clay pots that must weigh a couple hundred pounds apiece. Spring lilies in shades of pink and yellow and red showed off their trumpet-throated glory, vital despite blooming well out of season.

Violet stopped before the roses. Horatio settled down nearby.

Careful to cut only a few stems from each bush, she moved slowly along the row. She paused every now and then to brush her fingertips over a satiny petal or two, to breathe in an extra-deep draught of the intoxicating fragrance.

She was bent over a particularly magnificent specimen of palest pink, debating whether she should leave it untouched or clip it free of its stem, when Horatio let out a single, throaty woof.

She straightened and peered over her shoulder. Her brother-in-law stood a few feet away.

"Kit," she said, "I didn't hear you approach."

"I tread on cats' feet, or so I have been told." He walked closer. "Sorry. It wasn't my intention to startle you."

"You did not." She set her scissors in the basket, turned to face him. "At least not much. Did the vicar give you a few minutes' break or have you come in search of a new sanctuary?"

"I have been released for the day, thank the stars. Vicar Dittlesby feared the storm might worsen, and decided to travel home early. I am to continue the last lesson on my own." He rolled his eyes, then settled an intent look upon her. "Perhaps you could help me."

"Whatever do you mean?" She raised surprised eyes to his own, a tiny laugh escaping her. There it was again, she thought. That look. A frisson of alarm tingled down her spine.

"Nothing," he replied. "Just desperate, that's all."

She relaxed fractionally. "Is everything all right?"

"Yes, of course, why wouldn't it be?"

"I don't know. You seem . . . tense."

"Do I?" He reached down, touched one of the blossoms that lay inside her basket. "I shouldn't think why. Roses, hmm?"

"Yes. I am planning an arrangement for the family drawing room. I thought these would be cheerfully fragrant."

"Undoubtedly so. Rose is your middle name, is it not?"

She frowned for an instant before forcibly clearing her brow.

"Yes. Jeannette Rose."

"Roses are lovely, are they not?" he continued. "Such luxurious flowers, so soft and sweet-looking yet plagued with thorns. A cunning bloom, dangerous to the unwary."

A horrible dread raced through her. He couldn't know, could he? It wasn't possible.

"They're not like other flowers," he mused. "Take the violet, for example. An equally attractive flower in its own way, just as soft, just as sweet, yet curiously benign."

He trapped her in his gaze. "So which one are you? A rose or a violet?"

Her eyes popped wide before she could prevent the reaction, her heart fluttering like an erratic little bird trapped in a cage.

"What silliness are you spouting?" She turned away to dismiss him.

He stopped her, grabbed hold of the basket handle still hooked over her arm. "Don't bother with the charade. I know who you are." He leaned in close. "*Violet.*"

She made one final attempt to keep her deception alive. She laughed, a trilling noise that spilled upward into the rafters. "You think I am my sister? How remarkable. No doubt Violet will be exceptionally diverted when I write to tell her. The story will give her and Great-aunt Agatha a hearty chuckle."

A glimmer of doubt seeped into his gaze. Then as abruptly as it had appeared, it vanished. "Good try, but I'm not buying. I found your book. The one written in Latin that you have hidden beneath the seat cushion of your chair in the study."

"What book?" she prevaricated. "I know nothing about any book. I don't even like to read."

"Yes you do. *And* you know *Latin*. I heard you speaking it. You recited my lesson with me yesterday. You got the answers right too. All of them," he added, sounding affronted at the notion.

Heard her? Panic snatched at her throat like a suffocating hand. She remembered mumbling a word or two under her breath in the drawing room, but certainly nothing loud enough to be overheard. She supposed the impulse had come from her years of reciting Latin declensions aloud in order to memorize them. My God, how could she have been so stupidly careless?

"I have excellent hearing," he said as if he could read her thoughts. "Everyone in the family knows that. I've been accused on many occasions of being part basset hound. Great ears, sharp nose. But then, you are new to the family, are you not? How new? That's what I want to know. When did you and the real Jeannette switch places? How long has this ruse been going on? More to the point, why did you do it? Tell me. I want some answers."

She crumpled under his inquisition, shoulders slumping. The basket of flowers tumbled to the floor, metal scissors ringing as they struck the flagstones. "Please, you don't understand."

"On the contrary, I believe I understand quite well. Now, let's hear some truth."

Horatio sprang to his feet, positioned himself in front of her. Tense, he pressed his large dappled body against her skirts.

She laid a calming hand on the dog's head.

Kit flicked a downward glance at her canine champion. "It's all right, boy," he said in a soothing voice. "Everything's fine."

Horatio relaxed but did not lower his guard.

"I won't be put off by him, you know."

She debated how to handle the situation. "I know. Let me take him to Robert, then I will return and we can talk."

He nodded his assent.

Wanting to run and keep on running, Violet forced herself to stroll from the room. Back erect, she outwardly displayed none of the turmoil battering her system like a gale-force wind.

She located Robert within minutes, asked him to take Horatio for a walk. The dog resisted at first, whimpering, unwilling to be parted from her. She stroked him, long reassuring pats that made his muscles quiver with obvious delight. Soon he quieted, let Robert, his frequent companion, lead him outside.

She turned back, walking with the enthusiasm of a prisoner facing the gallows.

Kit had righted the overturned basket, neatly stacked the cut flowers back inside. She spared them barely a glance, her gaze flying straight to her brother-in-law.

"Would you rather sit or stand?" he asked. "There is a bench not far from here."

She trembled. "Sit, I believe." She feared her legs might not support her much longer.

And so they sat, beneath a graceful arch covered over in jasmine, the scent light and airy as a cloud. A full minute passed before she spoke. "She would not marry him."

"What?"

"Jeannette," she said, her voice low. "The morning of the wedding. She would not marry Adrian. She confided in me, only me, at the last minute. I could not persuade her otherwise. She was determined in her course, despite the scandal it would bring down upon my family and yours."

"So your solution was to switch places? Dupe Adrian with a false bride?"

"It wasn't planned, it just sort of happened. There was no time to really think anything through, and in that moment trading places seemed the lesser of two evils."

"With scant consideration for the wishes or feelings of my brother."

She flushed, threaded her fingers together in her lap. "Are you going to tell him?" Her words were strangled, moisture stinging at the back of her eyelids.

"Give me one good reason why I should not."

"Because I love him, if that makes any difference." She drew in a shuddering breath. "Whatever wrong I may have committed, it was never my intention to hurt Adrian. I've done my best to be a good wife. So far he hasn't seemed to object."

Kit met her earnest gaze, heard the truth of her words. From all appearances, she was right.

Just the other evening he had watched the two of them as they sat side by side on the sofa. He and Adrian had been discussing something ordinary—horses, he thought—while Jeannette . . . that is, Violet . . . listened as she sipped a cup of tea. When she set the beverage aside moments later, Adrian had gathered her hand into his. He'd stroked his thumb back and forth across the top of her skin in a lazy, absent glide. Apparently not even aware of what he was doing, as if his need to touch her was instinctual, visceral.

Kit remembered other instances. Casual glances. Brief touches and small gestures that spoke volumes about the success of his brother's marriage. Adrian seemed happy in a way he had never been before. Adrian had even remarked to Kit one afternoon that he found life with his new bride unexpectedly pleasurable and to his relief nothing at all like their own parents' less than satisfactory union. Did Kit have the right to disrupt that harmony simply because he had discovered a startling truth about the bride?

"He is living a lie," he argued, as much to himself as to her. "He'll have to know sometime."

"Will he? It's gone too far for regrets."

"So you are willing to live as another woman for the rest of your life?"

"If I must, yes. If that is what is required to keep both of our families from ruin. The shame of it could not be borne." Her ocean-colored eyes beseeched him. "She does not love him, Kit. She never did. But I do. Please, I beg of you, do not give my secret away."

"He may yet figure out your ruse all on his own. Adrian is no pea brain, you realize."

"I know. It's a chance I have to take."

He leaned forward, dangled his clasped hands between his knees as he weighed his choices. "I don't know. I just don't know."

"Will you take tonight at least? Say nothing until you have had a chance to think things through? What can a few more hours hurt?"

She looked desperate, features taut, her beautiful face more vulnerable than he had ever thought to see it.

He sighed. "All right. For tonight, then, you are still Jeannette. As to the future, we'll see. But I want it understood, here and now, that I will not lie to him for you if he should ever ask. If he questions me directly about your identity, I shall tell him the truth."

She nodded. "I understand. Why don't you meet me tomorrow at the folly. Say, ten o'clock. He'll be out inspecting the repairs made to the Oxleys' farm. He mentioned it to me this morning."

Kit frowned, uncomfortable with such skullduggery. "Very well. Tomorrow at ten."

Silence fell between them. What more was there to say? For now at least.

Kit departed, the echo of his footsteps ringing quietly behind him.

For a very long time afterward, Violet remained seated. She hung her head and let a pair of tears trace over her cheeks, desolation filling her heart.

Chapter Thirteen

The remainder of the afternoon and evening proved to be a tortuous ordeal.

She could scarcely bear to look at Kit, yet knew she had to behave as if nothing was wrong. As if he did not hold her world in his hands. As if he did not have the power to shatter that world utterly with only a few simple words come the morrow.

At dinner, she tried to eat, but each bite stuck in her throat, threatening to choke her. She tried to smile and converse. Her best efforts fell flat, sounding leaden even to her own ears. When Adrian expressed concern, she pleaded a headache and begged to be excused.

The brothers stood as she exited the room.

Once she reached her bedroom, she could not relax, pacing from one end of the spacious chamber to the other. Agnes arrived, alerted to Violet's condition by Adrian. Her maid bore a compress soaked in lavender water for her head and a glass of warm milk to help her rest.

She allowed herself to be cosseted even though it was the last thing she desired. Once Violet was changed into her nightgown, tucked between the sheets, Agnes finally departed. As soon as she did, Violet swung back out of bed, too overwrought to sleep.

She wrung her hands as she set to pacing once more.

She heard Adrian enter the adjoining bedchamber, the low murmur of his voice as he spoke to his valet.

Would this be her last night with him?

The thought nearly stopped her heart, so unbearable the idea. If Kit told him the truth, would Adrian turn away from her? She very much feared he would.

Perhaps she should simply tell him herself. Confess all, then throw herself at his feet and beg him to forgive her. Beg him not to cast her aside. Beg him to keep her as his wife.

She knew Kit was right. Adrian deserved to know the truth. But at what cost? She hugged her arms around herself.

Before she could give herself a second more to think, she yanked on her robe, strode across the room and pulled open the connecting door to his suite.

Adrian and his valet turned at her abrupt entrance.

In the course of their marriage, this was the first time she had come into Adrian's bedroom without prior invitation. She drew her robe closer around her body, suddenly self-conscious.

"My dear, is something amiss?" Adrian stood clad in his shirtsleeves and trousers, stockings on his feet. His discarded cravat and shoes dangled in his valet's grasp. The older man inclined his head in a respectful nod, then exercised discretion and moved away.

Her heart rabbited in her chest, her mouth turning dry as stale toast. Whatever words she had been planning to speak evaporated from her mind.

Adrian walked forward, drew her farther into the room. "How is your headache? I was going to come check on you once I had changed my clothing."

She fought to find her voice. "I . . . that is . . . it is much improved. The remedies you sent up with Agnes were very soothing. Thank you."

"I am glad you are feeling better, but your thanks

should go to your maid. The specifics of the treatment were her idea. I merely informed her you were unwell."

She nodded, lowered her head, stared at the patterned carpet beneath her feet. She dug her big toe into a velvety patch of midnight blue, aware of the silence hanging over the room like a shroud.

She drew a breath. "Adrian, I—" She broke off, recalling that they were not alone.

He turned, addressed his valet. "That will be all for tonight, Wilcox. You may retire."

"Yes, your Grace. Good night." Wilcox bowed, let himself out the door.

Adrian turned back to her. "Now, you were about to say, my dear?"

"I—" What had she been about to say? What was she doing, planning to give herself away? Perhaps she should, but . . . oh, she was such a dreadful coward.

She rushed forward instead, wrapped her arms around him, burrowed her face into his chest. "I missed you, that's all," she said, her words muffled against his shirt.

"Missed me? It's been little more than an hour since we were together in the same room."

She gazed upward into his vibrant eyes, into his irises of beautiful, luminous brown which never failed to stir her. She reached high, smoothed a palm across his cheek, finding it scratchy with stubble, strong and warm and impossibly masculine. "What I should have said," she murmured, "is that I want you."

His arms tightened at her back, desire firing his gaze. "Do you?"

"Yes." She brushed her lips across his jaw, scattering kisses here and there, down his neck, across the exposed skin of his chest.

His hands slid downward, stroked her bottom, gathered her close. "Let me finish washing up," he told her, dusting a pair of light kisses over her lips. "Shave this rough bristle off my face, and I'll come to you in a few minutes."

She tightened her hold. "No, I want you now." She arched onto her toes, tall as she could reach, and pressed against him, his arousal firm against her belly. She plunged one handful of fingers into his hair, tugged his head toward hers. "I want you just as you are," she sighed. "Always just as you are."

Hunger roared to life inside him, clawing with the razor-sharp talons of an untamed beast. She pleased him and surprised him. She'd never taken the role of the aggressor before, never initiated their lovemaking. But tonight she was like an unstoppable storm, hot, wild and willing. She yanked at his shirt, skimming it up over his head with a heedless toss to the floor, racing her hands across his naked flesh, arms, shoulders, chest and stomach.

He sucked in his breath when she touched him low, her slender fingers making quick work of his trouser buttons. His eyes closed, lips falling open as her hand curled over him. He throbbed in her grasp, burned like a supplicant beneath her caress. She kissed him everywhere, even there, sinking to her knees until he could bear it no longer and hauled her once more to her feet.

He captured her mouth, savage and needy, the room spinning into oblivion, her possession his only rational thought.

She reveled in his touch as his hands dived beneath her nightgown, sliding up her bare thighs, her hips and waist, over her breasts and down around the fleshy curve of her buttocks. Cupping her, kissing her, fondling her everywhere but the one place that ached the most for his touch.

She cried out, wanting him, needing him. If he was to be taken away from her tomorrow, she wanted this. One last memory to keep her warm on the cold, solitary nights to come. If the worst should happen. If her secret should be revealed. But now the decision was not hers alone to make. All she could do was show him how she felt and hope it would be enough.

He stripped the nightgown from her body, stripped the last of his clothes aside as they moved together toward the bed. They rolled over the counterpane, greedy hands, greedy lips, hungry and unable to get enough.

His unshaven cheeks burned and abraded her delicate skin, turning it a glowing pink as he kissed and suckled and licked her, tip to toe. But she didn't mind, the sensations, rough and soft, too tantalizing to resist. He flipped her onto her stomach, lavished the same attention upon her shoulders and back and buttocks until she bucked and moaned and shuddered. Calling out his name, her fists clenched in the sheets while exquisite pleasure buffeted her senses.

Then he touched her, using only the brush and stroke of his fingers to send her soaring up, up, up, until she shattered on an edge of primal delight. She convulsed, her body moist and mellow.

He turned her over, sank into her as far as his body could reach. She met him, matched him, catching his rhythm as he rocked into her. She smoothed kisses over his sweaty temple, his face buried against her neck, her legs looped around his back. He reached out, caught one of them in his hand and slowly stretched her, adjusting her thigh, her calf, her body and his, until her ankle rested on his shoulder. Then he moved her other leg.

She came instantly, the position taking him impossibly deep. But he wasn't through with her yet, bringing her to peak one final time before his body exploded into hers.

Her name was a hoarse shout upon his lips as he found his pleasure. "Jeannette."

She closed her eyes and let the heat and despair flood through her.

Slowly, he uncoupled from her, rearranging their bodies to snuggle her close. With her head cradled on his chest, they both fought to ease their labored breathing.

Her sister's name still rang in her head, always the same agonizing taunt. Would he have felt the same, shared the same hunger and pleasure in Jeannette's arms as he had just now in hers? Would their lovemaking have been meaningless if he knew her true identity?

She closed her eyes and held him, fighting away the tears. Yet they came anyway, squeezing from beneath her lids to leak in a salty puddle against his skin. She prayed he was asleep and would not notice.

He stroked a hand over her hair. "Are you all right?"

She nodded, snuggled harder against his chest, cheeks wet.

"Are you crying?"

She shook her head, certain her voice would betray her if she spoke.

Not fooled, he tugged her upright. "You are crying. What's wrong?" He paused. "I didn't hurt you, did I?" he asked, his tone absolutely appalled at the possibility.

"No," she said, rushing to reassure him. "I'm fine." She sniffed, wiped at her cheeks. "It's just the release."

"It's more than the release." He smoothed a hand along her arm. "What is it? Has your headache returned?"

"No, I told you, I'm fine. I just . . ."

"Just what?"

She stared for a moment, then wrapped her arms around him, decided to tell him the one truth she felt she could share. The most profound truth of all. "I love you," she whispered.

He leaned back. "Do you?"

He seemed momentarily startled by the idea.

"I do," she confirmed.

Finally, he quirked an eyebrow. "And that makes you cry?"

A laugh escaped her, despite her teary state. "Tonight it does."

He gathered her close, crushed her mouth to his. "Then I shall have to find a way to relieve your distress."

They tumbled backward upon the bed. Adrian, true to his word, found several inventive ways to drive away her sadness.

Only later, as she lay lax and dreamy beside him, did she realize what he had not said. An omission that confirmed the darkest of her fears. Justified the wisdom of her decision to keep her secret to herself, to maintain her lie.

He had not said he loved her back.

Autumn leaves crunched in dry, brittle clumps beneath Violet's shoes as she made her way to the folly the next morning.

Set some yards distant from the house, the circular pavilion rose in a splendor of white stone columns and fancy Baroque scrollwork, the roof a fine domed cap adorned by a whimsical stone cherub.

She stepped into the pavilion, hugged her cloak close against the cold while she waited for Kit to arrive. To the east, a small flotilla of ducks passed, paddling and quacking their way across the glassy sapphire lake that ranged beyond. A fish flashed upward from the lake's center. Its scales glinted silver in the daylight before disappearing once more into the water.

She willed herself not to tremble, half sick with nerves and dread.

She'd upset Agnes earlier, unable to eat more than a

single bite of toast and half a cup of tea for breakfast. Her maid fretted around her, warning against a putrid ague that was making its way through the neighborhood. She'd urged her to stay in bed and rest, especially considering her headache of the evening before.

But she could not rest. Nor could she laze the day away in bed. She had an appointment to keep, her fate to confront, whether it would lead to disaster or reprieve.

She heard him approach. The capes on his greatcoat billowed in a gust of wind, his hatless head bared to the elements.

"Brisk out here," Kit commented as he mounted the folly's steps. "It would have been far more comfortable meeting again in the conservatory, nestled warm among all the hothouse plants."

"I did not wish to risk us being overheard," she said without preamble. "Though if you have decided to expose my identity, the location of our meeting makes little difference, I suppose."

He rubbed his gloved palms together for warmth, nodded toward a short seating area that ringed the inside of the structure. "Shall we sit?"

She shook her head. "No, thank you, but pray do so if you wish."

Not one to stand on ceremony, Kit accepted her invitation and sat down.

She paced one way, paced the other, then stopped on a sharp turn of her heel. "Put me out of my torment. Tell me what you have decided. I can bear it no longer."

"Very well," he began. "It was not an easy choice, I'll tell you that. I did a great deal of thinking upon the matter last night and again this morning. Far more thinking, I must confess, than I am generally accustomed to engaging in. Made my brain fairly ache, what with all the strain I have been under of late."

"Blast it, Kit. Would you just tell me," she exploded in an outburst that surprised them both.

He arched an eyebrow, a gesture highly reminiscent of his brother. "This pretending to be Jeannette is really rubbing off on you, is it not?"

"Kit, please."

He relented. "All right. Against my better judgment, I have decided to keep your secret."

"Oh, thank the Lord." Weak relief shot through her legs, making her wish she'd taken his suggestion to sit. She clutched one of the columns, suddenly afraid she might topple over.

"You'll have to importune Him again," he told her with a quick glance toward heaven, "and do a great deal of praying if Adrian ever figures you out. I meant what I said before. If he asks, I won't lie to him about who you really are."

"But you will not tell him?" she confirmed.

"No, I will not tell him. Not unless he asks me directly." He sighed. "You've let her talk you into a real muddle, haven't you? I should have known you weren't Jeannette that very first evening I arrived. You were far too understanding about my predicament. Your sister, no doubt, would have laughed herself silly once she'd heard the particulars."

Knowing her twin, she guessed that is precisely what Jeannette would have done.

"And you're restful," he continued. "Don't know why Adrian hasn't cottoned on to that irregularity. Your sister would no doubt be elbow deep planning for a ball of some sort by now, wanting to fill the house with every neighbor for fifty miles or more, despite being a newlywed. Thing is, my brother barely tolerates large entertainments. Likely he's enjoying the peace and quiet so much, he doesn't want to question his good luck."

She clasped her hands, sank down onto the iron bench

beside him. "Is it so very noticeable, then, that I am mas-querading as my sister?"

His eyes glittered with irony. "It is now. Now that I can view everything through a lens of truth. But damn me if you aren't good at fooling everyone. If it hadn't been for your penchant for Latin, I very much doubt I ever would have realized."

"Mama always said too much book learning would bring me to ruin one day."

Her words settled between them, ticklish as feathers. They shared a smile that turned to a laugh, their former easiness with one another restored.

"In exchange for keeping my mouth shut," Kit told her, "I expect some recompense."

"Anything. What can I do?"

"Help me with my Latin translations, for one. That old man is likely to be the death of me."

She laughed again. "Gladly. What about Greek? How are you with that?"

He looked thunderstruck. "Good God, you know Greek too?"

She nodded. "Actually, I am more fluent in Greek than Latin. Greek's not a dead language, after all."

He shook his head in amazement. "I'll add that to your list of assignments."

A long moment of silence fell between them.

He twirled a leaf he'd found on the bench, then tossed it aside. "I still think you should come clean with Adrian. It always goes worse in the end when you try to brazen it out. Believe me, I speak from experience. With my brother, it's best to confess and face the fury. He'll go easier on you if you do."

But *would* he go easier on her, a woman who had de-ceived him in the most fundamental of ways? How did you tell a man he wasn't married to the woman he be-lieved he had wed? What did you say? "Darling, there is a trifling something you should know. I've been lying to you all this time. My twin and I switched places at the altar, isn't that amusing? You married the wrong sister."

The wrong sister. Is that what she was? Worse, is that what Adrian would think were he to discover the truth?

She shivered, but not from the cold. "I already told you. I cannot take the chance."

He made no further comment on the subject. "We'd best return inside," he said at length. "Wouldn't do for either of us to catch a chill."

"You are right," she agreed.

He stood, offered a hand to assist her to her feet.

She accepted it, held it for a brief moment before letting go. "Kit?"

"Yes?"

"Since you so obviously disapprove, why have you agreed to keep my secret?"

He tucked his hands into his pockets. "Ah, well, that's an easy one. You make him happy. What right do I have to interfere with happiness?"

Adrian reined in his horse, slowing from a gallop to a canter as he rode across the estate. A cool breeze swept over him, invigorating rather than chilly, his body well warmed by the exercise. The scents of autumn—dry leaves, half-frozen mud and dormant grass—were redolent in the air.

Cutting across the rear lawns that would eventually lead him to the stables, he saw the lake burst into view, fine and blue in the radiant daylight.

A sudden flash of red caught his eye. There, in the pavilion. He saw it was a cloak, and wrapped inside it, the familiar figure of a woman. Even from a distance, he recognized her.

His wife.

Leaving the warm haven of her arms this morning had been torture. Her long hair spread like sunshine over the pillows, her honeyed scent on the sheets and on his skin. If he closed his eyes, he could remember even now.

She loved him, that's what she had declared last night. A warm glow spread inside him at the thought. He shouldn't like it, hearing such words on her lips. But he did. He had to confess he liked it very much, selfish as such an emotion might be.

Did he love her?

He'd always considered love to be a lot of stupid, self-destructive rubbish, and yet lately he had begun to wonder. When he was with her, the notion no longer seemed so improbable.

He slowed Mercury to a stop, only then noticing she was not alone.

Kit.

He knew his brother's dark curls and lean, sturdy shoulders. He watched the two of them as they sat inside the folly. What on earth were they discussing? And why were they doing it out-of-doors on such a raw morning? It seemed out of character for them both.

Jeannette wasn't the intrepid type who liked to venture forth for a walk in any sort of weather. And Kit enjoyed his creature comforts far too thoroughly to risk a chill over a casual outing.

Then again, maybe they'd felt confined and in need of a draught of fresh air. He knew Vicar Dittlesby was driving his little brother to distraction, exactly as he had planned. He grinned to himself. Served the boy right for getting himself sent down. Perhaps next term at University would not seem so dreadful after a few weeks doing lessons with a deaf old man.

Mercury whinnied, tossed his head in an impatient gesture, hooves restive against the damp, cold ground.

Adrian reached out to pat a gloved hand against the gelding's sweaty neck, debating whether or not he should ride down to join his wife and brother.

As he looked on, Kit stood, extended a hand toward Jeannette to assist her to her feet. She accepted, placing her palm inside his. But their handclasp didn't end immediately; more words were exchanged before they separated.

Whatever Kit said brought a rich bloom to Jeannette's features, a spark of radiant delight that was plain to see even from a distance.

Obviously the two of them had formed a family bond. Close and comfortable as brother and sister should be. He was glad. He wanted his wife to get on well with his family. Still, he wondered what they might be discussing in so companionable a manner.

While he pondered, Kit jogged down the shallow stone steps of the pavilion and headed toward the house. Jeannette waited a full minute more before doing the same. Almost as if she did not wish the two of them to be seen returning at the same moment.

He watched his wife until she disappeared indoors. Then with a light nudge of his knees, he set his horse in motion and continued on toward the stables.

"More tea, Lady Carter?" Violet inquired.

Millicent Carter inclined her elegant silver-haired head. "Thank you, I believe I shall." She passed her cup.

Violet took a firm hold of the heavy Sevres teapot. The porcelain was pink, painted with delicate nosegays of yellow bellflowers. She poured, proud relief spreading through her when she managed the trick and passed back the cup without spilling so much as a drop.

"Another tea cake?" She lifted the plate arrayed with a varied selection of treats.

"No, thank you, your Grace, although they are most delicious. You must commend your chef. French, is he not?"

"Yes, François is a real treasure. He came over from Paris with the dowager's family a few years before the war. He's been at Winterlea since Raeburn's parents were married."

"I would like another tea cake," piped a masculine voice.

Violet turned her head toward the speaker and met her brother-in-law's twinkling gaze. No matter the occasion, solemn or light-spirited, Kit could always be counted on to eat. It was, he readily admitted, his one true avocation.

She passed him the plate.

Lady Carter swallowed a sip of tea. "How is the dear dowager? Fairing well with her daughter, I trust? Poor Sylvia must be nearing her time."

"The baby is due next month," she supplied. "Everyone is anxiously awaiting the birth. I shall send your regards in my next letter."

"Most kind." The older woman took another drink of tea, set her cup aside. "A shame they have not been able to enjoy the delights of the Little Season this year. Carter and I are going up to Town next week to partake of what remains, staying until nearly Christmas. Do you and Raeburn plan to do the same?"

Go to London? She sincerely hoped not. Although she supposed eventually they would have to go. But surely not before spring.

"Our plans are not as yet decided," she stated.

"Decided about what?" Adrian strode into the room, dashing as usual in a dark brown jacket and trousers. "Lady Carter. How good to see you." He bowed in greeting. "I was out overseeing one of my farms, or I should have joined you sooner. Is Lord Carter not with you today?"

"No, your Grace." The older woman inclined her head. "He sent his apologies. His gout is acting up quite dreadfully since the weather has grown so chill of late. I was just telling the duchess and your brother that we plan to leave for the city next week. Hopefully a change of scenery will improve Carter's health."

"Hopefully so." Adrian took a seat in the straight-backed chair that matched Lady Carter's, facing the sofa where Violet and Kit sat.

Without asking, Violet prepared Adrian a cup of tea—cream, no sugar, the way she knew he liked it—and handed the beverage across to him.

He rose briefly, accepting it with a grateful smile.

"Kit, pass your brother the crumpets," she murmured.

Kit dusted crumbs off his fingers and did as he was asked.

"The duchess said you haven't yet made plans for the remainder of the fall." Lady Carter turned a set of watery blue eyes upon Adrian. "You simply must come to Town. If you do, Carter and I shall be delighted to host an entertainment on your behalf."

Violet moved to squash the idea. "Why, that is a most gracious invitation, Lady Carter, but—"

"Yes, most gracious," Adrian interrupted. "Would you like that, my dear? You must be getting weary of being cooped up here in the country. A few weeks in Town would be a refreshing break. I had a letter from my sister Anna just this morning. She and Jameson will be there. They're bringing their oldest daughter with them to see the sights. Another year and Lydia will be old enough for her come-out."

Violet nearly choked on her tea. *"No,"* she wanted to shout, *"absolutely not. We're not going to London."*

She bit her tongue, stared down into her lap, desperate to conceal the terror she knew must be shining in her eyes. Jeannette, of course, would have been in raptures over the thought of London. Even more so at the idea of a ball to be held specifically in her honor.

She wanted to curl up in a corner and wish it all away.

Beneath the folds of her skirt, she clenched a fist, willed herself to do what she must. Pretend as she must.

She pasted a buoyant smile on her lips and looked up. "A trip to Town would be wonderful," she lied. "I only worry, darling, that it will take you away from your duties here at home."

Adrian relaxed back into his chair. "Actually, I have business in Town. I planned to inform you this afternoon, but Lady Carter broached the subject before I had the opportunity."

Her last spark of hope winked out like a doused candle. Cringing inside, she clapped her hands in false delight. "Well, then, is that not thrilling? Spending the last of the Little Season in Town. I'm all aflutter with excitement."

Adrian sent her a smile, visibly pleased to have made her happy. If only he knew the truth, she thought.

"Splendid," Lady Carter pronounced. "I shall start on a guest list immediately. Only the very best people will be in attendance, I assure you." She fluttered her hands. "How exciting. I simply love parties."

"Doesn't everyone?" Violet laughed to cover her distress, nerves turning her fingers to icicles.

Lady Carter joined in the merriment, while the men looked on.

Out of the corner of her eye, Violet saw Kit cross his ankles. She dare not look directly at him, knowing any sympathy she glimpsed there might prove her undoing. So she kept her eyes averted, her features as happily animated as possible, while inside she was squirming with anticipatory fright.

Lady Carter departed a few minutes later, scattering promises to see everyone again soon in Town. When her carriage rolled away, Violet allowed herself the small luxury of relaxing back against the sofa cushions.

"That's decided, then." Adrian rose to his feet, took the last sweet off the cake plate. The only one to have escaped Kit's notice. "When shall we leave?"

"Oh, I don't know. I'll have to consult with March and Mrs. Hardwick, apprise them of our decision. Staff will need to be sent ahead to prepare the London town-house for residence. Instructions must be left concerning the upkeep of Winterlea. It will be quite an undertaking."

"A week, then. Will that give you sufficient time?"

Certainly not, she thought, but it would have to do. A week's reprieve. She supposed she couldn't expect much more. "Yes, that will be fine." She pantomimed another sunny smile for his benefit.

Adrian popped the tart into his mouth and chewed. "Hmm, lemon."

"Kit will be coming with us, of course," she added.

Adrian stopped chewing, swallowed abruptly. "He has studies. He'll remain here."

She waved a dismissive hand exactly as her twin would have done. "Oh, fiddlesticks. Hasn't he been punished long enough?"

"His education is not a punishment." Adrian glowered.

She ignored the look. "That isn't how it has seemed to everyone else. No disrespect meant to the good vicar."

Kit cleared his throat. "Um . . . Jeannette, perhaps this isn't the time—"

"Of course it's the time," she interrupted. "Kit has

been quite a disciplined student since he's been here. Even you must concede he deserves a few moments of enjoyment now and again." She stood, crossed to Adrian. Gazing up into his eyes, she traced a palm over the stitching on his vest. "Besides, if he's here alone, who will watch to make sure he is continuing his lessons? Think of all the trouble he could land in, left to his own devices."

Adrian trapped her hand beneath his. "Why so concerned? He didn't put you up to this, by any chance?"

"How could he? The decision to remove to London was only made a few minutes past." She turned a winsome smile upon him, lowered her voice. "I simply hate to see people suffer, even him. Have pity, dear. He is your brother, after all."

His eyes moved past her, locked on his sibling. "No gambling. No drinking. No women. Is that clearly understood?"

Kit jumped to his feet. "Clear as glass."

"And you will continue to study. I will check your work myself."

"Check away."

"You'll be sitting for examination in January. The arrangements have already been made with the University. You *will* pass those exams."

"With flying colors, never fear."

"And if there is so much as one infraction, not only will you return home, I'll see to it you and the vicar do everything together. All day, every day."

Kit shuddered. "Don't worry. I won't disappoint you. And I really mean it this time."

Adrian shot him one last stern look. "Very well, under those circumstances, you may accompany Jeannette and me to London." His gaze moved back to his wife. "Satisfied, my dear?"

"Very. It seems so unkind to abandon him here all alone."

"Hardly alone. There are over a hundred servants on the estate."

"He can't socialize with the servants. It would make them feel ever so awkward."

Her words took a moment to sink in, then Adrian laughed. "I suppose this also means you'll want to take Horatio with us?"

"He can't be left by himself any more than Kit."

"I believe I have just been insulted," Kit complained.

"Not at all." She smiled. "You never need Robert to take you out for a walk."

Chapter Fourteen

She didn't have an opportunity to speak to Kit alone until the following day.

She found him in the library, an expression of disgust marring his pleasant features, a huge textbook open on his lap.

He looked up as she entered the room. "Dear merciful God, reprieved at last. Vicar Dittlesby stuck me in here an hour past with this bloody boring tome on the Hundred Years War. I ask you, after the first fifty, did any of them still remember what they were fighting about?"

He slapped the book shut. "Thanks, by the by, for springing me out of this place for a jaunt to the city next week. The vicar's nose has been out of joint ever since Adrian broke the news to him this morning."

"You are most welcome." She slid into the chair next to his. "But I didn't do it for solely altruistic reasons."

"Why'd you do it, then? I did wonder."

She leaned forward, lowered her voice. "Because I need your help."

His dark eyebrows scrunched together. "What kind of help?"

"The desperate kind." She clutched her hands together, her knuckles turning white. "You're the only one I can turn to, the only one who knows the truth.

"Oh, Kit," she lamented, "London is going to be an

utter disaster. I'll never be able to carry it off. I'll be unmasked at the very first entertainment I set foot into. They'll all know."

"No one has known so far. Why will London be any different?"

"Because I'm different. Because I am not Jeannette. It's one thing to fool a few country neighbors who've never even met her. It's quite another to convince a couple hundred of the Ton's elite, people who once anointed her their reigning belle, that I'm the Incomparable Lady Jeannette."

"You fooled Lord and Lady Carter. They'd already met Jeannette."

"But that's one-on-one, not in a large group." She rubbed fretful fingers over a sliver of lace trim on her dress. "Just walking into a crowd twists my tongue into a knot. My mind goes blank and I end up gawping like a fish plucked out of the water, gasping for air. You must remember how it is. You met me before, back in the days when I was still me."

Yes, he did remember. Shy, awkward, tongue-tied, she'd been exactly as she claimed. Despite her undeniable beauty, once the introductions were finished, people tended to look elsewhere because of her lack of animation, leaving her to fade into the background. One more timid flower forgotten amongst the other timid flowers that lined the ballroom walls, dwelling alone and unwanted on solitary chairs.

A brief wave of shame passed over him, brought face-to-face with the knowledge that he'd been no different in his original assessment and treatment of her than so many others. Now that he knew her, liked her, he realized how mistaken his first impression had been. Still, others might find no fault in their past actions, even if the truth were known to them.

"You do have a point," he mused. "Yet I believe you may be able to overcome it."

She shook her head vigorously. "No, no, it's quite impossible. Oh, Kit, whatever shall I do?"

He straightened, his features intent. "Have some faith in yourself, for a start. And in me, for that matter. You asked for my help, right?"

"Right," she agreed hesitantly.

"Then let me help. Up until now you've done a superior job fooling everyone, most especially my brother. If you can fool him, you can fool anyone. It's all in the attitude."

"Attitude?"

"Hmm. And the follow-through." He pressed a contemplative finger to his lips. "Let me do some strategizing on the subject, then we'll meet again to discuss."

"What about your lessons?"

"I'll take care of my lessons, so long as you keep clueing me in on the Latin and Greek. Say, that gives me an idea." He waggled his finger at her. "We should give you lessons."

"Me?"

"Mmm-hmm. With the proper instruction, I believe we can teach you how to prattle nonsense with the best of them. Now run on before someone begins to wonder why two such inveterate book haters would be huddled together in the library."

She nodded, climbed to her feet. She began to move away, then stopped, spun back. "Kit. Thank you. I mean, for everything."

He dismissed her gratitude with a negligent wave. "Don't worry. I'll simply add it to your tab." He grinned, then shooed her on her way.

* * *

"That wasn't bad, but let's try it again."

"Oh, Kit, it's no good." Violet groaned. "I'll never be comfortable making small talk with strangers. And you're not even a stranger."

She sprang up from the chair in her study, paced across the room. "This role-playing is all very well, but when the real event occurs I'll freeze up stiffer than that fireplace poker." She pointed a finger toward the hearth at the implement in question.

"Attitude," he stated. "It's simply a matter of attitude. You're a duchess. All you need do is remember that and act accordingly. Your sister certainly would."

"Yes, but it comes so naturally to her. I think she was born chattering animatedly to people. I, on the other hand, just lay there in the cradle, silent and staring. I probably didn't even wave my rattle."

"We've been through this before." He sighed. "You're letting your fears get the better of you, and there is no need for it. When you are at a social function, think, '*I* am the Duchess of Raeburn. There is no one superior to me in the room.' Say it."

She cleared her throat. "I am the Duchess of Raeburn." Her words sounded flat and wavery. "There is no one superior to me in the room."

"Chin up," Kit urged. "Say it again, more conviction this time."

She drew a deep breath, tried to add the confident inflection he wanted. "*I* am the Duchess of Raeburn. There is no one superior to me in the room."

"Good. Much better."

"What about Prinny?" she blurted.

"What about him?" Kit frowned at the non sequitur.

"He *is* superior to me in rank. He's superior even to Adrian. What helpful statements am I to tell myself if I run into the Prince?"

"Tell yourself he's just a man, then smile brightly and

flutter your eyelashes at him. From what I've observed of our esteemed Regent, he'll be too entranced by your beauty to care much about the words you are speaking." Kit leaned forward in his seat. "Now, once more with the statement, and really believe it this time."

She drew back her shoulders, holding her head up with pride. "*I* am the Duchess of Raeburn. There is *no one* superior to me in the room."

"Wonderful! Now, remember that next week when you appear at your first entertainment. Remember it and know it's true."

"There are only four days left until we depart." She resumed her seat, linked her hands tightly together. "Do you think I'll be ready?"

"You will. You'll have to be. Now, what are the two C's?"

"Condescension and conversation," she answered. "Only when I feel like conversation will I condescend to converse."

"Good. No-fail topics?" he coached.

"Weather. Pleasant observations about the party and its hosts. With women, fashions and feminine gossip. With men, horses, hunting and upon occasion world events, taking care not to be too knowledgeable about any particular topic. What about my sister's friends?"

"We've been over that. Let them do most of the talking and if anybody remarks upon your reticence, inform them that your elevated rank has given you a new appreciation for listening. Arrogance and authority go a long way toward squashing dissent."

"I know you are right, yet I fear my nerves will obliterate everything you've been drumming into my head these past few days."

"Which is why you require additional practice. The more practice you have, the less chance there will be of failure. You don't want to be found out, do you?"

"No." She shuddered.

"You don't want Adrian to find out?"

"Heavens, no."

"Well, then, buckle down and get it right."

She shot him a deadly look. "Just wait until you're sweating over those lessons of yours later today. You may discover I've left you all the really difficult translations to complete on your own."

His mouth fell open for a second before he snapped it shut, his skin blanching. "You haven't."

"No, but I could have done, so don't be mean."

"I am not mean, merely encouraging in a firm manner."

"Yes, well, please remember that when I refuse to provide you with all the answers to your assignments, I am simply encouraging you in a firm manner. After all, I am not the one who must sit for exams come the new year, am I?"

He grumbled briefly under his breath. "You've a cruel streak in you, do you know that? It's the reason I'm so certain you'll do fine in Society. Now, let's resume our work. Pretend you are attending a rout and the Duke of Wellington appears at your elbow. What do you say?"

"I give him the tiniest of polite smiles and say—"

A splintering crash sounded, a wailing cry carrying from beyond the closed study door. Both of them moved to investigate the commotion.

One of the housemaids stood in the music room, her eyes round as moons, hands clutched to her small breasts. Porcelain fragments and lilies lay scattered at her feet in a watery explosion.

Violet took in the scene. "Tina, what has occurred? Are you all right?"

The housemaid's gaze flew to hers. She bobbed a curtsey. "Yes, your Grace, I'm fine. But oh, your Grace,

I don't know how it could have happened. I'm ever so careful with fragile things, I swear I am. I was dusting and polishing in here. I'd set the vase over across the way as I always do when I clean the piano, didn't want to spill no water on that pretty wood, and when I went to move the vase back to its place, well, I don't know. One minute everything was fine, then the next my feet sorta caught under me and the vase came flyin' out of my hands." She emitted a fresh whimper of distress, knuckles pressed to her mouth. "I'm so sorry."

Violet cast another glance over the mess, puddles of water and wet flowers, the remains of a once lovely vase strewn about in a sea of white and blue shards. The winsome half face of a shepherdess winked a single eye up at her from a jagged ceramic sliver.

"Well, Tina," she began, "this is indeed a shame. But all there is to do now is—"

"Merciful heavens, what has occurred here?" Mrs. Hardwick marched into the room, the black bombazine dress she wore starched and unyielding as a suit of armor. She shot a hard, dark glare at the scene, then across to the young maid, whose cheeks had blanched to the color of flour.

"Tina," Mrs. Hardwick demanded, "is this your doing?" She pointed the cutting edge of her square chin down at the mess.

"Yes, ma'am," the girl squeaked, voice low and timid, eyes downcast.

The housekeeper angled her head. "Your Grace. Lord Christopher. I am sorry you have been disturbed by this unfortunate incident. I am here now and will make certain proper action is taken to set matters to right."

"Tina explained what happened, Mrs. Hardwick," Violet said, feeling rather like a schoolgirl herself, caught out at some mischief. "Clearly, this was an accident. The girl stumbled on the carpeting, it would appear. Perhaps we should inspect the edges for wear so as to prevent this in the future."

Mrs. Hardwick peered down her nose, then agreed with a faint nod.

"I was just about to tell Tina when you arrived," Violet continued, "that she should locate a mop and broom to clean up the damage."

"Oh, she will clean up the damage, then she will go."

Tina let out a keening wail, hugged her arms around her waist as two fat tears splashed over her pale cheeks. "No, ma'am, please."

"Not a word from you, miss," the housekeeper scolded.

"Mrs. Hardwick, I hardly think—"

"Your Grace, you needn't trouble yourself any further about this matter. It will be dealt with." The older woman crossed her hands in front of her, obviously waiting for Tina to depart.

Violet hesitated. "Well, I . . . I suppose. Yet what is your meaning? That she will go."

"Precisely as it sounds. The girl will be dismissed."

Tina let out a fresh wail, tears flowing in a stream.

"Dismissed?" Violet repeated. "But surely that isn't necessary. It was a simple accident with no lasting harm done. A vase broke, that is all."

Mrs. Hardwick straightened to the top of her five-foot six-inch frame. "That vase originally belonged to the second Duchess of Raeburn, his Grace's great-great-grandmother. She brought the piece with her from Austria upon her marriage to the duke. It is irreplaceable. His Grace will be most displeased when he learns of its destruction."

Violet cast a quick glance toward Kit, realized from his expression that he wouldn't be of much help. He looked nearly as uncomfortable as she felt. Oh, how she hated arguments and confrontations.

She met the older woman's gaze and did her best not to cavil. "Well, be that as it may, the girl didn't break it deliberately. Surely there must be some other manner in which she could make amends. Perhaps a small reduction in her pay until she has—"

"Pardon me, your Grace," the housekeeper replied in an unctuous tone. "It would take this lowly girl a lifetime of work and still she would be far from able to repay even a fraction of the value of the vase. May I suggest you return to whatever it was you were doing when the damage occurred and trouble yourself no further. I am the housekeeper, after all, and this is my purview. There really is no need for you to be involved in disciplinary matters concerning the staff."

The young maid whimpered again, sniffling loudly.

Mrs. Hardwick turned on her. "Stop your blubbering, girl. We've all heard more than enough out of you."

"I say, I don't care for your tone, to the girl or to the duchess." Kit started forward.

Mrs. Hardwick pinned him with a pair of beetle-black eyes.

He stopped dead in his tracks.

"You were saying, Master Christopher?" The housekeeper waited, arms crossed over her cadaverous chest.

He dropped his chin, lowered his gaze. "Nothing," he mumbled. In a whispered aside to Violet, he asked, "Shall I go find Adrian?"

She trembled, her body radiating and raw with nerves. "No, it will be all right."

She could either stand up to the detestable woman now, she decided, or slink away like a craven coward and forever concede the upper hand.

From the beginning, she'd known Mrs. Hardwick was a bully. Still, the older woman had held a high position in the household for many years, longer even than Violet had been alive. In most regards, she was an exemplary employee. And there was the fact that Adrian must hold the woman in some regard. Otherwise why would he have kept her on as long as he had?

What did she know about managing staff? she wondered. She'd only been a duchess for a little over three months. Perhaps such treatment of servants was to be expected. They certainly came and went in her parents' household. Yet an inanimate object, no matter how expensive, seemed poor reason to turn a girl out of service and ruin her life.

She thought of her sister, knowing Jeannette probably wouldn't have fought the housekeeper over the matter. Then again, her twin would never have allowed a servant—even an upper servant—to overrule her wishes or commands. Armed with that knowledge, Violet drew back her shoulders and raised her chin.

I am the Duchess of Raeburn, she repeated to herself. *There is no one in the room superior to me. I am the Duchess of Raeburn . . .*

"Go on, your Grace," the older woman insisted. "I shall see to this matter."

"Mrs. Hardwick, I believe you overstep yourself," Violet stated in a steely tone. "Perhaps you have forgotten to whom it is you speak." She linked her fingers together to control their shaking.

The housekeeper appeared momentarily taken aback. "No, your Grace, of course I have not—"

"If that is true, then why have you continuously interrupted me since you entered this room? Perhaps you believe your age gives you such a right?"

The older woman's lips tightened. "No, your Grace. I know my station."

"Do you? Then you will apologize to me. And you will apologize to Lord Christopher. He hasn't worn short coats in some years and as such deserves your respect."

Mrs. Hardwick's nostrils pinched tightly at the reprimand. "I beg your pardon, your Grace. Your lordship."

"Now, there will be no further discussion of dismissal—"

"But, your Grace—"

"Aah-aah!" she admonished, holding up a finger. "You are interrupting again. Not another word or it shall be your dismissal of which we speak."

A spark of malevolence flashed inside the housekeeper's eyes. "You have no cause to mention dismissing me, nor the right. His Grace is the only one who can take such an action."

"His Grace, *my* husband, defers to me in all matters of domestic concern," she brazened. "He will care nothing for your complaint."

The housekeeper began to visibly shake. "I'll have you know I have faithfully served this household for over twenty-five years. I know how it ought to be run. I know what a house such as this needs in order to function properly and efficiently. You come here, a slip of a girl who knows nothing about managing a grand establishment like Winterlea, and think to give me orders. Don't imagine I haven't seen the way you coddle the servants. How you let them get by with all manner of indiscretion and frivolity. It is intolerable, unsupportable, offensive. You should be thankful for my advice and my interference."

Violet forced her chin up another notch, though her stomach had turned to jelly. She'd started this confrontation, she couldn't afford to lose it now. She swallowed against the dryness in her throat.

"Well," she said, "it seems you have made your feelings quite clear. Now let me do the same. I have never liked you, Mrs. Hardwick. I find you cold and inflexible, lacking in humor, and more importantly, in compassion. You may know how to run a house but you do not know how to manage people. It is obvious you find me unacceptable as a mistress. Therefore, given the fact of your twenty-five years of service, I shall furnish you with a character reference. You may count on it to be in your possession by tomorrow morning when you depart. That will be all."

"I shall go to the duke about this." The housekeeper's fists tightened at her sides, her face florid as a cherry.

Violet knew Jeannette always matched one threat with another. She decided to follow her lead. "Go if you like. And when the interview is concluded, know that you will still find yourself dismissed. Only this time there will be no reference forthcoming."

Mrs. Hardwick blanched, then colored again as if she might explode from temper. She turned on her heel, stalked from the room.

Violet's shoulders slumped the moment the older woman was gone. "Dear heavens," she murmured. Only afterward did she notice Kit and the young housemaid staring at her goggle-eyed, slack-jawed.

Kit recovered first. "Bravo."

Tina sniffed, her eyes damp but no longer crying. She dipped a quick curtsey. "Oh, your Grace, thank you, thank you. I don't know what to say. How to express my gratitude. And I wants you to know, I'll repay every penny cost of that vase, no matter if it does take me my entire life to do it."

"Yes, well, it's all right, Tina. Now go along and fetch a mop and dustpan to clear away this mess. We will discuss what is to be done about the other at a later time."

Tina curtseyed again, hurried from the room.

"That was amazing," Kit declared. "I've never seen anyone stand up to old Hard-Arse before. Oh, beg your pardon," he hastened to add when her eyes widened at the crude nickname.

"Then I'm not the only one to find her difficult and unpleasant?" she ventured.

"Lord, no. She used to scare the liver out of my sisters and me growing up. And Adrian always steered well clear of her when he was home from school."

"Then why on earth has she been here so long?"

"Father hired her. I think he did it to spite *Maman* after one of their more spectacular fights. Once Mrs. H. was installed, no one ever had the nerve to remove her. Even *Maman* tiptoes lightly in her presence, and *Maman* doesn't cavil easily." He grinned. "I must say, Vi, you were bloody brilliant."

She shushed him. "I told you not to call me that, even when we're alone." She worried the corner of her lip between her teeth. "Do you think she'll go to Adrian?"

"Doubtful. She needs that reference too badly to risk it. No, she'll be packed and waiting with outstretched hand in the morning."

"But Adrian will have to be informed."

"Undoubtedly. He'll stand behind you on this one, though. He may even kiss you senseless for it."

"Kit!" she scolded, a pleased blush dusting her cheeks at the notion.

"You're top-o'-the-trees, sis." He grinned. "You'll take London by storm, just wait and see if you don't."

For the first time since this whole nerve-splitting masquerade began, a surge of confident hope sprang to life inside her. If she could go toe-to-toe against a fishwife like Mrs. Hardwick and win, then perhaps fooling the ne'er-do-wells of the Ton wouldn't be so impossible, after all.

Like Kit said, with the right combination of attitude and arrogance, a person could conquer the world.

*   *   *

Her hands began to perspire inside her gloves the moment the carriage crossed the city limits into London.

Unseeing, she stared at the narrow streets and the teeming throngs that ranged beyond the small glass coach window, too focused on her own problems and concerns to notice the activity around her.

Her day of reckoning was here at last.

Despite her buoyant spirits of four days' past, all her old fears and doubts came creeping back upon her, vicious as a mass of hideous fanged creatures. Acting for all she was worth, she put on a brave face, careful to let none of her trepidation show. Covering her dread with excitement. Smothering her anxiety in smiles.

Their coach rolled to an easy stop before the ducal townhouse. Typically grand, the structure took up the entirety of a city block, as well as a second block beyond for the gardens and stables.

With the exception of Agnes, Mr. Wilcox and Kit's man, Cherry, who traveled behind them in a separate conveyance, the rest of the household staff was already in residence in London.

March threw open the front door, a dignified yet welcoming smile upon his face as they exited the coach and ascended the stairs. "Your Graces. My lord. How was your journey?"

"Quite satisfactory." Adrian drew off his gloves and hat as he crossed the threshold, handing them to the majordomo. A footman hurried forward to assist with everyone's outer garments.

March turned to her. "Your Grace, what a pleasure to welcome you to Raeburn House."

"Thank you, March." She smiled.

"You will be delighted to know your return has not gone unnoticed, your Grace," March informed her. "Not even ten minutes after I installed the knocker this morning, a runner came by with an invitation. There have been six more since. Three of them, I am told, are for tomorrow evening. I have taken the liberty of arranging the cards for you in the salon."

Her stomach pitched like a ship on a rough sea. Valiantly, she pinned on a fresh smile. "How delightful. I will peruse them over some refreshments, if you would be so good as to alert the kitchen staff."

March bowed. "Immediately, your Grace. Oh, one additional item."

She paused, allowed Adrian and Kit to proceed her into the room.

"I have made arrangements with a highly reputable agency here in the city." At her confused frown, he explained in a hushed voice, "Housekeeper interviews."

"Oh, of course." Her lips curved upward, her smile genuine this time. "Thank you, March. Is there much gossip in the servants' hall about the matter?"

"Most definitely, and it is all running in your favor." They shared a conspiratorial grin. "I'll fetch that tea now, your Grace."

"Thank the stars Raeburn's seen fit to bring you to Town at last," Christabel Morgan gushed, fanning herself against the ballroom's warmth. "It's been frightful dull here without you, as I'm certain it has been for you, withering away in the wilds of Derbyshire, as it were."

Violet stared down her nose at her sister's boon companion.

The lively brunette had rushed up to greet her less than a minute after she and Adrian and Kit exited the receiving line. At Kit's whispered suggestion the day before, she'd chosen to attend Viscountess Braverly's ball, a sad crush with some five hundred people in attendance. As he had pointed out, the more people, the less opportunity for extended conversation with any single individual.

She lifted her lorgnette; another brilliant idea of Kit's. She'd purchased the odd thing this morning. A fashionable affectation that would allow her to see more easily, especially once she had an optician fit the glass with her prescription.

She peered through the lens. "There is much to be said for country living when it is done on as fine an estate as Winterlea. The grounds are some of the most beautiful to be found in the whole of England."

"Well, of course. I am certain they are," Christabel agreed.

"And the domestic management of the estate leaves little time for idleness now that I am Duchess. You would understand if you were married." Another of Kit's tricks, deflect unwanted comments or questions by the subtle use of criticism.

Christabel bristled, full bottom lip thrusting into a small pout Violet was sure the girl must practice by the hour in front of her looking glass at home. "I have a large number of admirers."

"Of course you do. Tell me, who are your latest favorites?"

She listened as Christabel waxed lyrical about her current matrimonial prospects, though it was the last thing she wanted to do. She took comfort, aware the subject totally occupied the other girl while giving herself a chance to stand quietly and observe the goings-on in the room.

She wished Kit were at her side to help buoy her up. Or Adrian. She would have much preferred to remain at his side the entire evening. But Kit had strictly forbade her from taking refuge beneath the protection of her husband's coattails.

A trio of gentlemen appeared. They signed her dance

card and Christabel's, then stood chatting about the large number of attendees and the delicacies to be had at the refreshment tables. She let them talk, nodding or smiling at the appropriate moments.

Adrian materialized at her elbow to claim the first dance. Still newlyweds, Society would think nothing of them spending a short while together before going their separate ways for the evening. With relief, she abandoned the now giggling Christabel, who was happily surrounded by men.

As soon as the waltz began, she melted into Adrian's strong, reassuring arms. Momentarily, she let herself forget the fear and strain she was under, Adrian's familiarity a comfort as he whirled her around the room.

All too soon the idyll ended. They strolled off the dance floor.

"Look there," he said, "I see a friend of mine."

He drew her toward a lean, brown-haired gentleman. Shorter than Adrian by half a head, the man's features were pleasant, patrician, yet unremarkable. It was his amber eyes, though, that caught her attention, left her transfixed like a fox to a dove the instant he turned them upon her.

She blinked to dispel the disturbing sensation. Strange, but for an instant she'd glimpsed intimacy in his look, as if he knew her. And knew her well. Then the look was gone, replaced by nothing more than casual, friendly interest.

She wanted to give herself a shake. Her overactive nerves must be making her see things that were not there, she decided.

"My dear," Adrian began, "you remember Toddy Markham. Old friend of mine from my soldiering days."

At least one mystery was solved, she thought. Obviously Adrian had previously introduced the man to Jeannette, during their engagement, no doubt.

She held out a gloved hand. "Yes, of course. Mr. Markham, how are you finding the evening so far?"

"Most enjoyable." He clasped her palm, bowed over it. "With so many beautiful women in attendance, a man can't help but enjoy himself."

He squeezed their joined hands, applying a firm, insistent pressure that lingered for a long, intense beat. Seconds passed, his face betraying none of the emotion expressed by his touch. Then he released her.

She drew her arm away, curled her fingers protectively at her side. *Imagining things, hah*. She hadn't imagined that touch.

She slid a fraction of an inch closer to Adrian.

The movement did not escape Markham's notice, a dagger's-edge glint winking at her out of those dangerous eyes.

"Do you stay long in the city?" she inquired.

"A while. My plans are of a fluid nature at the moment."

"Toddy abhors regimentation," Adrian volunteered. "Never plans past his next meal."

Markham quirked a grin. "That's right. I find that one misses out on far too many of life's unexpected surprises otherwise. Much easier to simply let our passions take us where they may, and not dwell on the uncertainty of our futures."

"Yet there is much to be said for plans," she countered, "as well as the good governance of one's emotions. After all, without plans, wouldn't we all still be living in caves?" As soon as the words were out of her mouth, she wished she could recall them. Jeannette would never have made such an intellectually provocative remark.

Both men studied her, different expressions upon

their faces: proud amusement on Adrian's, surprised speculation on Markham's.

She moved quickly to correct her mistake, laughing. "Then again, what would I know of such matters? Parties, shopping, amusing extravagances, those are the sorts of plans ladies like to make."

Markham studied her for another long moment before he relaxed and smiled. "Quiet right, your Grace. Speaking of amusing extravagances, may I request the honor of a dance with you this evening?" He reached out a hand.

Before he could grasp the dance card dangling from her wrist, she slipped it out of reach. "Ordinarily I would be enchanted, but my entire card has already been filled."

His face hardened. "Every dance? Perhaps you are in error and there is one that has slipped your notice." He reached forward again for the card.

She stepped away, eluding his touch. "No, I am quite certain. Not fifteen minutes past, Mr. Hughes remarked upon his disappointment at being turned away for the very same reason."

Markham gave a stiff bow. "Perhaps you shall have a set available next time we meet." He turned to the duke. "Raeburn. A game of cards later on this evening?"

"Sounds good. I shall find you in the card room after a while."

"Your Grace." Markham bowed once more to her, then turned on his heel and departed.

"What was that all about?" Adrian asked as soon as the other man was out of earshot.

"What do you mean?"

"You and Markham. I got the distinct impression you were brushing him off. Is your dance card really full tonight?"

"Yes, of course it is," she dissembled, aware there

were one or two blank spots remaining. "Just because I am married now doesn't mean I lack for admirers."

"So long as admiring is all they do," he warned with a teasing growl. He sighed. "I suppose that means you already have a partner for the supper dance? I was hoping the two of us could share it."

She'd hoped the same. How easy, how blissful, to pass the evening in Adrian's arms, at his side, sharing his table and his conversation during the elaborate midnight supper to come. But such exclusivity would draw unwelcome comment and attention, and she'd already taken one too many risks tonight as it was.

She tapped her closed fan playfully against his shoulder. "You know it wouldn't do. A husband and wife mustn't live in each other's pockets. There shall be plenty of time to see each other later. At home."

Lambent light flashed fire inside his dark eyes, the timber of his voice dropping low, whiskey deep. "I'll hold you to that promise. Don't dance too much and tire yourself out."

A faint answering flush tinged her cheeks. "I'll do my best."

A wave of melancholy washed over her, drowning her beneath its force as she watched him stroll away moments later. She wanted to call him back, bury her face against his shoulder and beg him to take her home. She hated the pretense, the brittle superficiality of it all. Even inside the lies she'd spun, when she was alone with Adrian some part of her true self remained. Here, there was nothing left of her. Everything falsehood and fabrication. As if she were only a shadow, a reflection without form or substance. As if the real her, the real Violet, didn't exist.

Sudden panic drained the blood from her head, leaving her dizzy, disoriented. Somehow she straightened, strengthened, as she remembered. She was here to make

Adrian proud. She must convince everyone she was Jeannette, the woman he'd chosen as his wife.

A gentleman appeared at her side; her next partner.

Pasting a bright smile upon her lips, she let him lead her into the dance.

Chapter Fifteen

The days to follow passed in a whirlwind of activity: morning calls, luncheon parties, afternoon teas, dinner parties, fêtes, soirées, balls and routs. Ices at Gunter's, promenades in the park, the theater, the opera and the ballet. There was scarcely a moment to breathe and even less time to rest. She danced until dawn. Slept until noon. And spent the rest of the time encircled by friends and acquaintances who buzzed around her like bees attending the queen in her hive.

Jeannette would have thrived on the attention.

Violet longed to find a quiet corner and curl up with a good book. She also longed for Adrian, the husband she rarely saw.

They shared a house and a bed. He still came to her at night, both of them often too tired to do more than turn into each other's arms and sleep. When he wasn't occupied by business or at one of his clubs, he escorted her to a variety of functions. Once there, however, they would go their separate ways, as husbands and wives were supposed to do.

There were times when an entire day would pass without so much as a glimpse of him. The imprint of his head on his pillow when she woke. The warm scent of him on the sheets when she slipped in late to find him already up and dressing for an early appointment that day.

She considered talking to him, asking if she ought to refuse a few more of the dozens of invitations they received. Spend an occasional evening, perhaps even an entire day, together quietly at home. But she knew she dare not broach the subject. It would be too unlike Jeannette. In the country, her differences were excusable. Here in London, they would never be believed.

She sipped a glass of champagne and studied the revelry around her through her lorgnette. She attended with only half an ear to the witty tale being spun by Mr. Moncrief, a blond, puppy-eyed youth who had become one of her retinue of devoted gentleman followers.

Adrian stood across the room, deep in conversation with Lord Liverpool, the Prime Minister. Adrian sported a faint crease between his eyes, a sure sign he disagreed with whatever was being said. She knew enough of his opinions to realize he was a Whig. The Prime Minister was a hard-nosed Tory. Although Adrian wasn't taking an active interest in his seat in the House of Lords, perhaps his mother was right, perhaps he did wish to pursue politics. Was he even now testing out his opposition?

Moncrief recited the punch line of his story. Everyone laughed. She laughed with them, her practiced response sounding hollow to her own ears.

Was this to be the rest of her life?

Her eyes drifted again over the bold, saturnine features of her husband, across the contours of his tall, proud, handsome frame. She sighed silently. If it took listening to a thousand such stories to make him happy, then listen she would.

She swallowed another sip of champagne and asked Lord Northcott about his new home in Sussex. He'd recently won it on the turn of a card, and never tired of retelling the tale or discussing his future plans for the property. The question was certain to keep him talking for half an hour at least.

Adrian observed his wife out of the corner of his eye, while he listened with half an ear to Lord Liverpool expound upon the illiterate masses and the dangers they represented to the Crown. He'd heard it all before, disagreed with it all before, and he knew better than to argue with the great man. There was no amiable way of winning an argument with the Prime Minister. And he preferred to keep on friendly terms with as many of his peers as possible. Even the ones with whom he was philosophically opposed.

It was all very well to banter politics over brandy and cigars. Quite another to trade in it on a daily basis, as some wished he would do. The notion of tossing his hat into the political arena made him shudder in horror. Politics might be his mother's, and a few of his cronies', fondest dream for him, but it wasn't his.

His wife laughed with her friends. She looked magnificent tonight—but then, she always did. Dressed in Prussian blue velvet, she reigned, the regal centerpiece in a tableau of elegant ladies and gentlemen.

Mostly gentlemen, he noted, an unwanted spark of jealousy stinging him like a hot cinder. He ought to be glad she was popular, having fun. Isn't that the kind of wife he'd wanted? A woman both personable and poised. A feminine jewel. Beautiful and refined enough to glitter on his arm when they were together, able to carry herself admirably when they were not.

Why, then, did he wish she was a little less sought after? Why did part of him long for her to cast aside Society's strictures regarding married couples and defiantly spend more of her time with him?

Since they'd left Winterlea, it seemed as if an ever-widening gulf had developed between them; he on the one side, she on the other. They lived in the same house. Yet some days it seemed as though they were no more than passing strangers.

He wished they might return home to the country. Yet how could he ask her to do so when they had only just arrived? When she was having such a grand time here in the city?

Across the room, her laughter rang out, radiant as sunlight on a crisp spring morning. For a moment he let it drown out every other sound in the room.

Then he turned his attention back to the Prime Minister. When a conversational opening appeared, he asked the other man if he might be interested in a game of cards.

Later that evening, Violet checked her image in a large wall mirror hanging in the ladies' withdrawing room. She sighed, nearly ready to return to the ball when her old friend Eliza Hammond entered the room.

She caught the other girl's reflection in the mirror, seeing features that would have been pretty had Eliza not been dressed in an unbecoming mustard-colored gown that drained every speck of color from her fair cheeks, leaving her sallow and plain.

The handiwork of Eliza's aunt, she suspected. A devout penny-pincher, the woman's choices were usually dictated by her pocketbook rather than any semblance of good taste. Sickly yellow had likely come cheap at the dressmaker's the day they'd shopped for this dress.

As she had a dozen times since her return to Town, Violet squashed the impulse to rush over and envelop her friend in a warm hug. She sat mute and let the other young woman disappear behind the privacy curtain that divided the room.

When Eliza reemerged a short while later, there were just the two of them, the room grown quiet after the departure of a quartet of chattering debutantes.

What could it hurt if she spoke to her? Violet thought.

Who would know except a single attendant, who looked too sleepy to care which ladies were in the room?

Giving in to impulse, she swiveled around on her padded stool. "How do you do this evening, Miss Hammond?"

Eliza stopped, blinked in obvious surprise at being acknowledged. She hesitated, then sank into a polite curtsey. "Your Grace. I am quite well. Thank you for inquiring. And yourself?"

"Well enough, though I'm finding it a trifle stuffy tonight. Too many warm bodies packed into too small a space. But that's a crush for you, isn't it?"

Eliza nodded, clearly ill at ease. No doubt she wondered what Jeannette—who'd rarely paused long enough to speak more than a handful of words to her in the past—could want. She wadded a lace handkerchief inside her palm as an awkward silence descended between them.

"Are you here with your aunt?" Violet asked.

"And her son," Eliza confirmed.

Violet knew all about Philip Pettigrew, an obnoxious toad who dressed like an undertaker and had less of a sense of humor than a corpse. He was studying to take ecclesiastic orders, and was actively searching for a prosperous living. Wherever he ended up, Violet pitied his future parishioners.

"I've had a letter or two from my sister. She's in Italy, you know." Her courage sank a little when she saw Eliza stiffen at the mention of her former friend. "She wanted me to convey a message."

"Oh? What might that be?"

"She asked me to express her apologies for her rather uncharacteristic behavior when last you met. She wasn't feeling . . . um . . . herself at the time."

Eliza unbent slightly. "Why didn't she write to tell me that herself?"

Yes, why hadn't she? She racked her brain for a plausible answer. She couldn't tell her it was because the letters would have been franked from Derbyshire and not Italy.

"She is . . . um . . . traveling a great deal. Great-aunt Agatha likes to keep on the move, and my sister feared her letter to you might go astray." She paused, gathering her breath and her thoughts. "To be candid, she wasn't entirely certain you would accept a letter from her. Truly, she regrets the unfortunate incident that happened between you, and asked me to say how much she values your friendship. She would like to continue that friendship, if you will still have her for a friend, that is."

Throat tight, she waited for the answer.

"Of course I will," Eliza said in a relieved rush. "I knew there must be something amiss. She seemed so very odd that day. Actually, she behaved more like y—" The girl broke off, her gray eyes widening at the gaffe she'd nearly made.

Violet forced herself to raise a haughty eyebrow in imitation of her twin. "You were saying?"

"N-nothing. I'm relieved, that's all. The loss of Violet's friendship has been a great sorrow to me."

She kept herself from stretching out a comforting hand. "As it has been to her."

"How long does she plan to remain in Italy?"

"Through the winter, I believe. Although her schedule is not yet fully decided." Violet rose to her feet, brushed an idle hand over her skirt. "Her direction is not firmly fixed. If you wish to write to her, you may give the letters to me and I will see them properly forwarded. And I shall do the same with hers."

Surprise shone once again on Eliza's features. "Thank you. I would be most grateful."

She inclined her head, wishing she could stay and talk, wishing she could put aside all pretense and reveal herself to her friend. But she didn't dare. It would be much too much of a risk.

"Well, I must be returning to the ballroom," she said. "I am promised to Mr. Canning for the next dance, and he will soon be searching everywhere for me. Good evening, Miss Hammond."

Eliza curtseyed. "Good evening, your Grace."

Violet returned to the party, to the press of the crowd, to the heat and light of a hundred blazing candelabras, to the scents of perfume and cologne and perspiring bodies. But the atmosphere did not weigh on her with its usual oppression, the load on her conscience lighter for the first time in months.

"There has been a tragic accident," Adrian announced the following morning. "Ben Yardley, one of my tenant farmers, has been killed. I must leave for home directly."

Violet turned from her place on the drawing-room sofa. "Oh, Adrian, how dreadful. Of course you must go. I shall tell March to notify the staff that we will be returning to the country."

"I can't say I wouldn't enjoy the company, my dear, but there's no need for you to come with me. You're having such a splendid time here in the city, I wouldn't want to spoil that. Besides, there's nothing you can do at home. The poor man is already dead."

He stilled her when she opened her mouth to protest. "No, you stay here with Kit." He cast a glance toward his brother. "He can escort you to any of the engagements you should like to attend. I won't be away long, a week at most. You'll scarcely even know I'm gone." He leaned down, pressed a kiss to her cheek. "Stay and enjoy yourself."

A hint of uneasiness clouded the brilliant translucent depths of her eyes. Then it disappeared as her lips curved upward. "All right, my love. If that is what you wish."

"Here is the translation I promised." Violet passed a folded piece of paper to Kit, then continued along the upstairs hallway toward the staircase.

He accepted the note with a smile, tucked it into his breeches pocket while he kept pace beside her. "Thanks, sis, you're a rock. If it weren't for your help, I'd be stuck here tonight racking my brain for answers instead of escorting you to Lord and Lady Taylor's bash. Not that you'd have trouble finding another eager gentleman ready to step in." He lowered his voice to a whisper. "You've assumed you-know-who's mantle quite admirably."

She stopped, turned to him. "Do you really think so, Kit? Sometimes I shake in my shoes waiting for one of them to notice. It would only take one, you know."

"Not to worry. On occasion, when I'm not paying full attention, you even fool me. And I already know." He patted her shoulder reassuringly, careful to keep his voice down. "As your mentor, I'm justifiably proud. If you weren't a duchess, I'd suggest you try out for the stage. You put Mrs. Siddons to shame."

His comment should have made her smile. Instead she sighed. "I wish Adrian would return. It's only been two days and I miss him dreadfully."

Which was foolish in the extreme, she thought, seeing how they'd barely spent two minutes together when he was here. Still, the bed felt empty at night. She hadn't realized how accustomed she had grown to having him beside her, so warm and strong and comforting in the dark.

"Never fear, he'll be back before you know it," Kit said. "This matter at home, sad as it is, can't take long to resolve. Now come on, or we'll be more than fashionably late." He coaxed her to the main staircase.

Resigned, she followed.

The soirée was well under way by the time they arrived. Several pairs of eyes turned in their direction as she and Kit strolled into the room. He excused himself as her usual crowd soon clustered around her. Not long after, young Mr. Moncrief dived into a sonnet he had composed in honor of her eyebrows. He'd entitled it "Angel Wings in Flight." His soulful blue eyes grew moist with pride as he began his recitation.

One of her brows shot up to hear such nonsense, eliciting a round of appreciative sighs from several of her other male admirers. All of them were competing to become her *cisisbeo*. They persisted in this quest despite her having informed them many times over that she was not in the market for an exclusive male "friend."

Christabel Morgan appeared at her elbow, anxious to pass on fresh snippets of gossip. Violet let her chatter away, making encouraging noises at the appropriate moments.

Short of giving Christabel the cut direct, which Jeannette would never do, Violet had tried every way she could think to gently rid herself of the girl. But Christabel was like a pesky garden vine that refused to go away no matter how many times you yanked it out of the ground. So she resigned herself and suffered her company as best she could.

The evening wore on, her slippered feet beginning to ache from too much dancing, her tongue pasty with the cloying aftertaste of one too many cups of sweet punch. In desperate need of solitude, she decided to brave the chill and slip out onto the balcony for a breath of fresh air.

The November night wrapped around her like a cool pair of arms. She stepped into its embrace, into the soothing, shadowy quiet that curled catlike along the edges of the house.

Suddenly, a pair of long, sinewy arms—real arms—grasped and turned her, pulling her flush against a solid, masculine body. Lips descended, hard and hungry, capturing her mouth in a steamy, passionate kiss.

She cried out in alarm, her distress muffled by the marauding mouth that had taken possession of her own. Too stunned to resist, she froze, her body corpse-stiff within the unwanted embrace.

Soon she regained her senses, ineffectually trying to twist free. But his imprisoning arms were as unyielding as steel bars. She was rallying herself to let out a scream that would bring everyone running onto the balcony, when he abruptly broke the kiss.

A splinter of light slashed across his face, illuminating his dangerous, familiar features.

"Mr. Markham," she gasped on a panting breath.

"Who else were you expecting?" Toddy Markham said on a near growl. "One of those puerile boys who trails after you, composing odes to your eyelashes?" He pressed another quick kiss upon her astonished lips. "I'm sorry if I scared you, darling, but when I saw you come out here, I couldn't let the opportunity slip past. You must know I've been in agony. Wanting to see you, touch you, while being forced to stand aside and do nothing except watch and wait."

Her mouth fell open. She blinked and sputtered, sure she must look like a freshly caught trout laboring for air.

"Mr. Markham," she repeated, sensible speech deserting her.

He turned a gimlet eye her way. "Oh, are we being formal, *your Grace*? You seem to be taking this new title of yours a bit too seriously, don't you think? 'Jeannette' was good enough for you before your marriage. 'Toddy' was fine when you cried out your pleasure in my arms.

Surely Raeburn isn't so skillful a lover you've forgotten what you had with me?"

Her eyes bulged. She actually felt them strain and scrape in the sockets. She sent up a prayer of thankfulness for the concealing darkness.

Markham tightened his hold, oblivious to her distress. "No, don't tell me, I don't want to hear about him." He drew a harsh, impatient breath. "What I do want to know about are these little games you've been playing. Acting as if you barely know me. Refusing to accept my invitations to dance. Avoiding me at every possible turn. Whatever sort of clever tricks you think you're up to, I don't care for them one bit."

Blood rushed, throbbing in her temples, pounding in her ears. For an instant, she thought she might faint. She knew her twin had amours. She'd just never expected one of them to appear in the flesh and confront her in such an obviously physical manner. Or for it to be Markham, of all people. He was supposed to be Adrian's friend. Obviously her instincts had been right on that count. She'd known from the moment she met him that he wasn't to be trusted.

What to do? What to do? she wondered, frantic. She had to think, only there wasn't any time to think. And if she didn't say something soon—other than his name— he might begin to wonder. He might start to question, start to notice a difference in her. Notice, for instance, that she was not the woman she claimed to be.

"L-let me go, someone might see." She pushed against his chest, using the defiant outburst to gather her scattered emotions as she stepped free. "D-do you want everyone to know?"

He reached for her hand, but she evaded him. "I wouldn't necessarily mind," he said.

"You forget. I am a married woman."

"No, my love, *that* I never forget." He scowled,

crossed his arms, his voice low, gruff. "Why did you go through with it? Why did you marry him when you said you couldn't bear the thought? And you've written me only once in all this time, urging me to be patient. How can I be patient when my heart aches for you? When my only recourse is to send letters to you at *his* house, since you've forbidden any other contact?"

Letters? He'd written letters. And she'd written back? She remembered the letter she'd passed on for Jeannette, forwarded to a post-office box in London. Her mind reeled at the implication.

"My God, you're K."

"Of course I'm K. What nonsense are you spouting? K. K for Kenneth, my middle name. We agreed to use it so no one would suspect. What's the matter with you?"

"Nothing, nothing is the matter. You've taken me by surprise, is all, jumping out at me from the darkness. Don't frighten me that way again."

"My apologies. I couldn't help myself, especially knowing Raeburn is away. Meet me tonight. Let me see you, touch you. It's been so long."

He stepped forward.

She stepped back. "I—I can't."

His jaw tightened, visible even in the shadows. "Can't? Or won't?"

"It's difficult. You don't understand. I can't just leave the house, someone will know. And Kit, he . . . he watches me," she lied. "Quite the little spy, Adrian's brother. Who would have thought?"

"You seem to have an affinity for spies." He reached out, traced a thumb over the curve of her cheek. "Very well, I'll wait. But not for long. You may be his wife, but that doesn't mean you aren't still mine to love." He swooped down before she could prevent it, planted another hard kiss upon her lips.

As quickly as he'd come, he was gone, disappearing like a wraith into the night.

She stood, her heart stuttering in her chest as if she'd just run a race. A shiver passed over her, cold seeping through the material of her dress. She hurried inside, anxious to be warm, desperate to be safe.

Scanning the crowd, she searched for Kit.

The Earl of Allensby intercepted her; it was time for his dance. She tried to slough him off, pleading a headache—which wasn't much of a lie, since she felt one coming on. Gentleman that he was, Allensby insisted on escorting her to her brother-in-law.

"Jeannette." Kit rose from the table where he was playing cards, tossed down his hand. "You look white as a sheet. Whatever has overset you?"

"Kit, take me home, please."

They thanked the earl, who bowed and wished her a speedy recovery then departed.

Without a word, Kit found a servant to retrieve their outer garments and alert their coachman they were ready to leave.

Only when they found sanctuary inside the carriage was she able to speak. She told him of her encounter with Markham, of her sister's involvement with him and about the letters.

"The villain." Kit's anger reverberated like harp strings in the air between them. "I ought to call him out."

"Oh, Kit, no. That would only make matters worse, don't you see?" She wrapped her cloak tighter around herself, hung her head. "I knew I shouldn't have said anything to you."

"Don't be silly, of course you should have." He leaned forward earnestly. "Don't worry. We'll think of some way to discourage the bounder. I only wish I could tell Adrian the foul nature of his friend." At her exclamation of dismay, he added, "Mum's the word. I won't divulge a thing. Now, let's get to thinking."

Five days later she barged in upon Kit while he was studying in the library.

She closed the door tightly at her back. "He wants to meet."

He peered up from a volume on the Peloponnesian War, a tome so dry he thought each copy should come with a stimulant. "He who?"

"Who do you think? Markham, of course. He says he's tired of being put off and that if I don't agree to meet him tonight in the conservatory at the Lymondham ball, he will have to take more drastic measures. Here, read for yourself." She thrust the note she'd received toward him.

He took it, scanned the contents. "Cheeky bastard, ain't he? Damned shame you won't let me skewer him. I'd relish having his blood on the end of my sword."

"Kit, please, be sensible. What am I to do?"

For nearly a week now, what she had been doing was hiding in plain sight. With Kit's wholehearted assistance, she'd been using him as a shield, of sorts. Keeping him close enough to prevent any unwanted advances, choosing entertainments that by their very nature squashed Markham's attempts to catch her alone and unawares.

Obviously that strategy had run its course.

Kit tapped the note against his thigh. "You should meet him."

Her mouth dropped open. "*What?*"

"Yes, I think it's time you told him how you really feel. Whatever the two of you shared in the past, it's over now. You've decided you want to make your marriage work. You don't want to see him anymore and you hope he'll understand."

"Are you insane?" she hissed. "He isn't the type to understand."

"Oh, I think he will, so long as you put it to him correctly. Tell him you loved him once but your feelings have changed. Adrian is your future. He is your husband and there's no possibility of divorce, especially now that you are with child."

"But I am not with child." A modest blush spread over her cheeks.

"Ah, but he doesn't know that. Having you enceinte with another man's offspring is bound to cool his ardor."

She paced a few steps, then stopped. "I'm not sure. What if he doesn't believe me? What if he doesn't care? After all, he isn't above having an affair with a married woman."

"He thinks he loves you. When you say you don't feel the same anymore, he'll have no choice but to go."

She paced a few more steps, stopped again. "All right. I suppose it's worth a try. But what about my sister? She won't like this. She won't like this at all." Brows puckered, she hugged her arms around herself.

"She should have thought about that before she convinced the two of you to switch places. You haven't any choice. Tell her it had to be done. Who knows, maybe Markham will meet up with *Violet* someday and fall in love with her."

She tossed him a withering glance. "God forbid. All right, I'll do it." She fluttered her hands, nerves showing. "I hope tonight is the end. Then I hope Adrian comes back, so everything can feel right again."

Chapter Sixteen

The coach and four raced through the evening darkness, the dimly lighted outskirts of the city coming into view.

He wasn't expected back in London for two more days, but Adrian had done everything that could be done about the tragic accident at Winterlea. He'd looked into the circumstances surrounding the farmer's demise. Consoled his grieving widow and her family. Paid his respects at the burial. Condoled with the community to set them once more at ease.

Death was never a pleasant business and he was anxious to put it behind him and return to Town.

The plain truth was, he missed his wife.

He thought of her at least a hundred times a day. Pausing at odd moments to reflect upon something he'd once heard her say or seen her do, committing to memory fresh topics and events he longed to share anew. The nights since he'd been gone were long. He hadn't slept soundly once. He'd never before realized how lonely his bed could be without her warm, womanly form curled beside him.

Before he'd left the city, the two of them had drifted apart, social obligation and convention doing its worst to lead them down separate paths.

But all that was going to change, he vowed.

As soon as he saw her, they were going to rectify the situation. He would convince her to cut back on the number of their engagements. Choose activities that would naturally keep them in closer contact, and spend a few more nights together at home. Society was wrong to dictate that husbands and wives should conduct their lives apart. He wanted to be with her, and conventional or not, he planned to be.

He would also tell her he loved her.

It was time. What was the point anymore of concealing the truth, from himself or from Jeannette? She'd revealed her feelings to him. He should be man enough to do the same.

He was grinning, his good humor bubbling over, when the coach pulled up to the townhouse.

March opened the door, eyebrows raised in surprise. "Your Grace, we weren't expecting you before Friday."

"Decided to come home early. Where's my wife? Has she already gone out for the evening?"

"The duchess and Lord Christopher departed some time ago. The Lymondham's ball, I believe."

"Tell Josephs I'll be wanting the carriage again in an hour's time. And send Wilcox up to prepare a bath and set out a change of attire. I'll be joining her Grace and my brother at the ball."

He bounded up the stairs, taking them two at a time. Halfway up, he paused. "Oh, March, did a messenger bring over a special-delivery package from Rundle and Bridge?"

"Yes, your Grace. It arrived yesterday and was placed in the safe in your study."

"Would you have it brought up to my room, please?"

"I'll see to it myself."

Ever efficient, Wilcox had a hot bath waiting by the time Adrian stripped down, and a fresh set of evening clothes laid out across the bed when he'd finished. A small plate of cheese, crackers and fruit, plus a glass of

Burgundy waited as well to ease his hunger after the long journey.

Refreshed and invigorated, he slipped into his formal attire. Breeches, cutaway coat and pumps—all black—contrasted with crisp white linen—shirt, waistcoat, stockings, neck cloth and gloves.

A velvet-covered jeweler's box lay discreetly on the dresser where March had left it. He popped the lid, gazed at the emerald, amethyst and diamond necklace he'd commissioned for Jeannette. Stunning, the piece was designed to resemble clusters of flowers, trailing leaves and sparkling dewdrops.

Perhaps he should have chosen a design that featured rubies or pink diamonds instead. Colors more closely matching her middle name, Rose. But when he'd seen the sketch for this necklace, he'd known it was the one for her. Oddly enough, it seemed to suit her better.

He imagined surprising her with the gift, envisioned her reaction. But when and where to do the deed?

Struck by sudden inspiration, he crossed into her bedroom. Lid open, he set the jewelry box in the center of her dressing table. The necklace glittered in the candlelight, so magnificent it would be impossible to miss. Tonight, when she arrived home, she would walk in and find it.

He grinned, imagining what he hoped would be her overjoyed response. Perhaps he could even persuade her to wear the necklace—and nothing else—tonight in his bed. His body quickened at the thought.

As he turned to leave, he sighted a piece of paper that had fallen out of the fireplace and onto the hearth. Ordinarily he would have ignored it, let one of the maids do the cleaning up. But Jeannette's name was written on the outside in a bold, looping hand, a single edge of the paper blackened to ash.

Curious, he scooped it up and flipped open the missive.

His heart slammed to a halt inside his chest.

My dearest love . . .

He looked away, a rush of blood swimming in his head, pounding between his ears. Swallowing past the tightness lodged in his throat, he forced his eyes to the page.

> *My dearest love, I cannot bear this agony a moment longer. Pray relieve my heart, my mind, and meet me tonight in the Lymondham conservatory. Be there at midnight and come alone. No more games. If you do not appear, I shall be forced to act in a manner neither of us would wish. I know your heart is mine. Do not despair, we shall find a way. Until this evening.*
>
> *Yours, K*

K? Who the hell was *K?*

The man his wife was having an affair with, that's who.

Adrian crushed the note in his hand, knuckles turned bloodless against the strain. He squeezed his eyes shut, attempting to fight the sickness that coated his insides like acid, the anguish that made him want to rage, to lash out, to scream and roar.

He cast the note into the fire and watched the flames feed until the paper had vanished like the happiness in his heart.

Midnight. The note had said they were to meet at midnight. He consulted the clock on the mantel, saw it was already well past eleven. If he hurried, he could intercept them. Discover the identity of her mystery lover, perhaps catch them in the very act. Is that what he wanted? Is that what he really wished to find out?

Anger, agony consumed him and he knew he had to have the truth. Had to see it with his own two eyes. Grim, he steeled himself for the hell that was to come and strode from the room.

Violet refused two separate offers to dance, carefully monitoring the time by the Lymondhams' magnificent grandfather clock.

Almost midnight.

She fought her nerves. Half sick with tension, she'd been unable to eat a single bite all evening. Hoping it would relax her, she'd drunk some wine, and regretted it. Instead of bolstering her courage, the alcohol had left her feeling muzzy-headed and unsteady on her feet. Luckily, she'd consumed it early enough in the evening for its effects to be wearing off.

She checked the time again.

Two minutes.

Better to slip away now while she could, before an acquaintance or a hopeful dance partner appeared. Kit had promised he would come with her despite the note's warning that she come alone. He'd promised to hide well out of range, close enough for comfort but far enough away not to be seen. Moving on lithe feet, she slipped into the conservatory.

A jungle of vegetation surrounded her, the syrupy fragrance of gardenias floating like a mist in the air. Deep shadows engulfed the space, her soft footfalls the only sound as she made her way deeper into the gloom. Low-burning braziers, ignited to keep off the chill, provided the room's only illumination.

As if materializing from nowhere, Markham stepped out from behind the cover of a large potted palm. "I wasn't certain you'd come."

"I'm here."

He reached for her hand.

She evaded his touch, her insides as wiggly as a blancmange. "What is it you wish to say to me?"

"Why so cold? Have you turned against me, love?"

"Don't call me that. I am not your love, not anymore." She scoured her mind to recall the dialogue she and Kit had rehearsed last night and again this morning. God, she hoped she got it right. "I . . . I am sorry, T-Toddy, but this romance between us cannot continue. I am a married woman now, and although I had feelings for you at one time, those feelings have changed. I love my husband and must ask that you accept that. I cannot see you ever again."

Markham's face turned dark as a thundercloud. She braced for the gathering storm, not at all comfortable with what she saw.

"I don't believe you." He balled his hands into fists. "You can't mean it. Has that interfering whelp of a brother-in-law put you up to this? He's been trailing you like a bloodhound these past few days. Is it blackmail? Has he threatened you? Because if he has, there are ways to remedy the problem."

"No," she said, aghast at the thought of what "ways" he might mean. "Kit has done nothing, so leave him alone. I asked him to stay close."

She decided it was time to play her trump card. She only prayed the lie would work. "If you must know, I'm with ch-child. Raeburn's child. Any future relationship between us is impossible now, you must see that. I belong with him. Please accept that and go away."

A shadow of pain washed across his face. He turned

as though she'd stabbed him, his eyes cast down. After a long moment, he drew in a deep breath, turned back. "It doesn't matter. Have the child, then come to me."

Come to him?

That wasn't what he was supposed to say. He was supposed to tell her good-bye. Oh, dear Lord, what was she going to do now?

She shook her head vehemently. "No, I've told you, it's impossible." Her voice rose to a high-pitched squeak. "It's over."

"No. I won't let it be over. I love you."

"Well, I don't love you." That was one statement she could make with utter sincerity.

"That's not what you said in your letter, when you begged me to wait. When you wrote that your heart would be mine forever and on into eternity."

She barely kept from rolling her eyes. Her twin could be so melodramatic sometimes. "I—I'm sorry, but my feelings have changed. I don't want you, not anymore."

He reached out, grabbed her by the shoulders. "I don't believe you."

She jumped beneath his touch. "Let me go."

He scowled, pushed her backward, closer to a pool of light shining from a nearby brazier. Then he stared, really stared, peering into her eyes as if he was trying to read her thoughts.

"Who in the bloody hell are you?" he demanded.

Her body jolted again. "Jeannette Brantford Winter, Duchess of Raeburn."

"You may be the Duchess of Raeburn, but you aren't Jeannette Brantford, not the one I knew at least."

"How dare you. Let me go."

"Not before I prove I'm right." Without warning, he spun her around, tugged down the sleeve of her gown to expose her bare shoulder and a portion of her back. "It's not there."

"What's not there?"

"Your birthmark. You remember, the one shaped like a little cat? We used to laugh about it because it seemed so perfectly suited to your nature. It isn't there." He traced a pair of fingers over the spot even as she tried to wriggle free of his touch. "It isn't there because you aren't Jeannette. My God, you're her twin, aren't you?"

She pulled away, yanked her gown back into place. Over Markham's shoulder, she glimpsed Kit rushing to her rescue. She met his eyes, gave a small warning shake of her head. He stopped, hovered, his frustration palpable. At her direction, he eased back into the leafy shadows of a nearby bush.

"I knew there was something odd about you," Markham said, "but I couldn't put my finger on it. The two of you switched. Her idea, of course."

Knowing there was no use dissembling, she gave a tight nod.

"Does Raeburn know?" He barked out a laugh. "Of course he doesn't, otherwise he would have booted you out on your lying derriere weeks ago. Incredible." He walked a few steps one way, then back. "Where is she? Where is Jeannette?"

"In Italy with our great-aunt."

He snapped his fingers. "Of course. She's pretending to be you. The strain must be killing her. I shall journey southward and see what I can do to ease her dreadful burden." He paused, eyes narrowing like a wolf's. "She didn't know about this, did she? This effort tonight to cast me aside?"

"She knew nothing about it." She twisted her fingers together. "What will you do about Adrian? Will you tell him?"

He raised a brow. "I ought to. It would serve you right for lying. But I fear it might spoil my fun on the Continent. Besides, if Raeburn is a big enough dupe not to realize the truth, then he deserves you. Rather funny that, having an imposter for a wife." He leaned in. "Are you really pregnant?"

Her cheeks heated at his query. "No."

He laughed again. "If you want to keep him, do yourself a favor and get that way. Once there's a child involved, he won't divorce you. Although he may hire a wet nurse and ship you off to one of his less hospitable estates to live out the rest of your days in lonely solitude." He patted her cheek. "Don't worry. I promise he won't hear it from me."

He turned, strode away.

Only when he'd left did she realize she was trembling.

Kit came to her, enfolded her in a consoling brotherly embrace. Glad of his support, she hugged him back.

"At least he's gone," he told her. "At least he's out of your life."

"It's having him in Jeannette's life that worries me. I pray it doesn't all turn to disaster."

Midnight had come and gone when Adrian strode into the Lymondham conservatory.

There had been a carriage accident on the way, his progress hampered while horses and drivers were sorted out and sent on their way. Once he'd arrived at the ball, he found himself waylaid by no fewer than a dozen people, all wishing to say hello and express their pleasure at his return to the city.

Quiet abounded as he walked through the greenery-laden room, a distant murmur of voices slowly intruding into the silence. His wife and her lover or someone else? He followed the sound, weaving his way amongst the exotic plants that were his host's pleasure and pride. He would confront them, but first he wanted to see the evidence. Positioning himself on the opposite side of a large, flowering bush, he peered through at the couple.

His heart took its second jarring kick of the evening.

There they were, Jeannette and Kit wrapped in each other's arms. For a moment, he didn't understand, couldn't comprehend what he was seeing. Then the words in the note stabbed into his mind, the cryptic signature at the bottom. *K.* That's how her lover had penned his name. *K* for Kit?

Sickness came upon him like a sweat. He turned away, fearing he might actually vomit, breath wheezing in and out of his lungs.

His brother and his wife? Impossible.

Yet he'd seen them together, holding each other. He'd seen them together another time as well, secretive and suspicious now that he considered, that day in the folly at Winterlea. He remembered too the way she'd insisted Kit accompany them to London. And he'd read the note tonight, the most damning evidence of all.

My God, what was he to do? Any other man he would have called out, met on the field of honor and done his level best to kill. But Kit was his brother. He couldn't call out his brother, couldn't murder his own flesh and blood.

Were they in love? His senses screamed at the thought.

Jeannette and Kit were of an age, less than two years apart. He'd witnessed their closeness, had been pleased to see their familial bond, little suspecting all the while that it might be something else.

What of her vows to him? Her words of love? Her pledges of fidelity?

Lies, all of it lies.

How far had it gone between them? Were they sleeping together? While he'd been away, had Kit taken his place in their bed? Had he been the one to bring a flush

of color to her skin, sighs of pleasure to her lips, ecstasy
cresting inside her body?

A red haze of rage swam before his eyes, his hands
trembling. He clenched them and fought for control.
Lord in heaven, what was he to do? How was he to bear
this?

He had to leave. Now. He had to be alone.

The idea of exchanging pleasantries and banal talk
for the remainder of the evening was an anathema that
could not be endured.

Footsteps quiet so Kit and Jeannette would not hear,
he retraced his steps. Making his excuses to his puzzled
hostess, he fled out into the cold night.

Violet rapped on the connecting door to Adrian's bedchamber. When she heard no reply, she turned the knob
and went inside. The room stood empty, bathed in a
mellow wash of firelight. A small branch of candles set
on a side table earlier in the evening had long since sputtered out.

She added another log to the fire, watched the flames
give a greedy, orange-red lick before she took a seat in a
nearby armchair. On her knees she balanced the black-
velvet jeweler's box she'd been stunned to discover on
her dressing table. Her breath had literally left her lungs
the instant she'd glimpsed the extravagant necklace.

Opening the lid, she traced reverent fingertips over
the pretty stones that sparkled even in the low light. No
one had ever given her such an exquisite present. And
for no particular reason either. It wasn't her birthday
and Christmas was still more than a full month away.

She desperately wanted to thank him. She'd never
seen something so extraordinarily beautiful in her life.

Adrian was back in Town. In addition to the jewelry,
one of the footmen had confirmed his arrival when she

and Kit returned home tonight. If rumor was to be believed, he'd put in a brief appearance at the Lymondhams' ball, though neither she nor Kit had caught so much as a glimpse of him. Odd that he would return from Winterlea only to immediately absent himself again.

The mantel clock chimed half-past three in the morning. Where could he be? She hoped nothing untoward had befallen him. Ignoring a small twinge of unease, she settled more deeply into the armchair to wait.

She startled awake, a soft gray predawn light scratching at the windows, the hushed murmuring of housemaids as they passed in the hallway to begin their day's work. She sat up, stretched, stiff from having fallen asleep in the chair.

Nearly seven o'clock. Her eyes flew to the bed, its coverlet undisturbed, as precisely made as it had been for all the days he'd been gone.

Adrian hadn't come home last night.

Alarmed, she hurried out into the hallway without considering her attire—robe and slippers, her long, sleep-mussed hair streaming down her back. He should be home by now, she fretted. Something terrible must have happened. An accident, an illness. Even now, he might be lying in pain, or worse.

She raced along the corridor. Betty was the first servant she found, the girl down on her hands and knees scrubbing the floor.

The maid looked up, clearly startled. "Your Grace, whatever's amiss?"

"Betty, thank heavens. Have you seen the duke this morning?"

"No, ma'am, I haven't but—"

She didn't listen any further, just hurried on.

She dashed down the main staircase, oblivious to the stares of the servants she passed. Entering the main hall, she rushed toward March.

The majordomo turned, his blue eyes widening. "Your Grace, are you all right?"

"Yes, yes, I'm fine," she panted, pausing a moment to catch her breath. "His Grace. He didn't come home last night and I'm dreadfully worried that something might have happened to him. Have you heard from him? Perhaps we should contact the authorities, his friends, anyone who might have seen him last."

A footstep sounded in the hallway. "There is no need of that, madam. As you can plainly see, I am fine."

She whirled at the sound of Adrian's voice. Setting a hand over her heart, she flew to where he stood in the doorway of the breakfast room, then threw her arms around him in a fierce hug.

His entire body stiffened. Too overcome with relief, she didn't immediately notice his lack of response.

With firm hands, he set her away.

"Such melodrama," he said, his voice cold as a frozen lake. "No doubt I am supposed to be moved by your concern. Look at my wife, March, so distraught over me she couldn't even be bothered to dress."

She flushed, only then realizing she stood in her nightclothes. She tugged the sides of her robe more tightly around her body. "I was worried. I waited up for you . . ." she lowered her voice ". . . in your room. You never came to bed."

"Perhaps we should discuss this matter where we can be private." He stepped aside, waited for her to enter the morning room. Dismissing the single servant inside, he closed the door, leaving them alone. He crossed to the breakfast table and resumed his seat in front of his abandoned plate.

She hovered, oddly ill at ease. "Where were you last night?"

"Would you care for one of these sausages?" He motioned toward a silver platter. "They're quite good."

"Adrian, please. What is wrong?"

"Nothing is wrong. I'm very well, breaking my fast with a hearty meal." He ate a forkful of scrambled eggs. "You must try some. Perhaps a cup of tea as well."

"I don't want eggs or sausages or tea. I want to know where you were last night."

He shot her a quick, hard glare, then lowered his eyes. He cut a piece of sausage, his knife scraping discordantly against the china. "At my club, since you are so interested."

"Your club? All night?"

"Yes. Mystery solved. Now, I suggest you go put on some suitable clothing. You have the look of a doxy about you this morn."

She gasped, her cheeks reddening. "I was concerned about you. I didn't think. I'm sorry." She hugged her arms around herself, stared down at the carpeting. She blinked back a sudden rush of tears.

Something was dreadfully wrong, she thought. Where was the man she knew? It was as if the real Adrian had gone away and a stranger had returned in his place. His harsh words, the chill in his eyes. For a moment, she'd almost imagined he hated her. A shiver passed along her spine.

"I'll go now," she murmured.

He set down his silverware, stared at her.

Why did he feel as if he'd just kicked a puppy? She looked so young, so beautiful. So innocent. If he weren't privy to the truth, he would have believed her and her distraught concern for his welfare. Would have believed she loved him, if not for the betrayal he'd witnessed last night.

"Why were you waiting for me?" The words escaped him.

"Oh. I . . . I wanted to thank you, for the necklace. It is so exquisite. The most beautiful gift anyone has ever given me."

The necklace. He'd forgotten all about the damned thing.

His features hardened as he remembered his naive, foolish delight, his happy anticipation over the present. How she would have laughed had she seen it.

"It is an attractive piece that will look well around your neck," he commented in a businesslike tone. "The family jewels haven't been updated for half a century at least. I thought it time they were refreshed."

She wilted, a small spark of pleasure dying in her eyes. "Oh, I see. I should return to my room now."

"Yes." He picked up his fork in dismissal. "My meal grows cold."

When she'd gone, he set the utensil down again. He pushed his plate away, no longer the least bit hungry.

Chapter Seventeen

Violet dressed for the Carters' ball. She wished she could beg off the engagement tonight and stay home. But the entertainment was being thrown in her honor—hers and Adrian's—so there was no escape.

Agnes slipped a beautiful gown of emerald satin with an overskirt of white-dotted Swiss gauze over Violet's head. The dress was low-cut and off-the-shoulder for evening, and it was a simple task to fasten the gown into place. Then it was on to her hair.

She sat at her dressing table, let her maid brush and arrange her long tresses into place. She stared at her own reflection in the mirror, studied her eyes and wondered if anyone else could see the unhappiness brimming within them.

Something was dreadfully amiss with Adrian.

Ever since his return from Winterlea last week, he'd been withdrawn. Abrupt, taciturn, humorless. She couldn't imagine what might have happened at the estate to overset him in such a way. She'd even questioned the servants—discreetly, of course—including Wilcox, his valet. Yet none of them was able to provide so much as a clue.

After his ghastly first morning back, she'd been reluctant to question Adrian directly. Finally, she'd gathered her nerve and asked him why he was so troubled.

Eyes cold, he denied any such condition, rebuffing her and her inquiries. Wounded, she hadn't asked again.

Neither had she asked why he no longer came to her bed. They hadn't slept together or made love since he'd left for Winterlea. She feared to hear his reason.

He'd changed toward Kit as well. For reasons no one could fathom, Adrian had taken to baiting his brother, often over the most insignificant of matters.

Last night at dinner, he'd torn into Kit over his so-called gluttony when the younger man helped himself to a second serving of trifle for dessert. Kit always ate seconds. His *not* doing so would have been more likely to elicit a comment. So Adrian's unexpected attack startled everyone, even the footmen on duty that evening, who'd watched in wide-eyed astonishment.

And two days prior, Adrian had lashed out at him over the purchase of a new waistcoat. How many striped waistcoats did one man need? he'd demanded in a scathing tone. Did Kit ever stop to consider the cost of such items? Surely he had better uses for his allowance than that. No wonder he was always so badly dipped, a hairsbreath from punting in the River Tick.

Kit's cheeks had flushed scarlet as he stood beneath the storm of Adrian's verbal castigation. She'd feared they might come to blows. Especially when Adrian impugned Kit's virility by asking if he was turning into a man milliner, an effeminate sort who thought of nothing but his looks and the attractiveness of his wardrobe.

With Adrian's sable brown eyes ablaze, his jaw fixed in a pugnacious tilt, she had gotten the distinct impression in that moment that Adrian *wanted* Kit to hit him. That he was inciting his brother to violence so he might have a chance to pummel him back. But why? It made no sense.

"Your Grace, would you like to wear your new necklace? The one his Grace gave you?" Agnes inquired, interrupting her musings.

She looked at the reflection of Agnes standing behind her in the mirror.

"Ooh, isn't it lovely?" The maid held up the exquisite piece. "It will be a perfect accent to your gown."

She stared at the necklace, reluctant to put it on. She'd loved it so at first. But Adrian's curt, impersonal explanation for its purchase had dampened her pleasure like a faceful of icy water. Perhaps it might placate him in some small way if she wore his gift tonight. Perhaps he might feel pride in seeing the newest of the family jewels gracing her neck. Maybe it would bring a small glint of pleasure back into his eyes. Eyes that no longer seemed to shine, at least not for her.

She nodded permission, the stones cool against her throat as they were fastened into place. She studied her reflection one final time and knew, without vanity, that she looked resplendent, every inch the Duchess of Raeburn. Silently, she prayed Adrian would find her beautiful, desirable.

Waiting in the foyer, he spared her barely a glance before assisting her into her cloak, his touch as impersonal as a servant's. Not by so much as an eyelash did she betray the aching disappointment that sliced through her like a blade. Head held high, she preceded him out to the carriage.

The trip to the Carters' was made in silence. Kit wasn't along to break the oppressive gloom, had he even been inclined to try. He'd accepted a dinner invitation with friends and planned to join her and Adrian at the ball later in the evening.

Adrian led her out for the first dance. She fixed a smile on her face, pretended all was well. Inside she wanted to weep. They spoke of trivialities, less intimate than strangers. Each step became a misery, each touch an exquisite torture.

She was losing him, she thought, and she didn't even know why. Worse, she didn't know what she could do to stop it.

When the song ended, she and Adrian parted, their duty done.

Lord Hamilton solicited her hand for the next dance. She placed her palm in his and let him lead the way.

She sat sipping a cup of negus, the evening nearly half over, when Eliza Hammond stole up next to her, quiet as a whisper.

"Pardon the intrusion, your Grace." Eliza curtseyed in a respectful greeting.

Violet inclined her head in reply.

"When last we spoke," Eliza continued, obviously reticent, "you said if I wrote to your sister, you would be willing to forward my letters on to her."

She set down her drink. "Yes, I did."

Eliza extended a thick piece of folded parchment. *Violet Brantford* was written in an efficient hand across the front.

She took the letter. "I'll see she receives this."

A smile spread across the other woman's face. "Thank you, your Grace. You're most kind." Then she vanished, winging away like some quiet brown sparrow.

Violet wanted to call her back, find a comfortable corner where they could talk and share confidences as they used to do. When Eliza relaxed, her reticence fell away, her conversation as entertaining and animated as the most lively wit. And Eliza knew how to listen, able to jolly away the blue-devils with a sympathetic ear and a well-needed dose of optimistic encouragement. If only people would take the time to look beneath the surface, they would see, as she did, what a wonderful person and loyal friend Eliza was. And right now, Violet was dearly in need of a friend. But Eliza couldn't help her. No one could help her.

She looked across to where the other girl stood, alone and forgotten. No, Eliza couldn't help her, she decided, but perhaps she could help Eliza, if only a very little.

When Kit arrived nearly half an hour later, she motioned him over to her side. "Ask Miss Hammond to dance," she said without preamble.

"Miss Hammond?"

She watched him scan the ballroom, saw when his gaze landed upon her friend. Seated on a straight-backed chair next to a pair of drowsy dowagers, Eliza looked as washed out as her gown of watered almond silk.

"Eliza Hammond, you mean?" He didn't sound enthusiastic.

"She hasn't danced all evening."

"She never dances."

"That's because no one asks her. Be a gentleman and stand up with her. And when you're done, get one of your cronies to take a turn with her as well."

"I say, I don't know if—"

"It's only one dance. I'm not suggesting you marry her."

Kit shuddered. "God forbid." He straightened his cuffs. "Very well. One dance, as a favor to you. And perhaps I can convince Suttlersbury to do the deed as well. He's always game for a dance. But don't think I won't remember this and call in my marker one of these days."

She chuckled. "Never fear. I know you too well to ever doubt that."

Adrian watched his wife and brother from across the room. *Look at them,* he thought, *their heads together, whispering thick as thieves, cozy as lovers.* His jaw tightened in a bone-grinding clench. Slamming down the tumbler of Madeira he'd been nursing, he stalked toward them.

Kit was just turning away as he approached. Their eyes met for a long, combative moment before the younger man gave a perfunctory nod and moved off.

The smile on Violet's face faded as soon as he turned his attention toward her, her reaction increasing his anger. "Dance with me, madam." He thrust out a gloved hand.

She hesitated, glanced to her left as a gentleman stepped forward. "I am sorry, your Grace, but I am promised to Sir Reginald for this set."

He pinned hard eyes on the other man. "What do you say, Malmsey? You don't mind if I cut in, now, do you? I want to dance with my wife."

Sir Reginald swallowed audibly, his pale complexion lightening a shade. "N-no, your Grace. Think nothing of it. More than happy to oblige." He gave a jerky bow, murmured something to her and scurried away.

Adrian held out his hand in a manner that brooked no defiance. "The musicians are beginning, madam."

She laid her palm in his, walked beside him onto the dance floor.

He swung her into a waltz, her body lithe beneath his touch, her hand soft and familiar within his own. He didn't know why he'd done this to himself. What had prompted him to demand they share a dance when he knew it would bring him nothing but pain? Yet it felt so traitorously good to hold her, to drink in her sweet scent, to gaze down upon her crown of lustrous golden hair.

Earlier that evening when she'd walked down the staircase at home, his necklace encircling her throat like a bouquet of glittering wildflowers, she'd stolen the breath from his body. It had taken everything he had not to let his feelings show. To behave as if he barely noticed, as if she no longer mattered to him. And damn it, she shouldn't. She shouldn't matter, not anymore. Yet somehow she still did.

Furious with himself and with her, he concentrated on keeping time to the steps of the dance, saying not a word.

Violet let him lead her around the room, the strains of violins and flutes sweet as perfume upon the air. He was tense. She could feel the barely leashed energy in his taut muscles. The fury that simmered just below the civilized surface.

She hazarded an upward glance, caught the hungry gleam of desire in his eyes. Startled, she looked immediately away, stared at his shirtfront as her heart quickened, gladdened. He hadn't shown any interest in her since his return to Town. Was it possible something had changed? Was it possible he might want her again?

Her pulse beat a rough tandem in time to the music. She stole another upward glance, disappointed to see the look no longer there.

All too soon, the dance ended. He escorted her back to her circle of admirers, bowed and strode away. He hadn't said a word the entire time, and for most of it he'd seemed resentful, angry. Why had he sought her out?

There was no understanding him these days. Yet she felt certain she hadn't mistaken that glance of his, or the longing in it. Now the question was, how should she respond?

She waited until she heard Adrian's valet leave, his room growing quiet on the other side of the connecting door.

She gazed down at herself, appalled at her own daring. She was wearing the scandalous red silk night rail from Jeannette's trousseau—the one garment she'd never had the nerve to don. The material clung to her body like a second skin.

Would Adrian want her?

Surely he would when he saw her like this. The gown was so shocking, she hadn't even let Agnes see her in it. As soon as her maid departed for the evening, she'd exchanged her nightgown for this one. She looked almost naked. Broad swatches of lace, interspersed with thin strips of silk that covered only the most essential parts.

The lewd thing was even slit up the sides.

She'd buoyed her self-confidence by remembering the last time she'd set out to seduce Adrian. That interlude had gone well—really well, as she recalled—so why should this time be any different?

Perhaps because he hadn't been angry and indifferent to her then, a little voice whispered. Perhaps because he'd still desired her then.

But there'd been that look in his eyes during their dance tonight. No matter how brief, she knew she hadn't imagined it. In spite of his recent coldness, some part of him still wanted her. Now she had only to revive that need and show him she felt the same.

Adrian tossed back the last of his brandy, set the snifter aside. He brooded, staring vacantly into the flames that snapped contentedly in the fireplace.

Jeannette.

He should never have danced with her tonight. Giving into impulse, to haste, to heat, had been a mistake. He spent his days trying not to think of her and ended up doing little else. His life had turned into an utter hell.

He was contemplating another brandy, so he might further drown his misery and have some chance of sleeping, when the connecting door opened.

There she came, gliding into the room on bare, silent

feet. Her body was garbed in a bloodred slash of silk that showed more flesh than it concealed. Glimpses of her bare legs showed as she walked. Her breasts were lush and firm, succulent fruits barely cloaked beneath a veil of passion-colored lace.

His body reacted of its own accord, instant lust priming him the way the scent of a ready mare would a stallion. He clenched a single fist and fought to maintain an impassive facade.

"What is it?" Deliberately, he made his tone sound bored and disapproving.

She halted, hesitated. "I saw your light. I couldn't sleep."

"It's late. You should ring Agnes, have her bring you some warm milk."

She took a few steps forward. "I don't want warm milk."

"Some brandy, perhaps." He grabbed his own empty snifter, rose from his chair, crossed the room. His back turned, he reached for a fresh glass, poured a large splash of liquor inside each.

He downed his own portion in a couple of healthy swallows. The alcohol burned its way along his throat, into his stomach, where it spread like fiery coals. He prayed the potent draught would deaden his senses, dull his carnal appetite.

He turned, held her glass out at arm's length, careful to keep his eyes averted. "Here."

"I remember the last time you plied me with liquor."

He remembered too, and wished he didn't. It made their current reality all the more painful to bear.

She moved closer. "What I need tonight isn't spirits."

"Take it anyway and go."

"Adrian, what is it? What's wrong?" She rushed forward, slid her arms around him, pressed the warm, pliant curves of her body against his. "Don't you want me anymore?"

Head buzzing from drink and desire, he stared into her eyes and began to drown. Without thought, without caring, he crushed his lips to hers, gave himself over to the hunger raging in his blood. The brandy snifter fell from his hand, liquor soaking into the carpet as the glass rolled away.

He poured all the need and want and frustration he'd been living under into his kiss, savaging her mouth in a hot, greedy mating that took more than it gave. She met and matched him, sighing beneath his touch as he stroked his hands everywhere. He lifted her, dying to be inside her where she was warm and wet. He couldn't resist. Couldn't deny himself what he had to have worse than his next breath.

They sank together onto the bed. Her hands caressed him, sleek and knowing, her mouth gliding over his neck and face and chest.

"Adrian," she whispered. "Adrian, I've missed this. Missed you. I love you."

He froze, desire dying in an instant. Memories beat viciously inside his mind. Finding the letter. Knowing she'd lied. Seeing her wrapped inside his brother's arms. Imagining them together as she spoke those very same words to him. *Kit, I love you.*

What was wrong with him? How could he be touching her? How could he want her? Yet he did, even now, even knowing what she was. Worse, he loved her, despite her hollow lies, her treachery. He was disgusted by them both.

"Get out." He rolled away from her, his words low, raw in his throat.

"What?" She reached for him again.

He flung himself off the bed. "Get out. Leave. Be gone."

"But Adrian, I don't understand—"

"Don't you? What is there to understand? I don't want you. Is that plain enough for you to comprehend, madam? I am no longer interested in sampling your fine feminine wares."

Tears sprang to her eyes, one coursing down her cheek. "Why? What have I done?" she pleaded.

"Please, don't persist in this charade," he said with obvious distaste and derision. "You gave it a good try, but it's over now. I *know* about you. I *saw* you."

He expected her to break, confess.

Instead she sat up on the bed, confusion heavy in her gaze. "Know about what? What did you see? I don't understand."

God, what an actress she was. "I found the note, the one from your lover."

Her face blanched.

"Ah, so you remember that, do you? You threw it in the fire, but it didn't burn. I found it and I read it."

"It's not what you think."

"Isn't it? I followed you that night, to the party. I saw the two of you together. I saw you in his arms."

He stalked away, to the fireplace, where he leaned an arm against the mantel, stared blindly into the flames. "How could you do it? How could you betray me with my own brother?" A sad, aching sickness filled him, a sorrow unlike any he'd ever known.

"Is that why you've been so beastly to both of us this past week? Because you believe I'm having an affair with Kit?" Astonishment rang in her voice.

"What else am I to believe?"

"He's my friend, nothing more. He gave me a hug that night. He wasn't . . . embracing me, not the way you think."

He whirled, confronting her. "Then what about that

note? Someone sent you that damned note. If not Kit, then who? Who in the hell is K?"

She linked her hands together, lowered her eyes. "I can't tell you."

"Can't or won't?" He charged forward, grabbed her by the shoulders and shook her. "Tell me who he is. Who is your lover?" he demanded at a near shout.

With one final furious glare, he wrenched himself away, afraid he might actually do her physical harm.

She rubbed her shoulder and climbed off the bed. "Adrian, please, I know it looks bad, but it isn't what you think. I—I don't have a lover. You're the only man I've ever—"

"No more." He threw up a hand. "I won't listen to another word. I've heard enough of your lies. Get out."

When she didn't move, he yelled at her, "Didn't you hear me? I said get out. Get out. Now!"

She flinched. With silent tears streaming over her cheeks, she raised her chin, looked him in the eye. "You're wrong. I haven't betrayed you. Please let me—"

He took a menacing step forward.

She swallowed the rest of her words, then fled, slamming the door behind her.

He crossed the room, leaned over to pick up the forgotten brandy glass. The carpet would need to be cleaned, he thought unimportantly.

He stared at the glass for a long while, until anguish rushed up inside him, burning and bitter as gall. With a shout, he flung the snifter into the fire, where it splintered into a hundred pieces. Something else to be swept away, put to rights.

If only their lives could be so easily restored.

Unutterably weary, he sank into the armchair. Sleepless, he listened to her sob till the wee hours of the morning.

Chapter Eighteen

They left for the country two days later.

Christmas would soon be upon them, and per tradition the entire Winter family, even distant relations, would congregate at Winterlea to share the holiday season.

News of the birth of Sylvia's newest baby had arrived in London only a few days before. To everyone's delight, the child was a girl. Despite being only recently out of childbed, Adrian's sister was determined to show off her prized infant. The dowager duchess would, of course, be returning with her daughter, Sylvia's husband and their sizable brood in tow.

Violet had received a note from her parents. They would be driving up from their estate in Surrey to join the celebration. Darrin planned to arrive from Scotland, where he'd been sharing a hunting box with friends. However, Great-aunt Agatha and "Violet" would be remaining on the Continent until spring. At sixty-five, Agatha's bones were simply too brittle to be subjected to the damp and cold of an English winter, even for the sake of Christmas.

And it was cold, blustery, with a few snowflakes twirling a giddy dance in the air. Violet watched them fall as she stared out the coach window, pulling the blanket higher on her lap to protect against the chill. She sat alone inside the coach. The men had decided to ride in spite of the weather. Though from what she could see, neither appeared to be enjoying the exercise.

Since that dreadful evening when she'd gone to him, she and Adrian had barely spoken to each other, passing less than a handful of minutes in each other's company. Given the things said that night, what remained?

He believed she was an adulterous liar. And to be fair, he was half right.

She was a liar.

She wanted to defend herself, prove to him she hadn't been unfaithful, but how could she? Not without giving away her other secret. In order to disprove one false-hood, she would have to reveal too much about the other. Like a loose thread in a tapestry, once picked free, the whole piece would soon come unraveled.

Perhaps she should simply admit the truth, confess her identity and end the charade. Then Adrian could de-cide to which of his many estates he would prefer ban-ishing her. Or would he divorce her instead and simply turn her out? She shuddered at the horrifying prospect, knowing she was damned no matter which path she chose. She sighed, watched more delicate snowflakes wing toward the earth.

Outside, Kit rode beside his brother. After nearly two hours of silence, he was fed up with being ignored. He'd rather be traveling inside the coach with Violet. It would certainly be a damned sight more comfortable. But once he climbed inside, he knew Adrian would insist upon joining them. Leaving the three of them knee to knee in misery for the rest of the journey.

Enough was enough, he thought. How many times did a man have to explain himself?

Violet had told him about Adrian's accusation the morning after the Carters' ball. He remembered his jaw literally dropping open at the news. The idea of a liaison with her was unimaginable. The pair of them were like brother and sister. Anyone with eyes could see that. Anyone, that is, except a lovesick fool too blinded by his own jealousy to recognize the truth.

The evidence—Markham's letter and Adrian's unfortunate witnessing of Kit embracing Violet—were damning indeed on the surface. Adrian demanded proof of their innocence, and with his own less than full explanation of events, his older brother's suspicions remained. Twenty-two years of familial trust, it seemed, weren't enough to sweep away a single night's worth of misunderstandings and falsehoods.

But he refused to unmask Violet.

He'd made a promise to her and unless Adrian asked him point-blank about her identity, he wasn't going to break that vow. He'd spent his whole life admiring his brother. Right now he just wanted to knock him a good one on the head.

"What a fool," he mumbled under his breath.

Adrian's head swung around. Kit's soft words had apparently carried on the wind. "I beg your pardon?" he said, his words as frosty as the air.

Kit squared his shoulders, raised his voice. "I said you're a fool. You're making yourself and everyone around you miserable over nothing."

A muscle ticked in Adrian's jaw. "You believe adultery is nothing?"

"She and I have both told you nothing happened. It's the truth, if you'd simply care to see it. As undeniably beautiful as Jeannette is, I don't find her even remotely appealing, not in a romantic sense, that is."

"How reassuring. Now, if you are finished—"

"I'm not finished." He plunged ahead, not stopping to wonder at his nerve. "That woman loves you, though God knows why, and you're cutting her out of your life over little more than a misconception."

"Misconception? Would that be the love letter I misconceived or seeing her wrapped in your arms?"

"I've already explained about that. I was giving her a hug, a brotherly hug, nothing more."

"And the letter? You haven't seen fit to explain about that yet, have you? If you aren't the missive's author, then who is? If Jeannette is an innocent in all of this, why the deception? The half-truths? The lies? What are you hiding? Who are you protecting?"

"That isn't for me to say. Ask your wife."

"I did ask, and she 'can't say' either."

"You ought to trust her nonetheless, no matter how things may appear."

A haunted shadow passed through Adrian's eyes. "Trust? I am to trust but not the other way around? I am to accept the weak excuses and convenient answers the both of you have provided me, all the while knowing you've been less than completely honest?"

"Adrian—"

"That is quite enough," Adrian commanded, his tone as chill and bitter as the wind. "There will be no further discussion of this matter, do you understand? We will not speak of it again." His horse, Mercury, trotted a few steps to one side. Adrian reined him in, moved him gently back into place. "When Christmas is over, you will return to University, and you will see to it you acquit yourself admirably, is that understood?"

Kit nodded. "Fully."

"As for Jeannette, how I choose to conduct my relationship with my wife is a private matter, and no concern of yours. I will tell you this, however." Their eyes met, challenged. "If you weren't my brother I would already have put a bullet through you. If I catch you with her again, brother or not, I will."

Adrian spurred Mercury into a canter, thundered ahead.

Kit watched them disappear into the swirling snow. *Well,* he thought, *that went splendidly.*

What an utter mess the three of them had made amongst themselves. If only he had the smallest idea how to make it come out right.

Huddling deeper inside his coat, he rode onward.

The house was a noisy hive of people. Children and adults scattered into bands of determined revelers. Amid much frivolity, Adrian had overseen the lighting of the Yule log in one of the older sections of the house, where the fireplace was large enough to accommodate the great length of wood. According to tradition, the log would burn for a full twelve days. Reduced to ashes by the conclusion of the holiday celebration on Twelfth Night.

The lighted Christmas candle held a position of prominence on the mantel in the first-floor drawing room, where the women and children spent their time fashioning paper ornaments and bows and streamers made from lengths of pretty gold and red ribbon. In the meantime, the men took to the fields to shoot game or ride over the frost-covered hills, returning flushed and famished in the evening. Tonight—Christmas Eve— everyone would exchange presents, sing wassailing tunes and drink syllabub and hot rum punch.

Usually Adrian loved this time of year. Visiting with his family and friends. Making rounds by horseback and carriage to call upon his neighbors and tenants, leaving gifts of food and drink to brighten their holiday table.

But this year he would be glad when everyone departed and the house grew quiet once again. Though Jeannette had agreed to pretend for company that all was well between them, the act was a great strain. Just the other day, he'd been forced to lie point-blank to his mother as everyone gathered to admire Sylvia's new baby, Emma.

A tiny bundle of rosy-cheeked joy, the infant gurgled and blinked at the sea of strange faces, waving a tiny fist in the air before falling into a deep slumber. Adrian's other sisters, Anna, Lysande and Zoe, all took a few minutes to hold the baby.

Then it was his wife's turn.

He couldn't help but watch as she bent over the child. Cradling the infant against her breasts, she cooed silly, soothing nonsense phrases. With the tip of a single finger, she stroked the baby's delicate cheek, an expression of pure pleasure lighting her face.

"When are the two of you going to give me one of those?" His mother came up beside him and laid a hand on his sleeve. "A woman cannot become a *grand-mère* too many times, you know."

A fist clenched inside his gut, a dreadful melancholy filling his heart. He forced a hearty smile and prayed his mother would not see through him to the truth. "We're working on it, *Maman*. We're working on it."

But they weren't working on it.

He no longer touched his wife and didn't know if he ever would again. He supposed eventually he would have to return to her bed to produce an heir. Assuming she didn't turn up pregnant before then. The thought, and others like it, left him in a constant state of agitation. A slow simmer of rage that boiled just below the surface, denying him any measure of peace or happiness.

And Kit. He couldn't look at his brother without wondering, questioning. He wanted to believe Kit's denials. Nearly did, especially when he watched him and Jeannette interact among the family. They did seem like brother and sister, not lovers. Yet every once in a while, he would catch a look, almost conspiratorial in nature.

And a fresh wave of fury would roar through him over the secrets they refused to reveal.

Just this afternoon, while the children played Hoodman Blind in the long gallery, he'd seen the pair of them standing with their heads together, whispering. Incensed, he'd watched his wife pass a note to Kit. Casually, Kit had tucked the slip of parchment into his pocket, then proceeded to act the fool, snatching the hood off his cousin Cicely's head in a way that set the whole crowd to laughing.

Another love letter? Grim with anger, he vowed to find out.

Keeping Kit in his sights, he bided his time until the adults assembled in the drawing room for tea. When Kit rose to make a return trip to the sideboard for seconds, he followed.

Slipping up next to him, he bumped into Kit just as his brother reached for a scone. Employing a sleight-of-hand trick he'd acquired during his espionage days, he purloined the note from Kit's pocket, using the "accident" as cover.

"Sorry, caught my footing wrong," he murmured in apology.

Kit turned, shot him a look, eyes narrowed as if he didn't entirely believe him. After a moment, he shrugged, filled his plate and returned to his seat.

Nearly two hours passed before Adrian found an opportunity to read the note. Alone at his desk in his office, he listened to the soft, rhythmic ticking of the mantel clock. He stared at the paper in his hand. He didn't want to read it. He didn't want to know what it said.

Finally, knowing he must, he forced his fingers to move.

Bewilderment surged through him as the words came clear on the page.

Latin?

The damned thing was written in Latin. Why would Jeannette give Kit a message written in a foreign language—and a dead one, to boot? It made absolutely no sense whatsoever.

He scanned the text, reading it with ease. Ancient languages had been one of his best subjects at University. Definitely not a love note, he decided. Rather, a translation—and a boring one, at that—about one of the lesser battles waged by the Roman Empire.

One of Kit's lessons? From every indication, yes. But what had it been doing in Jeannette's possession? And why had she passed it to his brother in such a secretive, clandestine fashion?

He puzzled over the curious question for what remained of the afternoon, and again when he went upstairs to dress for dinner. Still preoccupied, he tuned in with only half an ear to the conversation during the delicious Christmas Eve feast.

Time and time again, his eyes turned toward his wife where she held court at the opposite end of the lengthy table. He kept coming back to one question: If she hadn't betrayed him, if the love letter wasn't from Kit, then why all the lies and half-truths? What was she concealing?

He was no closer to a solution when the gentlemen joined the ladies in the drawing room after dinner. Over cups of wassail, Zoe was importuned to lend her skills upon the pianoforte. Everyone joined in a rousing chorus of holiday songs.

Somehow as the evening progressed, he ended up near the doorway, Jeannette at his side.

"Oh ho, look, everyone," his cousin Reginald declared, pointing a finger over their heads. "Mistletoe. Go on, Raeburn, you've been fairly caught. Kiss your wife."

He saw the bemused expression in Jeannette's eyes as

she glanced upward and realized the significance of the green and white plant dangling overhead. A wistful sorrow stole into her eyes as she gazed at him, his reluctance and her own understood without a word between them.

He tried to laugh off the suggestion, but with the entire family urging them on, he and Jeannette had little choice but to comply with tradition. Touching her for the first time in weeks, he bent down, dusted his lips lightly over hers.

"Is that the best you can do?" Reginald chastened. "I could kiss my own mother better than that."

"Watch your mouth, boy, or you'll find a piece of soap in it," his mother returned, sending everyone into a fit of giggles.

They all waited. Waited for him to kiss his new wife the way a loving, happy husband would.

Her eyes fastened upon his cravat, faint color staining her pale cheeks. He slipped an arm around her waist, fastened his mouth to hers and gave her a real kiss.

He meant to make it fast. A quick, healthy blending of lips that was all flash and no fire, designed solely to satisfy their audience. But as soon as his mouth linked with hers, sensory memory took hold, repressed needs, bittersweet longings rising to the surface. And he was lost.

Violet shivered, wanting him so, the near-forgotten beauty of his touch enough to make everything around her fade into oblivion. A rushing like the wind roared in her head, feverish heat scalding her flesh as her body turned compliant. So long, she thought, an eternity since she'd known this. She wanted, needed it never to end. She reached up a hand, stroked her palm over his lean jaw, his dear, beloved face.

Suddenly, he pulled away and she was free. She stood confused, bemused for a long, odd moment as voices buzzed like bees in her ears. For an instant, he'd made her forget who she was, forget their troubles, forget why they no longer lived as husband and wife.

A wave of intense heat swept through her, Violet finding herself embarrassed to be the cynosure of all. Then an arctic blast chilled her as she caught the grim set of Adrian's eyes.

An act, that's all it had been. Nothing had changed between them, nothing at all.

Giving a giddy laugh as though this were the happiest Christmas of her life, she pasted a beaming smile on her face, then crossed to the pianoforte to encourage another song.

Inside her heart wept.

Brilliant rays of sunshine cheered an otherwise damp, blustery January day. Violet lifted her face to the light, drinking in the radiance that gleamed brightly yet lacked any kind of essential warmth.

Rather like her life these days.

She shivered beneath her thick woolen cloak as she walked in the Winterlea gardens. Cold not in a physical sense but in an emotional one instead.

Lonely.

She was unutterably lonely; the house finally still after weeks of relentless, frenzied activity. The family had departed days ago, returning to their separate homes, their separate lives. Even the dowager duchess had left for the dower house, with promises to visit again when the weather turned more clement in the spring.

Kit was next to go. His University examinations awaited him, then the start of the new term. Assuming, of course, he passed the required tests. She had wished him luck, offering one or two final suggestions for what he ought to study. She watched, a lump in her throat, as her friend and only true ally rode away.

Adrian departed last. Urgent business in London, he claimed. But she knew the real reason. He wanted to get away from her, from their unhappiness. He'd made no pretense of inviting her along. And he'd strictly forbidden her from traveling anywhere on her own.

If she really were Jeannette, his edict would have sent her flying out of the house, if for no other reason than to prove she could. But no matter how she might pretend, she was not her sister. Anyway, where would she go? Lonely as it might seem, the estate was her home now.

She ought to be relieved Adrian was gone. Being alone with him was a misery, even in a house as massive as Winterlea. Yet his absence left a frightful void. They might not be on speaking terms these days, but still there was an odd sort of comfort in knowing he was near. A chance to catch a glimpse of him in one of the hallways, to hear his voice as he spoke to his secretary or one of the staff. And the nightly agony of sitting in silence as they dined, pretending to ignore each other down the length of the dinner table.

Now even that small contact was gone.

A year ago she would have reveled in her solitude. Plenty of opportunity to sleep and daydream. A world's worth of time to study and read without a single interruption or reproving word. Yet now that she could do all those things, they fell flat.

She'd written to her friend Eliza, giving some offhand excuse to explain away the lack of a foreign postmark. Jeannette was forwarding the missives for her, she'd said, so they wouldn't go astray. If Eliza found the delivery system strange, she didn't remark upon it, pleased to have reestablished their friendship, even if it was only through correspondence. What Violet would do when her twin finally returned to England, she hadn't yet puzzled out.

Otherwise, there was little to keep her busy around the house. The new housekeeper, Mrs. Litton, was a true marvel of efficiency. Warm and personable, but not above setting down a firm hand when needed, the tiny, no-nonsense whirlwind of a woman was an utter gem.

Dissatisfied with the "goings-on," as Mrs. Litton called them, at the new Marquis of Hartcourt's establishment—he being a distant relation who had inherited after her longtime employer passed away—she had been eager to find a new position. Unlike with Mrs. Hardwick, Violet had felt immediately at ease with the motherly woman. Without interviewing even one other applicant, she'd hired her on the spot.

If not for the older woman's expertise, Christmas would no doubt have degenerated into a disaster. Instead, it had been effortless. The housekeeper had aided her in anticipating everyone's needs, often before they were expressed.

In the garden, Violet paused to admire a bed of Lenten roses. The hearty winter-blooming plant added a refreshing dash of color to the otherwise dormant landscape. She leaned down, plucked a single blossom of dusky cream.

So pale and fragile, she mused as she let it rest in her gloved palm. By day's end, the petals would be wilted, their beauty nothing but a memory.

Is that all she was to have now? Memories? Was she to have nothing more than a brief taste of happiness as transitory as this flower?

Would Adrian ever forgive her without knowing the full truth?

Would he forgive her if he did?

She stared at the flower for another long minute, then crushed it inside her fist. When she opened her palm, a gust of wind carried away the remains, leaving her hand as empty as her heart.

"Another brandy, your Grace?"

Adrian glanced up from his silent ruminations. The White's Club servant stood at a respectful distance, awaiting his answer.

"Hmm, yes, Hoskins, I believe I will."

The man bowed, picked up Adrian's empty snifter and withdrew.

He ought to have refused the draught, Adrian chided himself. He was drinking far too much these days. He knew it, but couldn't seem to stop himself, drowning his sorrows a far easier solution than confronting them. What he should do was get up out of his chair right now, go home and get a good night's sleep. Trouble was, sleep had lately become his enemy. When he did try, he usually ended up staring restlessly into the dark. Or else he fell into a shallow doze, plagued by disturbing dreams of her, of Jeannette.

He needed to shake himself out of his brooding gloom and get on with his life as best he could. What was he doing here anyway, rattling around London in the dead of winter? He hated the city this time of year, cold and slick, void of any decent company. Although lately he wasn't fit for company, decent or otherwise.

Her betrayal had seen to that.

The staff at home was concerned, he knew. They'd taken to treading softly in his presence, tossing him worried looks they didn't think he saw. It was one of the reasons he'd come out to his club. No one to gawk at him here. No one to whisper and wonder about the problems between him and his duchess.

They all knew, of course. How could they not when

he and Jeannette barely spoke, no longer shared a bed, lived as husband and wife in name only.

His brandy arrived. He thanked the servant, then took a hearty swallow. The alcohol left a pleasant numbness in its wake.

Damn her, he thought. And damn him for still caring.

A man entered the room. He glanced up and had the unfortunate luck of catching Mortimer Landsdowne's owl-eyed notice as the other man surveyed the room. Downey Landsdowne—so named because of his soft, plump physique—made straight for him.

Blister it, he thought, there'd be no getting away now. He didn't even have a newspaper to hide behind.

"Raeburn, didn't know you were in Town. Deuced time of year to be visiting our capital city." Downey made himself comfortable in the chair next to Adrian's, ordered a libation when the waiter approached.

"Business takes no notice of the seasons," Adrian dissembled.

"Quite true, quite true. Nor family. Came up about m'wife's youngest brother. Got himself in a bit of a fix at the card tables, wouldn't you know. It's all been put to rights now, though. I'm taking him back home with me tomorrow." Downey swallowed a hearty sip of the claret that had been placed at his elbow, as if in dire need of fortification. "Did that lovely wife of yours join you?"

"No. She remains in Derbyshire. As you said, this isn't the best time of year for travel."

"Well, you must be anxious to return home. You still being newlyweds and all, eh? How was the honeymoon, by the by? Where was it you went again?"

"Dorset. I believe you provided some historical background and suggestions concerning sightseeing locales to the duchess."

"Your duchess?" Landsdowne's eyebrows rose. "Can't

say as I recall such a conversation, though I do tend to prattle on a bit wild at times. Dorset, you say?"

This time it was Adrian's turn to raise an eyebrow. "Yes, Dorset. You shared the history of Corfe Castle with her at our wedding reception."

"It wasn't me. Never heard of the place. Matter of fact, I've only been to Dorset once. The seashore at Brighton's more to my liking. Must have been some other fellow did the talking."

"Yes, you must be right," he murmured, positive he correctly remembered his long-ago conversation with Jeannette. At the time, she'd been very specific, mentioning Downey Landsdowne by name. Telling how he'd cornered her at the reception, bored her into a near coma with his discussion of the area.

"Can't think I'd discuss history with your wife anyway," Landsdowne continued. "She's not one to suffer through such tedious discussion without complaint. More likely find yourself cut off mid-sentence before she'd let one prose on too long upon such matters." He twitched a finger. "Sounds more like something her sister would do. Now, that one, that twin of hers, she's a real bluestocking. Thrives on that sort of heavy academic talk, history, literature, even languages."

A strange buzzing started in Adrian's head. "Languages?"

"Hmm, from what I hear, she's fluent in several, including the classics. She can read and write the stuff, both Greek and Latin, as unnatural as that may seem for a female."

An image of Kit's note popped into his mind, the inexplicable Latin translation he'd purloined from his brother's pocket a few weeks ago. A note Jeannette had passed to Kit.

Downey kept chattering.

Adrian heard his words as if from a very great distance.

"Reason I know so much about Lady Violet is from my cousin Harriet," Landsdowne volunteered. "The old gal and your sister-in-law both belong to the same ladies' literary society. Attended a number of lectures together. Harriet says Lady Violet is a model of self-education, knows as much as most scholars. Isn't any wonder she hasn't found a husband. She may look and sound exactly like your wife, but I've never seen two females so markedly different in every other way. You picked the right one of that pair, I'll say."

Suddenly an astounding idea took Adrian by the throat.

No. Impossible. It couldn't be true. Or could it?

"I say, Raeburn, are you all right? You've gone pale of a sudden. Has something disagreed with you?"

Disagreed? Yes, one might put it that way.

He lurched out of his seat. "You must excuse me, Landsdowne. I've only just remembered an urgent matter of business. I . . . ah . . . must bid you farewell."

"Oh, well, of course, old man. Don't concern yourself a bit on my behalf. Happy here with my claret."

Adrian strode out of the room, Downey Landsdowne forgotten the instant he turned his back.

"My coat," he ordered as he paced the club's front foyer.

"I'll call for your carriage, your Grace," the butler said. A page rushed forward with his garment.

He shrugged into the heavy greatcoat. "Tell my man to go home. I've decided to walk."

"Walk, your Grace? At this hour?"

He paid him no heed, hurrying down the stairs into the frigid night air. His long legs ate up the ground beneath him, his surroundings hazy, his mind in a whirl.

The idea was insane, preposterous. It couldn't be possible. His wife, Jeannette, could not be another woman. Could not in reality be her sister, Violet. Twins or not, a switch of such magnitude and daring would be beyond even their capabilities. Especially Violet's, who'd never been able to do more than stammer a few shy words at him at best.

No, he was mistaken.

Yet the more he considered it, the more probable the idea became.

Memories plagued him. Inconsistencies he'd shrugged off at the time, put down to nerves or exhaustion, or sheer moodiness. But now that he considered it, when had Jeannette ever been nervous about anything?

He remembered their wedding day. How she'd trembled, her skin blanched white as milk, her eyes large and startled as a doe caught in the woods, frozen as if too frightened to flee.

And their wedding night. Her maidenly reticence, her innocent touches and untutored kisses. *Her virginity.* He'd been so ashamed of his behavior that night, he'd dismissed all the signs, the signals. He'd lulled himself into seeing what he wanted to see instead of what had been there all the time, staring him right in the face. It was as if he'd had on a big pair of rose-colored glasses.

He stopped in his tracks.

Her glasses.

My God, how could he have been so blind? So stupid? Dear Lord, she really *was* Violet. Why else would she wear reading glasses? Why would she retreat to her study every afternoon to bury herself in perfect contentment? Why would she pass notes to his scapegrace brother—written in Latin, no less?

Holy Mother of God, he'd married the other sister!

He started walking again, the shock of the revelation sinking in. What an imbecile he was. What a gullible moron. A man who couldn't tell the difference between two sisters. He supposed the fact that they were so alike physically gave him some excuse. But as Landsdowne had pointed out, the two women were as different as the sun and the moon when it came to personality.

When had they made the switch? Before the wedding, obviously. He realized now Violet had been the one trembling next to him at the altar. But why?

Jeannette, of course. How she must have congratulated herself on her trick, on their trick. Duping him into marrying another woman. Even now Jeannette was in Italy, posing as her twin.

Of course, it all made complete sense. Jeannette's unhappiness about the canceled honeymoon to the Continent. Her week of tears and grumblings that she had so nicely recovered from after the wedding ceremony. Even at the time, he'd thought her sudden equanimity rather odd. Only it hadn't been, not for her, not for Violet. No wonder *his wife* hadn't complained.

And all this time she'd played out her lie. All this time she'd let him believe she was another woman. Sharing his life, sharing his home, sharing her body.

Raw fury gushed up inside him, his throat tight and burning. His feet pounded harder, faster against the pavement.

Kit.

Kit must know about her. Why else would he have sprung so readily to her defense? He really must love her. What other reason could he have for concealing the truth of her identity?

Adrian felt sick. A piercing ache lodged near his heart.

He stopped, stared absently at the entrance to his townhouse. For a long moment, he didn't realize he'd arrived home.

The front door opened. "Your Grace?"

He gazed upward at Smythe, the underbutler who'd

accompanied him on this journey. In sudden decision, he jogged up the stairs. "Tell Josephs to have the coach ready by first light. We'll be leaving for Oxfordshire at dawn."

He wanted answers, and by God, he planned to have them soon.

Chapter Nineteen

❧

"Out with it," Adrian demanded. "I've had enough of your excuses. I want the truth."

Kit closed the door to his University lodgings, closeting himself and his brother inside. Harold, his roommate, had scurried off only moments after Adrian's arrival. One look at the duke's face had been enough to send the younger man running, mumbling some excuse about his urgent need to study in the library. Kit wished he could have fled with him. Letting Adrian inside his rooms in his current humor was rather like inviting in a thunderstorm.

"The truth about what?" Kit asked, careful to keep his tone mild. He ambled across the room, took a seat by the window, as far out of harm's way as he could manage.

"You know what. My wife."

"I thought we weren't to discuss that topic again."

"Don't be flippant. Tell me about her." Adrian slammed his fist against the wall. The small equine painting that hung over Kit's bed rattled in its frame. "Tell me who she is."

Kit froze in surprise, choosing his next words with care. "She's your wife. Who do you imagine her to be?"

"*Not* Jeannette." Their eyes met, held, jousting like swordsmen. "Tell me if I'm right. I have to know."

Kit drew in a breath. "She's not Jeannette."

Adrian sank down upon the only other chair in the room, collapsing as if suddenly deflated. "How long have you known?"

"A few months. Violet preferred I not say anything."

Adrian's jaw clenched at the mention of her name, a muscle ticking beneath his skin. "No doubt she did. And would you have kept her counsel indefinitely? Didn't you think I might wish to know that the woman I've been living with all these months is an imposter?"

"She begged me not to tell you. At the time you both seemed happy, so I agreed to leave the decision in her hands. Perhaps it was an error on my part."

Adrian's silence hung between them like an ominous cloud.

"She loves you, you know." Kit leaned forward, gestured with a hand. "If it hadn't been for that blasted letter, none of this would have—"

"Ah, yes, the letter. I'd like to hear about that. Perhaps now you'll tell me who authored the damnable thing, since you say it wasn't you."

Kit lowered his eyes. "It was Markham."

"*What?*"

"Toddy Markham. Seems he and Jeannette were romantically involved prior to your marriage. The note was for her. He didn't realize it was Violet he was pursuing in London either. At least not until that evening in the Lymondhams' conservatory."

Adrian surged to his feet, striding like a caged beast, to and fro, in the small confines of the room. "The bastard. No wonder he could never find the man Jeannette was secretly meeting. He told me, did you know, that he suspected her of seeing someone else. No doubt he was trying to warn me off, hoping I'd cancel the wedding. To think it was him all the time. I ought to wring his lying, no good neck."

"You'll have to go to the Continent to do it. Blighter

left for Italy when he realized the truth about Jeannette."

"Hell and damnation, am I the only one who doesn't know about their switch?"

" 'Course not. Just Markham and I know, and her sister, of course."

"Of course." Adrian continued to pace, fists opening and closing at his sides.

"What do you plan to do now?"

Adrian stopped, faced him. "I haven't yet decided, but whatever it is, I'll thank you to stay out of it."

Kit raised his hands in a sign of surrender. "Wouldn't dream of interfering." He paused. "Don't be too hard on her, though. She has a good heart in spite of the mistakes she's made."

"Why is it you're always so ready to leap to her defense? Is it because you have feelings for her?" Adrian swallowed, his words low and choked. "Do you love her?"

"Love Violet?" Lord, Adrian was jealous, Kit realized. And besotted, to boot. "Yes, I do love her."

Adrian stiffened, his back ramrod straight.

Kit continued. "I love her as a dear friend and as a sister. In only a few months, she's become closer to me than any of my own sisters. Maybe because of our similar ages. Maybe because she helped me when I needed help. I passed my examinations, by the way, due in large measure to her. I don't know what it is about her for sure. But I do know this, you're a fool if you drive her away. She may not be perfect, but she suits you down to the ground. You'll never find a better woman than her."

Adrian pulled on his gloves. "See to it your term goes well. No infractions."

"Don't worry. Being sent down once was lesson enough for me."

Adrian nodded, then he was gone, striding down the corridor.

Kit could only hope his brother was headed toward his salvation and not his doom.

Two days later Violet entered Adrian's study at Winter-lea.

"You wished to see me, your Grace?" She smoothed a nervous palm over the skirt of her Clarence blue poplin day dress and hovered in the doorway.

He didn't look up from the letter he was writing, quill moving rapidly over the page.

She stiffened, wondering for the hundredth time why he had summoned her here.

Adrian had arrived home yesterday afternoon, yet this was the first she had seen of him. He'd made no effort to greet her upon his arrival and he'd failed to put in an appearance at dinner last night. The extra plate she'd had set for him had gone unused.

Finally, he laid down his pen. "Have a seat, madam." With barely a glance, he gestured her toward a chair. It was set in the center of the room, facing his desk.

She hesitated, then walked forward, feeling like a schoolgirl called before the headmaster. She sat, hands folded in her lap. "What's this about, Adrian?"

He looked at her, his eyes polar. "A few questions have come to light that I need to ask you, nothing more."

She did her best to relax, racking her brain as she tried to think what those questions might be. Perhaps some matter concerning the estate, or a bill that required explanation. She had purchased several new gowns during their time in London. Perhaps he disapproved of the cost.

"I found this missive." He extended a narrow sheet

of well-creased paper. "Perhaps you can enlighten me as to its contents?"

She had to lean forward in order to grasp it. "What is it?"

"You tell me."

"My pardon, but I'll need to put on my spectacles."

A muscle twitched in his cheek, an odd gleam sliding into his eyes. "By all means."

Fighting the sudden need to tremble, she reached into her pocket, slipped on her eyeglasses. She opened the letter.

An electric tingle ran down her spine. The note was written in Latin. It was one of the translations she'd prepared for Kit. She had no difficulty recognizing her own handwriting. Where had he come by this? She took a deep breath, forced herself not to panic.

"I'm sorry, but I haven't the faintest idea what this says." She nudged the note onto the edge of his desk. "It's written in some foreign language."

"Latin." His voice sliced like steel.

"Really? Is that what it is? Darrin used to struggle at it when we were children. I remember how he complained."

"You don't recognize the note, then?"

Her heart skipped a beat. "No, I don't believe so. Should I?"

"You gave it to my brother. I saw you do so over the Christmas holiday."

Dear Lord. "I don't recall," she lied. "I'm s-sorry."

"Seems these days there are a great many notes of which you fail to recall the origin, madam." He stood, walked around his desk. "Perhaps you'll have better luck with this one." He held out a single sheet of paper, crisp, folded precisely in half. "Read it."

Blood beat at her temples, her throat so constricted

she could barely swallow. Her fingers shook as she accepted the note. He moved away.

The office door closed. For an instant, she thought he'd left the room. But her relief was short-lived, sensing him as he waited somewhere behind her. She repressed the urge to peek around.

Knowing she had no choice, she opened the letter.

Five words, written in slashing black ink, leapt off the page.

I know who you are.

She blinked, trying to fully comprehend. Air whooshed out of her lungs as if she'd been hurled to the ground.

Suddenly, he was there, his lips against her ear. "Hello, Violet," he said, his voice silky as the devil's.

She jumped, then tried to rise from her seat. He held her in place, his fingers biting bruisingly into the flesh of her arms.

"Don't you have anything to say?" he demanded.

She flinched, tears springing to her eyes.

"Don't bother turning on the waterworks, madam. Your tears will have no effect on me."

He released her, circled around. "Well, have you nothing to say now that we both know who you really are?"

Her lips opened, but no sound came out.

"I talked to Kit, if you're wondering. And yes, he finally divulged the truth of your little ruse, so there's no point in trying to convince me I'm mistaken about you." He leaned down, thrust his face close to hers. "Speak. You didn't have any trouble chattering incessantly when you were pretending to be Jeannette."

She sniffed, her whole world shattering around her. "Adrian, I'm s-sorry."

"Sorry you've been caught, you mean."

"Yes. No. Oh, please, you don't understand." She

reached out a beseeching hand but he pulled away from her. "It's not what you think."

"It's exactly what I think. You and that harridan sister of yours conspired together to deceive me. No, don't tell me. She decided she didn't want to go through with the wedding on the morning of the ceremony and talked you into taking her place. I see by your expression I'm right. Was it the impending scandal or the money that made you do it? Or did you secretly long to be a duchess and couldn't pass up the golden opportunity that fell suddenly into your lap? All you had to do, after all, was prostitute yourself by pretending to be another woman."

She recoiled as if he'd slapped her, gripping the carved wooden arms of her chair for strength. "I did it because I loved you, and have done from the moment I first saw you," she said, her voice low and tremulous. "It was wrong, I know that, but I hoped I could make you happy. For a time, I think I did."

"You satisfied my lust, madam. What man wouldn't have been happy with that?" he drawled in a sardonic tone.

She knew he'd said it to hurt her, and he'd succeeded. She closed her eyes, fought to steady her tumultuous emotions. Then she looked at him again, pleading. "I realize you're angry, and you have every right to be. You've been deceived in the most basic of ways. I'm not the woman you thought I was. I'm not the woman you chose. But I am your wife and I can be still if you'll only let me."

"Are you my wife?"

"What? What do you mean?"

"We completed a ceremony together but you took vows using a false name. The banns read were for your sister and me, not for you."

"I signed my real name on the register."

He raised a brow. "How daring and unexpectedly forthright of you. But I doubt it will make any difference legally. Truly, I don't know which one of you I'm married to. *If* I'm married to either of you at all. My guess, my dear, is that you and I have been living in sin all these months. Which makes you little better than a kept woman in the eyes of the law and Society."

She felt the blood drain out of her cheeks.

"Are you pregnant?"

"What?" she asked, dazed, her thoughts reeling.

"I asked if you are pregnant. I want to know if I can expect my firstborn child to be a bastard. Assuming it would be *my* child."

She gasped. "I've never been unfaithful to you, I told you that. The note you found was meant for Jeannette, not for me. She . . . she was seeing someone else before the wedding."

"So I have been informed. My little brother is a wealth of information."

"I swear you are the only man I've ever been intimate with."

"In that, at least, I believe you." He leaned a hip against his desk. "So? Are you?"

"Am I what?"

"Pregnant. Are you with child?"

A flush heated her cheeks. She wished she were. She wanted his child, knew instinctively it might be enough to hold him. But she couldn't lie to him anymore, and in this there would be no concealing the truth.

"No." The single word rasped from her throat like a small death.

"That's a relief. At least we won't have to worry about ruining the life of some poor innocent child."

"Do—" She swallowed convulsively, then cleared her throat. "What do you intend to do about me?"

His eyes grew somber, reflective. "I don't know. I haven't decided yet."

"Let me stay, then." She moved without conscious thought, rising up out of her chair to fling herself against him. She wrapped her arms around his waist, pressed her face to his shoulder. "I beg of you not to send me away. I know you may never be able to forgive me, but I love you. In that, I've never lied. If you let me stay, I promise I'll be whatever you want, whomever you want. I can go on pretending to be her, if you can't stand the thought of me. No one will ever have to know."

He gripped her shoulders, pulled her back far enough to gaze into her eyes. "But *I* will know. And so would you. You're right about us being happy, for a while we were. But it was just an illusion, a part of your deception. The woman I believed was my wife doesn't exist. She's a fiction, a deceit. You're not the sweet girl who once stood weeping over a litter of drowned kittens, so shy she could barely say my name. And you're not your twin, I see that all too clearly now. You're really nothing like her. You're . . . well, I don't know who you are. But you've lied to me, used me, made a fool of me in ways I don't think I can ever forgive."

He pried her away, set her aside as if her touch disgusted him. A bleakness stole through her like a hollow wind, leaving her numb inside.

He retreated behind his desk. "I must consult my solicitor concerning the legal status of our union. I hesitate to call it a marriage, since I doubt that's what it is. Should I be in error on this point, suitable arrangements will be made. Otherwise . . . well, we shall see. It may prove necessary to consult your parents. I assume they are unaware of this matter?"

Slowly, as if viewing it all through a fog, she nodded.

"Very well, then. You may go."

And that was that. Interview over. Her life as she'd

known it, done. All that remained now was waiting to receive her punishment, her sentence.

She stood motionless for a long, long time, adrift inside her despair.

Agnes appeared suddenly at her elbow. Had someone rung for her? She heard Adrian speak, something about her being unwell. She kept her eyes lowered. She couldn't bear to look at him, not now, not anymore. March spoke, hovering around her in grave concern, then she was led from the room, led upstairs.

Her maid dressed her in a warm nightgown, tucked her into bed. The drapes were drawn against the bright afternoon sun. Horatio gave a single bark. Since her troubles with Adrian had begun, the dog had become a fixture in her rooms. Trailing after her during the day, sleeping with her at night.

He padded over to the bed, tunneled his cold, wet nose beneath her limp palm and whimpered in concern.

She curled toward him. Then she began to cry.

She spent the entire day in bed, hoping if she slept long enough, she would wake to find it had all been a horrible dream.

She rose the following morning, moving on bare feet to one of her bedroom windows to gaze out over the lawn. What she saw made the nightmare real. The traveling coach waited on the drive below.

Adrian was returning to London.

She clutched the curtains, her nails digging into the material as she watched him step into the vehicle. A muffled thud reverberated as the door was shut, the footman springing up onto his perch. Then Josephs snapped the whip and set the horses in motion.

A wash of pain squeezed inside her chest as the coach disappeared from sight.

Agnes bustled in a short time later, bearing Violet's usual morning tray. Putting on a cheerful show, the maid worked and talked. She laid out a lovely rose-colored day dress, matching slippers and a woolen shawl meant to keep away the drafts.

Violet choked down a few bites of toast, drank enough tea to keep it from sticking in her throat. Listless, she let Agnes help her bathe and dress for the day.

With Horatio trotting at her side, she wandered through the house, aware with each step that she no longer belonged, no longer had a right to call herself mistress here. If what Adrian suspected was true, she'd never even been his wife, duchess only by virtue of her ruse. Even now she could barely comprehend the fact that all of it, even their marriage, had been a lie.

She strolled into the portrait gallery, studied the faces of Adrian's ancestors. As she walked the long passageway, she noted the changing fashions and hairstyles, the similarity of a feature here and there.

Lawrence's magnificent portrait of Adrian hung in a central location. The painting had been completed not long after Adrian's ascension to the dukedom. Reed slender, only nineteen years old, he had not yet grown to his full maturity. How innocent he looked, she thought. How serious too as he posed out-of-doors, standing beside a favorite horse, Winterlea's tree-lined lake in the distance. He'd been weighed down by responsibilities even then, forced to accept duties that might have felled a lesser man.

A new portrait was to have been commissioned in the spring, along with a companion painting of her as his duchess. There would be no new paintings now, and the next time she saw him would likely be her last.

How many days, she wondered, before he returned to deliver the verdict? Before he banished her from his life forever? Agony tightened in her breast at the thought.

She'd shamed him, she admitted now, besmirched his heritage, his family, his name. The fact that she'd never intended to do so made little difference. Worse, she'd made an utter fool of him, and of herself. She'd demeaned herself, begging him to keep her, hoping against hope he might love her enough to forgive. But she should have known better. Theirs had always been a one-sided affection. She'd known the risks, now she must pay the price.

Waiting here like a dutiful wife would no doubt be the expected thing under the circumstances. But suddenly she didn't feel very dutiful. The idea of being returned to her parents like a naughty child who'd been caught in the act made her shudder.

An idea sprang fully formed into her mind, fear and desperation adding inspiration. No, she told herself as the thought took hold, she couldn't. But she had to look after herself now, didn't she? Adrian had made it clear he wanted nothing further to do with her. Once he returned, she would be dead to him. And she knew her family would feel the same.

Acting on instinct, she gave his portrait one last wistful look, then spun on her heel and hurried from the room.

"You may, of course, count upon my utmost discretion in this matter, your Grace. I shall file the appropriate motions once her Grace . . . that is, once Miss Brantford signs the annulment papers." Horace Jaxon of Jaxon, Jaxon and Pritchard, attorneys-at-law to the Dukes of Raeburn for three generations, handed a thick packet of documents across Adrian's desk to him.

"Legally the annulment shouldn't constitute a great deal of difficulty. From what you've told me, your marriage was invalid from the start. A true name must be given during the reading of the banns, which in this case clearly did not occur. However, since there was a true signature made in the register at St. Paul's—I went to the cathedral myself just two days past to examine the document—her Grace . . . pardon me again, your Grace . . . Miss Brantford must agree to the annulment."

"And if she refuses?"

"Then the issue would need to be argued before the court. A closed session with a single judge should suffice. Either way, the marriage will be dissolved with her consent or without."

Jaxon closed his leather satchel with steady fingers, little slowed by age. "The ecclesiastical courts must also be consulted in this matter. I've taken the liberty of broaching the subject with Bishop Canterly, a most knowledgeable and trustworthy individual. You've only to give your consent and he'll begin the annulment process."

Adrian nodded. "You may advise him of my consent."

"That concludes our business for today, then, your Grace. I'll leave you to your work." Jaxon rose from his chair, smoothed a palm over his thinning white hair. "If I may, your Grace, please allow me to convey my condolences on this sorry state of affairs. Most unfortunate, most unfortunate indeed."

Adrian gave him an implacable stare. "Thank you for your time, Jaxon. I shall be in touch. Smythe will show you to the door."

The attorney bowed, satchel clutched in a tight grip. He followed the servant, who appeared wraithlike at the office door.

Adrian shoved the packet of papers aside after Jaxon had gone.

Intolerable, he thought. Forced to discuss his personal life with a gaggle of bishops and lawyers. Compelled to reveal intimate details of his sham of a marriage, publicly expose his own gullibility and shame. Once the annulment was complete, he would be forced to endure worse. There would be little chance of concealing the news that he was not, and never had been, legally wed to either of the Brantford sisters.

All of Society would be agog. Astonished by the twins' deception, tittering over his inability to tell one woman from the other. He could only imagine the ribald jests it would spawn in the clubs and elsewhere. His hands curled into fists as fresh anger flooded through him. God, what a mess.

Jeannette and Violet would be ruined, of course. Particularly Violet, since she was indisputably damaged goods. He could almost pity her if he didn't know firsthand what she'd done. If he hadn't witnessed the brazen acts and deliberate falsehoods she'd perpetrated with such consummate skill.

He still couldn't fathom how she'd done it. She'd fooled not only him but everyone else, even her own parents. She'd deceived Society as well. A fact the Ton would not soon forget or forgive.

As for himself, he'd buried whatever love he'd once believed he felt. If a wound lingered, leaking a bit of blood now and again, it would heal. In time.

He would forget her too. In time.

He could always keep her, he supposed, to avoid the stigma of scandal. Marry her in a secret ceremony. Pay off the lawyers and ministers to keep their silence, then bundle her off to some remote location where she could live out the rest of her days in obscurity and solitude. Perhaps that would be the more prudent path. Yet he couldn't bring himself to give her that sort of satisfaction. To let her reap any kind of reward for the disgrace and pain she had wrought.

As for her sister, the beautiful, mendacious Jeannette,

she would do well never to let him set eyes upon her again. If she was really smart, she'd stay in Italy and lure Markham into marrying her. Toddy didn't have a farthing to his name, it was true, but under the circumstances perhaps money would matter less to her mercenary little soul than respectability.

He groaned and laid his head in his hands. Why had Violet done it? Had she really thought she could dupe him forever? She claimed to love him, but he couldn't let himself believe her. How could he believe anything she'd said or would ever say again?

Well, soon it wouldn't matter. Once she signed the papers—and by God, he would see to it she signed them—he'd pack her off to her family. Let them decide what was to become of her.

After that, he'd begin putting his life back together. Maybe he'd travel for a while. He owned a sugar plantation in the Caribbean. A few months baking beneath the hot, tropical sun might be exactly what he needed. He could sail. He'd heard glowing reports about the place. Crystal clear waters, magnificent blue skies and beaches lined in soft, pink sand.

There, England and all its misery would be a world away.

She would be a world away too.

Chapter Twenty

Adrian returned to Winterlea at the end of a two-week absence.

In his possession he carried the annulment papers from both the Church of England and the English courts. His visit would be brief, only long enough for Violet to sign the documents, pack her belongings and accompany him to her parents' estate in Surrey. Once there, he would explain the situation, then depart. Any further legal matters concerning the disposition of the marriage settlement could be argued over among their respective solicitors.

Upon his arrival, he changed clothes, ate a light meal and flipped through the stack of correspondence that had collected while he'd been away. When he could delay the interview no longer, he rang for March.

"Would you be good enough to ask my . . . um . . . wife to join me in the drawing room," he ordered.

Posture rigid, utterly formal, the majordomo fixed his gaze on a spot just past Adrian's shoulder. "I am afraid I cannot do that, your Grace."

Adrian scowled. "What do you mean you can't do it?"

Disapproval radiated off the servant in an icy wave.

In fact, since his arrival, he had noticed a distinct coolness emanating in his direction from the entire staff.

"I mean that the duchess is not in residence at present, your Grace."

"Beg pardon? What did you say?"

"Her Grace is not in residence—"

"Yes, yes, I heard that. Where did she go? Is she out visiting someone in the neighborhood?"

"No, your Grace."

"Then where the devil is she?"

"As I informed you, I do not know. Her Grace packed some of her belongings nearly a fortnight ago and left with her maid and her dog."

"A fortnight! And she took Horatio?"

"Indeed. She requested a carriage and had Warton drive her to a coaching inn in Derby."

His scowl deepened. "Then what?"

"She ordered him to leave. He, being rightly concerned for her well-being, insisted upon waiting until she and her maid were safely aboard the mail coach. Apparently there was a small difficulty about the dog, but she resolved it by purchasing all the seats."

"And he let her go?"

"Yes, your Grace. Short of manhandling her, there was little he could do to prevent her departure."

His blood raced with fury and something else, something worse.

Fear.

Where could she have gone? Unfortunately, he didn't need to ask why she had gone.

"In which direction was she traveling?" he demanded.

"South, I believe. Bristol was the destination her driver mentioned."

Bristol? Who could she know in Bristol? But, of course, she didn't know anyone there, he realized, the town was merely an embarkation point. From such a busy hub, she could journey anywhere in England. Anywhere at all.

"Why was I not contacted immediately?"

March hesitated for the first time. "She most specifically requested that I *not* contact you. Perhaps it is not my place to say, but the recent difficulties between you and her Grace have not gone unnoticed by the staff."

"You're right, it's not your place. You know nothing about the nature of our difficulties."

March straightened. "I know the duchess was near tears when she left. I know she has been abjectly despondent since that day she had to be escorted from your office. She requested that I give this to you." He brought forth a letter.

Adrian seized it. "I arrived here nearly two hours ago. What in the world took you so long to produce this?"

March turned a baleful eye upon him. "I wanted to see how long it would take you to notice that her Grace had left." He gave a clipped bow, then departed.

If good old March hadn't worked for the family since his father's day, Adrian might have dismissed him on the spot for his insolence. Instead he turned on his heel and stalked into the drawing room, where he'd planned to present Violet with the annulment papers.

He went to the window, stood where the sunshine provided the best light. He opened the letter.

Adrian,

When you read this I shall be gone. I have taken Agnes and Horatio with me; they shall provide adequate protection during my journey. I shan't tell you my destination, although I presume you no longer care where I go so long as it is away from you. Do not worry that I shall presume upon you again. I know you must hate me now. I hate myself for deceiving you, for bringing shame upon you and your

family. It was never my intention to cause you harm.
I know what I did is unforgivable and that I shall
spend the rest of my life trying to atone for the wrong
I have caused. Yet I would be lying if I claimed to be
wholly repentant. Love is what led me to make the
choices I did, and for that alone, I cannot regret the
time I shared with you. There are far too many beau-
tiful memories to cherish for that.

   I hope my father will repay the marriage portion,
though to my further shame I must warn you it is
likely spent. I have taken only a few personal belong-
ings. The rest I have left, including my wedding and
engagement rings. If we are not married, as you be-
lieve, then they were never mine to wear at all.

Please be happy.
Violet

He read the letter twice, finding not so much as a hint
of where she might have gone.

He crushed the note in his palm, stalked to the drawing room door. "March!" he bellowed. "Assemble the
staff. I wish to speak to them. Every single one."

Six weeks later, as Adrian walked through London, he
was no closer to locating Violet than the day he'd
learned of her disappearance.

Like a man possessed, he'd searched everywhere for
clues, starting with the servants. He'd questioned them
all, even the gardeners and the scullery maids. But no
one knew anything relevant, each and every one volun-
teering how much they adored the duchess, how they
were praying for her safe, speedy return.

He'd rifled her rooms, pawing through every drawer
and cabinet and wardrobe. He found her rings, remem-

bering the way they'd looked upon her slender hand. And the necklace he'd purchased for her, the one he'd once dreamed of seeing around her lovely neck as she lay in his bed. As she'd stated, she had taken very few possessions: a few clothes, a hairbrush, a toothbrush and other assorted toiletries. If he'd needed any additional proof of her identity, seeing all the beautiful gowns arrayed like a rainbow in her wardrobe was enough. The real Jeannette could never have countenanced leaving such elegant garments behind.

Frustrated, he'd driven to Derby, to the inn from which she'd departed. He questioned the hostlers, the innkeeper, a server who had brought her and her maid tea while they waited for the mail coach to arrive. They remembered her; not many ladies of quality stopped by, especially ones with dogs near the size of a small horse. Not a single one of them, though, had any notion where she'd gone.

Greasing a few palms over the next two weeks—including that of the mail-coach driver who'd taken the noteworthy trio on board—he managed to trace her as far as London.

After that, she'd vanished like a wraith.

He'd spent several days in London, visiting all her usual haunts, despite the futility of the attempt. Dolefully, he realized the places were mostly Jeannette's haunts and not Violet's. Without giving away his true intent, he'd probed a few of her friends—Jeannette's friends—for information. Nothing again. He'd even sent a query to her parents, concocting a tale about her calling upon friends in the Surrey area, and had she dropped by for a visit? Of course, she had not.

Finally, after swallowing a rather large measure of pride, he'd made a return visit to Oxfordshire to see his brother. Kit had given him a laconic stare, demanded details, then shook his head in sad derision.

No, he'd said, he hadn't seen her, wasn't harboring her and didn't know anyone else who might be. Then he asked a question of his own.

If Adrian truly despised Violet and wanted nothing more to do with her, why was he so desperate to discover her whereabouts?

Kit was right. Considering her wrongs, why did he care so much about finding her? She'd lied to him, used him, humiliated him. By rights, he should hate her. He did hate her.

At least, that's what he kept assuring himself.

Her disappearance ate at him, though, wondering where she was. What she was doing. Whether she was safe and healthy. Happy.

He dreamed of her nearly every night. Sometimes she was in terrible danger. Lost, penniless and frightened, at the mercy of some villain as she cried out for help. Failing to arrive in time, he would jolt awake. Skin damp, heart racing, he would stare into the darkness, his thoughts full of her.

Other nights the dreams were both sweet and seductive. Violet—he thought of her now as Violet—coming to tease him, tempt him, delight him. They felt so real, those dreams. *She* felt so real. And for a brief time she would be his again the way she had been in those first few wonderful months. Waking from those dreams was worse, his body stiff with unsatisfied desire, his mind haunted by the knowledge that even against his wishes, he wanted her still.

Yet how could he reconcile those needs with what she had done? For months he'd believed her to be Jeannette. She'd done everything in her power to deceive him. But now that his initial anger no longer burned so hot, he could look back and see the many ways she clearly had not been like her sister.

Her innocence. Her shyness. Her pretty, becoming

blushes. The forays into the library she'd thought he hadn't noticed. Her acceptance of his duties, understanding that he couldn't dance attendance upon her at all hours of the day. The peaceful quiet companionship she'd offered many an evening. Her kindness to the staff. Her appreciation of simple pleasures, nature, music, art. Her love for a great oaf of a dog who many others would have left to a life of misery and despair.

Looking back, he didn't know how he could have missed all the signs. Perhaps he'd wanted to miss them, afraid to see the truth. Afraid if he did, he would have to acknowledge what a mistake his original choice of wife had been.

Jeannette, the real Jeannette, would have made him miserable.

Violet had made him happy. And he'd driven her away.

Where was she? England surely wasn't so large an island that one small woman could not be found. Unless she was no longer in England. Had she gone to her sister? Were the two of them even now basking beneath the glow of a warm Italian sun?

He stopped, glanced up, only then realizing he'd arrived at Hatchard's Bookshop. He'd been so busy woolgathering, he'd scarcely been aware of his progress along the streets. He walked inside, a bell chiming birdsoft at his entrance.

He'd ordered a number of books some months ago; they'd finally arrived. While the clerk went to retrieve them, he wandered into the stacks to examine the other offerings.

A young woman turned at his footfall, glancing up from a book she had been perusing. She sank into a deep curtsey. "Your Grace, how do you do?"

He bowed. "Miss Hammond. I did not realize anyone else was here. Foot traffic is generally light this time of day."

"Yes, I know, that's why I like it." She paused, an awkward silence developing as the import of her admission sank in. She moved to cover the gaffe. "How is your family?"

"Well, thank you. And your own?"

"Fine. My aunt and cousin are currently debating the wisdom of remaining in the city. The expense of another Season, you see."

He did see. This would be Eliza Hammond's third attempt at the matrimonial mart. To his knowledge, she had not received a single offer all of last Season. He was about to find a polite way to end their conversation, when she issued a statement that riveted his attention.

"I had a letter from your sister-in-law," she said.

"From Violet?" Or did she mean Jeannette?

"Yes. She continues to enjoy the Continent. She and her great-aunt recently relocated to Rome and find the city most amiable. She says they will likely return to England soon."

"Did she? What good news."

"Please thank your wife, by the way, when next you see her. She has been most kind to forward Violet's letters to me."

A buzz arced through him. "Has she been? I was unaware."

"Oh, yes, for a few months now. I assume you will be joining her in Dorset once your business is concluded here in the city."

"Dorset?"

Eliza scrunched her brow. "That is where I have been sending my letters of late. She said she'd gone to the shore for a visit, to the lovely house you own there."

A rushing noise roared between his ears. Violet was at the house in Dorset. *My God.*

He hurried to cover his lapse. "Quite right. She went south for a few weeks. I plan to join her directly."

Most directly, he promised himself.

"Well, my purchase must be ready by now," he continued. "A pleasure, Miss Hammond." He bowed, turned away quickly. He raced from the shop, his book order forgotten, the clerk gawking at his abrupt exit.

Horatio loped through the grassy patches that dotted the cliffside fields, pausing every now and again to sniff at an interesting scent before racing on. Violet followed behind him at a more leisurely pace. A chill, stiff wind plucked at the pins in her hair and ruffled her skirts like some impish sprite bent on mischief. She didn't mind, letting the wind have its way, the tempest a perfect foil for her desperate, melancholic mood.

In the distance, the sea churned, whitecaps riding high atop steel blue waves as they raced toward the shore. The afternoon sun did its best to shine, without much luck, obscured by thick lumbering clouds that turned the sky a dingy gray.

After several minutes more, she called for Horatio, his ears flagging to attention. "Come, boy. Come here." The dog streaked toward her. It was time they were returning home, she mused. It was time she was moving on as well.

Facts were facts, her life with Adrian was through. Somehow, no matter how frightening the thought, she had to make her own way in the world, find the courage to act, to go on. She couldn't hide here forever, much as she wished she could.

When she'd arrived in a hired hack nearly two months before, accompanied only by her maid and her dog, the Grimms had taken her in with nary a question. Souls of discretion, they'd barely blinked at her request to say nothing to the duke about her stay. Ever the mother hen, Mrs. Grimm clucked and fussed, preparing a good, hot meal, coaxing her to eat when she would have only picked.

Rooms were prepared. One for Agnes in the servants' quarters. The master suite for her; the same room where she'd spent her honeymoon. Memories rushed at her from every corner, crowded with images of sweeter times past. Of Adrian when he'd still looked at her with desire burning in his eyes. When his cold hatred hadn't chilled her to the bone.

His memory was everywhere. In every room. Outside on the moors. In her bed at night as she cried until sleep overcame her.

She should never have come here, she knew.

Yet the house proved a comfort as the weeks passed.

Desperate, she hadn't known where else to go. Her parents were out of the question. Once they found out what she had done . . . well, she shuddered to consider.

Her brother would merely laugh if she applied to him, then turn her out.

As for Jeannette, her sister could offer her nothing, not even shelter since she had no property nor money of her own.

And Great-aunt Agatha would give her away, demanding to know why she'd fled England and left her husband. Before Violet knew it, Agatha would be writing letters to every acquaintance she knew.

No, there was no one in her family who would aid her.

She considered Kit. But as a single man—and a student at University—he wasn't in any position to help, even if he would.

As for her friend Eliza, even if Eliza forgave her all the lies and took pity, she could not aid her, since she, as an unmarried woman, lived wholly dependent upon her own relations.

Terrifying as it might seem, Violet was alone in the world.

With that in mind, she'd spent the past two months considering her options. She had a small amount of money saved from the generous monthly allowance Adrian had given her. If she lived frugally it could be made to stretch for several months. After that, she would need to acquire some sort of employment. Agnes would have to be let go, of course. She would write her a glowing letter of recommendation.

And Horatio. Her heart tore at the thought of leaving him behind, but what other choice did she have? He ate as much as a growing boy, and even if money were no consideration, his size was. Finding lodgings would be a problem with him in tow. And if she hired on as a companion or a governess, they would never let him come along. She would send him to Winterlea with a note asking Adrian to care for her dog. No matter how much he might despise her, she knew he would not be so cruel as to turn his anger against a helpless beast. Horatio would be cared for.

She paused in her walk, dropped to the ground beside the huge dog. She hugged him, laying her cheek against his warm, smooth flank. Eyes squeezed shut, she fought the bout of tears that threatened to overcome her.

When she'd recovered her emotions enough to escape comment from Mrs. Grimm's shrewd gaze, she rose and continued onward. The house came into view over a slight rise, gleaming like gold in a stray patch of sunlight. Then she saw the coach in the drive, the ducal crest emblazoned on its side.

She stopped dead, her heart kicking like a mule inside her chest.

Adrian had found her.

Chapter Twenty-one

He was waiting in the main parlor when she came inside.

She took her time removing her cloak, tidying her hair, resetting pins as she checked her reflection in a small mirror down the hall. The murmur of Adrian's deep voice floated to her ears. He was speaking to Horatio, who had rushed into the parlor in an exuberant dash the instant he realized Adrian was there.

Pinching her cheeks to put some color in them, she adjusted the spectacles she'd once again taken to wearing, then straightened her shoulders. She could do this, she told herself. She *would* do this and not fall apart. She'd made a fool of herself in front of him once. She did not intend to do so again.

Horatio's tail was still wagging when she walked into the room. He turned, padded up to her on huge paws, a big doggy grin demonstrating that his allegiance to her was as strong as ever. She stroked his head and sent him over to lie down near the fireplace.

A tea tray had been brought in, courtesy of Mrs. Grimm, an extra plate and cup laid for her use.

She glanced around the room, looking everywhere but directly at him. Finally, she spoke, aware she could postpone her greeting no longer. "Your Grace."

"Violet."

How odd it sounded, after all this time, to hear her

name on his lips. What she would have given, once, for him to speak her name and know who she truly was. Now that he did, she regretted the price at which that knowledge had come.

"How did you find me?" She moved farther into the room, striving to be her most elegant. She refused to cower.

"Tea first, I think." He crossed to the tray. "You look chilled."

"No, thank you." Her stomach lurched at the thought of food or drink.

Ignoring her, he lifted the pot. "Mrs. Grimm informed me you were out walking the cliffs."

"Yes."

Why was he being so polite? She'd expected anger or at least cold civility from him. Perhaps the worst of his outraged affront had faded during her absence. Perhaps in the intervening weeks, he'd come not to care at all.

Uncertain how long her legs would continue to support her, she crossed to the chair farthest from him and sank gratefully downward.

"Your tea." He extended the cup.

She accepted, pointedly set it aside. What did he want? Why was he torturing her? Why didn't he simply say whatever it was he'd come to say and have done with it. "Who told you I was here?"

He took a seat. "Your friend Eliza Hammond."

Her gaze flew upward.

"Forgive her. She didn't realize she was giving away your secrets. I happened upon her quite by accident in London. She mentioned she'd had a letter from you, sent from Dorset."

"I knew I should not have written her, but of all people, I never thought she'd have an occasion to tell you." She folded her hands together in her lap to keep them still. "Does everyone know? Have you told the world about me?"

He raised an eyebrow. "No. With the exception of my solicitor, one bishop and a few of their most discreet assistants. I was compelled to contact them concerning the validity of our marriage."

A lump swelled in her throat. She stared at her shoes. "And?"

"It is as I suspected. We are not legally husband and wife. Our marriage is invalid. Annulment papers have been prepared to make it official."

A last faint glimmer of hope went dark inside her.

"You gave me quite a turn, you know," he said, "when I arrived at Winterlea and discovered you'd run off. I was justifiably furious."

"You had my letter from March?"

"Yes, he gave it to me along with his opinion that I've been a brute to you. The remainder of the staff appears to agree."

"You will send my regards to them, I trust? Explain how sorry I am to have deceived them the way I did." Abruptly restless, she rose from her chair, crossed to stand at the window and stare out over the wind-tossed landscape. "I'll sign the papers and be gone tomorrow," she said, desolation plain in her voice.

"Where will you go?"

"North, I think, Yorkshire or Scotland, perhaps. They shouldn't be as fussy there about references and such. I hope to secure a position as a governess with a suitable family."

"What about your own family?"

She whirled. "I won't go back. Don't try to force me. They'll only cast me out again the moment you leave. I've never had the easy relationship you share with your mother and siblings. Once they learn what I've done, the shame I've caused, they'll want nothing more to do with me. I will be disowned, as good as dead to them."

"And Jeannette?"

Her lips quirked. "Jeannette is Jeannette. She will be fine."

"It won't work, you know," he said after a pause. "Your plan to become a governess."

"I fail to see why not. I am well educated for a female. I no longer fear to conceal that from you. I know languages: Italian, French, Spanish and a smattering of German."

"Don't forget Latin and Greek."

"Quite right," she acknowledged with a nod. "But those are boys' languages and I doubt they will come in much use, particularly if the family is in Trade. I know mathematics, geography, history and literature. I don't sew well, but I paint a fair picture and my penmanship is excellent. My credentials are exceptional."

"Your credentials won't be the issue."

"What, then?"

"Your looks."

She raised her chin. "What is wrong with my looks?"

"Nothing. And that will be the problem. No wife, once she sees you in the flesh, will let you anywhere near her family. The husband would be far too tempted."

"You never were." The bitter words gushed out before she could stop them. "All you could ever see was my sister."

He came toward her. "You're wrong. I did see you, even hiding behind your glasses. But I thought you were too shy."

"To be your duchess, you mean?" She gave a hard half laugh. "Apparently you were mistaken."

"Apparently I was. About a great many things."

She closed her eyes, turned her head to stem the tears

that abruptly threatened. "I don't blame you for hating me," she said in a throaty whisper.

He stepped closer. "Do you not? Funny thing that, much as I've tried to hate you—and believe me, I have—I can't seem to acquire the knack of it."

Her eyes sprang open, a tear sliding down her cheek.

He reached out, smoothed it away with his thumb. "Don't cry."

A fresh tear followed, then another, his kindness proving her undoing. Suddenly, she was in his arms. "Adrian, I'm sorry. I'm so sorry," she sobbed against his shoulder.

He cradled her near, rocking her against him. "Shh, it's all right. Don't cry. Don't cry, my dearest." He feathered kisses over her temple, rubbed his palm over her back in wide, soothing circles.

He held her until the flood subsided, tucking a handkerchief into her palm so she could mop at her eyes. She blew her nose into the silk in a most unladylike fashion, then nestled against him, exhausted.

They stood, quiet, in each other's arms for a long while.

Finally, he spoke. "Did you mean it?"

She sniffed. "Mean what?"

"When you told me you loved me? Is that truly how you feel, or was it merely a sop to ease my wounded feelings?"

Her gaze flew upward to meet his. "Oh, Adrian, can't you see for yourself? I adore you. That has never been a lie. If you believe nothing else, believe that."

"And if I asked you to leave?"

Her breath caught in her lungs. "Then I would leave. Is that what you want?"

He pressed her tighter, fit his cheek to hers. "No, I don't want that at all. I'm so grateful you came here, that you ran away. If you hadn't, I fear I would have made the biggest mistake of my life, by letting you go. I love you, Violet." He pulled far enough away to meet her eyes. "Shall we start over? Start afresh, no more untruths, no more lies between us?"

"Yes, if I'm the one you truly want. You said you didn't know me, couldn't tell the real me from the act. Are you sure you're in love with the right woman?"

"I never loved your sister, I know that. I think perhaps that's why I didn't question the differences between the two of you, the woman I courted and the one I wed. I was far too pleased, basking in my unexpected good fortune. I never dreamed I would feel this way about anyone, but I know I love you. Whatever else I need to know I can figure out along the way."

He bent to kiss her and bumped his nose against her glasses. He grinned. "I believe we'll start with these. Do you mind?" He set his fingertips against the wire frames.

She shook her head, giving her consent for him to remove them. Closing her eyes as he slid her spectacles free, she quivered at the sweet pressure when his lips merged with her own.

Ah, it had been so long. A lifetime. An eternity. How she wanted him. How she'd missed him. How she loved him. Bliss flowed through her, knowing in that moment she held everything she would ever want right here in her arms. He lifted her, fit her against him as hunger burned between them like a bonfire.

Her thoughts scattered, her limbs growing loose and liquid, completely his as she gave everything she was into his keeping. "Take me upstairs," she sighed.

He loosed her only long enough to tug her in his wake, their hands clasped as they raced on shaking legs through the house.

Horatio followed, whining in disappointment when they locked him out.

But all they could think about was each other. Being

close again. As close as two human beings could possibly be. They undressed one another slowly, reverently, taking their time to savor the sensations, dwell in the anticipation of the delight they knew was to come.

Seconds slowed to hours as they exchanged long, languid openmouthed kisses. Thoughts whirled, pulses hammered in syncopation. Hands glided in sleek, velvety strokes. Each inch of flesh caressed as it was exposed, clothing fluttering forgotten to the floor.

The fire burned low in the grate, casting a faint chill over the room. Neither of them noticed, too heated by their own inner fires, too lost in mutual passion and pleasure to care.

When they stood naked, he turned her around and reached for the pins in her hair, plucking them free, one at a time. He cast the pins after the clothes, letting them cascade to the carpet in a silvery rain. Sinking his fingers into her thick tresses, he massaged her scalp until she purred with pleasure. Tingling head to toe, she stood acquiescent, quivering, as he combed out her long locks, arranging them down her back, then over her shoulders. He slipped his hands beneath her veil of hair, cupped her breasts.

She covered his hands, held him there, as she basked in a heaven of carnal joy, his scent and her own saturating her senses. He slid one hand downward, riding over her belly, her hip and thigh, journeying lower still to part her tight curls and dip inside with a honeyed touch.

"I love you, Violet."

She came on that single endearment. Her toes curling into the carpeting, shuddering as she gloried under the skill of his touch, as he spoke her name in tones of love and longing.

Violet.

He said it again and again, as he drove her body higher. Propelling her up and over, and up and over once more, until she sobbed out her satisfaction and hung weak and quaking in his arms. He kissed her neck, her cheek and ear before he swung her around and crushed her mouth to his in a fevered mating, dark and wet and wonderful.

They sank to the bed.

She expected him to take her. Instead he played, savored, explored, leading her on an exquisite journey of passion, of ardor, of joining unlike anything she'd ever known.

When he came into her, finally, gladly, it was as a homecoming. An awakening. She gave him everything she possessed. He gave her everything in return. In those warm, intimate moments, lying beneath the spreading shadows of a waning sun, they took flight, locked in a love that righted all wrongs, forgave all transgressions.

In the quiet aftermath, they curled together on damp, twisted sheets. He pulled the covers over them, then lay stroking her hair, pressing languid kisses to her skin.

She smiled, flushed and floating, eyes closed in pure contentment. Less than a minute later, her eyelids flashed open. "Adrian, I just remembered."

"Remembered what?" he asked, his voice lazy, his body lax.

She sat up. "We're not married."

He crooked an eyebrow. "By Jove, you are right. And considering what just transpired in this bed, I believe we have good reason to be." He stroked a palm down her arm, over her bare breast, an impish twinkle lighting his eyes. "Unless, of course, you'd rather be my mistress?"

"Adrian!" Her cheeks heated.

He guffawed. "From your expression, I assume that option is out."

She thrust her chin into the air. "Indeed it is."

He laughed again, leaned up to kiss her. "Good, because I don't want you any other way than as my wife."

He rolled out of the bed, caught her hand to tug her so she sat on the edge of the mattress. Without warning, he lowered himself onto one knee, and naked as a babe reached for her hand.

She tried to pull away. "What are you doing?"

He clasped her hand tightly. "What I should have done the first time. Ask the right woman to marry me."

Her lips formed an O as his meaning sank in.

"Jannette Violet Brantford," he intoned in a solemn voice, "you are the brightness of my day. The sweet warmth of my night. The only woman I have ever known who could turn my entire world upside down and leave me glad she did. Perhaps we didn't begin precisely as we should. But, well, we are, both of us, human, and humans sometimes make mistakes. I promise to forgive you, if you swear to do the same for me when the need might arise. I love you. It took me some time to understand that, but I do now. I vow to spend the rest of my days showing you how much. Please say you'll make me the happiest man on earth and consent to be my wife."

A tear trailed down each of her cheeks as she smiled, lips trembling. "That's the most beautiful thing I've ever heard anyone say. Yes, oh yes, of course I'll marry you." She launched forward, looped her arms around his neck and smothered his face with kisses. "I love you so. I'll never give you cause for regret."

"And I shall have none, ever."

He laughed, crushed her mouth to his in a heady embrace. When they came up for air, breathless, he steadied her and rose to his feet. He crossed the room.

"One last thing." He returned, carrying a small, square jeweler's box that he'd dug out of his coat pocket. Opening it, he revealed a gold band set with the most vibrant purple amethyst she'd ever seen.

"It's beautiful, but why?"

"It's your engagement ring. The emerald was meant for another woman. This is expressly for you. It's not as expensive a stone, but I thought it suited—"

She sprang up, hurled herself into his arms. "I adore it. You couldn't have gotten me anything better. It's violet, like me."

He grinned, slipped the ring onto her finger. "That's right, and I'll never be in doubt of it again."

Five days later, they were married by special license in a small church on the outskirts of London. The ceremony was brief and extremely private, Kit the only family member in attendance. As soon as he'd been sent word, Kit had ridden down from Oxford, proud and pleased to stand as Adrian's best man.

The minister's wife, a friendly soul with a figure as round and soft as a peach, served as second witness. Impromptu weddings were her favorite, she cooed, her blue eyes a-twinkle. Such couples, she observed, were always deeply in love.

And she was right this time as well. As Violet joined hands with Adrian to recite their vows, their eyes met and held. Love shining plain for anyone to see.

"I, Adrian Philip George Stuart Fitzhugh, take thee, Jannette Violet, to be my wedded wife . . ."

"I, Jannette Violet, take thee, Adrian Philip George Stuart Fitzhugh, to be my wedded husband . . ."

Solemn words once spoken in duty and dishonor took on new meaning, expressed now in joy and devotion.

She did not tremble, her nerves rock steady. She had nothing to hide now, nothing to conceal.

And when Adrian slipped the ring onto her finger, he repeated her name—Violet—in a firm, clear voice that no one could mistake or misunderstand.

Now truly husband and wife, Adrian kissed her. And came up for air only after the minister loudly cleared his throat, his graying brows beetled in reproof.

She and Adrian laughed, his eyes twinkling, her color high.

The small wedding party repaired to a modestly decorated parlor, where cakes and tea awaited them.

Kit told amusing stories as he ate his way through the contents of the tea tray, much to the bemusement of the minister's wife.

A few minutes before they were ready to depart, Adrian drew the minister aside. Without delving too deeply into his reasons, he explained the need for silent discretion concerning the nuptials just performed. He would regard it, he said, as a personal favor if the minister and his wife were to say nothing about the ceremony should anyone happen to inquire. A healthy donation to the parish coffers and a handshake sealed the deal.

Prior to the ceremony, he'd taken care to make similar arrangements with his solicitor. Jaxon had moved swiftly to clear up all remaining legal difficulties resulting from Adrian and Violet's less than proper first marriage. Other individuals privy to the truth had been sworn to secrecy.

Ceremony concluded, the three of them returned to Raeburn House in London for a quiet, celebratory dinner.

Afterward, Kit said his farewells and set out for Oxford.

Hours later, Violet lay in Adrian's wide bed, flushed and radiant from lovemaking. Mentally, she reviewed the events of the past few days. "Do you think we're doing the right thing?"

He linked their fingers together, entwined hands cradled upon her belly. "About what?"

"Keeping my identity secret. Having me continue to pretend to be my sister."

He shifted slightly, angling his head to see her face. "It's what you wanted. Have you changed your mind?"

She remembered how firm her resolve had been only two days past. She'd argued her case to Adrian in favor of continuing the charade. He'd argued back. Willing, even eager, to let the truth be known to the world. She was his wife, he told her, his rightful duchess. Everyone from family to friends to casual acquaintances should know it.

But she had urged silence, fearful of the dreadful scandal the admission was sure to cause. She and Adrian had, after all, been living in sin all these months, even if they hadn't known it at the time. Even if they were now legally husband and wife.

For herself, she didn't care what other people thought. She could live out her days quite happily at Winterlea with her husband and her books and the children she hoped to have one day. Even if Society did its worst and shunned her as punishment for the impropriety of her actions, for having made fools of them all. Her true friends, like Eliza, would forgive her. At least they would once they got over the initial shock.

But there were other people's feelings to consider. People who would be affected by what she had done, whether they wished to be or not.

Her parents would be shocked, mortified. Likely, her mother would retreat to her rooms for a month or more. Her father, of course, would spend all his time riding and hunting—his two favorite pursuits—scarcely affected by the uproar to all outward appearances. But in the end, the damage would be done. Quite probably, many of their most influential friends would drop them. And trips to London, excursions that had once been so pleasant, would become an ordeal neither would be willing to endure.

Darrin, she suspected, would laugh off the entire misadventure. Then resume his usual profligate activities with newfound gusto, dusting up several minor scandals of his own.

And Jeannette . . . well, Jeannette would emerge battered but unbowed.

Then there was Adrian.

Although she had refrained from voicing her fears to him, knowing he would brush them aside, she worried most of all for him. By some blessed miracle, he had forgiven her.

Others might not be so kind.

Through her actions, she had cast a stain upon his name, his reputation. And despite his solid standing with the Ton, there were those who might choose to disassociate themselves from him.

Adrian would argue he cared nothing for such people, self-righteous, moralistic hypocrites every one. Yet if he hoped someday to pursue high political office, as his mother predicted, Violet ached to think she might be the sole cause of his failure.

So, to save them all a world of embarrassment and shame, she had convinced Adrian to stay silent, to keep their secret.

She rolled, leaned up to brace her forearms against his chest. "I haven't changed my mind. I know there may be difficulties. But I think it's best, for everyone, if we say nothing."

"What about your sister? What if she should wish to wed? What then?"

"Then she'll have to tell the man. Together they'll have to decide what is best."

He huffed out a breath. "I still think we should admit the truth, even if it would upset a great many people.

But since you're so opposed, I'll agree to continue the masquerade. But only when we're in Society. Here at home, you are to be yourself, fully yourself, is that understood?"

"Yes, your Grace, fully understood."

He brought his palm down across her bare bottom in a light, playful swat. "Don't be smart."

She laughed. "But I'm always smart, or hadn't you noticed?"

There were half a dozen books in three different languages scattered around the room, left on various tables and chairs. Since her return a few days before, she'd openly taken to reading again, though lately she hadn't had much time.

She leaned over, lifted her spectacles off the nightstand, slipped them onto her face. "There, I am being myself." She threw a leg over his hips, straddled him. "What do you think?"

His eyes heated to a deep, melted brown, swept up and down her naked form in obvious appreciation and undisguised lust. "I think those glasses have a hidden appeal I've never entirely appreciated before."

He smoothed his palms up over her thighs, then wrapped them around her hips to reposition her in a way that forced a moan from between her lips.

"Let's leave them on," he murmured as he fastened his mouth to her breast, "while we explore the issue in greater depth."

Chapter Twenty-two

Winter melted into spring. Tender green shoots thrusting from the dark, moist earth to blossom and thrive, spreading color and life onto every square inch of land. Animals shed their heavy coats for cooler, lighter ones. Birds sang joyous songs to welcome in the warmer days.

At Winterlea, the estate bustled from dawn to dusk. Gardeners and undergardeners tended the grounds, caring for old trees and young spring plants alike. Carpenters, painters and masons covered the great house like an industrious team of ants, making various small repairs to keep the property in its usual tip-top condition. While, inside, Mrs. Litton commanded the staff, sending them forth like a small army to do a thorough spring cleaning for the upcoming festivities.

In only four days' time, guests would begin to arrive for the house party Violet was throwing. Invitations had been sent out to neighbors, family and a few dozen close friends—most of whom would be in attendance only for the spectacular ball taking place on the final night. The celebration was being held in honor of Adrian's thirty-third birthday, and would mark Violet's very first solo foray into formal entertaining.

She listened now to the murmur and bustle of housemaids as she passed near the main ballroom. Several maids were down on hands and knees scrubbing and polishing the intricate parquet floors. While others un-hooked the heavy midnight blue velvet draperies, carry-ing them outside into the fresh air to beat them free of dust.

She couldn't deny a certain jittery fluttering every time she thought about the coming event. But hosting such an ambitious undertaking had been her idea.

All her idea.

When she'd broached the notion to Adrian, he'd urged her in a gentle voice to wait a few months. Begin with a small party at summer's end, he'd said. When the gentlemen could shoot, and the ladies might amuse themselves out-of-doors, dabbling at watercolor paint-ing or practicing their archery.

But Jeannette would already have hosted one party by now, if not more. And although she was under no pressure to do the same, Violet wanted to prove she could—to Adrian and to herself.

He said he didn't care about entertaining, and she be-lieved him. But she was his duchess, and being the Duchess of Raeburn came with certain social duties and obligations. She needed to live up to those responsibili-ties. Particularly now that he knew who she really was. She never wanted to give him reason to regret his choice. Above all, she wanted to make him proud.

And there was one more reason as well.

If what she suspected was true, she might not feel like hosting a party in late summer. If what she hoped was true, she would, by that time, be growing round with Adrian's child.

She put a hand to her belly, wondering, dreaming. She'd missed her flow at the end of last month and was now almost three weeks late. Always in the past, it had come quite regularly, like clockwork. If she went an-other week, it would be twice missed and she would know for certain.

Only then would she tell Adrian.

Of course, she was dying to tell him now. But if it turned out to be a false alarm, she didn't want to disappoint him by having to say there was no baby, after all. Besides, she'd decided the news would make a wonderful birthday present. If everything went as hoped, she planned to share her glad tidings with him the final night of the ball.

She hugged the knowledge to herself. Her thoughts drifting away into daydreams as they were wont to do these days, a silly grin lighting her face.

A half hour later, just as she and François were finishing their final review of the menus, a knock sounded on her study door.

She lifted her gaze toward March, who waited in the open doorway.

"Visitors have arrived, your Grace. Your family is here."

"Dearest, it's so wonderful to see you," her mother declared, enfolding her in a warm, gardenia-scented hug.

March had put them in the family salon upstairs, all four of them: her parents, Darrin, who stood by the window wearing his usual expression of boredom, and Jeannette—or rather, "Violet"—whose appearance came as a small shock.

Fashionably dressed, though still more conservatively garbed than the real Jeannette would ever have chosen for herself, her twin looked distinctly unhappy. Subdued, mouth turned downward at the corners, her eyes dull and sullen, half-hidden behind the square-cut spectacles perched on her nose.

And that came as the most surprising sight of all. Jeannette was still wearing "Violet's" glasses.

Violet returned her mother's embrace for a long moment, then pulled away. "It's good to see you too. Adrian and I weren't expecting you for a few more days."

The countess moved to take a seat on the wide sofa. "Well, that was our original plan, but it's done nothing but rain in London for the past week. So we decided to come up early and surprise you. Are you surprised?"

"Yes, very. But pleasantly so. Let me ring for tea and have your rooms prepared. You must be tired from your journey." She crossed to the bellpull.

"Fair number of ruts in the road," her father complained from where he sat sprawled in one of the wing chairs. "Must remember to have a word with Raeburn about that. Can't have people's coaches rattling apart on the way to and fro."

"As you say, it has been a wet spring." She knew first-hand that Adrian kept his own road in excellent condition. He'd had teams of men out only a few days past filling holes in the driveway with dirt, sand and rocks. She decided not to remark that Adrian had no control over the main roads, since she knew her father would only scowl and grow more irritable. He got that way when he was hungry.

"How is London?" she inquired as she took a chair across from the sofa. "I've been quite anxious for news of all the goings-on."

Jeannette moved silently into place beside their mother. Darrin maintained his stance at the window, brooding outward.

"The Season's been off to a slow start this year, though I can't say why," her mother began. "Hilary Asquith's chit is out. Whey-faced girl, shouldn't think she'll take at all. And the DeBrett child. Good complexion, tolerable eyes, but that voice. Lord, when she laughs it sends shudders down your spine. If her mother is wise, she'll advise her to keep her mouth shut until she finds a good match."

"And Italy. You haven't told me about all your grand adventures, Violet."

"Violet" looked up, an odd glint sparking in her gaze. "Italy was very pleasant. Aunt Agatha sends her regards."

And that was all.

What had happened in Italy? she wondered. Jeannette's first few letters from the Continent had been glowing. Then Toddy Markham had learned the truth, left for the Continent. There'd been no letters since. Had it gone badly between them? Was that the reason for Jeannette's less than sunny demeanor?

The countess patted Jeannette's hand. "I have great hopes for our Violet this year. Several gentlemen have seemed quite taken with her. And she's finally decided to show some interest in her wardrobe. Isn't this color most becoming?" Their mother nodded toward the peach-and-white-spotted India muslin Jeannette wore.

"Exquisite." She forced a further show of interest. "What modiste did you employ?"

"Lord save me from all this feminine folderol," her father cursed, scowling. "Where is that husband of yours?"

"Adrian rode out this morning with his estate agent, Papa. To inspect some tenant properties, I understand. He said he would try to return in time for tea, which I believe has just arrived."

A pair of maids entered the room, bearing two heavy silver trays stacked with refreshments.

"About time," the earl grumbled, perking up at the sight of food.

Darrin wandered over to take a plate.

Jeannette accepted a cup of tea and a single wafer-thin slice of Westphalia ham on a tiny biscuit. Nothing more.

"Not hungry," Jeannette murmured at Violet's questioning gaze.

Violet sipped at her own cup, her stomach lurching at the scents of deviled eggs and cold beef pie, which everyone else proclaimed delicious.

Further proof, she decided, that she might be in the family way.

Then Adrian arrived.

She shared a broad smile of welcome with him. He'd changed clothes, she saw. When he bent to press a brief kiss upon her lips, she caught the pleasant scent of shaving soap that lingered on his skin.

He turned to greet her family.

He went first to her mother, exchanging a warm, familial hug and words of welcome. Next, he shook hands with her father, then her brother. Both men managed somehow to tear themselves away from their plates long enough to obey the dictates of good manners.

Finally, he turned to Jeannette.

Adrian hesitated, shoulders stiff. Violet didn't believe anyone else noticed his reluctant displeasure.

Jeannette held out her hand.

He bowed over it, quick and perfunctory. "Lady Violet."

If Jeannette heard the razor-edged tone as he said her "name," she gave no indication, her smile pretty and sweet. "Your Grace. Or may I call you Adrian? We are brother and sister now, after all."

"As you will, my lady."

Duty done, he accepted the cup of tea Violet prepared for him, moved to take a seat on the sofa directly opposite the one on which Jeannette and the countess sat.

Adrian played the polite host, entertaining them all.

As he spoke, smiled and laughed, Violet noticed he barely glanced at Jeannette.

By the time Mrs. Litton arrived to escort them to their rooms, a line had settled between Jeannette's brows. She might be pretending to be Violet, but if there was one thing Jeannette could not abide, it was being ignored.

Thankfully, Jeannette held her tongue.

As the family moved after the housekeeper into the hallway, Jeannette slipped up next to Violet. "Come to my room this evening," she whispered. "We need to talk."

She met her twin's eyes for an instant, nodded a quick agreement before Jeannette moved away.

A familiar hand slid over Violet's shoulder moments later. "What did she want?" Adrian asked.

"To speak to me in private."

"No doubt she chafes beneath her role. Perhaps we should simply confess the truth to your family and end this farce."

She turned, gazed up at him. "No. All will be well, you'll see. Something happened in Italy. She's unhappy in a way I've never seen her."

"Hmm, that's exactly what worries me. Your sister is just spoiled and selfish enough to find a way to take her misery out on you. I don't want her ruining your enjoyment of this entertainment you've worked so hard to arrange."

"She won't. I won't let her." She rested her hands on his chest. "I love you. You love me. And nothing she says can disrupt our happiness."

"I wouldn't be too sure of that, but very well." He sighed. "I suppose she is your sister, and I'll have to resign myself to seeing her upon occasion."

"Yes, you will. And do your best not to ignore her completely. It only incites her ire."

"Good. She deserves feeling a bit of ire now and again." He leaned down, pressed his lips to hers, slow and sweet. "Still, I suppose I should be grateful to her."

"How so?"

"If she hadn't convinced you to switch places, I might be married to *her* now." He gave an exaggerated shudder.

She laughed, and looped her arms around his neck to bring his mouth back to hers for another long kiss.

It was late, the house grown quiet for the night, when Violet knocked softly upon her twin's bedroom door.

Jeannette peeked out. "Where have you been? I thought perhaps you'd decided not to come." She pulled the door wide for Violet to enter.

"I was delayed," Violet said as she crossed the threshold. "Mrs. Litton needed to discuss arrangements for tomorrow's breakfast. Then I had to change out of my evening gown."

They eyed each other. Both wore nightdresses and robes, their long hair brushed and tied back with ribbons. They were identical except for the color of their attire; Violet in deep blue, Jeannette in creamy white.

It brought back memories of their childhood days when they'd slept in the third-floor nursery, whispering together well after their bedtime. Often Nanny had to come in to shush them for their disobedience.

But they were grown women now, free to do as they wished. The days of girlish camaraderie long since past.

Jeannette gestured toward a chair. "Sit, sit. I have something for you."

Violet perched on the chair's edge and waited. "You didn't need to bring me anything."

Jeannette burrowed through some of the clothes in her portmanteau. "Don't be silly, of course I did. I wanted to. Here." She thrust out a small box, tied with a length of jonquil-colored ribbon.

Violet paused briefly, then accepted it. She opened the box, to reveal an intricately carved pin nested on a bed of velvet. "A cameo. It's beautiful."

"You like it?"

She traced a finger over a tableau of tiny birds and flowers carved into the carnelian oval. "It's exquisite. How could I help but like it."

"I knew you would." Jeannette beamed. "I found it in a small shop in Tuscany and immediately thought of you. I barely haggled with the shopkeeper over the price, I just had to have it."

"Well, thank you. It's gorgeous. Truly." She rose and gave her sister a hug. "I love it."

"Let's see how it looks." Jeannette fastened the brooch onto Violet's robe. "Perfect."

Silence fell between them.

"So, is the gift why you asked me here?" Violet asked after a time.

"Of course. And to visit," Jeannette added.

"Visit?"

"Yes, it's been almost a year since we've seen each other. I thought we'd chat. Can't a sister just want to chat?"

The notion took Violet by surprise since she and Jeannette had stopped sharing late-night confidences many years ago. "All right. What should we discuss? Italy, perhaps? You've barely mentioned your trip."

Jeannette sighed. "I haven't mentioned it because there's little to say. Except for some tolerable shopping, there's virtually nothing to do there. Aunt Agatha and I traveled around, looked at ruin after ruin, castle after castle. We ate strange foods with strange-sounding names like linguini and cannelloni. Half the time, we sat fanning ourselves against the heat and beating the pollen off our skirts from all the odious olive trees."

"From what you said in your letters, you seemed to be enjoying yourself. I thought there were a great number of parties and entertainments for you to attend."

"There were, and at first I did enjoy myself. But the novelty soon wore thin."

"No fascinating suitors? What about that prince you mentioned?"

Jeannette fluttered a dismissive hand. "I had plenty of suitors—even pretending to be you. They prowled around my feet like a pack of yowling tomcats."

"But you weren't interested?"

"I have no wish to inure myself permanently in such a hothouse of a country."

"So you missed England?"

"Of course I missed England."

"And nothing else occurred?"

"What do you mean?" Jeannette demanded, her eyes narrowed.

"Toddy Markham. I know he went to Italy to find you. Did he?"

Her twin rounded on her. "Pray don't mention that cad's name in my presence ever again. He's a contemptible swine. He's so low he doesn't even deserve to lick the bottom of my shoes. He . . . he—" She broke off, unable to continue. A tear trailed down her cheek.

Violet hurried to wrap an arm around her sister's shoulders. "Shh, you must tell me what he did to hurt you. Is that why you seem so unhappy? I couldn't help but notice."

They sank together onto the bed.

"I thought he loved me," Jeannette cried. "He said he couldn't live without me. Then he met *her*." She dabbed at her eyes with the edge of her robe. "The Contessa d'Venetizzo. Overblown Italian cow. She arrived at a

masquerade Markham and I were attending, and she seduced him away."

"I don't understand. Why would he suddenly change
his mind, switch his affections so abruptly?"

"I don't know," Jeannette moaned. "Because he's a
beast, a black-hearted, money-hungry beast. I can't remember all the particulars now, but I may have mentioned the fact that, as you, I would receive almost
nothing for a dowry. And as myself it wouldn't be much
better. Apparently he didn't realize Papa's pockets are so
badly to let. He envisioned a large settlement if we were
to marry. I said there would be none. After that, well, his
eye began to roam, and it landed upon her."

"Jeannette, I'm sorry." She reached out to lay a comforting hand over her sister's.

Jeannette shook off her touch, jumped to her feet.
"She's a rich widow. Young, and some claim, beautiful—
though I could never see the attraction myself—with
masses of dark hair, and breasts like overripe melons. I
suppose some men like that sort of thing."

She paced, working herself into a lather. "Well, he
can have her, and I hope they make each other thoroughly miserable. I hope she tires of him and kicks him
out into the streets to beg with the paupers. And to think
I gave myself to him," she wailed, tears starting again.
"Oh, how could I have been such a fool?"

Violet moved again to offer a consoling touch. "Shh,
it will be all right, you'll see. In time, you'll forget him
and find someone better. Someone you love who truly
loves you back."

"No, there'll never be anyone better. Nothing will
ever be right again." Jeannette sniffed, blew her nose
into a handkerchief, her tears gradually drying. "Which
is why I've come to a decision."

"What sort of decision?" Violet ventured, suddenly
wary.

"The things I did—leaving Raeburn at the altar, forcing you to switch places with me, forcing you to live my life in my stead. Well, it was wrong. The selfish and immature act of a foolish, desperate woman. So I've decided to make it right."

Jeannette straightened her shoulders, faced her. "I know how perfectly dreadful these past months must have been for you. How you must have suffered. Managing a household, coping with Society and the demands of being married to one of the most influential men in England. I know what a strain our deception has been for *me*. I can only imagine the nightmare ordeal you've had to endure."

"It hasn't been so bad." A nervous twinge of warning ran down Violet's spine.

"Oh, you don't have to pretend, not with me. You've done an excellent job, mind you, assuming the mantle of the Duchess of Raeburn. You've done so well, you've surprised even me. But it's a burden I'm prepared to lift from your shoulders. I'm ready now to do my duty, accept the responsibility that was rightly mine from the first."

Violet's brows creased in dawning disbelief. "I don't think I entirely understand."

"I'm here to rescue you, don't you see? I'm ready to be myself again, to switch back. You'll be Lady Violet Brantford again, and I'll be Her Grace, Jeannette Brantford Winter, Duchess of Raeburn."

Violet leapt to her feet. "No you won't."

"Of course I will. I am tired of pretending to be you. I want to be myself again."

"You may be tired of it, but switching back will never work. For one thing, you're not married to Adrian, I am. For another, he knows."

It was Jeannette's turn to frown. "Knows what?"

"About us. About you and me, and what we did. He

knows we switched places. He knows who we really are."

"Well, no wonder he's been staring at me in such a peculiar manner all afternoon and evening. When he bothers to look at me at all, that is. Don't think I haven't noticed the way he's been avoiding me. I was beginning to wonder just what it was you had done to offend him."

"I haven't done anything," she shot back, struggling to rein in her escalating temper. "It's what we did to-gether to offend him. He was very angry when he found out the truth." She shivered, remembering just how close she'd come to losing him. "Furious, actually, as he had every right to be. He nearly ended our marriage, or what we assumed was a marriage. Turns out we weren't legally wed."

"What?"

"I used a false name, remember? *Your* name, which voided the marriage in the eyes of the law. He and I had to take vows again to make it legal, but never mind that now. What you need to understand is that Adrian real-izes who I am. He knows I am Violet."

Jeannette's eyes were wide. "And Raeburn's willing to maintain this pretense?"

"I convinced him not to reveal the truth. Oh, Jean-nette, just think of the scandal. It isn't right to shame our families, hurt our friends, simply because we've per-petrated such an outrageous lie."

Jeannette resumed her pacing, a deep scowl creasing her forehead. "Which means, I suppose, that I am to go on living my life as you."

"And I as you. Maintaining our masquerade may not be the easiest solution, but it seems the only fair one."

"Fair? I see nothing fair about any of this." Jean-nette's lower lip quivered. "You never cared anything for Society but I do. I'm the one who was supposed to be the duchess. I'm the one who should be mistress of this beautiful house. And if we hadn't traded places the day of my wedding, I would be. It seems to me you're the one who's not being fair. You have no right being married to my husband."

Violet gasped. "Your husband? I'm married to *my* husband, the man you didn't want. The man you tossed aside and would have callously humiliated in front of the entire Ton. You betrayed and deserted him for another man. The day we switched places is the day you gave up all rights to Adrian."

She had to draw a deep breath before she could continue. "Besides, you don't even want him, not really. You only want his wealth, his title, his influence. Well, you can't have them or him. I'm his wife, the woman he married. The woman he loves."

A willful gleam shone in Jeannette's gaze. "Are you so certain of that? It seems to me Raeburn was content for months, believing himself married to me. Even now he can barely tell us apart. I'll bet if I quit wearing these silly spectacles of yours, he wouldn't know one of us from the other."

The accusation hit Violet like a hard slap. Old insecurities, old inadequacies springing back to life full-blown. She fought the doubts. *Not true,* she told herself, *not true at all.*

"He *can* tell us apart," she defended, rubbing the gleaming amethyst ring on her left hand like a talisman. "Adrian knows who I am. He loves *me.*"

Her twin shrugged. "Then you shouldn't mind trading places with me again to prove it."

Violet shook her head. "It's out of the question."

"Why? Afraid I'm right?" Jeannette taunted.

"No. I know you're *not* right, and putting him through some secret challenge is absurd," she dismissed, her words far more confident than she felt. "He's married to me, and nothing is ever going to change that."

"Perhaps not," her twin drawled. "Still, if I were his wife, I'd want to know. Personally, I'd find it quite dreadful spending my life wondering whether or not my husband could recognize the real me. The doubt and uncertainty alone would drive me mad."

Violet dashed a hand through the air. "Well, I need no such reassurances. Adrian has my complete trust, and as far as I am concerned, this conversation is at an end."

"If you wish, but remember you can always change your mind."

"I won't."

Shaking and half sick, Violet fled from the room. Down the hall, she found a chair and sat for a long time while she fought to compose her emotions. Only when her breathing was even, her body still again, did she make her way to bed.

Adrian was asleep. She removed her robe, the cameo she no longer wanted still fastened on its front. She slid in next to him, prayed he wouldn't wake.

Moments later, his arm curved over her waist from behind, tucking her up against him spoon-fashion. He pressed a sleepy kiss onto her neck. "Sorry I drifted off. How long were you gone?"

"I don't know, a while." Violet wrapped a hand around his forearm, snuggled closer into his warmth. "Go back to sleep. We'll talk in the morning." She closed her eyes, willed herself to sleep, knowing she wouldn't.

"What did Jeannette want?"

Her eyes popped open. She forced her body not to tense at his question. "She . . . she gave me a gift."

"What sort of gift?"

"A cameo. Carnelian. It's quite lovely. Then she told

me about her time in Italy. She's . . . unhappy. Apparently Toddy Markham seduced her, then ran off with another woman. Some rich Italian widow, a contessa."

"Scoundrel," Adrian swore. "I don't know how I could ever have considered him a friend. If he sets foot in England again, I'll see to it he's exposed for the bounder he is. A man like him shouldn't be tolerated in polite society."

"Luckily, no one knows she was involved with him. Please don't mention to her that I told you."

"Don't worry, I won't say a word."

A long moment of quiet fell between them.

"Anything else?" he asked.

She considered the question. Should she tell him? Reveal her argument with Jeannette? Divulge her twin's irrational and audacious demand to trade places again so that Jeannette could be his duchess? No, it would only make him angry. He might confront her sister. Start some dreadful row that would do nothing but embarrass the family, make this visit between them impossible to endure. Better to remain silent on the subject, even if doing so seemed tantamount to a lie.

"No," she lied in a small voice, "nothing else." She waited to see if he would press her any further.

"Well," he said, shifting position slightly behind her, "much as I'm sorry for her troubles, she isn't blameless in the matter. Perhaps in the end this will prove to be a good lesson for her."

"Yes, perhaps."

He yawned. "It's late. We should get some rest."

"Yes, I suppose we ought." She rolled onto her back, leaned up to kiss him. "I love you."

"Hmm," he murmured, already half asleep. "Love you too." He tucked his cheek against her hair and closed his eyes. Less than a minute later, his breathing grew deep and even, overcome by sleep.

She lay in the dark, his arms secure around her. Yet try as she would, the unpleasant quarrel with Jeannette kept repeating itself in her thoughts. Was her twin right? Would he be unable to tell them apart if put to the test?

An image of Jeannette lying here in her place slithered into her mind. She banished the thought as quickly as it came. No, she assured herself, Adrian loved her, and only her. Hadn't he already proven that through his actions, his words?

Still, the thoughts persisted, along with a twinge of doubt that wriggled its way beneath her skin like some vile, burrowing insect.

What if Jeannette was right?

Nearly an hour passed before sleep finally took her, troubled dreams chasing her through the night.

Chapter Twenty-three

Due to a bout of unusually warm weather, Violet decided to move the afternoon's luncheon out onto the east lawn. Cloth-covered tables had been arranged to afford a pleasant view of the folly and the glassy blue lake beyond. The surrounding trees provided patches of shade, branches spread green and full with tender young leaves.

All the house-party guests had arrived. In addition to several family members—Adrian's mother and two of his sisters, their husbands and children—several friends had driven up from London to join in the merriment. Adrian's friend Peter Armitage was among their number.

Violet thanked him kindly once again for the use of his house on the first night of her and Adrian's honeymoon. Green eyes twinkling, Armitage soon had her laughing and blushing over his saucy remarks. Eventually, duty pulled her away to make conversation with her other guests.

She'd considered inviting Eliza Hammond, along with her aunt and cousin, but feared it might elicit too many curious comments. It was an acknowledged fact that Jeannette and Eliza had never been more than polite acquaintances. Having her stay here at the house as an especial friend would raise more than one surprised eyebrow.

Then, of course, there was Jeannette. Expecting her,

in her role as Violet, to pretend to be close to Eliza, was frankly expecting too much. And Violet had worked too hard to reestablish her friendship with the other young woman to let her sister interfere with it yet again.

A refreshing breeze was playing on the air when Violet signaled everyone to gather so the meal could begin. As she turned to follow, her twin exited the house and strolled toward them across the lawn.

Jeannette's late arrival didn't surprise her in the slightest. Her twin's appearance did.

Their hair matched, swept upward in an elegant golden swirl, a few tendrils left to curl over each cheekbone. Worse, their gowns looked the same, or very nearly. The cut and style, even the color of Violet's pale-hued, Pomona green dress was virtually identical to the one her sister wore. Yet worst of all were the missing spectacles. Without them, Jeannette's ocean-tinted eyes sparkled like a mirror image of her own. The impish twinkle in her twin's gaze the only visible distinction between them.

They hadn't dressed alike since they were ten years old, when their mother had done them up for a party like a pair of matching china dolls.

How had Jeannette managed it? Violet wondered. Bribed one of the maids, perhaps? Watched out the window then run in a flurry to perfect an identical ensemble?

A harsh frown puckered Violet's brow. "What are you doing?"

"What do you mean?" Jeannette smiled, a picture of innocence.

"You know exactly what I mean."

"Oh, the wardrobe? I thought it would be fun." Jeannette angled her head. "Don't look now, but here comes Raeburn and his friend."

Slowly, dread plucking at her like a restless set of fingers, Violet spun around. She stood, ranged shoulder to shoulder with her sister.

Adrian continued forward, a grin on his face. It faded as he drew closer. He stopped. Hesitated. The question of which sister was which clear on his features.

Violet smiled at him, warm and inviting.

Jeannette did the same.

His eyes swept over her, over Jeannette, then across her once more.

Silently, Violet willed him to know her, to pick her. But his uncertainty remained. She watched, aware he was about to make a decision. What if he made the wrong one? What if he chose her twin?

Abruptly, she stretched out a hand, stepped forward. "Are you hungry, sweetheart? The food smells delicious even from here."

His relief obvious, he took her arm, looped it over his own. "Indeed it does. I'm famished."

They strolled toward the tables.

Armitage moved forward to escort Jeannette.

"What's she up to?" Adrian murmured once he and Violet were out of earshot.

"Just a prank," she assured him. "It's nothing."

Yet the damage was done. Another layer of doubt planted in her mind like a well-watered seed. Just as Jeannette had intended.

Three days later, on the morning of the ball, Violet tapped lightly upon her sister's bedroom door.

It opened a crack. Jeannette peered out.

"Are you alone?"

Jeannette nodded.

Violet pushed her way inside. "All right," she said in a rush. "I'll do it."

Shutting the door, her twin strolled farther into the room, one golden brow arched high. "Do what?"

Violet squeezed her hands together. "I'll trade places with you. But only for the ball tonight. When we come back upstairs afterward, everything will be as it was. I'll be the Duchess of Raeburn again and you'll be Lady Violet. Is that understood?"

"Oh, completely." Jeannette smiled like a cat with a mouth full of feathers. "What made you change your mind?"

"I know Adrian can tell us apart. I just . . . I want this issue put to rest for good, that's all."

"And if he fails the test?"

"He won't fail," Violet said, her words emphatic.

If only she were truly that certain.

The ballroom gleamed with the light of a hundred beeswax candles. Lively strains of music floated on the air as couples swayed in rhythm to the tune the orchestra played.

Violet stood on the sidelines, the world in sharp focus through the glasses perched once again on her face. How odd it felt to wear her spectacles in public once more. How odd it felt to be herself again. Yet not herself.

This evening seemed like a dream. Or rather, a nightmare. From the moment she'd come downstairs, garbed in the lavender dress Jeannette had planned to wear for tonight's ball, nothing had gone as it ought.

Most of the family had been assembled in the front hall, sharing a last few minutes of conversation before taking their places in the receiving line to greet arriving guests. Violet waited, quiet, nearly invisible again as had once been her way. No one noticed the change between her and Jeannette. Even Mrs. Litton crossed to consult with her sister about a last-minute detail for the party, completely unaware she was dealing with the wrong woman.

Then Adrian appeared, commanding all eyes as he descended the stairs. Proud and beautiful, he moved like some dark prince, resplendent in black. His linen—cravat, shirt, stockings and gloves—were snowy white; the only hint of color an emerald stickpin that winked like a large green cat's eye on his perfectly tied neck cloth. One of her birthday gifts to him.

She laid a hand over the other present, nestled in peace and security inside her womb. She was certain now. Come winter, she would bring Adrian's child into the world. His heir if it was a boy. The knowledge left her giddy with happiness and excitement.

As she cradled the wonderful secret to herself, she forgot for a moment what she had done. That she had exchanged places with her twin. Again.

Adrian strode forward.

She waited for him to come to her, to kiss her, his wife.

He passed her and took Jeannette's hand instead, brushing his lips over her sister's knuckles, a kiss against her smooth cheek. Jeannette smiled, murmured something that made him laugh.

Bile burned inside Violet's throat, scalding and raw. He didn't know her. After all they'd shared, everything they'd been through together, how could he not know her? How could he not see the truth staring at him from only a few feet away?

After that, the evening only grew worse.

The guests arrived, the party began, everything running like a well-wound clock. Compliments that should have been offered to her were given instead to Jeannette. Her sister beamed as boastfully as if she'd made all the arrangements herself.

Bitter, Violet endured, haunted by the knowledge that

she'd brought all this down upon herself. She should never have let Jeannette talk her into making the exchange. Never have allowed her sister to stir up doubts and insecurities and coax her into this foolish trade. But she'd needed to satisfy her curiosity.

Now it was satisfied.

Adrian had failed.

Her husband and sister whirled by, arm in arm. Jeannette looked elegant and vivacious in the golden gown Violet was supposed to have worn tonight. And Adrian, dearest Adrian, the man she loved more than life, was clueless, duped once again.

Unable to watch any longer, she turned and rushed from the ballroom.

Something wasn't right, Adrian thought.

All evening, a troubling undercurrent had been humming inside him. An uneasy awareness that made the tiny hairs on the back of his neck prickle at odd intervals.

On the surface, the ball was everything it should be. A magnificent venue crowded with convivial guests enjoying themselves as they ate, drank, danced and conversed with one another. Initially, he'd had reservations about hosting the house party and ball, but Violet had come through, doing a thoroughly splendid job. Lady Jersey, or any of Society's other patronesses, could not have done better.

He knew Violet had been determined to hold the event in order to prove her capabilities as his duchess—though as far as he was concerned, she had no need. He loved and admired her exactly as she was. Yet he was glad tonight had turned out to be such a success. The achievement would give her exactly the sort of confidence-building boost she needed and deserved.

He gazed down at her now as they waltzed around the room. The odd itch on the back of his neck returned full force. He met her eyes, eyes that usually gleamed with the depth and radiance of a warm, sunlit sea. Only, tonight that warmth was missing. Her eyes nothing but an attractive glaze of color, all surface with none of the underlying intensity.

The itch worsened, the odd internal hum he'd felt all evening shifting into a higher frequency.

A thought popped into his mind, one he instantly discarded. Then it came again, banging like a fist on a door.

"My dear," he said, his tone deliberately smooth and even, "have I congratulated you yet on this evening? It is a triumph."

"Mrs. Litton did nearly all of the work, but I'm glad you're happy. Is your birthday turning out to be everything you hoped?"

"That and more."

Her left hand rested on his chest. He reached up, covered it with his palm. He rubbed his thumb over the amethyst she wore on her ring finger.

"Do you remember when I gave this to you?" he asked, his voice silky, intimate.

Her lips curved upward in a sweet smile. "Of course."

"How we went to Rundell and Bridge together to pick it out? How you fell in love with it the moment you saw it?"

"It was so romantic. How could I ever forget?"

Jeannette.

My God, she was Jeannette, passing herself off as his wife.

The twins had switched places again.

Which meant Violet, in the ultimate of ironies, was portraying herself tonight. Anger roared through him like a blast from a fiery furnace.

"You couldn't forget," he whispered between clenched teeth, "because there is nothing for you to forget. It never happened." He squeezed Jeannette's hand.

She let out a small yelp.

"You've been caught in your own lie," he said. "Violet didn't pick this ring. I chose it for her. And at the time I gave it to her, we weren't anywhere near London."

Jeannette gasped, tried to pull away.

He held her tight. "Oh, no, *Jeannette*, you're not going anywhere. We'll finish this dance as if nothing is amiss, then you are coming with me."

She bristled, but stopped struggling. Her shoulders slumped as they continued their dance.

When it was done, he pulled her off the dance floor.

Adrian scanned the crowd for Kit, who'd driven up that morning to attend the ball and celebrate Adrian's birthday. He located him without a great deal of difficulty.

Kit stood on the sidelines flirting with the Lyles' eldest daughter, a pretty brunette just out of the school room. She giggled at something Kit said and fluttered her fan.

"Miss Lyle," Adrian said, "pray pardon the intrusion, but I need a moment of my brother's time."

"Oh, of course." The girl cast curious eyes over the family trio.

When she'd gone, Kit swung around, a look of mild annoyance darkening his features. "I hope this is important. Miss Lyle and I were just making plans to meet in the village tomorrow."

Adrian drew his brother and Jeannette into a quiet corner. "Your plans can wait. I have another task for you. Kit, meet your sister-in-law, Jeannette. The *real* Jeannette."

Kit's eyes widened.

"Watch her. Don't let her out of your sight."

Kit crossed his arms and glared. "Don't worry. She won't be going anywhere."

"Good. Now I just have to locate my wife and throttle some sense into her."

Adrian stalked away, then stopped suddenly and retraced his steps. Without so much as a by-your-leave, he grabbed Jeannette's left hand, twisted the rings off her finger.

"These," he told her, "don't belong to you. Never wear them again." He tucked them into his pocket and departed.

Violet wiped a tear from the corner of her eye and gulped a breath of cool night air. The scent of lilacs drifted through the garden on a sweet, succulent cloud.

She ought to return to the ballroom, she knew, before someone noticed she was missing.

The evening was growing late. Only a couple more hours to endure, then everything would return to the way it had been when she'd awakened this morning. She and Jeannette would switch back, no one the wiser.

Only, she would be wiser.

She would know the truth, and that knowledge would surely haunt her for the rest of her life. Her husband, the man she loved above anything, couldn't tell her from her twin. He claimed to adore her, said he understood her, knew her as only a lover could, yet still he'd been fooled.

Was she really so interchangeable? So generic? So dispensable?

Would Adrian, despite everything he said, be just as content married to Jeannette? Deep down she knew he would not. Still, an inkling of doubt remained, along with the obvious blow to her pride.

But that too would heal in time. She would go on

with her life, her marriage, and put this little matter aside. She would learn to forget. No use picking at it like a scab on a festering sore. That path would lead to nothing but disaster, poisoning everything that was good and honest about her love for him.

Adrian was her husband. Would always be her husband, she reminded herself. Her helpmeet and lover, the father of the child she carried and, God willing, all the others to come.

She would be content, happy, despite what she now knew.

She drew her shawl over her shoulders, resigned herself to returning to the party. A quiet sound of footsteps crunching in the gravel made her look up.

Adrian.

She nearly crossed to him, needing badly to be held.

Instead she retained her seat on the stone bench, painfully aware he believed her to be her sister. "Good evening, your Grace. What brings you out into the gardens at this late hour?"

He sank down beside her, stretched out his long legs. "The same as you, I would imagine. A breath of fresh air, a few moments away from the crowd." He turned his head. "Although you prefer crowds, as I recall."

Jeannette, she reminded herself, she was supposed to be Jeannette. "I love them," she lied. "But a party grows tiresome when one can't behave as one would wish. Violet says you know the truth, about her and me, that is."

"Hmm, I do indeed."

"She also says you were dreadfully angry with her when you found out, but you've forgiven her now." She paused. "Have you forgiven me as well?"

His white teeth flashed in the shadows. "I'm still deciding."

"Well, no matter. I'm just glad you and my sister are so happy together."

"Are you? I thought perhaps you might be a little envious, considering everything you passed up when you decided not to marry me."

"Not at all," she said with a forced breeziness. "You and she are far better suited. I'm only sorry I didn't realize it sooner."

"Sooner than our wedding day, you mean?"

"Yes."

"No doubt you are right." He gazed out across the garden for a moment, then turned his head, met her eyes. "Though on occasion I still wonder."

"Wonder what?"

He shifted a few inches closer. "What would have happened if you and I had tied the knot as planned." His voice grew mellow and husky. "If you and I were husband and wife now. Aren't you ever the least bit curious?"

A lump formed inside her throat. What was he saying? Surely he couldn't want Jeannette?

"No," she said on a rush, "not in the least."

"Really? You always struck me as the wild, passionate sort." He slipped his arms around her, hauled her close. "You and your sister are alike in so many ways. Makes me wonder how really alike you are. Perhaps we should experiment and find out."

He lowered his mouth to hers, but she turned her head away, evaded his kiss. She wedged an elbow between them to hold him off. But he was too strong and seconds later dragged her across his lap.

"Don't," she cried, her heart shattering into a thousand pieces. "No."

He crushed her mouth to his, commanding her, bending her to his will. A knot of agony twisted inside her chest. Try as she might to resist him, she couldn't. She loved him, wanted him still. For a moment she gave in and let him take her mouth. His tongue swept inside to sip like a bee gathering nectar.

Finally, she gathered enough strength to shove him away. "Stop," she sobbed on a harsh whimper, tears sliding down her cheeks. "Stop."

"Why? What's wrong, my love? Don't you like kissing your husband?" He skimmed his lips over her wet cheeks, nuzzled an especially sensitive spot behind her left ear.

She shuddered at the sensation, pleasure racing through her. Then his words became clear in her mind. "W-what," she stuttered. "What did you say?"

He pulled back, far enough to meet her eyes in the moonlit darkness. "You heard what I said, *Violet.*" He gave her a shake, his jaw taut with anger. "Yes, I recognize you. Did you think I wouldn't know? Exactly how long was this charade supposed to continue?"

"Tonight. Only for tonight during the ball. When we all went upstairs for the evening, we were to switch back."

"And have a good laugh together first at having duped me again." He set her off his lap none too gently.

She wrapped a restraining hand around his arm to keep him from stalking away. "No, it's nothing like that. I didn't want to do it. It's just that Jeannette said you couldn't tell us apart and I . . ."

"You what? You believed her? Wondered in some deep part of yourself if she might possibly be right?"

Suddenly ashamed, she lowered her eyes. "You didn't seem to know which of us was which that day at the picnic when she . . . when she deliberately dressed like me."

"And because of that, you decided to lie to me again?" he thundered.

"It was wrong. I realize it was wrong, but I had to know."

"Know what?" He laid his hands over her shoulders.

"Know that I see you as an individual and not some duplicate of your sister? That I cherish you and only you? That I can look into your eyes and tell the difference between you—the only woman I'll ever love—and your sister, a woman who would never have made me happy? Is that what you wanted to know?"

She nodded, a fresh tear of vulnerability racing down her cheek.

He wiped the moisture away with his thumb. "Violet, why can't you trust me? Believe me when I tell you I love you and don't want anyone else?"

"I do believe you. I will from now on. It's just . . ."

"Just what?"

Her voice lowered to a near whisper. "No one's ever picked me over her. Our whole lives it was always her first, then me. Even you didn't originally pick me. You unknowingly wound up with me that first time down the aisle."

"Well, I didn't unknowingly wind up with you the second time." He enfolded her in his arms. "I chose *you*. You, who I recognize as my love, my only love. And I *do* know you. I could pick you out blindfolded if necessity dictated that I do so."

She smiled as the last of her tears dried. "You think so? Then what took you so long tonight?"

"You've got to give a man some maneuvering room when you deliberately set out to deceive him. You two are twins, after all."

She laid a hand over her heart. "I didn't want to deceive you. I wanted to prove to Jeannette you can tell us apart. And you passed the test most admirably." She paused for a moment, then poked a finger at his chest as she remembered. "And what about the trick you played on me? Making me believe you were seducing my sister."

"It wasn't anything you didn't deserve after trying

again to deceive me." He glowered. "Speaking of which, you'd better never play that little switching game on me ever again."

"I swear I will never, ever lie to you again. Jeannette and I are done trading places, you have my most solemn vow. I mean it, Adrian. I'll never mislead you about this or anything else again."

"I'm going to hold you to that. Otherwise, I may resort to my original method of punishment."

"Which was?"

"Paddling your bottom so hard you wouldn't be able to sit down for a week. In fact, I think I might give you a few thwacks now just for good measure." He tugged her toward him as if he really meant to go through with his threat.

"Don't," she cried out. "You might hurt the baby."

He halted. "Baby? What baby?" His eyes skimmed over her frame. "Are you with child?"

Her face lit up and she nodded. "I was going to tell you later tonight."

He gave a loud whoop, jumped to his feet and grabbed her into his arms. He swung her around in wide circles until they were both laughing and dizzy.

"I take it you're happy." She beamed, her arms locked around his neck.

"Ecstatic. You?"

"The same."

She grinned at him. He grinned back, the two of them behaving like a pair of giddy fools. He kissed her long and deep, until they were both breathless.

"We'll have to tell the family," he stated when he'd recovered enough to speak. "*Maman* will be overjoyed."

"Perhaps we should keep it to ourselves for a little while longer. I only just found out myself."

He shook his head. "No. No more secrets, no more

lies, not about anything." He set her on her feet, then grabbed her hand, pulling her in his wake.

"Adrian, what are you doing? Where are you taking me?"

"Back to the party."

"But we can't go, not together. Everyone thinks I'm Violet."

"You are Violet."

"You know what I mean. You're supposed to be married to Jeannette."

He stopped, turned toward her. "Well, I'm not married to Jeannette and I'm tired of the world thinking I am. Oh, I nearly forgot." He dug a hand into his pocket. "Here, put these on."

On his palm lay the rings he had taken from Jeannette, gold and gemstones gleaming faintly in the moonlight.

"But I can't."

"Of course you can. They're your rings. Put them on and swear to me you'll never take them off again."

Her hand trembled, hovering. "We shouldn't do this."

He met her eyes. "Yes, we should. No more games, that's what you promised me tonight."

"But what about our families? Our friends? What about your career?"

"What career? I'm the Duke of Raeburn, I don't have a career."

"Your political career. Your aspirations to one day hold high government office."

He huffed out an exasperated breath. "I have no political aspirations, no interest in any office, either high or low. Wherever did you come up with such a nonsensical idea?" He held up his other hand. "No, wait. Let me guess. My mother."

"She said your dream was to rise in the House of Lords, maybe even become Prime Minister one day."

"God forbid." He shuddered. "Politics has long been my mother's dream for me, not my own. Dear *Maman* means well, but on this point she's just dead wrong. Please never believe such spurious suggestions again, for both our sakes."

"So you really don't want to be Prime Minister?"

"No. Most emphatically not." He cocked an eyebrow. "Been protecting me, have you?"

She nodded. "Trying a bit."

"Well, you needn't bother, not on this score. And next time you have a question about my dreams, just ask me. I'll tell you whether or not they're really mine." He jiggled his palm. "Now put your rings back on."

She did as she was told, feeling easy and fully herself for the first time in a long while. She raised her eyes to his. "Are you sure?"

"Completely." He dropped a kiss onto her lips. "No matter what happens, remember that I love you."

She captured his face in her hands. "And I love you. So much, Adrian, so very much."

After one last kiss, they walked hand in hand into the ballroom.

Inside they found Jeannette seated along the room's periphery, her lower lip protruding in an unhappy pout.

Kit occupied the chair next to her, swinging an elegantly shod foot in time to the music as he cheerfully shooed away any would-be dance partners who approached his sister-in-law in hopes of escorting her out onto the ballroom floor.

He'd just sent another man packing when Adrian and Violet drew near.

"You found her, I see," Kit said, raking his eyes over the errant pair. "And?"

"And nearly everything has been resolved. Just one

last item remains to be seen to." Adrian extended a hand to Jeannette. "My lady, if you would, please be so good as to come with your sister and me."

Jeannette crossed her arms, thrust her chin into the air. "I don't see why I should, not after your abominable treatment of me. Going away and leaving me a virtual prisoner of this insolent puppy."

"Puppy? Who're you calling a puppy?" The foot Kit had been swinging hit the floor as he straightened abruptly.

"You, you lap dog."

"Enough," Adrian commanded, silencing the bickering pair. He pinned a fierce glare on Jeannette. "Now, either come with us willingly or be dragged along. The choice is entirely up to you. But know, either way, you will be coming with your sister and me."

"To do what?" Jeannette challenged.

"You'll find out soon enough."

A small, silent battle of wills ensued. Just when it looked as if he would have to resort to force, Jeannette rose to her feet and fell into step beside him and Violet. Adrian led them to the front of the ballroom, signaling the musicians to stop their playing.

"What's he doing?" Jeannette whispered under her breath to Violet.

But Violet didn't have time to answer as Adrian drew her away. He lined the three of them up, one twin on each side of him, a hand on each of their arms.

The entire assembled crowd turned their eyes upon the trio.

Visually, Violet located her parents, her brother, the members of Adrian's family, including his mother, all of whom looked on with mild interest and curiosity. Kit stood to one side, an expression of keen expectation on his face.

"Ladies and gentlemen," Adrian began, "thank you

for attending tonight's celebration. It is a pleasure to have you in our home. I hope each one of you is having an enjoyable evening. There is a small announcement I would like to make, a matter of some importance that has long needed correction. As you know, all the credit for tonight's festivities, indeed the entire week of splendid activity, belongs to my wife. A woman I admire, respect and deeply love."

Violet raised her eyes, met his as they swept warmly over her. She squeezed his arm, asking in silent, intimate communication if he was completely certain he wanted to continue.

The look he returned confirmed he did, without reservation or fear.

She rallied, drawing strength from his confidence.

He resumed his speech. "What you do not know is that the woman you've assumed to be your hostess this evening is not my wife."

A murmur went up from the crowd.

Jeannette gave a squeak and tried to pull away. He held her firmly in place.

"The woman you have been offering thanks to this evening is actually my sister-in-law, Lady Jeannette Brantford."

More murmuring, this time in obvious bewilderment.

"I don't blame you for being confused. I know many of you attended my wedding, witnessed the ceremony where I appeared to marry Lady Jeannette. In actuality, I wed another woman."

He clasped Violet's hand, grown cold from nerves, and stepped forward.

He released Jeannette, who scuttled back and away.

"My wife," he announced, "the woman I married, the woman I love and am proud to claim as my own, Violet Brantford Winter."

A chaos of frenzied exclamations erupted.

Above it all rose a piercing wail.

Violet's gaze flew across the room in time to watch her mother faint, and be caught in her father's arms. He lowered her mother's prostrate form to the floor in a pool of silk and feathers. A pair of her female friends hurried forward, armed with fans and hartshorn.

"You might ask how all this is possible," Adrian continued in a powerful voice. "It's quite simple really. The twins switched identities, and yes, fooled even me for a brief time. But by then it was too late. My heart had been fairly captured by the most wonderful woman I have ever had the good fortune to know." His eyes sought hers, and for a moment Violet forgot the tumult around them, happy and secure inside his love.

They exchanged smiles.

Then he turned once more to the assembled guests. "And there's one more announcement we'd like to share, one for which I hope you will wish us happy. Just tonight, my lady wife informed me we are to have a child." He slipped an arm over Violet's shoulders, hugged her close against his side. "A new Winter will be born sometime late this year."

Her mother, who was finally coming out of her faint, awakened just in time to hear his statement about Violet's pregnancy. She let out a fresh wail, then dropped off into another swoon.

Violet laid her head against his shoulder. "Well, you've done it now," she remarked. "But if we are to be ruined, at least we'll have each other."

He gazed down and they shared a tender smile. "Never doubt it, my love. Never doubt it."

And then, there in front of their family and friends, Adrian kissed Violet, spectacles and all.

Get caught in the trap!

Read on to catch a sneak peek at the next
charming novel in the Trap series
by Tracy Anne Warren . . .

The Wife Trap

Available from Ivy Books

Ireland, June 1817

Lady Jeannette Rose Brantford gently blew her nose on
her handkerchief. Neatly refolding the silk square with
its pretty row of embroidered lilies of the valley, she
dabbed at the fresh pair of tears that slid down her
cheeks.

I really need to stop crying, she told herself. *This un-
remitting misery simply has to cease.*

On the sea voyage over, she'd thought she had her
emotions firmly under control. Resigned, as it were, to
her ignominious fate. But this morning, when the coach
set off on the overland journey to her cousins' estate, the
reality of her situation had crashed upon her like one of
the great boulders that lay scattered around the wild
Irish countryside.

How could my parents have done this to me? she
wailed to herself. How could they have been cruel
enough to exile her to this godforsaken wilderness?
Dear heavens, even Scotland would have been prefer-
able. At least its land mass had the good sense to still be
attached to Mother England. Scotland would have been

a long carriage ride from home, but in Ireland, she was separated by an entire sea!

Yet Mama and Papa had remained adamant in their decision to send her here. And for the first time in her twenty-one years, she'd been unable to wheedle or cajole or cry her way into persuading them to change their minds.

She didn't even have her longtime lady's maid, Jacobs, to offer her comfort and consolation in her time of need. Just because she had told Jacobs a little fib about her identity when she and her twin sister, Violet, had decided to exchange places last summer was no cause for desertion. And just because Jeannette's parents were punishing her for the scandal with this intolerable banishment to Ireland was no reason for Jacobs to seek out a new post. A loyal servant would have been eager to follow her mistress into exile!

Jeannette wiped away another tear and gazed across the coach at her new maid, Betsy. Despite being a perfectly sweet, pleasant girl, Betsy was a stranger. Not only that, she was woefully inexperienced, still learning about the proper care of clothing and how to dress hair and recognize the latest fashions. Jacobs had known it all.

Jeannette sighed.

Oh well, she thought, training Betsy would give her new life purpose. At the reminder of her *new* life, tears welled again in her eyes.

Alone. Oh, I am so dreadfully alone.

Abruptly, the coach jerked to a tooth-rattling halt. She slid forward and nearly toppled to the floor in a cloud of skirts.

Betsy caught her, or rather they caught each other and slowly settled themselves back into their seats.

"Good heavens, what was that?" Jeannette straight

ened her hat, barely able to see with the brim half covering her eyes.

"It felt like we hit something, my lady." Betsy twisted to peer out the small window at the gloomy landscape beyond. "I hope we weren't in no accident."

The coach swayed as the coachman and footmen jumped to the ground; the low rumble of male voices filled the air.

Jeannette gripped her handkerchief inside her palm. *Drat it, what now? As if things weren't bad enough already.*

A minute later, the coachman's wizened face and sloped shoulders appeared at the window. "I'm sorry, milady, but it appears we're stuck."

Jeannette's eyebrows rose. "What do you mean, 'stuck'?"

" 'Tis the weather, milady. All the rain of late has turned the road back to bog."

Bog? As in big-wheel-sucking, muddy-hole kind of bog? A wail rose in her throat. She swallowed the cry and firmed her lower lip, refusing to let it so much as quiver.

"Jem and me'll keep trying," the coachman continued, "but it may be a while afore we're on our way. Perhaps you'd like to step out while we . . ."

She shot him an appalled look, so appalled obviously that his words trailed abruptly into silence.

What was wrong with the man? she wondered. Was he daft? Or blind perhaps? Could he not see her beautiful Naccarat traveling dress? The shade bright and pretty as a perfect tangerine. Or the stylish kid-leather half boots she'd had dyed especially to match prior to her departure from London? Obviously he had no common sense, nor any appreciation of the latest styles. But mayhap she was being too hard on him since, after all, what did any man really know about ladies' fashion?

"Step out to where? Into that mud?" She gave her head a vigorous shake. "I shall wait right where I am."

"It may get a might rough once we start pushing, milady. There's your safety to consider."

"Don't worry about my safety. I shall be fine in the coach. If you need to lighten the load, however, you have my leave to remove my trunks. But please be sure not to set them into the mud. I shall be most distressed if they are begrimed or damaged in any manner." She waved a gloved hand. "And Betsy may step down if she wishes."

Betsy looked uncertain. "Are you sure, my lady? I don't think I ought to leave you."

"It's fine, Betsy. There is nothing you can do here anyway so go with John."

Besides, Jeannette moaned to herself, *it will be nothing new since I am well used to being deserted these days.*

The gray-haired man fixed a pair of kindly eyes on the servant girl. "Best you come with me. I'll see you to a safe spot."

Once Betsy was lifted free of the coach and the worst of the mud, the barouche's door was firmly relatched. The servants set about unloading the baggage, then began the grueling task of trying to dislodge the vehicle's trapped wheels.

A full half hour passed with no success. Jeannette stubbornly kept her seat, faintly queasy from the vigorous, periodic rocking of the coach as the men and horses strained to force the carriage out of its hole. From the exclamations of annoyed disgust that floated on the air, puncturing the rustic silence, she gathered their attempts had done nothing but sink the wheels even deeper into the mire.

Withdrawing a fresh handkerchief from her reticule, she patted the perspiration from her forehead. Blazing from above, the sun had burned off the clouds but was doing little to dry the muddy morass around her. Afternoon heat ripened the air, turning it sticky with a humidity that was unusual for these parts even in midsummer, or so she had been informed.

At least she wasn't crying anymore. A blessing since it wouldn't do to arrive at her cousins' house—assuming she ever did arrive—looking bloated and puffy, her eyes damp and red rimmed. It was humiliating enough knowing what her cousins must think of her banishment. It would be a far worse ignominy to greet them looking anything but her best.

A fly buzzed into the coach, fat and black and repugnant.

Jeannette's lip curled with distaste. She shooed at the insect with her handkerchief, hoping it would fly out the opposite window. Instead it turned and raced straight for her head. She let out a sharp squeal and batted at it again.

Buzzing past her nose, it landed on the window frame, its transparent wings glinting in the brilliant sunlight. The insect strolled casually along the painted wooden sill on tensile, hair-thin legs.

With equal nonchalance, Jeannette reached for her fan. She waited, running an assessing thumb over the fine gilded ivory side guard. As soon as the creature paused, Jeannette brought her fan down with an audible *thwap*.

In a single instant, the big black bug became a big black blob. Gratified by her small victory, she inspected her fan, hoping she had not damaged the delicate staves since the fan had always been one of her favorites.

Catching a fresh glimpse of the squashed insect, her lips twisted in revulsion before she quickly flicked the carcass out of her sight.

"Sure and you've a deadly aim, lass," remarked a

mellow male voice, the lilting cadence as rich and lyrical as an Irish ballad. "He didn't stand a chance, that fly. Are you as handy with a real weapon?"

Startled, she turned her head to find a stranger peering in at her through the opposite window, one strong forearm propped at an impertinent angle atop the frame.

How long had he been standing there? she wondered. Long enough obviously to witness the encounter between her and the fly.

The man was tall and sinewy with close-cropped, wavy dark chestnut hair, fair skin, and penetrating eyes of the bluest blue, vivid as gentians at peak bloom. They twinkled at her, those eyes, the man making no effort to conceal his roguish interest. His lips curved upward in silent, unconcealed humor.

Devilish handsome.

The description popped unbidden and unwanted into her mind, his appeal impossible to deny. Her heart flipped then flopped inside her chest, breasts rising and falling beneath the material of her bodice in sudden, breathless movement.

Gracious sakes.

She struggled against the involuntary response, forcing herself to notice on closer observation that his features were not precisely perfect. His forehead square and rather ordinary. His nose a bit long, a tad hawkish. His chin blunt and far too stubborn for comfort. His lips a little on the slender side.

Yet when viewed as a whole, his countenance made an undeniably pleasing package, one to which no sane woman could claim indifference. And when coupled with the magnetism that radiated off him in almost visible waves, he looked rather like sin brought to life.

And a sin it was, she mused on a regretful sigh, that he was clearly not a gentleman. His coarse, unfashionable attire—plain linen shirt, neckerchief, and rough tan coat—betraying his plebeian origins along with his obvious lack of manners before a lady. One had only to look at him to know the truth as he leaned against her coach door like some ruffian or thief.

She stiffened at the idea, abruptly realizing that's exactly what he might be. Well, if he was there to rob her, she wouldn't give him the satisfaction of showing fear. She might burst into tears on occasion, but she had never been a vaporish milk-and-water miss. Never one of the frail sort given to wailing for her smelling salts at the faintest hint of distress.

"I am well able to defend myself," she declared in a resilient tone, "if that is what you are asking. Be aware I would have no difficulty putting a bullet through you should circumstances require."

What a fib, she mused, deciding it wisest not to mention the fact that she had never fired a gun in her life and had no pistol with her inside the coach. The coachman was the one with the weapon.

Where was he anyway? She hoped he and the others weren't, quite literally, tied up.

Surprise brightened the rogue's eyes. "And why would you think you've cause to shoot me?"

"What else am I to imagine when a strange man accosts me in my own carriage?"

"Perhaps you might assume he's here to help."

"Help with what? Help himself to my belongings?"

His eyes narrowed, glinting with a dangerous combination of irritation and amusement. "You've a suspicious mind, you have, lass, painting me immediately as a thief." He leaned closer, his voice growing faintly husky. "Assuming I were a thief, what is it you possess that I might find of value?"

Her lips parted involuntarily, alarm and something far more treacherous quickening her blood. "I have my clothes and a few jewels, nothing more. If you want them, they are in the trunks outside."

"If I were of a mind to want such things, I'd have them already." His eyes locked with her own, momentarily holding her prisoner before his gaze lowered slowly to her mouth. "No, there's only one thing I'm craving after. . . ."

Her breath caught in her lungs as he paused, leaving his sentence tantalizingly, frustratingly unfinished. Did he want *her*? she wondered. Did he intend to force his way inside her carriage and steal far more than belongings but kisses instead, and maybe other intimacies as well? Given the circumstances, she ought to be screaming her lungs out, ought to be terrified beyond measure. Instead she could only wait with her heart thundering in her ears for him to continue.

"Yes," she prompted in a near whisper, "what is it you crave?"

The corner of his lips curved upward. "You, lass, hauling your fine backside out of this coach so your men and I can free it from the muck."

A long moment of incomprehension passed as his meaning gradually sank in. Surely she could not have heard him right? Had he actually told her to *haul her backside out of the coach*!

Her mouth dropped open, her shoulders and spine turning stiff.

Why the gall of the man! Never in her entire life had she been spoken to in such a disgraceful, disrespectful manner. Just who did he think he was?

"And what is your name, fellow?"

"Oh, my pardon for not introducing myself sooner," he said. "If my dear ma were still alive, God rest her soul, she'd cuff me but good for my lack of manners." He straightened to his full, impressive height, touched a pair of fingers to his forehead. "Darragh O'Brien at your service."

"*Darr-ah?*" She crinkled her brow. "Rather an odd-sounding name."

He frowned back. " 'Tisn't odd, 'tis Irish. Which you'd know if you hadn't just made the crossing over from England."

"And how can you tell that?"

"Well, you haven't a sign on your forehead, but you might as well since it's plain as the nose on your pretty face that you're English and new to this land."

He could discern all that from a couple minutes of conversation, could he? Well, at least he had the grace to offer her a small compliment, even if it was wrapped around a criticism.

"Now then, lass, you know my name, so what's yours? And where is it you're bound? Your men didn't say."

"Nor should they have since my plans are really none of your affair, most particularly if you are indeed some sort of rogue."

"Ah, a rogue, am I now? No longer a thief?"

"That remains to be seen."

He barked out a laugh. "Sure and you've got a wicked tongue in your head. One that could slice a brigand to the bone and leave him fleeing in terror."

"If that is true," she asked with a teasing half smile, "then why are you still here?"

He flashed her an irreverent grin, obviously amused by her words. "Well now, I've never been one to run from danger. And I don't mind dipping my toe into an interesting spot of trouble when I chance upon one every now and again."

Up went her eyebrow at his salvo. Was he implying that *she* was just such a spot of trouble? Come to think of it, maybe she was at that.

"I stopped to offer my help as I tried to tell you before," he explained. "I was riding past when I noticed the sorry state of your vehicle. Thought you and your men could do with an extra hand."

His words reminded her of her servants' conspicuous absence, some of her earlier suspicions returning. "And where exactly are my men?"

"Right there." He gestured with a hand. "Where they've been all this while."

She leaned forward and shifted on the seat, then looked over her shoulder through the window. And there they were, all four of them—coachman, two footmen, and her maid—grouped around her luggage on a patch of dry road. She thought they resembled castaways on a small, deserted island, looking hot, bored, and in absolutely no fear for their lives.

"Satisfied?" he questioned.

Clicking her tongue with a barely audible tisk, she settled back into her seat.

"Now then, I've shared my name. What might yours be, lass?" He leaned in again, resting both muscled forearms along the windowsill.

"My name is Jeannette Rose Brantford. *Lady* Jeannette Rose Brantford, not *lass*. I would prefer you do not refer to me in such familiar terms again."

His smile broadened at her lofty reply, his vivid eyes twinkling with a boldness that made her heart squeeze out an extra beat.

"Lady Brantford, is it?" he drawled. "And where would your lord be then, this husband of yours? Has he sent you out traveling on your own?"

"I am presently on my way to my cousins' estate north of Waterford, near some village called Inis . . . Inis . . ." She broke off, racking her mind and drawing a complete blank. "Oh, fiddlesticks, I can't remember now. It's Inis-something-or-other."

"Inistioge, do you mean?" he suggested.

"Yes, I believe that is it. Do you know the place?"

"Aye, I know it well."

Assuming he was not a rogue—though she still had her doubts on that subject—she supposed he might be a decent sort. A local farmer or some such, a freeholder mayhap or possibly a merchant. Although she couldn't imagine Darragh O'Brien serving anyone, not with that brash, ungoverned attitude of his.

If he knew the village near her cousins' home, though, perhaps she hadn't too much farther to travel. Heaven knows she longed to arrive at her destination so she could climb down from this coach and shake out her skirts.

"I am to stay with my cousins there," she said. "And though it isn't actually any of your concern, my title is one of birth, not marriage. I am presently unwed."

The gleam in his expressive eyes deepened. "Are you not, lass? I always knew Englishmen were fools, but I didn't know they were blind into the bargain."

A renewed ripple of awareness quivered in her middle. She buried it with a stern inner rebuke, reminding herself that no matter how attractive he might be, O'Brien was not the kind of man with whom a lady of her rank would consort.

"I believe I told you not to address me by the term *lass*," she said, her tone too breathless to sound much like a scold.

"Aye, and so you did." He grinned at her, visibly unrepentant. "Lass."

Then he did the most astonishing thing—he winked at her. An audacious, irreverent wink that sent a flood of warmth rushing through her veins like the unleashing of a rain-swollen dam after a heavy storm.

If she'd been given to blushing, the way her identical twin sister was, she'd be stained scarlet as a poppy now.

But thankfully blushing at every passing remark was one of the rare physical traits she and her sister, Violet, did not share.

The summer heat, she concluded, *that* was the cause for her untoward reaction. The steamy, unseasonable weather must be affecting her already overburdened senses. If she were back in London, she wouldn't have given him so much as a second look. Well, maybe a second, but not a third.

"Come along with you then," O'Brien declared in a no-nonsense tone. "We've talked long enough, and I need to get you out of this coach."

"Oh, I'm not getting out. Perhaps my coachman didn't mention it, but I have already had this discussion with him. We agreed that I would remain precisely where I am until the barouche can be set on its way."

O'Brien shook his head. "I'm afraid you'll have to step out, unless you've a wish to start living inside this vehicle. In case you didn't know, the coach is muck-mired up to its wheels, and your men can't push it properly with you inside."

"If it's my safety you are concerned about, do not be. I shall be fine."

A bit queasy, mayhap, but fine.

"It's more than your safety, though, that is a concern. There's the matter of your weight."

"What about my weight?" Her eyebrows jerked high.

With a bold, assessing gaze, he scanned the length of her body, from the brim of her hat to the tips of her half boots. "I'm not implying you're fat or anything, if that's what you're thinking. You've a fine womanly figure make no mistake. But even a few stone can make the difference between lifting this coach out of its hole or sinking it deeper."

She sat, momentarily speechless, his rudeness beyond measure. Imagine discussing her weight and her figure in nearly the same breath! Why a gentleman would never dare. But then this man was no gentleman. He was a barbarian. From his tone he might have been discussing farm animals that needed to be shifted from one pen to another.

A long moment passed before he continued. "Of course, if you'd rather, you can stay here while I ride on. I'll carry word to your cousins to let them know you're in need of help. I don't expect it'll take above four or five hours to set you on your way again."

Four or five hours! She couldn't stay in this coach that long. Maybe he was exaggerating, using subterfuge to lure her out of the coach. But what if he wasn't? What if her insistence upon remaining inside the barouche did make the difference between traveling onward or remaining stranded? Why in four or five hours it would be dark!

She shivered at the thought. God only knows what sort of dreadful creatures might lurk in the vicinity, ready to creep from their hiding places after nightfall. There could be wolves—did Ireland have wolves?—or some other equally dangerous beasts. Hungry beasts who might not mind nibbling on a young lady.

Deliberately she kept her voice from quavering, trying one last argument. "If all this is true, why are you here telling me and not my coachman? I should think if things were so dire he would be delivering the news himself."

"He was gathering up the nerve to tell you, as I understand it, when I happened along. He didn't like bearing the bad news, so I offered to deliver it myself."

She peered again at the surrounding ocean of mud. "But where would I wait? Surely you can't expect me to sit atop my luggage in the middle of this bog while the sun toasts me to a crisp."

The humorous gleam returned to his gaze. "Don't be

fretting yourself. There must be a spot of shade some-where hereabouts. I'm sure we'll find one that suits."

She sincerely doubted it, but what choice did she have? Either she vacate the coach or risk still being here, virtually alone and unprotected, come eventide.

O'Brien shot her a sympathetic look, clearly aware of her dilemma and the internal war being waged. Opening the barouche door, he stepped forward. "Come along with you and save your stubbornness for another day. You and I both know the quicker we get you out of this coach, the quicker you'll be on your way."

"Has anyone ever informed you that you are imperti-nent?" Grudgingly, she climbed to her feet.

He chuckled. "A time or two, lass. A time or two. Now gather whatever it is you need and let's be going."

She hesitated for a long, indecisive moment then bent to retrieve her reticule where it lay on the coach seat. With it barely in hand, he reached inside and whisked her up into his arms. Shrieking, she almost dropped her purse as he swung her clear of the coach, his strength and balance the only things separating her from harm's way.

He cradled her against his solid chest, carrying her as though she weighed no more than a feather despite his earlier remarks to the contrary. His nearness washed over her, engulfing her, surrounding her, the scent of fresh air and horses teasing her nostrils along with something else, something indescribably, deliciously male.

Surreptitiously she tilted her head to catch a deeper whiff, the illusive fragrance uniquely his own, she real-ized. She closed her eyes and for the briefest second con-sidered pressing her nose against his neck. Instead, she held herself rigid in his arms, distressingly aware of the thick brown ooze that encircled them like a slick, squishy sea.

"Don't you dare drop me," she admonished, catching up the edges of her skirts to keep them from falling into the mire.

Methodically he slogged forward, mud slurping in noisy protest against his tall boots as nature fought to maintain its tenacious grip upon him. They were halfway across to the oasis where the servants anxiously waited and watched, when O'Brien teetered, his knees dipping precipitously downward for a sudden heart-stopping instant. She screamed and wrapped her arms around his neck, unprepared for the plunge into the tepid muck below.

But just as quickly as O'Brien faltered, he recovered, his feet as steady as if he'd never wavered at all.

Her heart threatened to thunder out of her breast, throat dry and tight. An instant passed as the truth slowly dawned. A glance at the wide, wicked, totally un-apologetic grin on his face confirmed her conclusion.

"You beast." She cuffed him on the shoulder. "You did that deliberately."

"Oh, aye. I thought you could use a bit of jollying. You scream all high and funny like a girl, did you know that?"

"I *am* a girl and that was not funny." Or it wouldn't have been if he'd miscalculated and actually dropped her. She tightened her hold.

He laughed again.

If only he knew who she was, he wouldn't laugh or taunt her. Back in England, before the scandal, she'd been used to gentlemen hurrying to do her bidding. Wealthy, refined men, who catered to her slightest wish, who fought one another for a chance to satisfy her most fleeting desire. She'd been the Ton's Incomparable for the past two Seasons. And she would be again, she vowed, once her parents came to their senses. It wouldn't be long before Mama missed her and Papa's temper cooled. Soon the pair of them would realize what a horrible mistake they'd made, sending their beloved daughter away to this rustic frontier.

Until then she supposed she would be forced to endure unspeakable indignities, such as being carried about by disrespectful, provincial Irishmen like O'Brien.

Her servants stood in a mute cluster, their eyes round as planets, when O'Brien set her on her feet among them. Betsy hurried instantly to her side, an act for which Jeannette was silently grateful, and made a shy attempt to pluck Jeannette's reticule from her grasp.

O'Brien moved to turn away.

"Are you leaving me?" she asked.

He paused, swung back. "Aye. I've got to help your men with the coach."

"But you promised me shade and a comfortable place to sit."

He planted broad hands on his narrow hips, made a show of scanning the area, then he locked his gaze with hers. "It's sorry I am to tell you, but the only shade to be had is over in that little glade just there." He pointed to the spot, a small cluster of silver fir trees standing several yards distant. "And I suspect the ground beneath those trees is just as muddy as the ground here. If you've a parasol, I'd have your maid open it out for you to keep you from the sun.

"As for the comfortable seat, I never promised you such as I recall. If I were you, I'd have a sit-down on your strongest traveling case. Otherwise, you've a fine pair of feet on which to stand. After all the hours you've been in that coach, I'd think you'd be craving a good stretch by now."

With that he turned and strode back toward the foundered barouche. One by one, her men stole away after him, the warm summer stillness broken only by the undulating hum of insects singing in the fields.

Jeannette stood immobile, stunned to speechlessness. She didn't know whether to stamp her feet in frustration or burst into another noisy bout of tears.

But she wouldn't give him the satisfaction of seeing her so upset.

Dastardly man.

And to think she'd considered him attractive.

Aware no one was looking, she stuck her tongue out at O'Brien's back. Feeling slightly better for her childish act of retaliation, she turned to find a seat.

Fall in love at first sight—
and second, and third . . . with the
captivating new Regency romance trilogy

by TRACY ANNE WARREN

The Husband Trap

When shy Lady Violet Brantford agrees to
switch places with her vivacious twin sister,
Jeannette, she finds herself married to the
dashing Duke of Raeburn. Unfortunately,
the Duke has yet to learn the true identity
of his new bride...

The Wife Trap

London socialite Jeannette Brantford is banished
to the Irish countryside in the aftermath of a
Town scandal. But when she meets Darragh
O'Brien, the devilishly handsome architect
transforms Jeannette's punishment into a delicious whirlwind of wits, words, and undeniable passion.

The Wedding Trap

Bluestocking Eliza Hammond inherits a
fortune and an endless line of gold-digging
suitors all in one moment. But when dashing
bachelor Kit Winter steps in to help make Eliza
over for her new role, the last thing either of
them expects is to fall for each other!

 Ballantine Books • www.ballantinebooks.com